PRAISE FOR *THE PARIS ASSIGNMENT*

"Rhys Bowen's multitude of fans will love *The Paris Assignment*, a story of love and war, of bitterness and brutality, of bravery and forgiveness, woven together with a rich sense of time and place, and characters only a master storyteller could create."

—Jacqueline Winspear, *New York Times* bestselling author of *The White Lady* and the Maisie Dobbs series

"No one writes a wartime historical novel as well as Rhys Bowen. *The Paris Assignment* is a gripping, evocative, and skillfully plotted read, with a heroine you will root for right up to the satisfying conclusion. I couldn't put it down!"

—Deborah Crombie, *New York Times* bestselling author of the Duncan Kincaid / Gemma James novel series

"Gorgeous, authentic, and absolutely riveting. There is no better storyteller than Rhys Bowen! *The Paris Assignment*, like all her novels, is meticulously researched, brilliantly told, and endlessly captivating. Bowen's extraordinary ability to synthesize history and present it as essential and heartbreaking human drama is unmatched. I read this in total awe, as it honors reality and cinematically brings it to life again. *The Paris Assignment* is emotionally and historically immersive, and no reader will be the same after they turn the final page."

—Hank Phillippi Ryan, *USA Today* bestselling author, Mary Higgins Clark and five-time Agatha Award winner

"*The Paris Assignment* is a sweeping story of love, bravery, and ultimately hope. Rhys Bowen masterfully weaves an immersive story that carries us through the crucible of war with characters that capture your imagination and heart. Traveling through Paris, London, and Australia, *The Paris Assignment* is a story about the things we do when we believe there might be nothing left to lose, about the irrepressible love of a wife and mother, and about courage in the face of great and terrible odds. Historical fiction at its best, *The Paris Assignment* is a rich and absorbing experience."

—Patti Callahan Henry, *New York Times* bestselling author of *The Secret Book of Flora Lea*

PRAISE FOR RHYS BOWEN

"Rhys Bowen is a gift to all who love great writing, rich and complex characters, and a plot that grabs from first words."

—Louise Penny, #1 *New York Times* bestselling author of the Chief Inspector Gamache novels

"Thoroughly entertaining."

—*Publishers Weekly*

"A truly delightful read."

—*Kirkus Reviews*

"Keep[s] readers deeply involved until the end."

—*Portland Book Review*

"Entertainment mixed with intellectual intrigue and realistic setting[s] for which Bowen has earned awards and loyal fans."

—*New York Journal of Books*

"[A] master of her genre."

—*Library Journal*

"An author with a distinctive flair for originality and an entertaining narrative storytelling style that will hold the reader's rapt attention from beginning to end."

—*Midwest Book Review*

"Bowen's vivid storytelling style holds readers enrapt."

—Historical Novel Society

THE PARIS ASSIGNMENT

ALSO BY RHYS BOWEN

In Farleigh Field
The Tuscan Child
The Victory Garden
What Child Is This
Above the Bay of Angels
The Venice Sketchbook
Where the Sky Begins

CONSTABLE EVANS MYSTERIES

Evans Above
Evan Help Us
Evanly Choirs
Evan and Elle
Evan Can Wait
Evans to Betsy
Evan Only Knows
Evan's Gate
Evan Blessed
Evanly Bodies

MOLLY MURPHY MYSTERIES

Murphy's Law
Death of Riley
For the Love of Mike
In Like Flynn
Oh Danny Boy
In Dublin's Fair City
Tell Me, Pretty Maiden
In a Gilded Cage

The Last Illusion
Bless the Bride
Hush Now, Don't You Cry
The Family Way
City of Darkness and Light
The Edge of Dreams
Away in a Manger
Time of Fog and Fire
The Ghost of Christmas Past

With Clare Broyles

Wild Irish Rose
All That Is Hidden

ROYAL SPYNESS MYSTERIES

Her Royal Spyness
A Royal Pain
Royal Flush
Royal Blood
Naughty in Nice
The Twelve Clues of Christmas
Heirs and Graces
Queen of Hearts
Malice at the Palace
Crowned and Dangerous
On Her Majesty's Frightfully Secret Service
Four Funerals and Maybe a Wedding
Love and Death Among the Cheetahs
The Last Mrs. Summers
God Rest Ye, Royal Gentlemen
Peril in Paris

THE PARIS ASSIGNMENT

A NOVEL

RHYS BOWEN

LAKE UNION PUBLISHING

This is a work of fiction. Names, characters, organizations, places, events, and incidents are either products of the author's imagination or are used fictitiously.

Published by Lake Union Publishing, Seattle

www.apub.com

ISBN-13: 9781662504242 (hardcover)
ISBN-13: 9781662504235 (paperback)
ISBN-13: 9781662504259 (digital)

Cover design by Shasti O'Leary Soudant
Cover image: © V_E / Shutterstock; © Stephen Mulcahey / ArcAngel

Printed in the United States of America

First edition

I am dedicating this book to Mary-Fran McCluskey, who earned the right to appear in this story by being the high bidder in a charity auction to provide scholarships for young women to attend university. Although she was never a courier in WWII, she did go by the name Marier-France when she lived in that country.

CHAPTER 1

Paris, 1931

Madeleine Grant met Giles Martin at the end of her first month at the Sorbonne University in Paris. She was a tall, slender girl with dark, hopeful eyes and unusual red-brown hair that she wore shoulder-length and unpermed. Having been a student at Westfield College, a small residential women's college of the University of London, she'd only known civilized tutorials with female professors. She had come to Westfield straight from a girls' boarding school and felt safe and comfortable there amongst young ladies from similar backgrounds. It was, indeed, an extension of her school life. So the Sorbonne, with its large, draughty lecture halls, its loud male students, was a huge shock to her system. She watched groups of young people of both sexes surging between buildings, arguing expansively with much gesticulating, or laughing together at outdoor cafés and wondered if she would ever be part of a group like that. It seemed like another world that could never open up to her. She was beginning to wish she had never come, but at least one term of study abroad was required for her degree in French. And it was heady and exciting to know she was in Paris. But she longed to be one of those confident French girls who smoked and tossed their scarves nonchalantly, laughing and arguing on equal footing with the boys.

Until now she had sat, quiet as a mouse, at the back of a lecture hall, trying to understand the professor's rapid French, taking copious notes, hoping not to be noticed, terrified of being called upon. At the end of that first month, the lecture was halfway through when a sudden draft announced that the door behind her had opened, and someone slid into the seat beside her.

"What's this lecture on?" a male voice whispered in her ear.

She looked up, surprised, to see herself staring at a mop of unruly dark hair and a pair of alarming tiger eyes. "*Racine,*" she whispered. "He's talking about Phèdre."

"Oh her." The eyes flashed amusement. "Horrible woman, wasn't she? All those ancient Greeks and their guilty passions! Too much time on their hands, if you ask me. And why Racine needed five acts for her to agonize over her passion for her stepson." He shook his head, grinning. The professor must have sensed a disturbance at the back of the lecture hall because he broke off from his monologue and looked up, frowning. The young man beside Madeleine winked, nudging her. "Do you want to come for a cup of coffee?"

"I should be taking notes," Madeleine whispered. "There will be a paper to write."

"How can there be anything new to learn about a play written three hundred years ago? Come on. I have friends who are fourth-year students. They will share the papers they wrote after this class. It's only the same old stuff rehashed every year."

Madeleine hesitated, torn between wanting to be the dutiful student, making the most of her time in Paris, and the desire to go with this attractive young man. The latter option won out. She folded her notebook, stuffed it into her bag and crept out after him. Once in the hallway outside, she looked up at him and gave a nervous laugh. "I shouldn't be doing this," she said.

"Rubbish. Why does anyone need to study Racine, anyway? How can he be relevant to us in the twentieth century? All those plays about great and noble people who end up killing themselves. We need more plays about real people, with real problems, like how to pay for next week's rent."

"So why are you studying French literature, then, if you don't find it relevant?"

"To tell you the truth, I am not. I just ducked into that lecture hall because I saw a chap to whom I owe some money. I have dabbled in various subjects, but currently I am studying philosophy and politics."

He put an arm around her shoulder as if it was the most natural thing to do. "Come on. Come and cheer me up. I've had a depressing week so far."

She allowed him to steer her down the echoing stone staircase and out into the brightness of an October day. The buttery yellow stone of the buildings surrounding the courtyard glowed in the slanted sunlight.

"So which is your favourite café?" he asked.

The courtyard was empty, since lectures were in progress. From a tall open window came the droning of a professor's voice. "And we notice in the year 1357 . . ."

Madeleine gave an embarrassed shrug. "I haven't really tried too many cafés yet. I get my midday meal at the cafeteria here and my evening meal at the hostel."

"You're new? How long have you been here?"

"Yes, I'm new. Only a month. And I have not been brave enough to visit more than a few cafés alone."

Something about the way she phrased this statement made him look at her critically. "You're not French?"

She felt herself blushing. "No, I'm English."

"That explains it. You use words that only professors might use. Or elderly nuns. But your French accent is remarkably good. Usually the English have horrendous accents—quite incapable of blending in."

This made her smile. "My mother was half-French. When I was a little girl, we used to visit a relative in Paris. And my mother spoke to me in both languages. I understand quite well, and I used to be fluent. But I'm afraid I only have the vocabulary of a child, *vous comprenez*." She used the polite form of the word "you," noting that he had also done this. She still wasn't quite sure when one verged into the familiar. "More recently I've been studying French at school and at university in London, but I'm not familiar with everyday spoken French."

"Your mother stopped speaking to you in French?"

She looked away. "The Great War came, and we couldn't go to France any more. And then my mother caught the Spanish flu and died when I was ten. So no more visits to Paris."

"And now you have a new chance," he said, beaming at her as if she had given him a present. "How marvellous. You can connect with your French roots again."

"Yes." She looked up at him, smiling too now. "A new chance, as you say. I'm very excited."

They came out to the rue des Écoles and turned towards the bigger boulevard Saint-Michel. "If you have not experienced our Parisian cafés, I should take you somewhere iconic," he said. "The Café de Flore if you don't mind a little walk."

"I love walking," she said. "I must have walked every inch of Paris already. At home in England, we walk everywhere. My college is near Hampstead Heath, and we young ladies are encouraged to take healthy walks between lectures."

He looked amused. "You attend a college for young ladies?"

She nodded. "It's part of the University of London, but most of my classes are within the college—only female professors."

"Mon Dieu!" He looked appalled. "How unhealthy. How are you supposed to learn how to snag yourself a husband?"

"I don't think one goes to university to snag a husband," she said, giving him a reprimanding frown. "Surely an education gives one the option not to get married, if one chooses. Besides, it is comforting to study amongst female friends. Safe."

"That's what you want to be? Safe?" He shook his head, making his dark curls dance. "How are you ever supposed to know about life?"

She considered this. "Perhaps you're right," she said. "I was at a girls' boarding school. We were encouraged to apply to ladies' colleges where we would be safe and protected."

"But one should never be safe and protected," he said. "To live with danger is to know that you are fully alive."

She looked at him with awe. He had said something she had never really considered before. "You are right," she said. "I've been shut away all my life, and now I haven't even dared to go to coffeehouses on my own. But I want to live. I want to know what danger feels like." She corrected herself. "I remember what it felt like at the time of the Great War. Bombs fell near us in London. And just when it felt safe, the Spanish flu and Mummy getting so ill and dying very quickly. And I thought I never wanted to go through times like that again. But since then, it's been a safe little cocoon."

He grabbed at her arm and yanked her back as she went to step out into the street and a taxicab came hurtling towards them. A horn blared out. "If you wish to stay safe, remember the traffic goes on the other side of the street," he said, laughing.

Then he seemed to realize he was still holding her. "I should perhaps know your name if I'm to rescue you from passing taxis and take you to cafés."

"It's Madeleine," she said. "Madeleine Grant. My mother wanted a name that was equally good in both French and English."

"Madeleine." He pronounced it in the French way and nodded approvingly. "Yes. It suits you. And I am Giles. Giles Martin." And he held out his hand in proper fashion.

"I'm pleased to meet you, Giles," she said, her voice suddenly shaky because she was aware of the warmth of his hand and realized he was terribly attractive.

They crossed the boulevard Saint-Michel and continued past the faculty of medicine until they joined the wider boulevard Saint-Germain. Here the leaves of the sycamore trees lining both sides of the street glowed golden to match the buildings. There were attractive little boutiques, and Madeleine glanced into windows as they passed them, recoiling in horror at the price of a pair of shoes.

"Where do you stay?" Giles asked.

"At a women's hostel that belongs to the university on the rue Saint-Jacques. It's rather dreadful, actually. Disgusting food and depressing rooms. And mostly foreign students—not much chance to improve my French."

"Why don't you find a place of your own? There are many in the city that are not expensive. And you can eat in a café as cheaply as your hostel, I am sure."

"I wouldn't know where to start," she said. "I haven't been to Paris since I was a small child." She paused. "I used to have a great-aunt here, who lived in a little flat in the Marais. But I don't have her address. She must be very old now—if she is still alive."

"The Marais is where I live," he said. "A good place. Full of life. Is your aunt Jewish?"

"No. I don't think so." She looked confused.

"Because the Marais is the traditional Jewish quarter."

"Are you Jewish, then?"

"I stay there because the rooms are cheap." And he laughed. "Money is always a problem, is it not?"

"Your family is poor?" He didn't behave like a person with no means. There was a certain confident swagger to the way he walked and talked, using his hands expressively.

"Not at all," he said. "But my mother controls the funds and likes to keep me on a tight leash. She thinks I am not studying hard enough—which is true. Also, she despairs of me because I am a Communist."

Madeleine looked up in surprise. "But aren't Communists horrible people? In Russia they have slaughtered millions and sent many more to camps in Siberia for disagreeing with the government."

"They are not true Communists," he said angrily. "They used the term to attract the masses, to get them to rise up in revolution, but now those in power behave as badly towards the people as the tsars did before them. A true Communist wants to share all things equally. There is really plenty to go around." They paused before crossing another street. "Take my family's house, for example," he said. "We have fourteen bedrooms, and currently one person sleeps in them. That is a disgrace when other people sleep six to a bed."

Madeleine digested this. "You must have a big house."

He nodded. "It's actually a château. My family survived the revolution rather well."

"What about your father? Does he run the estate?"

"No, that would be my mother. She is a formidable character—quite terrifying, actually. My father ran off with a dancer, years ago, and now lives in sin in Monte Carlo. Maman tells people that he died a hero in the Great War. She's terrified that I'll take after him and not take my responsibilities seriously. I'm supposed to be studying law, since it is considered a noble thing to study." He laughed. "My mother does not realize that most lawyers are crooked."

"Do you have brothers?"

"No. I'm an only child. Father ran away before he could produce more."

"Won't you be required to run the estate some day?"

"Over my mother's dead body." He laughed. "Literally. She'd be terrified I'd invite the local peasants to live in the summer house and share the produce—which I would, of course."

They seemed to be walking a long way, and Madeleine was aware that she might miss her next lecture, too. A whole morning with no studying. She had always been the dutiful student, not sneaking out through the window at night to go to parties or on dates like some of her fellow classmates at Westfield. This felt a little like the first step on a road to sin, but it also felt terribly exciting.

They came at last to a corner with two cafés facing each other. They had colourful awnings over outside tables. "That's another place you must try," Giles said, pointing to their right. "Les Deux Magots. Good food. Not expensive. But this is the one we are going to now." He crossed the street, then ushered her to an outdoor table. The sign on the awning read "Café de Flore." Most of the tables were occupied, and the scent of herby French cigarettes wafted across. Giles snapped his fingers, and a waiter came over to them. He didn't ask what she wanted and ordered two coffees and a basket of pastries. She found herself wondering for a second whether this was going to be expensive and whether she should offer to pay her share. She, too, did not have money to spare.

Giles leaned back in his chair, crossed his legs and examined her. "Your French is really quite good," he said, "but I'll have to teach you some slang or you'll sound like a nun, newly escaped from her convent. And some swear words, too. One always needs to swear occasionally. Or in my case more frequently."

She found that she was also examining him. He was not terribly tall but well built, and his face was decidedly French—aquiline nose, sharp features, dark eyes that lit up with amusement. Altogether an appealing-looking young man. He caught her looking at him and grinned, making her blush. A tray was brought containing cups and two pots, one with coffee and one with hot milk. Giles poured equal measures of both and passed a cup to her. Then he offered her the basket, and she took a curly *pain aux raisins*. He took a croissant and promptly dunked it into his coffee.

"This is divine," she said, taking a large bite of warm, flaky pastry. "We have stale bread and jam at the hostel."

"We should start work on finding you a place of your own," he said. "I could come and visit you. I'm sure no men are allowed at your hostel."

"Certainly not." She smiled. "It's very strict. But I don't think it's worth looking for my own flat. I'm not going to be here long. It's only for one term. I go home at Christmas."

"Back to university in London?"

"That's right."

"That is not long enough to experience Paris. Why not stay and finish your degree here? I'm sure it's more agreeable."

Madeleine gave a nervous laugh. "Oh, I don't think my father would go for that. I'm supposed to get my degree as quickly as possible and then become a teacher like him, earning my own way."

"Your father is a teacher?"

She nodded. "He teaches Latin and Greek at a famous boys' school in London. He's a scholarly type—quite unworldly, actually. And old, too. He was in his forties when I was born, so he probably should have retired by now, but he enjoys the teaching too much. And I don't think he'd want to spend all day with my stepmother."

"Ah, your father married again?"

Madeleine's expression changed. "He did. Quite soon after Mummy died. He married a war widow. Eleanor. He wanted someone to take care of us, and she wanted someone to pay the bills. She's not my favourite person."

"*Alors*—the wicked stepmother." He laughed. "How very traditional."

"That's probably not fair," Madeleine said. "She's not a bad person. She's a complete snob who claims to come from a noble background—although whether that is true is debatable. She's really mean with money, and she doesn't like me very much."

"Did she have children of her own? You have stepsisters?"

"Oh no. She didn't have any children from her previous marriage, and she was too old for that sort of thing when she married my father. And I suppose I was an awful child when she met me. I was still so upset by my mother's death. I adored her. She was warm and wonderful. And then this woman arrived, and I probably did not behave well. Certainly made it clear that I didn't want her as a new mother. She couldn't wait to send me off to boarding school."

"Your father had no say in this? She rules the household, does she?"

Madeleine sighed. "My father, as I said, is quite unworldly. Anything for a quiet life. And she's clever at getting him to see things her way." She looked up and met his gaze. "I was quite happy to be away at school and after that at college. And I'm also happy to be here. It's all rather wonderful."

"You're right. Paris is wonderful. I felt quite intoxicated myself when I first arrived."

"How long have you been here?"

"Four years now," he said. "This is my fifth."

"Should you not have graduated by now?" She paused. "I'm sorry. That was rather rude, wasn't it?"

He laughed. "Of course I should have completed my studies. But I am in no hurry. I like this life too much. No responsibilities. Good friends. Plenty of wine. I guess you can see why my mother threatens to cut off funds."

"Does plenty of wine go along with communism? It sounds rather hedonistic."

"Of course. One does not have to be miserable to be a Communist, although I have to agree that some of them are horribly earnest. I shall be a merry Communist and hand out bread and wine to all." He paused. "One day I shall take up the challenge seriously, of course. But for now . . ." He looked at her, and his expression became more serious. "I should warn you," he said, "that you should not fall in love with me. I am not a reliable type. I'll probably get myself involved in some kind of Communist uprising and wind up in jail or on Devil's Island. And I have no money of my own. A hopeless cause, actually."

"Don't worry," she replied, trying to keep her voice light and steady because the statement had unnerved her. "I have no intention of falling in love with anybody before I've completed my studies. And I'll soon be gone." But as she said this, she was thinking that it was probably too late. She was already a little in love with him.

CHAPTER 2

Madeleine really didn't expect to see him again. The Sorbonne was a big university. She was hardly likely to bump into him, and she suspected he had just invited her for coffee because he wanted companionship at that moment. But the next day he was waiting in the hallway when she emerged from a lecture on the Romantic poets.

"Ah, there you are," he said. "Was Romanticism more pleasant than the crazy Phèdre?"

"How did you know where to find me?"

A wicked smile crossed his face. "It is not hard. I asked a friend who studies French literature what classes there were this morning. And I worked out that you would not approve of Émile Zola and the Romantics were more your style. Shall we get some coffee again?"

"But I have my medieval literature class," she said.

"Boring. All those troubadours and unrequited love and noble quests. Come on. It's another lovely day, and who knows how long the weather will hold at this time of year. Besides, I'm horribly hungry and thirsty."

"You're a bad influence," she said as they pushed their way down the stairs, against the flow of students coming up. "I think you're leading me astray."

"Oh, I do hope so," he said, making her blush furiously.

This time he took her up the boulevard Saint-Michel, crossing the Seine on to the Île de la Cité, stopping for coffee in a tiny coffeehouse on a back street close to Notre-Dame. She tried a *pain au chocolat* and offered to pay. Giles waved her away. "It is always up to the seducer to pay," he said, laughing. "You have visited Notre-Dame, I suppose."

"It's the most beautiful church I've ever seen," Madeleine said.

Giles shook his head. "What about the Sainte-Chapelle?"

"I don't know that one."

He looked horrified. "Then we must remedy it instantly." He took her hand and led her swiftly through back alleys, past grim, medieval-looking buildings and eventually into a narrow courtyard before pushing open a door. The smell of incense wafted towards them, and the murmur of voices. A Mass was in progress. But Madeleine wasn't aware of the priest or the altar. She gave a little gasp of awe as she saw the rainbows of coloured light streaming in through impossibly tall windows and painting stripes on the stone floor. High above them the arched ceiling was made of blue tiles, like the sky. The whole chapel was so ethereal that the ceiling seemed to float.

"It's the ancient royal chapel," he said. "Marvellous, don't you think?"

"It's not as big or impressive as Notre-Dame," she ventured, "but definitely more lovely."

He nodded. Madeleine was experiencing an odd sensation, surely déjà vu. She had been taken here once before. She remembered her mother staring up at those same windows, lost in contemplation. She remembered getting impatient, tugging on her mother's hand. *Come on. We've seen it, now let's go.* But her mother, still gazing in wonder, refused to budge for what seemed like an eternity.

A bell rang at the altar. Giles paused, knelt and crossed himself. He gave an embarrassed shrug when he stood up. "I come to Mass here sometimes. How can one not feel spiritual in a place like this? You are a Catholic, with a French mother?"

"My mother was only half-French," she admitted, "but she was raised a Catholic herself. She had me baptized as a Catholic, and I attended Mass with her sometimes. But when she died, I was sent to a Church of England boarding school, and we had to go to church, but

I can't say I've much faith at all. I felt that God let me down when he took my mother from me."

Giles looked at her with understanding. "I felt that way when my father went. But it can't hurt to pray, can it? To remind God we are still around."

"I suppose not." She glanced uncertainly at the altar, where the priest was now holding up a host. After the simple services of the Church of England, it seemed rather exotic and mysterious, like a wizard chanting a spell.

As they walked back towards the university, she paused on the bridge over the Seine. A barge was passing beneath, a woman sitting at the back, steering it while a baby crawled at her feet. Madeleine took a deep breath before she dared to ask the question that had been plaguing her.

"Why are you being this nice to me? Giving up your time? Do you usually show foreigners around as an act of charity?"

Giles grasped her shoulders and turned her towards him. "Has no one ever told you that you are beautiful?"

She gave a nervous laugh. "Don't be silly. At school they said it was a pity I was so skinny and plain. My hair is dead straight. My nose is straight, too. Not a nice little button."

"It is a classic French nose," he said. "And your bone structure is perfect. If I was still studying art, I'd make a sculpture of you, in white marble."

"Don't." She looked away. "Please don't tease me."

"But I'm not teasing. One thing you should learn is that I always say what I mean. Yesterday I was intrigued. Why is this girl speaking like someone from the age of Racine? I thought. It seemed rather interesting, as if you might have been dropped into the class through a time warp from the past. But then I found myself thinking, *This is someone I'd like to spend more time with. Someone quite unspoiled, not trying to flirt, to show off like the other girls. Someone who listens and understands.*" He paused. "*Someone with whom I can be myself.*"

"I'm going back to England in just over a month," she said, not wanting to meet his gaze.

"Then let us make the most of the time we have," he said. He took her hand as if it was the most natural thing in the world, and they walked back along the boulevard Saint-Michel in silence.

After that it became a normal habit to go to coffee or to eat lunch with him. He rarely took her out in the evenings, and she wondered why this was—whether he had another girlfriend, or a group of friends he wanted to keep separate from her. She had never had the chance for a proper boyfriend. At the university in London, there had been formal dances and she had exchanged pleasantries with suitable young men, who shuffled her around, as nervous as she was. She realized that the British education system, with its single-sex schools, left young adults hopelessly in the dark about communicating with the opposite sex. Some boys had stammered, blushing, and talked about rugby while others had tried to steer her up to the balcony and made awkward attempts at kissing and groping. But there was not a single one, until now, who had just seemed to appreciate her company or whom she had wanted to get to know better.

When she looked at herself in the mirror that evening, she wondered what he saw in her. Surely she wasn't beautiful. He was clearly not lacking in friends. Other students called out and waved to him as they passed. He also had not apparently been lacking in girlfriends. One boy greeted him, then noticed Madeleine. "You're no longer with Yvette?" he asked.

"Obviously not," Giles said. But he didn't introduce her, and she wondered whether his evenings were devoted to another girl. But when she examined this, it seemed better this way. A pleasant young man to have coffee with, and at the end of her time here, she would go home with no regrets. And, she added to herself, her conversational French was improving by leaps and bounds. She even understood the lectures more easily.

It wasn't until the week before she was due to go home that he kissed her.

"Where does your great-aunt live?" he asked. "It seems rude to be in Paris and not visit her."

She gave an embarrassed grin. "I really don't remember. I was really young. The last time I was here must have been the spring of 1914. I was only four. All I can picture is we went in through a courtyard and there was a rickety lift like a birdcage."

"That could describe fifty percent of the buildings in Paris," he said.

She thought some more. "I think there was a big park nearby. With houses all around it and some kind of archways. I remember chasing pigeons."

"That might be the Place des Vosges," he said. "Come on. Let's go and take a look."

They crossed the Seine, then walked along the quay, past the imposing town hall, and eventually turned up a narrow side street lined with interesting-looking little shops. At the end of the street, they stepped through an archway and out into a broad area of green, the buildings around it old and elegant looking with covered cloisters.

"Yes," she said, nodding with pleasure. "I think this was it. She didn't live far from here."

"Neither do I," he said. "I have to walk through the Place des Vosges every day to come to class. It gives me great pleasure, and every time I come through, I tell myself I should change my subject to architecture and design something like this."

"Or the Eiffel Tower?" she suggested.

He laughed. "Paris does not need more than one Eiffel Tower. This used to be an upper-class part of the city. Where nobles lived. Now I'm afraid it's quite run-down, which means one can rent a room very cheaply. When you come back after Christmas, we must find you a room here."

"But I told you, I'm not coming back," she said. "I had to do one term abroad, and this was it. Now I have to go home, study hard and pass my final exams."

"Then be a good, studious teacher until you marry a similarly studious male teacher and live happily ever after?"

"Something like that." She looked away.

"Do you want to teach? Do you adore children?"

"I don't dislike children, but I'm not sure that teaching is what I would have chosen. I suppose one takes what is available. For a woman it's either teacher or secretary. And in case you haven't noticed, there is a depression on. Jobs are hard to come by."

"So I'm told by my mother. She never fails to remind me how fortunate I am that I am attending a university and have the chance for a profession. She doesn't care which profession I choose. She just wants to say, 'my son the attorney, or doctor.'"

"Or architect?" she suggested.

He nodded. "Perhaps. But no. Too much mathematics. I'm horrible at mathematics."

"I was, too. But it was badly taught. You could always go into the priesthood. That's a profession."

He burst out laughing. "I don't see myself as the celibate type. I like women too much. I enjoy sex."

Madeleine felt her face burning with embarrassment.

"Oh, I'm sorry. I should not have said the naughty word, is that it?" He put a friendly arm around her shoulder. "I told you, I always say what I mean. Probably not a good trait. One makes enemies. And embarrasses sweet and innocent young girls."

They came out the other side of the square. "Do you think your aunt's building was around here?"

Madeleine frowned. "Somewhere like this. I'm really not sure."

"My room is on the little street to the right," he said. "Come up and see it."

Madeleine was all too aware of what he had just said about sex. "Oh, I don't think . . . ," she began.

"I promise to behave," he said. "And it's the middle of the afternoon. If I made love to you, I'd want candlelight and a moon shining in through the window. You see, I am a romantic at heart."

Giles steered her along a cobbled side street and in through a narrow doorway. A steep stone stair led upward. There was a smell of drains and cooking with garlic. Up two flights and along a dark hallway. He put a key in a door and ushered her inside. "It's not a palace, but it meets my needs," he said.

The room was surprisingly neat. There were several prints of works by post-impressionist painters on the walls. On one side was an iron bedstead. A desk and chair in the window, and on the other side a sink and gas ring. "Is this not better than the hostel?" he asked.

"Much better. Twice as much room, to start with. And look. From your window you can see a nice wide boulevard with a statue. Very Parisian. My window looks on to another wall."

"We will find you a similar room when you return." He went across to the sink, filled a kettle and put it on the gas ring. "Take a seat. Do you like peppermint tea?"

She perched, nervously, on the bed. "Giles, I'm really not coming back."

"That is too bad, because I shall have to come to England after you. Because my English is poor, I shall not be able to study or get a good job but shall have to be a porter or a chimney sweep or even a beggar. I shall have to suffer for you."

"Don't be silly," she said. "Of course you must finish your studies here."

"But don't you see how much more useful it would be to you to stay here, improve your French and have a degree from the Sorbonne?" he asked. "If you went back to England later, you could be a translator, for a publisher, maybe. And it costs almost nothing—books, food. Surely your family could not object."

"I'm sure they would," she said.

"Do you actually want to go back to the girls' college and listen to old women spouting about French literature?"

Madeleine toyed with this before answering. The dorm room at the women's college did have a certain appeal—coffee together in the evenings, a sort of cosy isolation from the real world. But here was Paris, and excitement, and Giles. Then she shook her head. "No, I don't want to go back, but one has to do the sensible thing, doesn't one?"

"I never have." He gave her a challenging grin.

The kettle boiled. He poured hot water into two mugs. While he worked, Madeleine looked around the room. There, on the desk, were some photos. One of a woman with a little boy at her side, standing outside an impressive country house. His mother and Giles when he was small, she thought. And then one of a dark girl with lots of flyaway hair, holding up her hand to shield her face from the sunlight and laughing. And Madeleine realized she had seen that girl at the university—had sensed the girl watching her as she went down the stairs.

"Is that Yvette?" she asked.

He looked up, startled. "How did you know about her? But yes, that is Yvette."

"She was your girlfriend?"

He nodded. "She was."

"And she lived here with you, in this room?"

"For a while. How did you guess?"

"The room looks as if it has had a woman's touch."

He shrugged. "For all you know, I might be a very tidy and artistic man. But you are right. She did choose the paintings for the walls. And the rug."

"And you broke up with her?"

A spasm of pain or annoyance crossed his face. "She broke up with me. She said I did not pay her enough attention, I was never home in the evenings."

"Where were you?" She surprised herself at her boldness.

"I work." He gave an apologetic smile. "I told you that my mother likes to keep me short of cash. I work in a bar. A rather disreputable bar. Not the sort of place I could take you. And eventually Yvette tired of me, and she found someone with more money and more time for her."

"I'm sorry."

"Are you?" He looked amused now. "You and I would not have met if Yvette had not discarded me. Actually I came into that lecture hall because I saw her coming down the stairs and did not want to pass her."

"So you broke up recently?" She realized that she might be pressing him too much.

"Very recently."

"I see." She considered this. "And then you decided to pick up another girl to show that you didn't mind. Any girl. Any girl at all . . ."

He went over to her and put a hand on her shoulder. "Madeleine, no . . ."

"I noticed her looking at me once. You latched on to me only to walk past and show her . . ." She blinked back a tear. Stupid. She was not going to cry.

"Yes. To start with, yes." He almost shouted the words. "But then I found you interesting . . . and I found I did not want you to go home. I meant what I said, Madeleine. I will follow you to England if you go back. I don't want to lose you."

"Really?" She looked up at him.

Instead of answering, he pulled her towards him and kissed her. The kiss was not a tender brushing of the lips but a passionate embrace, his mouth hungry and demanding against hers. It left her breathless, her heart pounding. She was unaware that such feelings existed, especially the feeling of desire in the pit of her stomach.

"Now do you believe me?"

"I suppose I must," she said.

"Will you come back in the new year?"

She sighed. "I really don't know, Giles. I want to. I'll have to think about how I can persuade them. My father wouldn't mind, but it will be a case of making Eleanor believe that it will cost her less and be more beneficial in the long run."

"I'm sure you'll come up with a way," he said. "Put your whole mind to it on the boat going home for Christmas. Otherwise I shall have to become a street sweeper in London."

"You said chimney sweep last time." She laughed.

"I remembered I am claustrophobic," he said, taking her into his arms and laughing, too.

CHAPTER 3

Madeleine was in a turmoil of indecision on the journey back to England for the Christmas holidays. She wanted to return to Paris. Of course she wanted to return. She wasn't quite sure that Giles would go through with his threat and come to London just to be near her, but she suspected that he might. After all, he had told her he never said anything he didn't mean. That would wreck his own chances of earning a degree and would make his mother even more furious with him. Part of her longed for the simple security of that room in the hall of residence at Westfield, where meals were served at long tables in the refectory and where friends gathered for coffee and chat every evening. All of her needs were met, leaving her with time and room to study. Well, not all of her needs, she reminded herself. There was no Giles.

As the train crossed the bleak and bare winter countryside, her thoughts went back to him. The previous evening they had strolled together along the Seine, even though the weather was bitter with the promise of snow. His arm was around her, and she snuggled into the warmth of the fur collar on his coat. As they passed under a bridge, out of the full force of the wind, he took her chin in his hand, drew her towards him and kissed her, the warmth of his mouth melting the cold on her lips.

"How shall I survive for three long weeks without you?" he asked.

She laughed. "You're being dramatic. You'll go home to your château and have a huge Christmas celebration with goose and champagne and *bûche de Noël* and forget all about me."

"No," he said quietly. "I don't think I can ever forget about you. I knew you were special from the first moment I saw you. Promise me you'll come back. Don't listen to them."

"I want to come back," she said. "I'll do my best."

"No, better than best. We must always fight for what we want in life." He let go of her, reached inside his coat and brought out a small package. "I have a little Christmas gift for you."

Then of course she was embarrassed because she had nothing for him. "Oh dear," she said. "But I have nothing for you. I didn't think . . ."

"My gift will be if you promise to come back."

She took the small package. "Thank you. I'll open it on Christmas Day and think of you."

"Now I think we really must get out of the cold, or they will find two frozen figures standing here, locked in passionate embrace." He hugged her to him again and they walked on. I will remember this moment forever, she thought. Just in case I never see him again. I'll remember that I met the most wonderful man in the world.

~

"Well, here you are. Back safe and sound." Her father greeted her warmly as she came into the warm drawing room of their house on the common at Blackheath, a pleasant suburb to the south of the city. "Had a good time? Learned a lot of French?" He held out a hand to her. "You're looking peaky. Have they been starving you?"

"The hostel food wasn't good," she agreed, "but it was a rough crossing. Everyone was being sick."

"Well, you're home now. We'll tell Cook to fatten you up," he said. "Although Eleanor won't like that. She claims Cook's food is too fattening for her. Blames Cook that she is putting on weight." He chuckled.

The room and familiar surroundings felt so comforting that she wondered why she had told Giles she was not happy at home. Here was her father, being welcoming.

"Oh, I thought I heard voices." The temperature in the room seemed to drop as her stepmother came in. "You're back, are you? I hope you weren't wasting your time over there. You need to pass your final exams on time. And with good marks. There is a lot of competition for jobs, you know. Too many people out of work. They say even top scientists and professors are taking teachers' jobs now." She ran a finger over the surface of the bureau and examined it for dust. "Your father hasn't been well," she said. "It's his chest again. I told him we should move to the country. The London air is not good for him. He is old enough to retire, after all."

"But I enjoy my job. I enjoy the boys," her father said. "What would I do in the country? And how would we live on my pension?"

"We would get by. A house in the country would cost less than this place. And be cheaper to heat, too." She turned to Madeleine. "Don't just stand there. I expect you've got a suitcase to unpack, haven't you?"

"The child has hardly arrived, Eleanor. Give her a chance to settle in. A nice cup of tea would be a good idea."

"It's past teatime, isn't it? Dinner is in an hour." She bustled around the room and then walked out. Her father gave Madeleine an apologetic smile. "She's really glad you're home safely," he said. "She just doesn't like to say it."

Madeleine went up to her room, the familiar bedroom of her childhood. There were the dolls her mother had given her, the tea set for the dolls' tea parties, the French books she had read with her mother. It all seemed so long ago it was like a beautiful dream. She changed out of her travelling clothes and wondered how and when she would tell them that she was going back to Paris.

~

Madeleine put off facing them until after Christmas. They went to midnight service, and afterwards she opened Giles's package. She had half hoped it would be jewellery, but instead it was a tiny leather-bound book of love poems. She read the first one, and tears came to her eyes. The fact that he had selected this, sent her these sentiments, made it very special.

Christmas Day was a modest celebration with a roast chicken, a small tree and paper chains in the drawing room. She was given a scarf and some writing paper. She suspected the scarf was an old one of Eleanor's she no longer wanted since it came with a lingering hint of perfume. But it was not unattractive, and she accepted it gracefully. In turn she had brought wine and chocolates back from France. Eleanor drew her aside. "How thoughtless of you," she said. "You must know that your father has a problem with drink."

"Daddy?"

"Drinking far too much. It's become a real concern," Eleanor said. "And here you are encouraging him."

"I didn't know. I'm sorry," Madeleine stammered.

"How could you know? You're never home. And also that I am battling middle-age spread and therefore staying away from sweet things," Eleanor went on, pointing to the chocolates. "And now you tempt me with these."

Madeleine studied her father after that. Was he drinking too much? She couldn't blame him for wanting to escape into an alcoholic stupor. But his behaviour seemed quite normal to her. And she realized that it was a case of the pot calling the kettle black. Eleanor herself drank too much. And became belligerent when she was drunk. Madeleine only discovered this the hard way. She had waited until after the holiday celebrations before she broached the subject of going back to Paris.

"When does your new term start?" her father asked her as they sat with the port after dinner. "You'll be off soon, I suppose."

Madeleine took a deep breath. "Actually, I am going back to Paris," she said.

"What?" They both sat up straight, staring at her.

"Did the term there not finish before Christmas?" her father asked. "They are on a semester system?"

"Daddy, I've made the decision that I'd like to finish my studies over in France. At the Sorbonne. It's much better to have lectures about French dramatists given by Frenchmen and not old English professors who have no proper feel for the culture of the country."

She had rehearsed this statement ahead of time, and it came out in a rush.

"But will that university accept the courses you've already taken? Will it take longer for you to finish your studies?"

"It's utterly ridiculous!" Eleanor said, so forcefully that Madeleine realized too late the outburst was alcohol-fuelled. "Of course she can't go back to Paris. Tell her, William. She's supposed to finish her degree and get out into the world. Get a job. Stand on her own feet. Not be dependent on us until she's an old maid."

"I'm not asking you for any more money," Madeleine said. "In fact the cost of everything is less in Paris."

"And pray what use will a foreign degree be to you when you come home and want to teach, eh? You think any decent school, like the one your father teaches at, will want to hire a teacher with a dubious foreign degree?"

"I hardly think the Sorbonne counts as a dubious foreign institution." Madeleine fought to control her temper. "It's one of the oldest universities in the world, you know. And most distinguished. Besides, I might not even want to teach. There will be other things I can do—more interesting things—like translating, interpreting."

"I'll tell you what other sorts of things you can do," Eleanor shouted. "You can become a bloody servant like your mother. They do say bad blood will always out, don't they?"

"Louise was not a servant, Eleanor," Madeleine's father said quietly.

"What was she when you met her, then? Certainly not a debutante."

"She was a governess," her father said quietly. "A governess to a good family—to my family. My young nephews."

"Not much better than a servant," Eleanor sneered. "She wasn't allowed to eat her meals with the family, was she? A governess is nothing.

She was lucky she managed to snag herself a proper gentleman—although you've always been a pushover with your kind heart. You probably felt sorry for the girl, and she worked on your sympathies."

"She was very beautiful," William said, "and had such a sweet nature. A man could not help loving her, even if it caused a rift with my family."

Madeleine had been trying to stay calm "And I doubt that you were ever a debutante yourself," she said, regretting the words as soon as she said them.

"I?" Eleanor's face turned beetroot red. "My family goes back to William the Conqueror, I'll have you know. We have all sorts of titled ancestors. So many men who did great deeds. And my first husband was a major general."

"The very model of a modern major general?" Madeleine asked. Her father smiled. Eleanor did not.

"You have learned some very bad manners during your time away from home. The sooner you are back in a decent women's college, the better. There is no question of your returning to France."

"Daddy?" Madeleine turned to him.

"It does make more sense to finish your degree when you are so close," he said. "Take time afterwards to travel on the Continent if that's your wish. You do come into a little money on your twenty-first birthday this year."

"I'm sorry, but I've made up my mind. I'm going back to Paris."

"Please don't expect any money from us." Eleanor spat out the words. "And don't expect to be welcome here when you come home with your tail between your legs."

The threat felt dire. Madeleine almost gave in, but pride wouldn't let her.

"Very well," she said. "I think I'll go up and pack. I'll leave in the morning."

"Sweetheart . . . !" her father called after her. "Let's discuss this when we've all cooled down."

And her stepmother's voice, floating up the stairs. "Bad French blood. Let her go back there. Good riddance, I say."

~

There were many times during the journey to Dover and then on the ferry across the Channel that Madeleine questioned her actions. She was, after all, returning to a foreign country simply because of one young man—a man who had told her himself that he wasn't particularly reliable. What if she arrived in Paris only to find he showed no more interest in her or had taken up with another girl? Would she have to return with her tail between her legs as Eleanor had predicted? And yet she realized she was dying to see Paris again, dying for her own room in one of those old buildings and a life of freedom. She had no idea how she was going to fund this but was prepared to wait and see. She had been to the post office and withdrawn her small savings before she left—enough to keep her head above water for the first few weeks. Also her father had stopped her as she came down the stairs with her suitcase in her hand.

"I really wish you'd reconsider this, my dear," he said. "I think it is a foolish decision and one you will come to regret. You know Eleanor. She does not forgive or forget easily." He put a hand on her arm and drew her closer to him, lowering his voice. "But I want you to know, between ourselves, that I will send you money. I don't want my only child to starve. Your mother would have wanted me to take good care of you."

"Hasn't she gone yet?" Came Eleanor's voice. Madeleine hugged her father, then picked up the suitcases and hurried out of the front door.

CHAPTER 4

It was raining hard when the train pulled into the Gare du Nord. Madeleine couldn't risk splurging on a taxicab, but instead left her suitcases at the left luggage office and then walked down the long boulevard towards the Marais. The rain had now turned to sleet, and the driving wind stung her cheeks, making her gasp as she walked. Her plan was—she realized she didn't really have a plan. She had left in a hurry, driven by her stepmother's scornful fury. If she'd paused to consider, she would have written to Giles, asked him to look for a room for her, and then returned to Paris. Now she was counting on him being home, taking her under his wing, making everything all right.

It wouldn't be too late to go back to Westfield, a voice whispered in her head. *Term hasn't started yet. Your old room. Old friends.* It did sound very tempting, but she acknowledged that she had written to the college, announcing her intention of spending the rest of the year at the Sorbonne. That seemed to be a good halfway measure. Students were certainly allowed to spend a whole year abroad, only it would push back her graduation date a year. Not too terrible. Then she pictured her stepmother's face. "I knew she'd come slinking home and want us to fund another year of study for her."

No. She wasn't going back. She strode out resolutely. She was going to see Giles, and everything was going to be all right. She put her hand into her pocket, and her fingers closed around the tiny book of love poems. Her heart was beating fast as she climbed the second flight of stairs to his room. She tapped on the door. No answer. Tapped again. All right. He wasn't home. She tried the door, but it was locked. Reluctantly she retreated. There must be a concierge, she told herself. All these French buildings had a resident caretaker. Music was coming from a radio inside one of the ground-floor rooms. Madeleine tapped on that door, and it was opened by an alarming old woman, dressed in black, with a big, hooked nose. Almost a caricature for a witch.

"Yes?" she asked.

"I'm sorry to disturb you, madame," Madeleine said, "but I'm looking for Giles Martin."

"Aren't we all," the woman said. "He is gone, mademoiselle. Disappeared." She spread her hands with a shrug in a classic French gesture of hopelessness.

"Gone?"

"He was supposed to pay the rent on January first. But no sign of him and no rent. I don't know how much longer I can keep his room. If he wished to delay his return, why did he not write to me? Why did he not send a check to cover the rent, huh?"

"I don't suppose you'd let me stay in the room until he returns, would you?" Madeleine asked. "I'd pay you the rent for this month."

"You're a family member?"

"No. Just a friend."

The woman looked at her with scorn. "Too many friends have visited that room, mademoiselle. I do not approve of the bohemian lifestyle. Take my advice and be on your way."

"Oh no," Madeleine stammered the words. "I only came to visit him, not to stay here. He was supposed to help me find a place to live . . ."

The woman now looked at her with pity. "I can't help you. We have no vacancies in this building. You are a student at the university?"

"Yes."

"I suggest you ask there."

Madeleine came out into blowing snow. She would have to find a cheap hotel for the night. Unless . . . She stood on the doorstep, pausing to consider. Before she left home, she went through the French books her mother had read to her—fairy tales she had loved so much:

Cendrillon, La Belle et la Bête—Cinderella and *Beauty and the Beast.* As she flicked through the pages, remembering her mother's soft voice as Madeleine nestled against her, the sweet smell of her hair brushing against Madeleine's cheek, she came upon a page from a letter. *My dear niece*, it said, written in an antique French script that was hard to decipher. *I am relieved to find that you and your little family have survived this terrible war unharmed. I, too, have come through it, although after many deprivations, my health is not what it once was. Problems of the chest with not enough heat and no nourishing food. But let us hope for better things now. You say you hope to bring your daughter to see me next summer. That would be a great treat. I look forward to seeing how she has grown. Does she still speak our language?*

It was signed, *Your devoted aunt, Janine du Bois.*

By that next summer, Madeleine's mother would have died in the flu epidemic. Her father had also been very sick but survived, and as the epidemic raged, there had been no talk of travel anywhere. Then her father had married Eleanor. Madeleine had been sent to boarding school and had never visited Great-Aunt Janine again. But now she had the address. She had looked it up on her city map and found it was not far from Giles's place. Did she dare go to see the old lady now, in the hope that she might have a temporary place for Madeleine to stay? It seemed awfully rude, and she remembered Tante Janine as old when she last saw her. That was seventeen years ago now. It was hardly likely that she was still alive. But better than nothing, and at this moment there were few options. So worth a try.

Ironically her address was the rue Saint-Gilles (although this was spelled with two *l*s.) As Madeleine checked house numbers, she finally came to a building that looked familiar. Yes, there had been potted bay trees on either side of the front door. They still stood there, looking forlorn with a dusting of snow. All in all it looked more civilized than where Giles lived, the building in better repair and the front step scrubbed. What's more, there was a bank of doorbells beside the door, their names beside them. And on the third floor lived a du Bois.

Madeleine took a deep breath and pushed the bell. After a long wait a buzzer sounded, and she realized that this was opening the front door. Tentatively she pushed it open and stepped into a murky foyer. There was no electric light, and she had no idea where the switch might be, but in the middle of the foyer she made out the black cage of the lift. After much fumbling she managed to open this, felt her way inside, then jumped as the door slid shut on her with a resounding bang. After more searching she found the button to make it go up. It rose, creaking and groaning, just as she had remembered it, still equally terrifying.

At last it juddered to a halt. Madeleine wrenched the door open and came out. One door on the landing was open, and a sliver of light streamed out from it.

"Hello," said a frail female voice. "Who are you? What do you want?"

Madeleine saw the hunched little figure standing there, a shawl around her shoulders. "Tante Janine, it is I, Madeleine, the daughter of Louise," she said.

The old woman seemed to straighten up. "Madeleine, my dear child. What a surprise. What a lovely surprise. After all these years. I thought . . . I thought you must have perished with your dear mother. But no, here you are. Come inside, come inside, do."

She was ushered into a large room, quite unchanged after all this time. Madeleine recognized instantly the velvet curtains, draped with a fancy swag, the faded silk chairs, the Victorian knick-knacks, but then she turned her attention to her great-aunt. Tante Janine had seemed old when Madeleine had last seen her in 1914. How old could she be now? And yet the face was not horribly wrinkled, and the eyes that examined her were bright.

"Yes, I see your dear mama in you," she said. "But why have you left it so long? Why all this time before you come to visit your old aunt?"

"I'm sorry," Madeleine said. "There was the war, and then Maman died, and my father married again, and I was sent to boarding school. I suppose I felt that my connection to France died with my mother."

Tante Janine nodded. "I understand. Well, I'm glad to see you have not quite forgotten our language. And now you return to Paris?"

"I have been studying at the Sorbonne," Madeleine said. "I didn't have your address. And to be truthful, I thought it unlikely you were still alive after all this time. But then I found a letter from you in a book belonging to my mother, and here I am."

"Where are you staying?"

"Ah." Madeleine hesitated. "I have to find a room. I was in a hostel before, but I don't want to go back there. I had expected a friend to be in Paris, but he has not returned."

"You are looking for a bed for the night? Is that it?"

"If it wouldn't be too inconvenient," Madeleine said. "I'm sorry, but it's snowing, and I really thought . . ." She had a horrible feeling she might cry.

"Sit down, child. I will make us both a tisane," Tante Janine said. She left the room. Madeleine looked out at the snowflakes now driving past the tall windows. She shivered, although the room itself was warm. Her great-aunt returned with a tray. Madeleine leapt up to take it from her and put it on a low gilt table. There were two cups on it, each containing an interesting pink liquid, and beside them some plain biscuits. Madeleine took a sip. The taste was not unpleasant.

"Rose hip," Tante Janine said. "Good for the blood." She put her cup down. "Now," she continued, "you were expecting to meet a young man here? But he has not shown up."

Madeleine nodded.

"Your young man?"

"I don't know if he's mine," Madeleine admitted. "He begged me to come back after the holiday and said he'd come to England to be with me if I didn't return. I thought . . ."

"My dear, I have found that young men say a lot of things they don't mean. I would advise you to choose carefully. A lot of them are scoundrels and charlatans. Take my sister, your dear grandmother. She fell in love with an English fellow when we were at the seaside, recovering from a sickness. She ran off with him, back to England, but it turned out that he had not been truthful about his prospects there. She had a hard time of it and died young, leaving your poor mama to have to go to work as a governess. Quite beneath her. It was only luck that your father was a member of that household and rescued her. I warn you, be cautious. Young men usually only want one thing. And when they get it, why they often move on to new pastures."

Madeleine was feeling quite sick, some of it with hunger but also with the realization that Tante Janine might be right. She had given up everything for a man she hardly knew. She had no way of contacting Giles. He had never given her his home address, nor did she know where his friends might be found.

"You never married, Tante Janine?" she asked, diverting the focus from herself.

The old woman shook her head. "I never found a man who lived up to my father, who was a good and noble man in every way. I inherited this apartment and a small private income, and I live quite frugally, so life has not been unpleasant, apart from the war, when we couldn't get fuel or food." She eyed Madeleine critically. "But you, my child. I suppose you want something to eat? You look quite pale."

"Yes please," Madeleine said.

"Usually I take my evening meal early, on account of digestion. A boiled egg. A little custard."

She would not let Madeleine help with the preparation, but they sat together in the tiny spotless kitchen to eat. Madeleine was still ravenous after the boiled egg, two slices of thin bread and a little cup of custard, but she thought it would be most rude to ask for more.

"What will you do now?" her aunt asked when they had cleared away the meal. "Find your own place to live? Go back to the hostel?"

"Definitely not that," Madeleine said, shaking her head. "I really don't know what to do. I should probably return to England and my old university there, if they still have a place for me."

"I suggest you sleep on it tonight. Things will look brighter in the morning," Tante Janine said. Madeleine helped her make up a bed in the small spare room that smelled of mothballs and lavender. Her suitcases were still at the train station, so she lay in her underclothes, curled into a ball, her mind in turmoil.

~

She awoke to strange yellow light and found the world blanketed in snow. Tante Janine was already up, and there was an enticing smell of coffee. What's more, there was a basket of croissants on the breakfast table. Madeleine looked at it in wonder. "You didn't go out in the snow to get these?"

"No, my dear. I have a kind neighbour who brings me fresh bread every morning. I told her I had a visitor, and she brought croissants."

Madeleine tucked in with relish.

"What is your plan for the day?" Tante Janine asked.

"I suppose I must go to the university and see if they have a list of rooms for rent."

"You've decided to stay in Paris, then? Even if this Romeo does not return?"

"I can't go home," she said flatly. "My stepmother—she is not the easiest woman. She said some horrible things."

"And you walked out in a huff?"

Madeleine nodded.

"And your father? Your kind father? What does he say about this?"

"He was sorry to see me go. But she is the dominant one now. He seems rather weak and old, and she bosses him around."

"So your pride will not let you return home?"

"Maybe." Madeleine gave an embarrassed shrug.

Tante Janine studied her. "What is it you really want? Where do you want to be? If there were no young man in the picture?"

Madeleine considered this. "I really like it here in Paris. I find the lectures stimulating. I think I'd quite like to stay."

"Then stay." Her aunt spread wide her hands. "You may use my spare room until you find a situation to your liking. I shall not turn you out into the snow."

Madeleine reached out and touched her aunt's hand. "Thank you. You are most kind."

"You are Louise's child," the aunt said simply.

~

By the time Madeleine ventured out, the pavements had already been swept clean of snow. She took a bus back to the Gare du Nord and retrieved her suitcases. Then she stopped at a corner grocery and bought sliced ham and cheese, wanting to provide her share of the food. Tante Janine always took her big meal in at midday, she said. Much healthier for the digestion. What she served was a hearty soup, and Madeleine relished it.

"You are a good cook," she said.

The old woman smiled. "I have a few dishes that I have mastered over the years, but one can't go wrong with a vegetable soup. You just throw everything into the pot, and voilà."

After lunch Madeleine made her way to the university. She had an uncomfortable interview at the admissions office, during which she was advised to remain a visiting scholar for the rest of the year. If she decided to remain in Paris after that, she could apply for admission as a resident, realizing the standards would be more demanding. Madeleine agreed. If she stayed until the summer, she could go back to London and finish her degree as if nothing had happened. It would give her time to think.

After the interview she examined notice boards for rooms to rent. She didn't have much luck. Most rooms had been rented for the academic year. She bought a newspaper and studied the ads, but everything seemed more expensive than she could afford.

The next day classes began. She tried to concentrate through a lecture on medieval French poetry. She kept looking up as if she half expected Giles to materialize as he had done before. But at the end of the day, she returned home to her great-aunt with no Giles and no room. Each day her great-aunt was polite and welcoming, but Madeleine could tell that it was a strain on the old woman and that she wanted to return to her usual routine. By the end of the week Madeleine decided she would go back to Giles's landlady. If he had, indeed, not returned, then the room would be free, and she could rent it. If they looked inside they could see whether he had taken all his belongings with him, indicating he was not coming back ever. The very thought of that made her feel sick and empty.

She sat through her Friday lectures only half listening to the drone of the professor's voice. Coming out, she made up her mind. She would skip lunch and go to Giles's flat right now. Get it over with. Know where she stood. As she started down the stairs in the midst of a crowd of students, she saw him coming up towards her. No mistaking that head of unruly curly hair. He saw her at the same time and fought his way through the crowd like a salmon swimming upstream.

"You came back!" they exclaimed at the same moment and fell into each other's arms, blocking the stairs, not caring for the mass of humanity that tried to pass them.

"I thought you'd gone and wouldn't come back," she said as he dragged her aside and they sat on a bench in the hallway together.

"I'm so sorry." He stroked away a tear from her cheek, brushing the hair back from her face. "I didn't know where to write to you. I didn't quite believe you'd have the nerve to go through with it. I was ill, you see. I got a really bad flu right before Christmas. Missed the whole celebration, lying there with a fever. Even my mother was quite worried I'd die. She became quite gentle and solicitous for a few days. Until I recovered, that is. Then she told me I'd better come up with a plan to graduate by the end of this year or there would be no more money. I staggered back here, and here I am."

She took in his face, clearly thinner and paler than when they last met. "I was afraid I'd never see you again, that I'd come all this way for nothing," she said.

"Did your parents agree? There was no unpleasantness?"

"Oh, much unpleasantness," she said. "My stepmother was horrible. Said horrible things about my mother and told me if I went to Paris, I need not bother to come back."

"And yet you came. You really must care for me."

"Of course I care for you," she said. "You are the best thing that ever happened to me."

His look became serious. "I'm probably not a good bet, in the long run," he said. "I don't have good prospects, and I'm not the most reliable of men. But for now we're together, and that's all that matters, right?"

"Right," she agreed, his warning echoing in the back of her brain. Not the most reliable of men. Was he telling her not to trust him?

CHAPTER 5

After a cursory hunt for a room, it became obvious that nothing close enough to the university was available, at least not that she could afford and in a safe enough neighbourhood.

"Of course, you could always move in with me," Giles said with a half laugh. Then he looked directly at her. "I mean it, Madeleine. You and I—we like each other, don't we? We have something special."

"Yes, but moving in with you. That's a big step," she said. Thoughts raced through her head: surely one found a boyfriend, went to the pictures and took walks in the park. It got serious, and he visited the family and finally asked for one's hand, and then, but only then . . . "A big commitment. I hardly know you, Giles. Oh, I've had a wonderful time being with you, but living with you—that's different. It's . . . not something that girls like me do. I mean we haven't even . . ." She couldn't finish the sentence, looking away in embarrassment.

"Look at it this way," he said. "If you and I continue to see each other, we will, inevitably, make love soon. I am not the type who can hold hands with and write poems to a woman he desires forever. I want you. You know that."

Madeleine flushed at his frankness.

"And why not?" he demanded. "You are a free woman. I am a free man. You enjoy your time with me, yes?"

"Yes," Madeleine said tentatively.

"Then let us enjoy our time together. Give it a try. All right?"

Madeleine took a deep breath, almost not wanting to say the words. "All right."

~

"You have found a suitable flat nearby?" Tante Janine asked. "That is good news."

Madeleine couldn't meet her gaze. She knew her great-aunt would not approve of her moving in with a boy. She was sure her father and stepmother would not approve, so there was no way she could ever tell them. She didn't exactly approve of it herself, but she also knew that Giles might soon tire of her if she played the demure virgin. And she had to admit she felt an arousal of excitement at the thought of a man wanting her, an attractive man, and she tried to picture what being in his arms would be like.

Their first week together was everything she had dreamed of. Giles was a patient, attentive lover. Waking up in his arms was the most wonderful thing she could have imagined. He took her around Paris, showed her secret corners, hidden treasures, flea markets where she could find designer clothes for pennies. And they laughed a lot. He introduced her to his friends, who clustered in noisy groups in cafés, debating the state of the world. It was all heady and improbable, and she soaked up every moment of it.

Giles himself was an enigma. At one moment a dedicated Communist, talking passionately about justice for all men, overthrow of corrupt governments, and at the same time a devout Catholic. On their first Sunday together he had woken her early.

"What's the matter?" she asked blearily. "Isn't it Sunday? We don't have classes."

"I go to Mass," he said. "Aren't you coming?"

"Mass? I haven't been since I was a small girl. I told you that I don't have much to say to God."

"Come anyway." He took her hand and pulled her up. "It will be good for your soul."

She went with him, feeling strange and out of place with the forgotten rituals of her childhood.

All went well until after three months the inevitable happened. She became pregnant. Having grown up without a mother in such a sheltered environment, Madeleine was completely naïve about such matters. Giles had said he'd take care of such things, and she believed him. A missed period was not so unusual. But when she vomited into the toilet one morning, she suspected that something was wrong. When it happened again the next morning, realization began to dawn on her. The news made her feel both excited and scared. She went for a long walk along the Seine, trying to grapple with what this meant for their future. Surely now they'd marry and live happily ever after. Giles was an honourable man, wasn't he? He had said he loved her . . .

She stood watching the barges go past. One was being steered by a woman while a toddler crawled around at her feet. A baby. It would mean the end of Madeleine's studies. Of any plans for a career. And what about Giles? How could he support them? What if he didn't want to support them? Told her it was her responsibility . . . She felt a cold sweat coming over her. She was far from home, from a stepmother who would tell her she had made her bed and now had to lie in it. Only an elderly great-aunt to turn to, but she'd, too, disapprove. She started walking again, faster and faster, trying to practice how she should break the news to Giles.

When she told him at supper that night, Giles took the news in his stride.

"I suspected this, you know. When I heard you throwing up this morning." He sucked in a long breath, considering. "I should get a real job, I suppose," he said. "If I have to provide for a family."

"Shouldn't you finish your studies first?" she asked. "The baby isn't due until the end of the year. I intend to finish my own university courses."

"We have to think of the future," he said. "We can't raise a child in a situation like this. I'm going to write to my mother. This might change everything."

This sounded hopeful to Madeleine: they might be invited to move to the château, and her child would grow up in pampered surroundings. But the reply, when it came, was short and not at all sweet.

I have no interest in meeting any of your mistresses. And if you are stupid enough to have put one of them in the family way, it's up to you to take care of it. May I remind you of your commitment and obligation, from which you cannot simply walk away.

"What does she mean?" Madeleine asked.

He turned away, looking out of the window. "She means I can't marry you."

"What?"

"I'd like to," he said. "I fully intended to. But I'm engaged to someone else."

"And you never thought to mention this small fact to me?" She heard her voice shake.

"It was never relevant until now."

"To me it might have been! I would not have allowed myself to share the bed of a man who had an obligation to another woman. How could you do this to me, Giles?"

He ran his hand through his hair like an embarrassed little boy. "You have to understand it's different for my kind of people. An understanding was made between our families when I was a boy—too young to know my own mind. But at her coming out party when she was sixteen, her family made the announcement to all who were present. She and Giles Martin would marry at a suitable time."

There was a long pause. Outside a cart rattled by over cobbles. "Do you love this girl?"

"I hardly know her. I have no feelings for her at all, but that is the way it is done in France. One marries for family expectations and keeps a mistress for companionship."

"Companionship?" She spat out the word. "That's how you think of me? And your child? You want your child to be a bastard? Never to have your name?"

"Of course not. I want to marry you, but you don't know that family. They are powerful in our part of France. They will sue for breach of promise, I know. Sue enough to ruin our family. My mother would not survive the scandal."

"You care more about your mother than about me." She would not look at him now.

"That's not true. I do care about you. Very much. But I hadn't expected this to happen. I hadn't dared to think of the future yet. I was here in Paris and so were you, and you were warm and wonderful, and I was happy. That's all that mattered. Now everything has changed."

"I suppose when the time comes you will leave me and go to her," she said. "And I—I have to go home to England and beg forgiveness of my stepmother? Beg her to take me in? And if she refuses, try to get some lowly job to provide for my child?"

He put both hands on her shoulders now. "I will never abandon you, Madeleine. I promise you that."

"I'm meant to continue in a secret apartment somewhere as your mistress? Is that right?"

He shrugged, not knowing the answer. "I want to be with you," he said. "I'm sorry this has happened now. I'll do my best."

At least Giles was true to his word in that. He came home one day looking excited. "I have a real job," he said. "I am to be employed by a newspaper—a very left-wing newspaper. Of course they do not pay much, but I will be writing articles and doing interviews on the treatment of the working class. Just what I'd always wanted." He paused, looking at her. "I thought you'd be happy for me. It could lead to bigger and better things. A job with a better newspaper, with a labour union."

"I am happy for you," Madeleine said. "But all I can think of is that you can walk away whenever you feel like it, whenever your mother snaps her fingers, and I'll be left with nothing."

He wrapped his arms around her. "I promise I will never leave you," he said. "We will get through this somehow."

"If I went with you to see your mother, would she not realize that I am a good and decent person?"

He shook his head. "You are not what she had planned for me. Therefore you could be St Bernadette, and she would still not make you welcome. She is a difficult woman who has had a hard life."

"A hard life—in a château?"

"The disgrace when my father abandoned her. It nearly killed her. Her pride, you know."

~

Madeleine had been to visit Tante Janine regularly, noticing that the old woman enjoyed her company, but since the news of her pregnancy, she had not dared to face her. She pictured her great-aunt's look of disdain, heard her saying, "I told you so."

The months passed quickly. Madeleine went to classes, wearing an oversized jacket that hid her growing bulge. Giles also tried to attend classes as well as his new job, about which he was increasingly enthusiastic. "I have met union bosses," he said. "They are impressed with me. They like my vision for the future."

He began going off to meetings with other Communists, coming back late at night. Most of the time Madeleine fought off fear, but as she lay alone, it threatened to engulf her. Was she doing the right thing by staying here? Wouldn't it be better to be safe at home in England? And what could the future possibly hold for her and the baby that now kicked and squirmed inside her?

She passed exams with good marks and wondered if she could go on studying when the autumn term commenced. She broached this with Giles, who was becoming increasingly preoccupied with his labour unions and newspaper. "What's the point?" he asked. "You are never going to be a schoolteacher now. It would make more sense if you found yourself a little job until the child arrives, so we have money to move to a better address and buy the necessary equipment."

"All right," she said. "If that's what you want."

"What I want is to make enough money to provide for us properly," he said. "At the moment I'm not doing that."

Madeleine put an advertisement in the paper to teach English lessons. She visited several shops, putting a card in their windows, and then it occurred to her that she might visit Great-Aunt Janine again. Someone who had lived in Paris all her life would have contacts. Again she hesitated, hating the feeling of knowing she had let her family down. But she imagined what her mother would have done. Maman would not have judged, she was sure. She would have wrapped her arms around Madeleine and whispered, "My poor darling. But don't worry, we will get through this somehow."

Madeleine blinked back the tears at the thought of this. She set off for Tante Janine's with a basket of fruit and pastries as a peace offering.

"Well, this is a surprise," the old woman said. "I was sure you'd gone back to England after all."

"I should have listened to you," Madeleine said. She opened her coat to reveal the growing bump.

"Mon Dieu!" Tante Janine put a hand to her throat in horror. "You returned to the wayward young man, and now he has abandoned you?"

"No, I'm still with him. But he can't marry me, Tante. He is promised to another woman. He's from an old family, you see, and they've been promised for years. He doesn't love her. He doesn't even know her, but he says he has to go through with it. But he will take care of me and the baby."

"Sit down, child. Sit down," she said. "I am sorry for you. I won't say you made your own bed and now must lie on it, because the young never listen and have to learn by experience. But if you need a sanctuary, I am here."

"What I really need is a job. We don't have much money, and I thought I could work until the baby comes. I'm sure you know a lot of people."

Tante Janine shook her head sadly. "A lot of old people, I'm afraid. But let me think. You should not be on your feet all day. What skills do you have?"

"I speak English. I'm well educated."

Tante Janine sighed. "I understand the world is still in the grips of the Depression. Too many people with skills but no jobs. I suppose I could employ you part-time . . ."

"You?"

"My eyesight is failing, but I love to read. You could come and read to me every day. You could answer my correspondence for me. Do my shopping for me."

"Gladly," Madeleine said, "but I wouldn't want to take your money."

The old woman smiled. "I don't have much, but a small income for life that takes care of my needs. And you would be doing me a great service. You could go to the library and choose new books for me . . ."

"I'd love to be of service, but I still don't think you should pay me. My mother would not have wanted . . ."

"Listen, my dear. You need work. I need assistance. Perfect. No more to be said. Come every day at three, and we shall take tea together and you shall read to me. And some days I'll give you a small shopping list. Is that agreeable?"

"More than agreeable. I'll start tomorrow." Madeleine almost bounded home. It wouldn't be much, but it would be a joy.

Giles did not seem as impressed as she hoped. "She's just doing it to be kind to you," he said. "I don't think you should take an old woman's money. Times are hard."

"I said the same thing, but she said I'd be doing her a service. She's lonely, Giles. She'll welcome the company."

"I may have something better for you," he said. "There is a chance for some translation work, from English Communist writings. You'd be good at that, wouldn't you?"

"I would. But I can probably do both. I'd only be with my aunt for a couple of hours."

"Very well," he said. "It's your choice."

Madeleine started her daily visits. And was surprised when Great-Aunt Janine invited her to bring Giles for Sunday lunch. Equally to her surprise, he accepted, and what's more, he hit it off immediately with the old woman. They sparred good-naturedly about the merits of Communism.

"Of course, Jesus was a Communist," Tante Janine said. "And I have always followed him devotedly. But it can never work in real life because people are greedy and fearful of those not like them and do not want to share."

"You are right!" Giles slapped his hand on his thigh. "People are driven by fear. How wonderful if they knew that there was enough to go around and nobody would ever need to starve. How wonderful if we would all share our surplus."

"A beautiful dream, my boy," she said softly. "Cling to your dreams. You may need them."

After that the Sunday lunches became a regular occurrence, but Giles became moodier and more withdrawn. Madeleine looked at him, worrying that he was trying to find a way to break up with her. Then one day in November he burst into their room, his eyes flashing, his face animated.

"I went for a long walk along the Seine," he said. "I needed to think, and I have made a decision!" he said.

Madeleine recoiled in alarm.

"I don't care what anyone says. I don't care what the world says or my mother or anybody. I love you, and I'm going to marry you before our child arrives. Come. We'll go to the *mairie* for a license."

He pulled her up from the chair, bustled her into her coat and almost dragged her down the stairs. They had a civil wedding and afterwards cake and champagne with Aunt Janine. Giles wrote his mother and received a letter in return.

You are no longer my son.

CHAPTER 6

Olivier Louis Martin was born the week before Christmas. He was a tiny baby, red and wrinkled and crying lustily. It had not been an easy birth, and Madeleine lay exhausted in her hospital bed while Giles held her hand.

"He's an ugly baby," Giles said, staring at him. "Let's hope he improves with age."

"No, he's not. He's beautiful," Madeleine replied. "Absolutely perfect. Look at his little fingers."

The doctor who had delivered the child came to speak to them, a worried frown on his face. "She has lost a lot of blood," he warned. "She must stay here for a while until she recovers."

"I can take care of her at home," Giles said.

"There is a danger of infection. It would be better for her to be in our care. And I must warn you both: you were fortunate it was a small baby this time. A bigger baby could not have passed through the birth canal. There would be a danger of the baby getting stuck and both mother and child dying." He shook his head. "I would advise no more children. The risk is too great."

~

Madeleine recovered after a stay in hospital and brought tiny Olivier home. Fulfilling Giles's wish, he developed into a beautiful child with large, dark eyes and a serious expression as he stared at their faces. Madeleine was entranced with him. So was Giles. He sent a snapshot of the baby to his mother but heard nothing in return. They sent a snapshot to Madeleine's father and received a long letter and a hefty check. *My dear child. Why did you not let us know you had married? We would have wanted to attend the wedding. Are you ashamed of your husband? Or of us? And now this adorable grandchild. I would like to meet him. Please bring him over when he is old enough to travel. In the meantime, here is a little something to help his life to start out right.*

Madeleine blinked back tears when she read it. She should have kept in contact with her father, whatever Eleanor had said and thought. The check enabled them to move to a small apartment near the Bois de Boulogne. Life developed into a pleasant routine. Giles was getting more work for the newspaper. Madeleine pushed the baby in his pram around the park or took him on the bus to visit Tante Janine. The old lady took great interest in him. "Such an intelligent-looking little face. As if he understands every word. You must make sure you speak to him in both French and English, so he can move between both worlds."

Madeleine did this and enjoyed watching his alert little face as he listened to songs in both languages, trying to make sense of the words. The first sentences came out as a lovely, jumbled mixture: "Look, Maman. A *cochon*." But before he turned three, he was fluent in French and English. A bright little boy, excited to learn and discover—sometimes too much, as when he dismantled the clock.

Giles was becoming a rising star of the left wing. He had sensibly realized that Communism, and all that it represented, could never take hold in a moderate and urbane country like France. He had gone to work for a Socialist politician and was sent all over the country on fact-finding missions, reporting on workers' conditions, strikes, factory disasters. Then he was sent abroad, reporting back on the struggle between Communism and Fascism in Germany. Things looked bad there, he reported. A strange little man called Hitler had seized power and was arresting Communists by the dozen, sending them off to prison camps. Giles was determined to do something about it: to whisk them out of Germany to safe havens.

"Please be careful," Madeleine begged. "You have enough to do here without worrying about what's going on in Germany."

"But the Communists there are our brothers." He shook his head. "Actually, I've been warned not to go to Germany any more. It's not just Communists they are rounding up. It's Jews. It seems that this Hitler has a personal hatred of Jews, for some reason." He shrugged. "I suppose a lot of people do. That's why . . ." He paused. His eyes met hers. "I never told you before, but my father is Jewish. I am half-Jewish. Your son is a quarter Jewish. In France we keep quiet about such things."

"As if it matters to me," Madeleine said. "But I do hope you take the warning and stay clear of Germany."

She didn't know whether he did this, as he didn't always tell her where he was going or what he was doing. She suspected that he was not always faithful to her, from a hint of perfume on his shirt, but she didn't confront him. When he was home, he was a loving husband and father, delighting in their growing son. Their life became mildly prosperous. A woman came in to clean once a week. Madeleine shopped for clothes, learned to find great bargains at flea markets, and met other young mothers for tea. They could afford to go back to England to visit her father. She teased Giles about it. "You're not a very good Communist, you know. Here we are eating oysters and drinking wine. Aren't you supposed to live plainly and be miserable?"

Giles shook his head. "Your great-aunt said Jesus was a Communist, and he turned water into wine, remember. He enjoyed a good feast as much as anyone. As long as we give what we don't need to the poor and work to improve the conditions of the needy and downtrodden."

He really is a good man, Madeleine thought. *How lucky I am to have married him.*

~

All this changed in 1939. On September 3, Britain and France declared war on Germany. Giles came home one day with a sombre face. "The inevitable has happened," he said.

"Will you join up and fight?" She heard her voice shake.

"I will do my part," he said. "But I want you to do something for me."

"Anything."

"I want you and Olivier to go back to England."

"Now? But we don't even know what might happen. France has built the Maginot Line. Surely that will keep the Germans out. They say it's impenetrable, don't they?"

Giles shook his head sadly. "Do not underestimate the Germans, my love. We may be safe for now, but France will surely be invaded soon, and it will be worse than the Great War. I can't do what I have to if I am worried for your safety."

"But I don't want to leave you . . ."

He took her hands in his. "I will not be around to take care of you. The Germans might come, and . . . I want you to be safe."

"Are you going to join the army?"

He shook his head. "I have other plans. I'll escape conscription because I'm a journalist. I've talked to some fellows, and . . . the army won't stand a chance. I've been in Germany enough. I have seen their build-up of arms. They are a trained fighting machine. I think they will try to swallow the world."

Madeleine shivered. "England, too, do you think?"

"At least they have a better chance, being an island. And with a decent army. So please go when I ask you."

"Then come with me. Join the forces in England if you want to do something brave."

He shook his head. "Someone has to stay here and do what they can."

"But you told me you were half-Jewish. You know how Jews are being treated in Germany. Think of Kristallnacht. All those windows smashed and people attacked."

He gave her a sad little smile. "My darling, if they catch me working to stop them, I don't think they'll take it too kindly anyway."

"Must you really do this? Abandon your wife and son?"

"Somebody must," he said simply.

For a while the world held its breath. Nothing happened. There was talk and sabre-rattling, but in France life continued as it always had. People sat in cafés, music sounded from windows. Madeleine held out hope that it might all fizzle out and she wouldn't need to go. But British forces started arriving in France. Frenchmen joined the army, and there were parades of men in uniform past cheering crowds. From the east, terrible news filtered in. Battles and massacres in Poland. Fierce fighting before the country fell to the Germans.

Madeleine continued to visit Great-Aunt Janine and told her that Giles wanted her to take Olivier to England.

"Very sensible," her great-aunt said.

"Will you come with us?" Madeleine asked. "There is room at my father's house."

Tante Janine gave a sad smile. "My dear, what would I do in England? I have lived in this flat for fifty years. Besides, if the Germans invade, they will not bother an old woman. They respect the elderly."

Christmas came and went with people in Paris trying to celebrate as if nothing had changed. Although the country was already rationing food, Madeleine tried to make it special for Olivier, knowing too painfully it might be the last holiday they would ever spend together with his father. Giles had started to go away for days, returning with a worried frown. Spring came to Paris with its usual glory—blossoms and flowers in all the parks, pavement cafés opening up, spring fashions on the streets.

Only Giles remained tense and watchful. "Soon, my love," he said. "You don't want to find it's too late and you're trapped here."

"They have turned their attention to other places. They are invading Norway. Perhaps they are not interested in us."

"Oh, they are interested," he said with a sad smile. "These others are just a precursor. They want France and they want England."

"You really think they will breach the Maginot Line and our forces won't be able to keep them out?"

"I really do. I think it's inevitable. Our leaders have their heads in the sand."

"All right. If you want me to, I'll go. Soon." She gazed up at his face, taking in every detail. *How I love you,* she thought.

She went to see Tante Janine, telling her that they would be leaving.

"Go with God," her great-aunt said. "I shall be praying for you. You can pray for me, too, if you like. And we shall meet again when this madness is over."

Reluctantly Madeleine kissed the old woman's cheeks and said goodbye.

Then came the news Giles had expected. The Germans had swept around the Maginot Line through the forest of the Ardennes in Belgium and were now pouring into the northeast of France.

"Go now," Giles commanded. "Do not wait a moment longer. I must be ready, too."

In a daze of shock, Madeleine packed up their belongings. Giles decided against keeping on the flat, so they sold their few pieces of furniture.

"Where will I find you?" Madeleine asked as their sofa went out of the door. "Where can I write to you?"

"I'll write to you at your father's and try to give you updates when I can," he said.

"I could always write back to you at Tante Janine's."

He shook his head angrily. "I wouldn't want to expose her to any danger."

"You'll be in danger?"

"Quite possibly, I'm afraid."

"Then don't do it. Come with me now. There will be things to do in England."

"You don't understand. Someone has to do it. And in a way I'm quite looking forward to it. A chance to do something brave and daring like the comic books I read when I was growing up."

~

On the day before they were due to leave, Giles took Madeleine up to Montmartre. Olivier had gone to school as usual, and they were both aware that this would be their last time alone together. It was a beautiful spring day—the scent of blossoms was in the air. Birds sang, pigeons cooed. They climbed the steps together without speaking. At last they came to the gleaming whiteness of the new basilica and stood on the terrace with the whole of Paris spread below them.

"How I will miss this," she said. "What a beautiful city." Then she looked up at him. He was staring out across the city, and there were tears on his cheeks. "How I will miss you."

He turned her towards him. "Madeleine, I want you to know . . . I have not always been the perfect husband to you. It was all too soon, wasn't it? I expected to enjoy freedom, travel, finding out what I wanted from life, and I'm sure you did, too. But Olivier came, and we were stuck with each other."

"Don't say it like that," she said. "Olivier has been the most wonderful gift, and being with you is all I've wanted. I'm sorry if you felt you were stuck with us and we spoiled your dreams and plans."

"You didn't let me finish," he said, gazing down at her. "I was going to say that I realize now that I could not have hoped for a better life than the one we have had. You are the love of my life, Madeleine. I can't bear to let you go."

"Then we'll stay."

He shook his head. "No. It's because I love you so much that I want you to be safe. I have a hard enough road ahead. I need to know that my wife and son are well and happy and that we will see each other again as soon as possible." His voice cracked with emotion at the end of these words. His arms came around her, holding her fiercely to him. She felt his heartbeat against her and took in the familiar smell of him, the feel of her cheek on his shoulder, and tried to remember every tiny detail. They stood there for an eternity, locked in each other's arms, oblivious to passers-by, until at last they walked down the steps together, hand in hand.

The next morning they went together to the Gare du Nord. “Take care of Olivier for me. Make sure he remembers his papa. And his French language.”

“I will.”

He took her face in his hands. “I love you,” he said. “I have loved you since the day I first met you, and I don’t regret a moment of our time together. I will come to you whenever I can.”

Madelcine nodded, afraid she would cry if she tried to say a word. Giles scooped Olivier up into his arms. “Put me down, Papa. I’m a big boy,” Olivier said.

“But I want to hug you one last time before you go away.”

“Why won’t you come with us?” the boy asked.

“Because I have to stay in France and fight for our country. You must be brave, too, and look after your mother, yes?”

Olivier nodded solemnly. “All right, Papa. I’ll be brave.”

“Good lad. Now off you go. You don’t want to miss the train.”

Giles loaded them and their luggage into a compartment. Madeleine dropped the sash window so that she could still touch him. They exchanged a final kiss. A whistle blew. The engine let out a great hiss of steam. The train started to move. Giles waved. Madeleine waved and kept on waving until the train entered a tunnel and the platform was lost to view.

I will never see him again, said a voice in her head.

CHAPTER 7

London, May 1940

Madeleine's father seemed delighted to see them.

"My little grandson. What a treat. Why, you look just like your dear grandmother who died a long time ago."

The reception was frostier from Eleanor, but she agreed that it was not sensible to remain in France.

"Finally you've come to your senses," she said. "I always said no good would come of living abroad, or of marrying a foreigner."

"But a lot of good did come out of it," Madeleine said patiently. "I have a wonderful husband who is now going to fight for all of us, and I have a perfect son."

Eleanor studied the little boy, who was looking around the sitting room with curiosity. "Yes, well that remains to be seen. Just as long as he doesn't touch things. Does he speak English?"

"I speak it very well, Grandmother," Olivier said in his solemn little voice. "My mother always reads to me in English."

Even Eleanor was slightly impressed. "Well then," she said again. "As long as the child knows his place, stays in his room and is in bed by seven, I think we'll get along for a while. Just until you find a place of your own, and a job."

"I'll be volunteering for war work," Madeleine said, "as soon as I've found a suitable school for Olivier."

"And you'll need to apply for ration books," Eleanor said. "We can't feed you on our rations." She frowned as she studied Olivier. "I don't know about him. He's not a British subject, is he? Will they give him a ration book?"

Olivier shot a worried glance at his mother.

"I'm sure it will all work out just fine," she said. "You are the child of a British subject, Ollie. Don't worry."

~

By the end of the first week, Madeleine had sorted things out. She and Olivier both had identity cards and ration books—she as a British subject and he as a refugee. And she had enrolled him in a small preparatory school nearby—St Mark's, which, in spite of its name, was not run by a religious order. It had small classes and was within walking distance of the house, which would be necessary if Madeleine were to work. Olivier had been used to walking alone to school in France and thought nothing of it, although Madeleine had to remind him about crossing roads with the traffic coming from the other direction.

Instead of war work, Madeleine quickly found a job teaching French at a local secondary school. The male teachers had all been called up for the armed forces, and there was a bad shortage, so the fact that she had no degree from an English university was easily overlooked with her certificate from the Sorbonne. She saw immediately that the work was not going to be easy. These were not the bright students who went to the grammar school or to private schools. They were the ones who wanted to be out at fourteen, getting a job and earning for the family. Rough kids from the dockland in Greenwich, they had no interest in learning another language and thought French sounded sissy.

"If we have to learn something, it had bloody better be German," one of the cheekiest boys said. "We can talk to them when they invade."

"They ain't going to invade," one of the girls retorted. "My dad's joined the Home Guard. They'll stop them Germans."

The rest of the class laughed. "Your dad? Do you reckon he'll be out of the pub long enough to stop an invasion?"

~

Madeleine soon noticed that the mood was pessimistic everywhere. People thought Britain didn't stand a chance in warding off the might of Hitler's army. She thought of Giles doing some kind of undercover resistance and wondered what chance of survival he might have. It all felt hopeless.

Olivier, too, was not having an easy adjustment to life in England. He was used to being a good student. His spoken English was good, but he had little experience in reading and writing and came home fuming with red lines all over his exercise book. "I was one of the bottom ones in the class," he said. "I didn't know *threw* in *he threw the ball* and *he went through the door* were spelled differently."

"Of course you didn't, darling," she said. "I'll have a word with your teachers and explain that you have attended a French school until now. Maybe they can give you some special tutoring."

"That won't make any difference," he said. "They all think I'm strange."

After a week at the school, he announced that he had changed his name. He was now Oliver Martin—pronounced the English way and not *Mar-tan*. The boys made fun of his English, he said. He didn't know their slang words, and he couldn't understand some of the London speech. He hadn't read their comic books or seen the films they liked.

Madeleine put an arm around him. "I know it's hard right now. It's hard for me, too. I'm trying to teach a lot of children who don't want to learn and think French is a waste of time. We just have to stick it out for now. But it will get better, I promise. You will make friends."

"I hope so," he said, "because it's not fun right now."

~

Life in London continued not being fun. Coal was rationed and in short supply. Madeleine's father had become rather frail and developed a nasty cough. If he drank too much before the war, as Eleanor had insisted, that had now been curtailed, as it was hard to buy wine or spirits. Madeleine had heard nothing from Giles for a while now. She had received two letters at the beginning, saying that he was joining up with a group of comrades and going into the field. She understood that he couldn't risk writing to her, as it would give away his position. And as the Germans swept across France, there was no more postal service between England and France. The successful invasion culminated in the disastrous retreat of the British forces to Dunkirk, when the whole country held its breath as thousands of men were rescued from the beaches by any boat that could cross the Channel.

And then, in the autumn of 1940, the Blitz began. Nightly bombing of London. Madeleine's father had an Anderson shelter constructed in their back garden—a corrugated iron shell over a dug-out trench, the shell covered over with turf from the lawn. They went down into it at the sound of the first air-raid warning, but Olivier panicked at being in the dark, damp hole.

"Take me out," he cried in French. "I can't breathe."

"But it's dangerous, darling. Bombs are falling," Madeleine whispered in French.

"I don't care. Take me out." He was near hysterics.

Madeleine held him close until the all-clear sounded, but the next time, he utterly refused to go into the shelter. They rigged up a bed in the cupboard under the stairs, which would be safe from flying glass and probably safe if the house collapsed. Madeleine and Olivier slept there together while the world shook with the muffled thumps of falling bombs. In the morning, walking to school and work was impeded by broken glass and debris on the streets and the sight of bombed houses with only one wall still standing.

"We should get out of London," Madeleine said to her father. "It's not safe for any of us here."

"Blackheath should be safe enough," he said. "It's not as if we're in Central London."

"But we are close enough to the Greenwich docks. And Olivier isn't sleeping. He's terrified of the bombs."

"But this is my home," her father said. "I've lived my whole life here. I'm close enough to my old school to come in and teach when they need help." He gave her a pleading look. "It's not as if we're near an industrial or military installation. Any German plane will see we are a quiet suburban street. They won't deliberately bomb civilians. They are a civilized society, after all."

But he was proved wrong. During a particularly fierce bombing raid at the beginning of 1941, a house at the end of their street took a direct hit, killing three people.

"We have to try to move, Daddy," Madeleine said. "It's just not safe."

He gave a heavy sigh. "You're right. I'll try to find us a house to rent in the countryside," he said. "Although at the moment everyone who can is trying to move out of London."

Madeleine worried about a move to the country, finding a suitable school for Olivier and another job for herself. But then the matter was settled for them. At the end of teaching one day, she was summoned to the headmaster's office. She went cautiously, worrying what she might have done wrong, or if it was some kind of bad news. Instead the headmaster indicated that a man had come looking for her. A man from the ministry, he said. He didn't know which ministry. Madeleine went into the hallway, where a middle-aged man in civilian dark suit stood up from the chair where he had been sitting and held out his hand to her. "Mrs Martin?" he asked.

"It's *Martan*," she said, pronouncing it the French way. "It's French."

"Quite so." He nodded. "Might we have a word together?"

"What's this about?"

"All will be made clear in a minute, if we could find somewhere private to talk." In spite of the civilian clothes, everything about him shouted military, from the neat little moustache to the upright bearing. Her heart was racing. Did he have news about Giles? She led him down the corridor until they found an empty classroom. It was stuffy, smelling of chalk and unwashed teenage bodies. "Well?" she asked. "May one know which ministry you represent?"

"I suppose you could say the War Office, but that's not entirely true." He smiled. "But you don't need to know any more at this moment." He cleared his throat. "We understand that you have lived in France for several years?"

"For eight years," she said.

"And you are fluent in French?"

"I grew up speaking the language," she said. "My mother was French, and I was taken to France as a child."

"Could you pass as a Frenchwoman?"

"I believe so. I have done so for the past eight years."

"That is good news," he said. "Of course there will be tests, a selection committee, you understand."

"For what?"

"Your government can use you, Mrs Martin—*Martan*," he said. "In various capacities: as a translator of intercepted radio broadcasts, as a radio operator sending out fake broadcasts, or as an infiltrator."

"Infiltrator of what?"

"Of France."

"As a spy, you mean?" Madeleine gave him an astonished look.

"Something like that."

Madeleine gave an uneasy laugh. "Oh no. You're looking at the wrong person. I have a small son. He's already traumatized enough by having to move away from his home to a strange country and a strange school. I'm not going to go anywhere."

"Then I'm sure we can make use of your language skills in London for now. When your son has settled in, maybe . . ." He left the rest of the sentence hanging.

"I'd like to be useful," Madeleine agreed. "But my son comes first at the moment."

"Quite." He nodded. "Let me give you my card. My secretary will answer the telephone. You ask for Major Carlson."

"Is that your name? Major Carlson?"

"That is the name you ask for."

"I see. You apparently know all about me, but I know nothing about you."

"It's better that way." He held out his hand. "I look forward to seeing you at Whitehall in the near future. I'm sure you can be of great service to your country."

He strode away with long, military strides.

~

Madeleine toyed with the card when she got home. Translating in London was one thing, something she'd be prepared to do. But what if there were long hours, or night shifts, and she was away from Ollie? He'd panic without her in an air raid. Once you worked for the government, especially in something rather hush-hush, you did what you were told. *Stay safe and bored teaching at the school*, a voice whispered inside her head. And then the matter was simplified for her. Olivier came home from school with a letter from the headmaster:

> *Dear Mrs Martin:*
> *Our school sustained damage from a bomb last night, meaning that we can't use some of the classrooms. Given the extreme danger to which we are exposing our students with nightly bombing raids, I have decided the only course of action prudent at this time is to move the school out of London. Fortunately I have managed to secure an unused wing of a girls' boarding school in Sussex. It is already set up to house and feed students as well as give instruction and should take care of us until the situation in London improves.*

Should you not wish your son to be part of this great adventure, and want to withdraw him from the school, please let me know your decision by the end of the week. I hope to make the transition as soon as possible.

Madeleine read the letter out loud to Olivier and his grandparents.

"Very sensible," her father said. "So many children are being sent out of London at the moment, and he'll be well supervised."

Madeleine looked at Olivier. "Do you want to go?" she asked, sensing that his answer would be no. "If you don't, that's just fine. We'll find you a new school near here."

Olivier frowned, weighing this. "Then I'd have to make friends all over again," he said. "The boys might be rougher than they are at St Mark's. But I think it might be quite fun to be out in the country. I've never lived in the country before. I'll see cows and sheep and things, won't I? And go on walks through the woods."

"I expect you will," Madeleine said. "Should I tell your headmaster that you want to go?"

"It won't be for long, will it?" His voice echoed sudden uncertainty. "Because I wouldn't want to be away from you for too long."

"I really don't know, darling," Madeleine said. "I don't think the Germans can keep up this level of bombing indefinitely. Your grandparents and I might also try to move out of London. I have no idea what will happen. But you can write to me, and if you don't like it, I'll come and fetch you."

A relieved smile crossed his face. "All right then," he said.

CHAPTER 8

February 1941

With Olivier's future taken care of for the present, Madeleine telephoned the number she was given for Major Carlson. She was invited up to Central London to an interview at the St Ermin's Hotel at a time and date convenient to her. She said that she would be bringing Olivier up to Victoria Station on the twentieth, to put him on his train, and it would be convenient to visit the St Ermin's Hotel after that. Then she turned to the business of getting her son ready for what he called his "big adventure." They were not allowed to take much. One small suitcase light enough for them to carry, the letter said. Only their school uniform, change of underwear, gym clothes, shoes, toilet bag, and gas mask. A favourite photo was encouraged, plus enough pocket money that they could buy writing paper and stamps as well as visit the tuck shop.

Madeleine tried not to let her son see that she worried about his going. Part of her was glad he was out of danger in the countryside and would have access to better food and fresh air, but she knew he had never been the most outgoing of children. He was a quiet, studious little boy, the type others love to pick on. She lay awake at night fighting back her worries. What if he was bullied and miserable but too proud to tell her? What if the Germans invaded and she was cut off from reaching him? But what was the alternative? There was no other suitable private school within walking distance, and she didn't want him to rely on buses. The only other option was the local primary school, and she had seen the rough working-class children who went there. Besides, it would mean starting over for him, trying to make friends and fit in at yet another school. She tried to gauge his mood as they packed his suitcase together.

"So you'll be quite happy about going to the country?" she asked.

He tried to give her a cheerful smile. "Yes. I think it will be interesting. Mr Horton said we'll have a big field for games, and we'll start rugby. And I've never seen a cow being milked. Do you think they have cows nearby?"

"I expect they do," she said. "But what about the other boys? Sharing a dorm room with them? Will that be all right?"

He shrugged. "I suppose. They are not so bad now. They've sort of accepted me. I'm a fast runner—they want me on their team. And a couple of the chaps are quite decent."

She noticed he had already refined his vocabulary. "It shouldn't be for too long," she said. "I'll miss you, but now I can get on with important work to help our country."

He nodded. "That's good, isn't it? Everyone has to do their part. That's what Mr Horton says."

She looked at his serious little face and wrapped her arms around him. "My darling boy," she whispered.

"Aw, Mum. I'm too old for that now." He pushed her away. "And when we're at the station, please don't make a fuss, will you? I don't want the other chaps to think I'm a sissy."

"I'll try not to." She smiled. "And anyway, we're not to come into the station with you. Your headmaster says we are to meet at the side of the building where the bus station is, and then you'll all march together on to the platform. He says there will be other schools travelling with you, and he doesn't want parents to add to the chaos."

Madeleine's father hugged Olivier fiercely. "Take care of yourself, little man. I'll be thinking of you. You will write, won't you?"

"Of course, Grandpa. My teacher says we must write home once a week." He looked embarrassed at his grandfather's tortured face. Then he shook hands politely with Grandma Eleanor. She did not try to hug him.

They set off for Victoria Station, taking a bus to the tube station. Olivier insisted on carrying his own suitcase. "I'll have to do it the rest of the way. I need to get used to it." In truth it was sadly light. None of his favourite Meccano sets or drawing pads. He had refused to take his stuffed dog, fearing the other boys would laugh. They arrived at Victoria Station. There was already a group of boys waiting on the side street.

"Ah, Oliver, there you are." The headmaster ticked his name off the list. "Jolly good. Ready for a fun adventure, eh?"

Olivier nodded.

"Here you go. Make sure you wear this." He handed Olivier a label on a string. It bore the name Oliver Martin, the name of the school he was going to and his destination, Haywards Heath.

"Remember that, won't you? Haywards Heath. I imagine the train will be quite full. If we get split up, that's where you get off. Now remember there won't be any station names on the platforms. They have all been removed in case of invasion. But someone will call out the name when the train stops. Your teachers will call it out and make sure you get off. All right?"

Olivier shot a frightened glance at his mother as the label was put around his neck.

"Now you look like a piece of luggage," she teased, making him smile.

Big Ben started to chime ten o'clock.

"Time to be off, boys," the headmaster said. "The train leaves at ten fifteen. Say goodbye, boys."

They did as they were told. There were no tears, all of them trying to be brave. Madeleine hugged Olivier. "Have a wonderful time," she said. "Give my best wishes to the cows."

He managed a smile. Then the headmaster blew a whistle. Olivier lined up beside another boy his own age. Another whistle, and off they went. Two by two. Olivier looked back, and Madeleine blew him a kiss. He thought about blowing one back but decided not to. Instead he waved. They passed around the corner towards the front of Victoria Station and were gone.

~

One by one the parents dispersed, bleak looks on their faces. Madeleine would have liked to visit the station ladies' room and spruce herself up before her interview, but she didn't want Olivier to think she was spying on him. Instead she collected herself and headed for the St Ermin's Hotel. She had looked it up in the A-to-Z directory and seen that it was not far away. Within walking distance, anyway, along Victoria Street and up towards Buckingham Palace. A swank address, obviously.

Even in this neighbourhood close to the palace, there were signs of destruction. Sandbags blocking off a street, one building standing as a blackened shell, another with the windows blown out and now covered in plywood. The St Ermin's Hotel, however, seemed untouched, its red brick with white trim glowing in morning sunlight. Madeleine stood at the entrance, admiring it. She was not familiar with grand London hotels, having never moved in those social circles during her years in London, and hesitated before walking up to the front door. She expected to see a glittering foyer with marble tables and chandeliers. Instead she found that the hotel had been taken over by the War Office. The former foyer now blocked off with plywood partitions. A desk had been set up to intercept anyone trying to enter. When she asked for room 055, she had to show the letter and her identity card and was told to go up to room 236. The lift wasn't working, and she had to use the stairs, so she was quite out of breath by the time she arrived at the second floor. The door was opened by the man who called himself Major Carlson, and she was ushered into one of the plainest and most dreary little rooms she had ever seen. Even the room at the hostel was bigger, and at least it had a rug on the floor. This room consisted of four walls, a window that looked out on to an inner courtyard, a plain wooden table and two chairs.

"Good of you to come, Mrs Martin." He shook her hand. "And good of you to answer the call of your country. Please take a seat."

She sat opposite him. He put a piece of paper in front of her. "Before we go any further, I must ask you to read and sign this."

"What is it?" She glanced down at the sheet of paper, then gave him a suspicious stare.

"It's the Official Secrets Act. You have to sign that you will never divulge anything about your work to anyone, including your nearest and dearest. If you do, you could be shot for treason."

"Golly." Madeleine realized she sounded like a schoolgirl.

"It's wartime, Mrs Martin. We can take no chances with whom we take on. Tell me, do you now consider yourself French or English?"

"English. Definitely English," she said. "I feel comfortable in France, but I feel at home here."

"And your husband? Tell me about him. How does he feel about the British and the Germans?"

"From what I know and can glean, my husband is currently with a group of Communist Resistance fighters, working undercover against the Germans. I had two letters to begin with but only one since Paris fell. It was so heavily censored that I couldn't make out what he was saying. I haven't heard from him for a long time. I have no way of knowing if he's still alive or dead."

"And if I told you he is still alive?"

Her eyes lit up. "You know that? For a fact?"

"We have information to suggest that is the case."

"That's wonderful." She gave a little sigh. Giles. Still alive. The words rang in her head. She almost got up and hugged the man opposite her.

His expression did not change. "And you—would you consider yourself patriotic?"

"Absolutely. These bombing raids have made me furious. I'd like to do what I can to help, but as I've told you, I have to consider my son. His school is being evacuated to Sussex for now, so I'd be free to work in any capacity you thought fit."

"But not to be trained to go abroad?"

She shook her head. "I have to be within reach if Olivier needs me. I can't take risks because I'm all he has."

"You live with your parents, don't you?"

"My father and stepmother," she said. "My father has become rather old and frail, I'm afraid. And my stepmother—well, she was never the warmest of people. We tolerate each other now because she needs our ration books and my income as a teacher." She hesitated. "I presume I'd still be paid if I did some kind of war work?"

"You'd still be paid."

"How do you think you could use me?"

He gave a small chuckle. "Young lady, I'm supposed to be interviewing you. Let me ask the questions. But to answer that one, I cannot tell you whether we'll want to use you or not. We are extremely choosy in my department. Oh, we could give you a job easily enough doing office work, filing, typing . . ."

"I'm a rotten typist."

"So what would you say your skills were?"

"My French is almost as good as my English. I'd be a useful translator. I know Paris well."

"Are you good at crosswords?"

"Reasonably."

"And mechanically?"

"My son is definitely better than I am." She laughed. "He can take anything apart in seconds. And you should see what he builds with his Meccano set. But I'm not completely helpless. I've fixed a leaking pipe in our bathroom once. Does that count as mechanical?"

He managed the ghost of a smile. "Good. Honest answers. Do you count yourself as an honest person?"

"Oh definitely. My parents raised me to tell the truth."

"Could you lie if you had to?"

She considered this. "It depends on the lie. If a German soldier broke into my house and asked me if I was alone, but I knew my son was sleeping upstairs, I could easily lie to him."

"And what about keeping a secret? This form we will ask you to sign—how hard will it be not to tell others what you are doing? Let's say, for example, that your difficult stepmother says to her friend that you are doing mindless office work when their daughter is in uniform? Will it be hard not to tell her the truth—that your work is more valuable than the Auxiliary Territorial Service."

Again she was slow to answer. Then she said, "I didn't tell my father or stepmother that I was living with my boyfriend, that I became pregnant and finally married. I only wrote to them when Olivier was born. I can keep a secret when necessary, I suppose."

"Tell me about your friends."

She sighed. "I don't have any really close friends in England any more. I've kept in touch with my old roommate at Westfield College. She married a vet and now lives in the North of England with her husband and four children. Another Westfield friend went to Australia when she married, and we write to each other. I was friendly with other young mothers from my neighbourhood in France, but nobody I was really close to, except my great-aunt. I get on well enough with the other teachers at the school, but I can't say we're friends. We don't go out for drinks or anything."

"You're not the sort of person who develops close attachments, would you say?"

Madeleine considered this. "I suppose not. When my mother died and Daddy married again really quickly and I was shipped off to boarding school, I sort of shut down. I think I didn't want to get too close to anybody ever again. Except Giles, that is. My husband was my life. And my son, of course."

Major Carlson tipped back his chair and sat staring at her until she began to feel quite uncomfortable. "Well, Mrs Martin, I believe we can find somewhere to use you. There will be a month's basic training at a house outside London, where we assess your skills and aptitudes. But we don't go any further until you sign this sheet of paper."

He sat up abruptly, his chair making a loud bang on the bare floor, and pushed the piece of paper towards her.

She met his gaze. "You guarantee that I won't be sent abroad against my will? That I won't be required to do anything that would put my life in danger?"

"All our lives are in danger, every day. We never know when the next bomb is going to fall, do we? And if we're invaded, we'll all be required to do our part and fight in any way we can. You'd be prepared to do that, wouldn't you?"

"Oh, definitely."

"Then I suggest you sign this piece of paper, and we'll get to work."

He handed Madeleine a pen. She took the paper, gave it a cursory read and then signed. She had just handed the paper back to him when they heard the familiar wail of the air-raid siren.

"Oh, not again," Major Carlson said with a sigh. "These damn daylight raids are becoming a nuisance."

"Should we go down to the cellar or something?" Madeleine asked.

"Oh, we don't normally bother," he said. "They're not really interested in the West End, apart from that time the blighter hit the palace."

He looked out of the window. "I don't see any aircraft. I'll see you down to the foyer and maybe wait there until the all-clear."

They made their way down the stairs, joined by the occupants of other offices. Madeleine noticed they chatted easily, as if a raid was nothing to really worry about. Once in the foyer, some of the workers went down another flight, below ground. From the distance came the thump of a bomb falling, followed by another.

"Nowhere near here," someone said. "I think they're heading south. We can probably go back to work."

At that moment the all-clear sounded. Everyone sighed, nodded and dispersed. Major Carlson shook Madeleine's hand. "I hope we have the pleasure of working with you in some capacity, Mrs Martin."

"I hope so, too," she said.

He opened the door for her, and she stepped out into sunshine.

CHAPTER 9

Oliver

Olivier Martin, now referring to himself as Oliver, marched into the station beside Gerald Hopkins. Gerald wasn't a particular friend, but he was harmless, quiet and rather shy like Olivier. They glanced at each other, gave each other a reassuring grin, but didn't say anything. Olivier liked the sound of their feet, marching, echoing from the pavement as they turned into Victoria Station. Like soldiers, going off to war. It made him feel important and useful. Inside the station was chaos: whistles, shouts, hissing of steam, slamming of doors, hundreds of children trying to squeeze on to one platform. Olivier felt his first jolt of fear. His life had been sheltered thus far: a pleasant life in Paris, a school where he was one of the better students, and then his grandparents' home on a dignified suburban street. Apart from Bastille Day, and when they went to the Arc de Triomphe to watch a parade of soldiers with General de Gaulle leading them, he had never been in such crowds. He moved closer to Hopkins and hurried to catch up with the boys in front of them.

"Stay together, boys," the headmaster called over their heads. "We're going on to the platform now."

He handed the ticket collector at the gate their pass, and they were waved through. Another school came behind them, their students rowdier and not in uniform. They barged on to the platform, pushing Olivier forward. Soon he was swept up into the crowd. He tried to find Hopkins but couldn't. He tried to pick out the striped caps of his school uniform, but he wasn't tall enough to see over the taller children from other schools.

He felt panic rising. *Stay calm,* he told himself. *I know where to get off. It will be all right. They won't leave me behind.* As he stood waiting, another boy came up beside him, looked at his name label and let out a whoop of laughter.

"Look at you." His voice was not refined like those of his grandparents and schoolmates. It had a rough cockney edge.

"What?" Olivier tried to sound defiant.

"Oliver Martin, right?" He pointed at the label on Olivier's blazer.

"That's right." The label was spelled the way he was now known at school.

"Well, we've got the same name. I'm Oliver Martin Jones. How about that?"

"That's funny." Olivier knew better than to tell the boy that he was really Olivier Martin, pronounced *Martan.*

"You know what," the boy said. "We should swap labels. And when they call the rolls, you answer for mine and I'll answer for yours!"

"Oh no. I don't think we'd better do that," Olivier replied. He had always obeyed rules.

"Come on. Don't be a spoilsport. Bit of a laugh, eh. We'll swap back afterwards."

Still, Olivier hesitated. "What are you, a goody-goody?" The boy sounded belligerent now. "Or a cowardy custard?"

Olivier could sense other children looking at him. His cheeks were burning with embarrassment. He looked for one of his teachers. "Come on. What's the harm in it? Bit of a giggle," the boy said. "We all need a giggle right now, don't we?" He reached over and yanked off Olivier's label, then stuck his own around Olivier's neck.

"St Mark's School?" A voice shouted out. "Answer to your names. Oliver Martin?"

"Present," said the other boy and burst into laughter. Olivier tried to smile, too.

Other schools were called. "New Cross Road primary school? Oliver Martin Jones?"

The boy nudged Olivier. "Present." He could hardly get the word out.

The boy was laughing again. "I like fooling the teachers, don't you? Teach 'em a lesson."

A train was pulling in to the platform, gliding in with a hiss of steam.

"Wait for it, children," a commanding voice shouted. "Nobody board until I say so. Make sure you've all got your tags on."

But some children were not waiting. They were surging forward towards the open doors.

"Hey, wait a minute," Olivier called. "Give me my label back."

But Oliver Martin Jones was already climbing on to the train. Olivier tried to see which carriage he was getting into before he was propelled forwards by a tide of eager children. He was swept up into a corridor, already packed with bodies. He tried to move along it, squeezing past other boys and girls, but his suitcase impeded him.

"'ere, watch where you're going," a bigger boy threatened. "You ain't getting my spot."

He looked for the other Oliver but couldn't find him. He looked for any familiar uniforms from his school but couldn't see any. *It doesn't matter,* he told himself. *I can remember Haywards Heath. I can get off at the right stop and find the others. It will be all right.*

~

A whistle blew. "All aboard" was shouted. Doors slammed shut. The engine let out a big hiss of steam. The train gave a jerk and started to move forwards. The children packed in beside Olivier cheered. Out of the station the train moved cautiously, crossing points, stopping, then starting again. It crossed the Thames, and Olivier had glimpses of a power station, big black buildings as it moved through Vauxhall, many of them bombed into rubble. The train moved on to Clapham, passing small back gardens where washing flapped on clotheslines and small children played amongst the rubble in the streets. The noise level on the train was almost overwhelming, children shouting to each other. It was loud enough that nobody heard the drone of approaching aircraft or the wail of an air-raid siren. Daylight raids were not usual but had been happening more frequently lately. The train came to a halt as a thump sounded nearby.

"Blimey," a boy said next to Olivier. "We're being bombed."

There was a whistling sound, a flash and the train received a direct hit.

CHAPTER 10

Madeleine came out of the St Ermin's Hotel and stood on the empty street, wondering which way to go. She could return to Victoria Station and take the tube back home, or she could enjoy the unexpectedly mild and sunny day. There was no rush, after all. She had taken the day off work, and nobody would be expecting her. She decided to walk up to Buckingham Palace and through the park. Maybe she'd even walk as far as Oxford Street and treat herself to lunch in one of the department stores. She set off, noticing the spring in her step. Soon she'd be doing something useful, not teaching disinterested and rude children. Also she realized that the lightness of heart came from knowing that Giles was still alive. Maybe he'd survive this whole nightmare and they'd be together again. It gave her renewed hope. She strode out and stopped in surprise when she found herself in front of the palace. She knew it had also been bombed, but from the outside it still looked pristine, and the royal standard was flying, indicating that the king and queen were in residence. She nodded with satisfaction. England was lucky to be ruled by good people, people who cared.

From the palace she headed up to Hyde Park Corner and made her way through the park. Londoners were coming out from nearby Mayfair, making the most of the mild weather and the all-clear after the raid. Secretaries sat on benches, eating their sandwiches together. Young men lounged on the grass. A couple of nannies pushed babies in prams. It was a pleasant scene, a brief interlude in a war.

Madeleine had underestimated the size of Hyde Park and was quite tired by the time she reached the Marble Arch and Oxford Street. Her stomach reminded her it must be lunchtime, but she didn't feel like walking along Oxford Street all the way to D H Evans or John Lewis. She was pleased to see the word *Lyons* opposite Marble Arch. Maison Lyons—one of the Lyons company's upmarket restaurants instead of its normal tea shops. She decided to splurge and went in, finding that the food did not live up to the art nouveau décor. The roast beef on the menu was in reality two ultra-thin slices of warmed-over meat plus a pile of swedes and mashed potatoes, covered in glutenous gravy. It reminded Madeleine painfully of the French food she was missing. Nobody in France would stand for this, she thought, but then she corrected herself. Maybe in France conditions were worse than here, now that the Nazis occupied the country. And again her thoughts went to Giles.

At least Olivier should have good food in the country, she told herself. Surely they'd get fresh vegetables supplied by farmers and maybe even extra eggs. This made her feel better. She had not wanted Olivier to see her concern before he left, but she had worried about him. He was such a small boy to go away on his own. Not the type who easily made friends, even in Paris. Would he be teased, bullied, when they were safely away from home with no parents nearby? But she told herself that he'd grow big and strong with plenty of fresh air and room to play sports. It would toughen him up—something he'd need in this difficult world.

She finished her lunch with a cup of tea and a biscuit, paid and came out to find the early sunshine was now clouding over. She looked down Oxford Street. Should she do some window shopping? She wondered. Then decided against it. There was little point in new clothes. Nowhere to go. Nobody to impress. There wasn't much to buy anyway, even if she had two coupons in her ration book. As she entered the Marble Arch tube station, the placard at the newsstand read, *Schoolkids Killed in Bomb Strike*.

"Bloody Germans," she muttered to herself. Who would want to bomb children? What did that achieve? She bought a ticket, went down the steps and got on to the train.

~

"You've taken your time," Eleanor remarked as Madeleine came in through the front door. "I thought the boy had to be at Victoria at ten?"

"That's right." Madeleine had perfected keeping her composure so as not to let the older woman know how she annoyed her. "After I saw him off, I went for an interview."

"What kind of interview?"

"It seems I might be working for the government."

"Leaving teaching?" Eleanor's voice sounded sharp. "Where do you think they are going to find teachers with all the men gone?"

"But my government needs me more," Madeleine said sweetly.

"Doing what?"

"I'm not quite sure yet." Madeleine took off her coat and hung it on the hall stand. "Something like translating, probably. Or helping with broadcasts from the BBC to France. Either would be preferable to facing a classroom of rowdy students every day who make fun of French pronunciation and are quick to talk about how the French capitulated and didn't fight."

"Quite right," Eleanor said. "They did."

"What chance did they have when the British retreated to the coast and left them in the lurch?" Madeleine snapped now. "Anyway, I hope to be doing something useful, even if it is backup office work."

"They will pay you, I hope?"

Madeleine headed for the fire in the living room, suddenly feeling chilly. "Don't worry. I should still be bringing in money."

Her father was sitting close to the fire, which glowed with only enough heat to warm the immediate area, since coal had become rationed. He was wearing a scarf and gloves, as he felt the cold badly. He looked up with a smile as Madeleine came in. "Well, here she is. Did the boy get off all right, then?"

"He did. He was very brave. Not a single tear." She sat down in the armchair opposite him, holding out her hands to the warmth of the fire. "And I'm probably going to be working for the government."

"The government, eh? Using your language skills, I suppose."

"Exactly. It seems they need all sorts of translators at the moment." She remembered the Official Secrets Act that she had signed. Translating was a harmless occupation that would raise no questions.

"Your school will miss you," he said. "There are few teachers around. I might volunteer to come back from retirement."

"Don't be silly, William," Eleanor said. "I'm not having you going out in all weathers at your age. And with your weak chest, too. In fact I think Madeleine was right. We should try to move out to the country and away from this awful bombing. There were planes going over today. Enemy planes. I saw the black crosses on them. I don't know where they were headed. We certainly didn't get the warning, but it must have meant another daylight raid somewhere. Now I can't even go out to do the shopping without worrying. We need to go."

"I don't know how you think we can afford to take a place in the country," Madeleine's father said. "We'd never get anyone to rent this house, would we? Not being so near to the docks. And I don't want to leave the house unoccupied. We'd find squatters in it when we returned, you mark my words."

"Fine, stay here and we'll all be bombed in our sleep," Eleanor snapped.

"But Madeleine will need a place to stay if she's working at a ministry in London. We should stay and ride it out. It can't go on forever. Hitler has turned his attention to Russia, hasn't he? Maybe he'll lose interest in bombing Britain."

"Don't count on it," Eleanor said. "He aims to bring us to our knees."

"Shall I make us a cup of tea?" Madeleine asked, not wanting to dwell on her own worries.

"You can turn on the radio, dear," her father said. "Almost time for the five o'clock news."

Madeleine turned it on, going through to the kitchen, where she put the kettle on the stove and spooned tea leaves into the pot. She was just putting cups on to the tray when she heard the rich, fruity voice of Alvar Lidell saying, "This is the news from Broadcasting House in London."

The water in the kettle came to a boil with a loud whistle.

"A great tragedy occurred earlier today when a train full of school-children being evacuated to the country took a direct hit from an enemy bomb. The incident occurred near Clapham Common."

She rushed through into the sitting room, still carrying the sugar basin.

"It is feared there are a large number of fatalities."

Inside the kitchen, the kettle continued to shriek as it boiled unheeded on the stove.

CHAPTER 11

"Who would know? Who do I telephone? Where do I go to find out?" Madeleine's voice was near hysteria.

"Calm down, my dear," her father said. "We don't know that it was Olivier's train."

"How many trains of evacuees could there be in one day?" She shook her head as if trying to wipe out the image. "I must go and find him. Where would the nearest hospital be, do you think?"

"South of Clapham Common did they say?" Her father frowned, looking at his wife. "Wandsworth, I think?" he said.

"Don't go rushing to any hospital," Eleanor said. "It will be chaos there. Crowds of people milling around. They wouldn't let you in."

But Madeleine was already heading for the telephone in the front hall. "Operator, I need you to connect me with Wandsworth Hospital. Would you know if that's where the casualties have been taken? My son was on that train."

The operator sounded flustered. "I'm sorry, ma'am. The lines are flooded with calls at the moment, so I have to assume that you've got the right place. Let me try to connect you."

Madeleine waited, about to explode with impatience, until at last a voice said, "Wandsworth Hospital."

"The train. The little children . . ." Madeleine could hardly get the words out.

"That's right. They are being brought here. More arriving all the time."

"My son," Madeleine said. "Can you tell me if you have an Oliver Martin amongst your casualties?"

"Let me check for you." A long, awful pause. From the background came the incessant ringing of an ambulance bell. And then, "We have nobody of that name, I'm afraid."

"Might that mean that he's all right? He's safe somewhere?"

"It might well. The end carriages were untouched, so we're told. It was the middle ones that got the worst of it."

"How would I find out?" Madeleine almost whispered the words. "If he's still alive?"

"I wouldn't come in person at the moment. It's been chaotic all day, and they are not letting family members in. If your son is one of the lucky survivors, I'm sure you'll be notified as soon as possible. I recommend that you stay by the telephone. And in the morning we may have a better picture for you."

"Is there anywhere else where casualties might have been taken?"

"The lesser wounded might have been taken further afield." The woman sounded unsure. "We haven't been given much information yet. Look, I'm sorry to sound unhelpful, but as you can imagine, it's been a nightmare all day."

"It was the train that left Victoria just after ten, wasn't it?"

"I believe so." The woman paused. "We received our first casualties just before noon. Poor little kids. I just hope your son was one of the lucky ones."

Madeleine put down the receiver. "They don't have him there, at Wandsworth Hospital. But if he's been taken somewhere else, why haven't they telephoned us?"

"There may be so many children that they are overwhelmed," her father said. "It's utterly beastly to have to wait like this, but there isn't much else we can do."

"Go in person? Go to the local police station? Ambulance station? Wouldn't somebody have lists?"

"What about the boy's headmaster?" Eleanor said, sounding helpful for once. "He'd know."

"Yes." Madeleine let out a little sigh. "He'd know, wouldn't he? But he would have been on the train, too." She grabbed for her overcoat. "I'm going to the school. Maybe there is someone still there who might know something."

She walked out into the falling light. It had started to rain, a cold, driving rain that threatened to turn to sleet later. She pictured Olivier still lying trapped, waiting to be found, while freezing rain fell on him. "Oh my baby," she whispered. "Why did I let you go? I didn't want to . . ."

The school stood in darkness, one corner blackened by the bomb strike. She looked for a caretaker or anyone else who might have information, but she realized the teachers didn't live at the school and anyway would have accompanied the boys on that train. She came home and telephoned the hospital again. No, her son was still not on a list of survivors. And the headmaster? "Mr Anguin? I'm afraid he was one of those who was killed."

Another name popped into her head. The small, serious boy standing beside Olivier. Mum, this is Gerald. "Gerald Hopkins? A boy at the school?"

"He does not appear on any list. Maybe he came through unscathed."

Madeleine went through ten different Hopkins families in the telephone directory before she found the correct one. Mrs Hopkins answered. Her boy was safe and well, luckily not in the carriage that took the hit. Her husband had gone to bring him home now, although whether they'd find a train or a bus this late in the evening was debatable. "But at least he's with his father."

"Can you ask him if he knows anything about Oliver Martin?" Madeleine asked, feeling renewed hope. "They were walking in pairs, and Oliver was with your son."

"I'll ask him when he comes home," Mrs Hopkins said. "And I'll telephone you right away if I have any news."

It was eleven that night when Mrs Hopkins telephoned. "I'm afraid Gerald can't tell you anything about your son. He said there were so many children on the platform that they all got split up, and everyone tried to get on to the train at once. He said the teachers blew whistles, but the children from other schools didn't listen and kept surging forward. Gerry thought he was going to be left behind, and he was lucky that one of the teachers lifted him into the last carriage. But he didn't see Oliver at all once they were on the platform. He said there were a lot of bigger children, and it was impossible to see over their heads."

"Thank you." Madeleine took a deep breath. "Where was your son held until he was picked up?"

"Taken to the hospital to start with and then on to a local vicarage. St Andrew's, I believe Gerald said."

Madeleine hung up, then managed to be connected with St Andrew's vicarage. A tired voice affirmed that yes, there had been a lot of children there, but most of them had been picked up by their parents. And no, there was no Oliver amongst them.

A sleepless night was spent with Madeleine calling the hospital three times and being told that no new survivors had been brought in recently. She made up her mind to go to the hospital first thing in the morning, whatever anyone said. She pictured Olivier lying unconscious and nobody knowing who he was. At first light she caught a series of buses across London to Wandsworth. It was a frustratingly complicated journey. At the hospital, the admitting sister was sympathetic but firm. They did have two unidentified patients, but they were much older than eight. Apart from those, everyone was accounted for.

"But they are still finding survivors?" Madeleine's voice shook.

"It's still possible, I suppose." Her voice showed uncertainty. She looked grey and exhausted and had presumably been on duty all night.

"Do you have a list of the dead? I'd rather know. I need to know. If he was alive, he'd have found a way to contact me."

"Let me call the morgue for you." The nurse looked at her with understanding. "What was his name again?"

"Oliver Martin. It's actually Olivier Martin because he was born in France, but he's changed it to Oliver to fit in with the other boys."

The waiting seemed to last an eternity. Several times the sister glanced up briefly at Madeleine, nodded and looked down again. At last she said, "Oh, I see." She put down the telephone. "I am very sorry to tell you that your son was amongst those who did not survive."

"Are they sure? Absolutely sure?"

"His name label was still round his neck."

"Where is he?" Madeleine almost shouted the words. "Let me go to him!"

"I'm afraid you can't do that, Mrs Martin. His carriage took the direct hit. I don't think you'd want to see him. All the occupants were beyond recognition."

"But you said he was wearing his name label. That must mean . . ."

"Bombs can do strange things. I've seen complete destruction and yet spectacles that survived, a vase that survived. At least it would have been a mercifully quick death."

"How can any death be merciful?" Madeleine shouted now. "He was my son. A little boy with his whole life ahead of him. Such a bright little boy. Such a fun . . ." And she burst into tears. Everyone was very kind. A cup of tea was brought to her. The hospital chaplain arrived and said comforting words.

"I'd like to have his body, please," she said. "I'd like to give him a proper Catholic burial. His father and I would want that."

The chaplain shook his head. "From what we have been told, it wasn't possible—I mean it was a powerful bomb. Some of the dead will never be identified, poor little things. I'm sure my fellow Catholic chaplain will be happy to give the remains a blessing, but . . ."

She understood what he was trying to say. Her son had been blown to pieces. There was no body left to bury. She stood up, rushed past him and was violently sick in the hallway. After she came out of the hospital, she went to find the nearest telephone box and pulled out Major Carlson's card.

"I've changed my mind," she said when he was put on the line, "I am ready to volunteer for whatever you want me to do. Anything at all. I've nothing to live for here."

CHAPTER 12

Oliver

Oliver opened his eyes and blinked as the light hurt him. He moved his head to look around, and the very action of moving hurt him, too. Tall white walls. High windows letting in grey light. A strange smell that was somehow familiar but that he couldn't identify and associated with something unpleasant. A picture came into his head. He had fallen over, and Maman had had to clean the gravel out of his knee. She had put something on that stung and said she was sorry but she had to clean all the nasty stuff out. He tried to sit up and winced in pain. "Mummy?" he called out.

Instantly a figure dressed in white with a white headdress appeared at his bedside. "Oh, you're awake, little man. That is good news. Don't try to move, and we'll have doctor come and take a look at you."

He identified the figure in white as a nun. He had seen plenty of nuns in Paris, but not any in England, so he was surprised. "Where's my mummy?" he asked. "Where am I?"

"You're in hospital, dear," the nurse said gently. "You were in a bad accident. In the train. Don't you remember?"

Oliver frowned. Train. He remembered something about a train, but he couldn't bring it into focus. Gerald Hopkins. He remembered walking beside Gerald Hopkins and waving to Mummy. But then nothing. "I was going away?" he asked.

"That's right. You were going with your school to be evacuated. I'm afraid your train took a direct hit from a bomb. Lots of children were killed. You were one of the lucky ones."

"Is my mummy coming to see me?" Oliver said.

The nurse looked uncomfortable. "Not right now," she said. "You have to rest and try to get well quickly. That's your job. I'll go and get the doctor."

The doctor was a worried-looking man with a deep voice.

"What's your name, young man?" He glanced at his chart.

"Oliver Martin," Oliver said, pronouncing both the English way.

The doctor checked his chart and nodded. "Well, Oliver Martin, let's take a look at you."

He examined Oliver, listened to his heart, then checked the rest of him. "You gave us a scare there, young fellow," he said. "You've been asleep for almost a week. Hit on the head. Nasty concussion. And I'm afraid you've broken your leg as well. Cracked your collarbone. Lots of cuts and bruises. We'll have to take good care of you, and soon you can be up and playing football again, eh?"

Oliver nodded. He noticed now that his head did hurt him when he tried to look around. He saw he was in a long ward with maybe twenty beds, each one occupied by another child.

But the doctor sounded cheerful and confident, so he lay back, waiting for Mummy to visit. The nurse appeared at his bedside again. "I expect you must be hungry?"

Oliver considered this. "Yes. I think I am."

"We'll start you off on something easy to digest, shall we? Some soup and some jelly and custard? How does that sound?"

"That sounds good, thank you," he said and noticed a strange look from the nurse. One of intense pity.

Several days passed, each the same as the other. A trolley was brought round in the morning with porridge or another hot cereal, a small glass of orange juice and a spoonful of cod liver oil that tasted horrible. Then a nurse washed him. Sometimes changed his pyjamas. Held a bedpan for him to pee. He had been mortified to find he was wearing a nappy when he first woke up and begged to be taken to the toilet.

"I'm afraid you can't walk yet, dear," he was told. "We have to let that leg heal. But don't worry, the doctor will let you get out of bed soon."

And every day he asked when his mother would be allowed to visit him. And every day nobody answered. The first time he was brought colouring books and comics, he realized that he didn't have his glasses. No wonder everything looked indistinct.

"Excuse me, but I think my glasses must have broken when I got bombed," he said. "I can't see properly without them."

"Oh no." The nurse looked surprised. "We had no idea you had worn glasses. It's not on your chart. Let me see what I can do about it. We'll have doctor examine you."

A different doctor came in, checked Oliver's eyes and admitted that yes, his eyes were weak, and he did need spectacles. They'd have new ones made, but in the meantime they'd find him a pair that just magnified things so that at least he could see to read. A pair was brought. They were a bit too big and slipped down his nose, but at least he could see to read with them.

The days seemed awfully long but on the whole not unpleasant. He chatted to the girl in the next bed. She was a cheerful cockney and told him funny stories. He was brought puzzles and various crafts to keep him occupied. But the nights were bad. He learned that some of the children in the ward were much more badly injured than he. One girl had lost a leg. Others had been burned, and they cried out at night, sometimes calling for a parent who didn't come.

Other parents did come during visiting hours, bringing treats and sitting at bedsides. But Oliver's mother was not amongst them. At last a man who looked like a priest came to his bedside.

"Oliver?" he said.

Oliver nodded.

"I want you to be very brave," the man continued. "We haven't told you this before because the doctors wanted you to be strong enough first, but I'm afraid your family has been killed in a bombing raid."

Oliver stared at him, trying to take this in. "All of them? Mummy and Grandpa and Grandma Eleanor?"

The man with the priest's collar nodded. "I was told it was everybody in the house. It took a direct hit. I am so very sorry."

"But why didn't they go down to the shelter?" Oliver asked. "I wasn't even there. They didn't have to worry about me."

The clergyman gave a little sigh. He had had to do this so many times. "I don't know, son. Maybe it was a surprise daytime raid. Maybe they didn't think they would be affected. I can't tell you. I only know that they were all killed." He put his hand over Oliver's. "I know there is nothing I can say that makes this easier, but we have to trust that God has a plan and we'll all be together again in heaven one day, and that God will send down an angel to take special care of you."

He looked at Oliver's face, waiting for a nod, but Oliver was too stunned to react. *Mummy gone,* he thought. *Grandpa gone. Eleanor gone.*

"What will happen to me?" he asked. "Where will I go?"

"Do you have other relatives we don't know about?"

Oliver frowned. "My daddy. He may still be alive in France."

The clergyman frowned. "Your daddy? I don't think so, my dear. Your daddy was killed in the evacuation from Dunkirk. Don't you remember?"

Oliver frowned. "But Mummy said that he might still be alive."

The clergyman smiled. "I think she was just trying to be kind. To give you hope."

"Oh," Oliver said. Grown-ups did things like that. They didn't always tell you the truth and thought they were being kind. Like not telling him about everyone dying. Letting him think for all this time that his mummy might be coming in through those big doors at the end of the ward, carrying chocolate biscuits or one of his other favourite treats.

"What about in England?" the clergyman asked. "Do you have other relatives in England we could contact for you?"

Oliver frowned again. He thought that Grandpa had mentioned that he had a brother, Charles, but Oliver had never visited him. And he had never seen any of Eleanor's relatives. Besides, if they were like her, he'd prefer not to go to them.

"My mummy's mother died when she was a little girl," he said. "I don't think she knew any of her relatives in England. There's Tante Janine in France, but she's very old."

"We'll search around and see what we can find," the clergyman said, "but in the meantime you're well cared for here. We'll let you heal before we decide what would be the best thing for you. All right?"

Oliver tried to nod, but he couldn't. He couldn't even cry. It was as if he was frozen into stone. He lay back, staring at a ceiling that had water marks on it where rain had once come in. He had stared at that ceiling before, picking out a dog and a butterfly in the stains. Now as he stared he could see goblins and wolves—a whole ceiling full of dangerous things.

~

Day followed day. Oliver tried to think of one cheerful thing, but he couldn't. He wondered what would happen to him when he healed. Where would he go? Who would want him? The word *orphan* came into his head, and he toyed with it. He remembered seeing a group of children in Paris, all dressed in blue smocks, walking in two straight lines with nuns at the front and the rear, and Maman had said they were orphans. They hadn't looked too unhappy. Would he be sent to a place like that? Would he be allowed any toys? Books? He realized with a jolt of sadness that all of his things were gone. His favourite stuffed dog, that he hadn't taken with him on the train because he hadn't wanted the other boys to laugh at him, had now been blown to smithereens like his family. It was strange about that train. He could remember going into the station, the hiss of the steam engines, the sound of whistles, a lot of children all arriving at once, and then . . . Nothing. He wondered about his headmaster. Had he been hurt? If not, why hadn't he been to see Oliver in hospital? Why had nobody from his school come? Had he been in a carriage with Gerald Hopkins? He couldn't remember. But he hoped Gerald had survived and was now happily at home with his parents.

And Oliver realized that all he had now was the present. No past. No future. Nothing to hope for. Nobody to hug him ever again. Nobody to sing him that special song at night. And at last Oliver wept.

CHAPTER 13

Madeleine went through the next days like a sleepwalker, unable to escape from a nightmare. Nothing seemed real. She longed for Giles, to feel his arms around her, to know that something made sense. Her school had granted her compassionate leave, but she couldn't bear to be at home. Every room in the house reminded her of Olivier: his egg cup sitting on the shelf, a drawing he had made for his grandfather's birthday. Her father seemed to have sunk into a profound silence, sitting staring out of the window, while Eleanor was at her annoying worst.

"No sense in moping around," she said. "Terrible things happen in wars. We just have to get on with it. When my first husband was killed in the Great War, I refused to give in to grief. I got on with my life."

Madeleine couldn't stand it another minute. She went out, even though it was a bleak, rainy day with a cold wind blowing up the Thames. She kept walking down the hill until she had reached the river and stood staring at the angry grey water. Another scene came to her mind—the day she had walked along the Seine trying to come to terms with finding herself pregnant. She'd been hopeful, excited and terrified at the same time. And everything had worked out so well. Olivier had been born. They had been a happy family, and he'd been such a bright little boy.

So unfair. So stupid. So mindless. She shouted the words into the rain that now blew into her face. As she stared down at the churning waters, another thought came into her mind. End it all, now. It would be easy to climb over the wall and slip into those cold waters and never have to feel this terrible pain again. She sat on the wall, about to swing her legs over, when an image of Giles came into her head. If it was possible he was still alive, why make him suffer doubly with the loss of a wife and a son? If she was indeed sent to France, might she possibly find him again? It was the smallest glimmer of hope, but she seized on it. She'd go to France, and if she could stop one German, one atrocity, it would be the start of revenge.

~

Madeleine was told that she needed to finish the spring term at school so that a replacement could be found before she reported for training. She informed her father and Eleanor of this.

"What work could be more valuable than teaching young minds?" Eleanor said, always searching for the negative. "And presumably we won't be getting your ration book if you are away?"

"But I won't be eating here either," Madeleine replied. "I want to do something useful. You have to understand that. I want to make myself feel that Olivier did not die for nothing. I've got to stop those bastards from taking more sons."

Eleanor gave the sort of patronizing smile Madeleine was used to. "Do you aim to stop the Germans single-handedly? Very commendable."

"Don't mock the girl, Eleanor," her father said. "Let her do what she feels is right. She needs something to aim for right now. We all do. And it's bloody hard to think of anything positive. I'm a useless old crock. They don't even want me back at the school, even if I could make that journey every day. I'd volunteer for Maddie's position if my French was good enough."

"I never did see the point of teaching French to dockland hooligans. Why, they can't even manage to speak English properly. And soon enough they'll be out of school and forget everything."

Madeleine felt this was true enough, but she wasn't going to give Eleanor the satisfaction of being told she was right. Every day seemed interminable. Sullen faces staring at her, glancing at the clock. Waiting for the lesson to be over so they could go to lunch. All she could think as her mouth spouted French verbs was that these boys were alive and her son was dead. Boys who didn't want to learn. Who wanted to get out of school and earn money and go to the pub when her bright, funny little son would have gone to the Sorbonne like his parents, would have been a witty, passionate man like his father. It seemed so horribly unfair. She wanted to shout at them, "Why are you here?" But then one of them came to school one day with the news that his dad had been killed. Another had his house bombed. And she saw they were all living through the same hell, one way or another. Soon enough they'd turn eighteen and be sent off to fight. And she felt more kindly about them.

"Look, I know you don't want to learn this," she said one day to the most difficult of her classes—the leavers. "I know you think it's a waste of time. I might be thinking it's a waste of my time teaching you, when I could be helping my government win the war. But we all have to get through this somehow. I don't think it really matters if you know French verbs or not. You tell me what you want to know."

"Tell us about Paris, miss," one girl spoke up.

"You used to live in Paris?" another boy asked.

"That's right. My husband is French, my mother was French, and I lived in Paris for a long while. And it was wonderful."

And they listened while she described her happy memories—specially attentive to the food.

"Is it right that they eat frogs, miss?" one girl asked.

"People do eat frogs' legs in France," she said. "I've tasted them. They taste a bit like chicken. Not horrible at all. And they eat snails, too."

"Eeeewww. Disgusting," came a collective groan.

"They are not bad either. They are specially bred snails. They are quite clean, and they are cooked with lots of butter and garlic. I've never cooked them personally."

"Then what was your favourite food?"

Madeleine thought, and a smile crossed her face. "The pastries. You should see the pastry shops. *Pâtisseries.* That's the French word. Repeat."

She described the pâtisseries—the rows of perfect little tarts and cream cakes filling the windows, and the breakfast pastries, warm from the bakery, and for a moment she was back in the little flat, sitting around the breakfast table at a time when she was happy. By the end of the lesson, the class had learned how to ask for coffee and the bill afterward. To address someone politely. To believe that maybe it would be possible, even for them, to go to Paris one day.

At the end of the lesson, one of the bigger, more disruptive boys stopped to talk to Madeleine. "You know, miss," he said, "I'm going to be joining up before long. I'm going make sure I'm one of the ones who drives that bugger Hitler out of Paris."

His naiveté and earnestness brought tears to her eyes. *You'll probably be cannon fodder,* she thought.

~

Coming home after school had been equally grim. Madeleine's father had sunk into a quiet depression. He sat, staring at the fire or out of the window, his mind not able to concentrate on the book or crossword on his lap. He and Eleanor both lamented that it was impossible to find French wines and had switched to gin and tonic, which were also becoming hard to acquire. Madeleine could hardly bring herself to eat or drink anything. There seemed no point. But Giles was still alive, she kept telling herself. He was clever. He'd survive somehow, and they'd be together again. She might even meet him if she was parachuted into France. And that thought gave her enough hope to get through to the next day.

~

Easter came with no celebration beyond three boiled eggs, procured on the black market. Eleanor insisted on going to church, because it was expected on Easter Sunday, although she lamented she hadn't had a new hat in three years. Madeleine's father went with her, reluctantly, she felt, but he usually gave in to his wife's bossiness. Madeleine herself refused.

"How can there be a God?" she demanded. "No loving God would take my son. Take all those boys." As she said it, she remembered one of her first conversations with Giles. She had told him that she felt God had let her down when her mother died. He said he felt the same way when his father abandoned them, but he still went to church, just in case, because it couldn't hurt to remind God who he was. For a worldly cynic, he had such a simple faith. "Oh Giles, if only you were here," she whispered. But soon . . .

She had received an official communication telling her to report to an address in Whitehall on the Tuesday after the Easter bank holiday. She was told to bring the minimum of possessions, a change of clothes, an overcoat, stout shoes, a toilet bag. As she packed these into a small suitcase, she stared longingly at the clothes she had acquired in Paris. They had never had much money, but they had lived comfortably enough. Giles had helped her to find wonderful items at flea markets—the classic Chanel black dress, a Chanel suit, high-heeled shoes . . . all useless now. She would probably never wear them again. She closed the suitcase with a sharp snap. She was about to go downstairs when on impulse she went into Olivier's room. She had kept the door firmly locked since the awful news. Now she went in and stood, taking in every detail—a half-finished Meccano model. A drawing of a desert and camels on the table. A pair of his shoes left on the floor—such small shoes, scuffed from the sort of play boys do. And on his pillow, his beloved stuffed dog, the one he had slept with every night until going off on that train. She was so tempted to take it with her but realized personal possessions would not be allowed. She hugged the dog, fighting back tears, then kissed it and put it back on the pillow.

"You stay there and take care of his grandfather, you hear?" she said in French, as the dog understood that language better. Then she picked up the suitcase and carried it downstairs.

"Well, I'm off, then." She attempted to sound bright and breezy. She saw her father turn towards her and read the distress on his face. And a great wave of compassion came over her. He had never been a demonstrative man. Upper-class English schoolboys were raised not to show emotions. She had always taken this to mean he didn't care, but she saw now that he did. He had grieved for the wife he loved. He was grieving Olivier as much as she was, and now he was going to grieve for her. Impulsively she went over and wrapped her arms around him.

"I love you, Daddy," she said. "I'm sorry. I never said it often enough. But I do love you. Take care of yourself until I come back."

He hugged her fiercely, then held her shoulders, looking at her for a long minute as if he wanted to memorize every detail.

"You're going to go to France, aren't you?" he asked at last.

"I can't tell you that," she said. "At the moment I have no idea what they want me to do, and even when I do know, I can't tell anyone. But if they ask me to go to France, yes, I will go. I will do whatever they ask me to."

"Then all I can say is God go with you."

"I wish I could believe that," she said. "On the whole I think the Greek and Roman gods you used to teach about were more use than our current one. At least they intervened to make battles come out the right way."

This made him smile. "They didn't always pick the right side."

"Maybe there wasn't a right side in those days. But now there clearly is. Hitler is a monster. We must all do what we can to stop him." She stopped, shrugged at her outburst, then kissed the top of his bald head. "I must go. I can't be late on my first day, and who knows how long the bus will take."

She turned to see Eleanor standing in the doorway with a look on her face that might have been jealousy. *She resents that my father loves me,* Madeleine thought, and realized with a jolt that perhaps it was because he had never loved Eleanor.

"Goodbye Eleanor," Madeleine said softly. "Please take care of him until I come back."

"I've always taken the best care of him," Eleanor said stiffly. She held out her hand. "Have a good trip." Almost as if she was going on holiday. Madeleine almost laughed.

As she opened the front door, she looked back to see her father gazing at her with such longing that she almost ran back and hugged him again, but she closed the door behind her and strode out firmly in the direction of the bus stop.

CHAPTER 14

Big Ben was striking nine o'clock when Madeleine joined a group of women assembled outside the building in Whitehall. About twenty of them, all young, their dress ranging in style from expensive and chic to what her father always called "cheap and cheerful." Some of them were chatting, others stood in silence, looking around nervously. Madeleine put her suitcase down with relief. In spite of the limited contents, it had still become heavy in the walk from the tube station.

"Hello," she said, nodding to the woman standing beside her. One of the chic ones, the jacket decidedly French.

"Bonjour," the other replied curtly. "Are we not expected to speak French from now on?"

"I've no idea," Madeleine said. "I've been told nothing. I don't have a clue where we are going or what we'll be doing."

The other gave her a withering look. "You're English," she said, her accent clearly French. "You won't be much use, will you?"

"But my mother was half-French. I am married to a Frenchman and lived in Paris until recently," Madeleine replied in French. "So if you wish to use this language, it is fine with me." And she gave a very Gallic shrug.

The other woman held out her hand. "My name is Solange," she said.

"Madeleine."

"Your husband, did he come over here with you?"

"No. He stayed behind to fight. He couldn't tell me, but I think he must be with the Resistance. I haven't heard anything from him for a long while now, but someone seems to think he is still alive."

Solange gave her a pitying look. "That's what they always say to make you volunteer. My lover is also in the Resistance. I have also heard no news for a while, but they want me to believe I might see him again."

"Is that why you are here? The hope of seeing your lover again?"

"That is certainly an incentive. But no, I am here because I want to drive the Nazis out of my country. I want to kill as many as possible, preferably with my bare hands."

Madeleine tried not to show her shock. It had not occurred to her that she might be called upon to assassinate Germans personally. Before the conversation could continue, a rather old-fashioned-looking coach pulled up beside them. A young army officer got out of it.

"Right, girls," he said. "Who's ready for a day at the seaside? Got your buckets and spades? And your pennies to buy rock?"

This broke the tension, and everyone laughed. He held a clipboard and started to read off names. They were an interesting mix of French, Dutch, English and even German. He pronounced *Martin* correctly, the French way. Madeleine boarded the bus, wondering if she should save a seat for Solange, but then put her suitcase in the overhead rack and took a window seat. Another woman slid into the seat beside hers.

"Well, this is exciting, isn't it?" the woman said. "I've been waiting to do something for ages, hoping they'd call me. But I think there was a lot of resistance from the higher-ups to using women for anything that could be dangerous. You know, we're supposed to stay home and knit socks for the soldiers, aren't we?"

Madeleine was surprised to hear that her accent was decidedly Irish. "I'm Madeleine," she said. "Madeleine Martin."

"Are we allowed to give our true names?"

"Well, that officer just called them out for all the world to hear, so I suppose it's all right."

The other woman laughed. She was tall, slim, blonde. Not at all Irish in features. "In that case I'm Marie-France. Marie-France McCluskey. They don't exactly go together, do they?"

"Not exactly. Are you half-Irish, half-French?"

"No, entirely from Northern Ireland." She grinned. "Named Mary Frances at baptism. Mary Fran for the first part of my life. Then I became a dancer. And I got a job in Paris. At the Moulin Rouge, no less." Madeleine tried not to register her surprise, but was not quite successful. Marie-France nodded. "You should have seen my parents' faces when I told them. They said I was going straight to hell." She leaned closer to Madeleine. "Well, to be honest, I had no idea to begin with that it would be that sort of dancing. I was mad keen for a stage career. I'd been to several auditions, and then this man came to me and asked if I'd like to dance in Paris. Off I went, thinking it would be more like musical theatre or maybe even a ballet company. I confess I was a bit shocked myself when I found I'd have to take my clothes off. But you know it wasn't bad. The manager was really protective of us. Didn't allow any of the stage-door Johnnies to annoy us. And the pay was good. I lived in Paris for ten years. French lover, the whole bit. And you can't have a dancer doing the cancan called Mary Fran, can you? So I became Marie-France. I like it much better."

She likes to chatter, Madeleine thought. *That might not be a good thing for a spy.* "Is your French really good?"

"It is. And of course I have all the Parisian street slang, which is an advantage. I'll fit right in."

"Do you think we'll actually be going across to France, then?"

Marie-France shrugged. "I have no idea. A man came to me and asked if I'd like to help the war effort, then he made me sign a piece of paper and told me nothing more. But I presumed it had to do with France, although it could be a job as something like a radio transcriber here. We'll just have to see, won't we?"

The coach had filled up, and the army officer slammed the door shut. It took off with a rumble, a rattle and a burst of diesel fumes.

"What were you doing before this?" Madeleine asked. "Did you go back home after we had to leave France?"

"I did, for my sins," she said, giving a little chuckle. "Not for long, though. I couldn't take it. Hardly the jolliest place to be. I left and came to London. I've been working at the war ministry, doing office work—filing mainly. Boring as hell. And you?"

"Teaching French in a secondary school. Not a grammar school but dockland kids who could not have been less interested. I, too, was glad to leave."

"And now we're going to have a jolly, fun time, eh?" Marie-France asked.

The coach had passed over Westminster Bridge and was heading south.

"Do you have any idea where we're going now?" Madeleine asked.

Other women must have been thinking the same thing because a girl leaned across the aisle to them. "You don't think they are taking us to the coast now, do you? Ready to ship us across to France?"

"Not with no training," Marie-France said. "They wouldn't be that stupid. I bet it's some secret training centre they've got hidden away. It might even be a nice country house, and we'll have good food for a while."

Madeleine saw relief on the girl's face. She looked absurdly young—eighteen at the most. Surely the government wouldn't send someone like that?

Inner suburbs with rows of grimy houses became outer suburbs with semi-detached homes with neat front gardens and then the fringes of the city with sports fields, market gardens and big, impressive houses. They must have had lovely gardens once, Madeleine thought, but now lawns and flower beds had been dug up in favour of vegetables. Even so the scene became more attractive as they journeyed south into the Surrey countryside. Apple trees in blossom. Primroses in all the hedgerows and even the first bluebells in the woods. Lambs in the fields were frolicking as if there wasn't a war on. A young girl was riding her pony over tiny jumps. It was all so wonderfully timeless and English that Madeleine was annoyed at herself she had never appreciated it until now.

At last they left the main road and turned on to a narrow lane bordered by high hedgerows. Then they came to an impressive gateway with pillars on either side, and stone lions on top. A sentry stood on duty, and he went forwards to open the big wrought-iron gates. The coach passed through the gates and followed a drive between flowering rhododendron bushes until a large red brick house came into view.

"There you are. What did I tell you?" Marie-France said. "A big posh house. We'll be eating well here. Like having a holiday."

The bus came to a halt in the forecourt. The army officer opened the door and stood waiting for the women to disembark. When they were all outside, an older man in army uniform appeared at the front door.

"Welcome to your training centre, ladies," he said. "Leave your baggage in the front hall, and follow me to the briefing room."

They trooped up a flight of steps and into a marble foyer, where they stood looking around, some of them open-mouthed in wonder. There was a suit of armour, vast portraits on the walls. A marble staircase curved up one side. From a room to their left came the clatter of typewriters, but they were ushered into the room on their right. It must have been the main drawing room, with a big fireplace at one end and a portrait of a man on horseback over it. But no fire was lit, and it was rather cold. All the original furniture had been removed, and it was now full of rows of collapsible chairs.

"Take a seat. As quickly as possible," came the snapped order from a man who stood there in army uniform.

The women obeyed.

"Welcome, ladies," the man said again. "You may call me Major Branson." He was probably in his late forties, and he had tired bags under his eyes. "Your country appreciates your desire to serve. But I have to warn you right now that this will be no picnic. You will be on the go all day. It will be hard work—a series of tests and challenges to see what abilities you might have and how we can best use you, if we can use you at all. I have to tell you right now that only about six to ten of you will progress to the next stage. We have to be sure that we take no chances with our recruits. Those who are not chosen for our particular needs will be reassigned. But I must point out now that you have all signed the Official Secrets Act. You are now in the service of your country, the same as any soldier or sailor. You obey orders. You share nothing of what goes on here with anyone. You are not allowed to leave this place, or to communicate with anyone outside. To betray what goes on here will be considered an act of treason and you could be shot. Is that clear?"

Madeleine heard the young girl beside her give a gulp of fear.

The major looked around the room, assessing their reactions. "Having said this," he continued, "you have the right to opt out if you decide this sort of thing is not for you. Nobody is forcing you to be here or to continue at any stage. We want willing volunteers. If you decide that you don't wish to continue, you will come and see me in private, and I'll arrange for you to be taken away. Not to be taken home, I have to point out. Anyone who leaves here will be put to work in another of our facilities—maybe in office work, translating, wherever you'll be most useful to us. But nobody here is going home for quite a while." He looked around again. "Do you have any questions at this stage?"

A hand was raised. "Is it true that we'll be sent over to France?"

"Let's face that hurdle when we come to it, shall we?" he said. "First of all, we want to see what you're made of, what you can handle and where we can best use you. Let's get right to work. Go back into the hall and pick up your suitcases, then you'll be taken up to your rooms. Find yourself a bed and come straight down again. We will meet again at eleven hundred hours. Company dismissed."

There was a scraping of chairs on the parquet floor. Madeleine followed the others up the staircase. Nobody spoke, but some of the girls glanced at each other with reassuring grins. A female in army uniform was waiting at the top of the first flight of stairs.

"Up the second flight, ladies," she said. "Rooms on your right and left. Choose a bed quickly. On your bed you will find the clothing you will wear while you are here. Get changed. Leave everything for later to be put away. Lavatories and bathrooms at the end of each hall. Go quickly if you need to go, then report downstairs."

They went up a second, and not so grand, staircase to a plain, whitewashed hallway.

"I bet this is where they used to put the servants," a woman behind Madeleine said. "And I bet they take the good rooms downstairs for themselves."

The rooms were indeed plain and simple. Each one had two sets of bunk beds, a chest of drawers with a mirror on top, a small wardrobe and an electric fire. Madeleine stepped into what she thought was an empty room, assessed quickly that she'd rather have a top bunk and hoisted her suitcase up on to it.

"'ere, watch it! What the bleedin' hell do you think you're doing!"

Madeleine jumped back in horror as a face appeared, glaring at her. A young face, surrounded by dark curls.

"I'm sorry," Madeleine stammered. "I thought I was the first one into the room and . . ."

"It's all right, ducks," the girl said. "I was just trying out the bed to see how I felt about sleeping up so high. I'm a bit claustrophobic, so I didn't like the thought of anyone lying on top of me—although I've enjoyed that before now, if you know what I mean." And she gave a cheeky smile.

"I'll take the other upper, then." Madeleine moved her suitcase across to the other side of the room. "Are you one of us? I mean, one of the women who . . ."—she fought for the right word—"volunteered?"

"Cos I don't talk posh, you mean?" the woman laughed. She looked absurdly young. Then she added, in perfect French, "If you'd rather that I speak French, I can do that, although you sound as if you're English, too."

When Madeleine registered her surprise, the girl sat up, swinging her legs over the side of the upper bunk. "My mum's French. She met my dad when he was a wounded soldier in the Great War. She took care of him and nursed him back to health, and then she went back to England with him. And I came along. Then the old bastard walked out on us, so it was just my mum and me, and she took me back to France. But by the time I was sixteen, I'd had enough. We lived in a village, you know. Nothing to do. Only boring farm boys. So I left her to it and scarpered back to London. Been living on me tod in the East End, working in a munitions factory. But I didn't fancy getting blown up, so I thought speaking French might help me get something better."

"I don't know if parachuting into France would be better or not." Madeleine lifted the pile of clothing from the top bunk. She held each item out. The stack consisted of a pair of heavy wool trousers, a white open-necked shirt and a khaki jumper.

"Not exactly going to win no fashion awards with those, are we?" The young woman jumped down nimbly beside Madeleine. "I'm Annie, by the way. Really Annemarie, but I never liked that."

"I'm Madeleine." She nodded as she held the trousers and wondered if they were expected to strip off right here. But Annie was already doing so.

"You don't think we can do this in the bathroom?" Madeleine asked.

"What all these girls and two bathrooms? I don't think so. Come on. Get a move on. It's not as if we ain't seen a pair of legs before."

"Oh, it's you." Marie-France came into the room. "And I see you've taken the top bunks, you bastards." She paused, watching them. "Is that what we have to wear?"

"Afraid so," Madeleine said. "And they are awfully rough, too."

"Is there a bed still free in here?" An elegant woman with perfectly Marcel-waved hair poked her head around the door. "Oh good." She made her way to the empty bed beneath Annie's. "I thought I'd found an upper bunk in another room, but the woman who joined me in there positively stank, darlings. I mean, as if she hadn't washed under her arms for decades. And there are limits, aren't there? So I beat a hasty retreat." She looked from one face to the next, smiling. "I'm Portia, by the way. I don't think we need to bother with last names, do we?"

"Madeleine."

"Marie-France."

"Annie."

Portia heard the British intonation in their pronunciation. "So everyone is English except Marie-France?"

"I'm Irish," she said. "But Northern Irish, so I'm one of you."

"Well, that's a relief." Portia smiled. "I thought we'd have to speak French day in and day out, and it does get rather tiring."

"My mother is French, and I lived in France for eight years. I'm married to a Frenchman," Madeleine said.

"My dear, how frightfully glamorous," Portia said. "Are they as good at it as one hears? I was dying to find out for myself, but I got sent home because of the war."

Madeleine gave an embarrassed laugh. "Mine was a wonderful lover. I can't speak for the rest."

"Those boys in my village were hopeless," Annie said. "All talk but not much there, if you know what I mean."

"But I can attest that there are plenty of Frenchmen who are good lovers," Marie-France said.

Portia reacted to the Irish accent.

"She used to dance at the Moulin Rouge," Madeleine said.

"Gosh." Portia looked quite impressed. "What an interesting bunch we are. And do we really have to wear these things? If I telephoned Harrods, do you think they'd send me something less scratchy?"

"We are not allowed to call the outside world, remember," Madeleine reminded her. "And it is a sort of uniform, isn't it?"

"Come on, you lot. Less talking and get downstairs now," came the stern warning from their doorway. They hastily pulled on jumpers.

"But what about shoes?" Portia looked down at her shiny black pumps with a little heel. "I can hardly go slogging through swamps in these. My brogues are in the suitcase."

"Shoes will be provided downstairs." The army sergeant blew a whistle. "Everyone down now."

There was a lot of scrambling and scurrying from various rooms as the young women ran down the staircase. When they reached the briefing room, they found a big table had been placed along the windows with gym shoes on it.

"Find your size, or something that approximates your size," the sergeant said. "If we don't have enough of a particular size, make do for now and we'll see what can be done later."

Madeleine took a pair of size fives, found a seat and put on the canvas shoes. Portia sat beside her. "At least they aren't army boots," she whispered. "When I saw the trousers, I was afraid, you know."

"I know." Marie-France joined them. "At least these won't wreck my feet if I want to dance again."

"Move up, please." Solange joined them, saying the words in French. They obliged, and she sat beside Marie-France. "Are these not the ugliest clothes you have seen in your life? Of course I wear trousers. I am a modern woman. But silk pyjamas. Linen sailor trousers. Not what the farmers wear in fields."

"You know, I think this is on purpose," Portia said thoughtfully. "I think we are supposed to feel uncomfortable. They want to make sure we understand that what lies ahead is going to be worse. If this training is no picnic, then the real thing is going to be absolutely bloody."

The women exchanged a glance, taking this in.

CHAPTER 15

Conversation was broken off as a woman came into the room. She was slim, attractive and dressed in a well-fitting suit and high heels. She looked as if she would be more at home going into the head office of a bank as an efficient private secretary to the chairman. She carried a clipboard, looked around the room and smiled at the upturned faces.

"Don't look so surprised. If women can be recruits, then it makes sense to have women as your trainers. You can call me Vera. And frankly I have to confess that we are all as new at this as you are. The idea of using women operatives in various underground capacities has been floated since France and the Low Countries were occupied but has met with fierce resistance from the old brass. As you know, women are not allowed in combat roles in any of the armed forces. So this is really going in defiance of military orders. However, it is very necessary."

She put down the clipboard on the desk at the front of the room and started to pace as she spoke. "We have long believed that women can make the best spies and undercover agents. A strange man, out of uniform, is immediately suspicious, whereas a woman is often invisible. You walk past carrying your shopping basket or wheeling your bicycle and nobody would think to search you to find out that the shopping basket carried explosives.

"We used women in the last great war, although few people have heard of it. You'll have heard of one such woman—Edith Cavell, who was captured and shot. There were others who did not fare much better. We think their training was weak. We aim to make sure that any woman we send into the field this time is trained to the best of our ability. Having said this, most of you won't be going abroad. You'll be aiding in our propaganda mission, in decoding messages from France, in sending such messages, in translating intercepted documents. All valuable and vital."

She paused again, looking around the room. "But I must also tell you that we are extremely picky. You will be put through a series of verbal, physical and psychological challenges. But it won't always be the smartest and fittest who go through. It's the temperament we want, the ones who won't crack. So"—she picked up the clipboard again—"let's get started, shall we?"

She handed a sheaf of papers to the person on the end of each row. "Pass them down."

She waited until this was accomplished.

"You have exactly one hour to answer all the questions in the language for which you have been selected. The questions mention France, but please substitute Belgium or Holland if you need to. There is a box containing clipboards and pencils under the table. Two of you hand them out." She looked around. "You two." And she pointed to Solange and the woman in front of her. Solange got up with a sigh. "It is like being in primary school again, is it not?" she muttered as she stood up. "Next we will have to draw happy faces."

The papers and clipboards were passed around, and Madeleine studied her paper, wondering what kind of test it would be. But she saw that the questions were all biographical. Where was your mother born? Where was your father born? What are your first memories? When was the first time you went to France? Your experiences? What part of France are you familiar with? What was the best thing about living there? What childhood games did you play? What books did you read? What was your favourite food?

All the questions were very simple, but Madeleine saw the point of them. They wanted to assess how fluent in French she was, and how well she knew France. She answered the questions with ease but saw others were frowning as they worked. She suspected some might be fluent in spoken French but not so hot on French grammar.

When the papers were collected, the women were sent out for a run around the estate—a mile's course that had most of them panting by the end. Madeleine had developed a stitch in her side. Others were close to collapse. Vera met them on their return and gave an exaggerated sigh. "I can see there is some conditioning to be done here. How far would you get if you had to run from the Nazis? How far could you carry a ten-pound radio? Or drag an unconscious airman?

"Well, by the time you leave here, you'll be able to do those things. Conditioning starts tomorrow. Calisthenics on the front lawn at O-seven hundred hours, sharp. Shorts and shirts will be delivered to your bedrooms tonight."

"What if it's raining?" a voice asked.

"Do you not think you might have to undertake assignments in the rain?" Vera sounded scornful. "Please don't send us any airmen tonight because I'd get my hair wet."

Everyone laughed. Madeleine was feeling a little faint and realized how long it had been since she had eaten. She prayed there would be no more physical assignments that morning and was relieved when Vera said, "Right. Lunchtime. Dining hall straight to the back of the building. Grab a plate. Serve yourselves. Report to the briefing room at fourteen hundred hours."

"Bloody 'ell." Annie fell into step beside Madeleine. "This is worse than the army, ain't it? I had no idea we'd be doing this type of thing, did you?"

"I had no idea about anything," Madeleine said. "I suppose we have to be extra fit before we're any use to anyone."

"Not if we have to operate a radio. I think I'll volunteer for that."

"You'll still have to do all the training." Madeleine laughed. "Like Portia said, we are supposed to be uncomfortable all the time."

"I hope the food's good," Annie said. "I'm ruddy starving, aren't you?"

"I am, actually." Madeleine joined the procession up the front steps and then along the central hallway and into a room. It was plain with whitewashed walls and had one long scrubbed pine table in the centre. On a sideboard were tureens and a stack of plates beside them.

"I see we haven't been given the family dining room." Portia came up behind Madeleine. "This had to be the servants' hall. We have one like it at home."

Madeleine glanced at her—tall, elegant, probably a former debutante. Why would she want to volunteer for a thing like this? Maybe for a lark? She wasn't able to ask as they were propelled forwards towards the serving dishes. There was a dish of some kind of stewed meat, another of boiled potatoes and a third of greens. The smell was not unappetizing.

"At least we're not meant to suffer with our food," Portia muttered as they carried plates to the table and squeezed in next to other women. She was right. It was a treat to get any kind of meat, but Madeleine couldn't identify it.

"What sort of meat is this?" she whispered to Portia.

"It's rabbit," someone else said. "I bet the estate is teeming with them. We'll probably have rabbit morning, noon and night."

"Well, it doesn't taste bad," Madeleine said. "All right with me. It's been a while since we've had any sort of meat except offal in London. And the food they served us for school dinners was quite disgusting."

"You were a teacher?" a woman across the table asked.

Madeleine nodded. "Yes. Teaching French."

"I'm surprised they let you leave. There's an awful shortage of teachers now the men have joined up."

"I hope I'm going to be more useful doing this," Madeleine said. "Whatever this turns out to be."

There was a steamed pudding with custard to follow, and Madeleine was feeling full and sleepy when they had to report back to the classroom. This time the test was one of puzzles and logic. If Mary's sister was twice as old as her brother when Mary was three . . . Which of these designs comes next in the pattern? Which of these words is the odd one out? Solve these anagrams . . . It was hard to concentrate, and she felt her head would explode as she stared at the patterns on the paper. She couldn't help noticing that some women breezed through them. *I'm not going to pass,* she thought. *I'm going to be sent to do office work or dreary transcription . . .*

They handed in their papers and then had to listen to a lecture about the current state of affairs in Europe. A map of France was displayed, showing the occupied zone to the north and west, including the entire Atlantic coastline, and the free zone to the south.

"Free in name only," the lecturer, a short, balding man with a paunch said. "The Vichy government is firmly under Germany's thumb, and there will be Gestapo agents stationed routinely throughout the region. If any of you are dropped in either zone, you will never be far from danger, never able to let down your guard. Something to think about, right?"

The day ended with a propaganda film on the Nazi invasion of France, Hitler's triumphant arrival in Paris, German tanks rolling through the countryside.

"That could be here next if we don't find ways to slow down the enemy," the presenter said.

The women filed out silently, their minds full of the images they had seen.

Am I up to this? Madeleine wondered. She pictured all those tanks, all those soldiers. Planting explosives on a bridge as they went past. Making friends with Nazis and learning their secrets. It seemed all too improbable.

~

The evening meal was a combination of tea and supper with bread, jam, tea and baked beans on toast. Nursery food, Portia called it. Then they were told that because it was their first night they would have a free evening to unpack and get settled into their rooms.

"I ain't half-tired, and I'm dying for a fag," Annie said, climbing up to her bunk and then collapsing on to it. "Do you think we're allowed to smoke?"

"Not in the bedrooms," Madeleine said. "There's a notice outside."

"Blimey. If I have to go all day without a smoke, I'll be a jittering wreck. Do you reckon every day will be as bad as this?"

"Worse, probably," Portia said cheerfully. "They'll make it awful at the beginning to weed out those whose hearts aren't really in it."

"Is your heart in it?" Madeleine asked.

"Oh, absolutely." Portia looked up from the suitcase she was unpacking.

"I would have thought a girl like you could get out of war work," Marie-France said, "or at least do some kind of genteel volunteer work—supervising jam making or handing out clothing."

Portia smiled. "I expect we could all be doing something different and equally useful," she said. "In my case it's personal. My father is in a German prison camp."

"Your dad? Ain't he too old for the army?" Annie asked.

"He's a career soldier," Portia replied. "He was overseeing the withdrawal of British troops and the retreat to Dunkirk, and typically my father, he wanted to be the last one to leave, making sure no solider was left behind. And they captured him. The Germans were delighted because he was a great prize. So he's being held in an awful castle called Colditz. So that's why I want to do something to stop these monsters."

There was an embarrassed silence in the room. Portia looked at the others. "What about you?"

"I grew up in France," Annie said. "I've no idea what my relatives are going through—my little cousins, you know. My grandma. I'd like to do something to help."

"Me too," Marie-France said. "The best years of my life were in Paris. When I saw that little toad Hitler strutting through my city, I thought, *I'd like to find a way to drive those Nazis out.*"

"And you?" Portia turned to Madeleine. "Why give up teaching? You're doing a valuable service there."

Madeleine stared out of the window as the last glow of twilight silhouetted the trees. "My husband is French. I lived in France until I had to return home, but Giles stayed. I think he's working with the Resistance now, if he's still alive. I've had no news in a long while. A man from the ministry approached me and asked if I'd be interested in this sort of thing. I told him there was no way I could leave my son." There was a long pause. Chatter from other rooms drifted towards them, a woman's loud laugh. "Then my son was killed. So I have to do something to make sure his death wasn't for nothing."

"I'm so sorry," Portia said at last. "How beastly for you. I can't imagine how you handle that grief. My brother is flying for the RAF, and every day I worry that he might be shot down. But your son . . ." She reached out and gently touched Madeleine's shoulder.

Madeleine turned away, frightened she might cry. But at that moment, their door burst open and Solange came in.

"Oh, thank God," she said in French. "I thought I'd go mad in that room. Why did I not come in here with you? I saw a bed by the window, and I thought that would be nice, but those awful women. Chatter chatter non-stop. Always in English, too. And one of them smells so bad. I don't think she has had a bath in weeks. And another has cheap perfume. Ashes of Roses, I fear. Is there no way you could squeeze another person in here?"

"I regret not," Madeleine said. "You see we have four beds and four people. Why don't you check the other rooms to see if there is a spare bed anywhere? They can't have known exactly how many of us would show up in London, so there must be extra beds."

"You're right." Solange beamed at her. "You are a genius. I will check further down the hall. And if not, I will demand of the supervisor that she find me a new bed. One in a room that does not smell."

And she stalked out again. The four women exchanged grins.

"She's going to be trouble, that one," Portia said. "And I'm not at all sure she's suitable for the task ahead. Doesn't she realize we may not be able to bathe for weeks ourselves? We may have no change of clothing?"

"I tell you one thing," came Annie's voice from the bunk above. "I ain't half-glad we don't have no extra room in here!"

And they all burst out laughing.

~

How strange, Madeleine thought as she lay in her top bunk later that evening. *Four of us are so very different, and yet we seem to have formed a bond already.* She realized how long it had been since she had enjoyed a close friendship with other women—not since her college days in London when they had sat together drinking cocoa. And a tiny sliver of warmth crept into a heart she had thought was completely and irrevocably frozen.

CHAPTER 16

Oliver

A manor house in Surrey, spring 1941

Oliver was in hospital for a month. Gradually his wounds healed, his bones knit together. His headaches went away. New glasses were made for him.

"You're as good as new," the doctor said cheerfully when he examined the boy.

Oliver thought the man must be really stupid. How could anyone be as good as they were when they no longer had any family or anywhere to go? One by one the other children in the ward were collected by parents and off they went. Oliver wanted to know what would happen to him next but was afraid to ask. Everyone had been so kind here, but he had read about orphanages in books—one bowl of gruel a day (whatever gruel was) and lots of beatings.

But then he was told that he was being sent to convalesce in the country. He needed fresh air and the chance to fatten up and get strong again. New clothes were brought to him: a shirt, a pullover and corduroy shorts.

"What happened to my blazer and my cap?" he asked. "My own clothes?"

"Sweetie, they were blown to pieces in the bombing," the nurse said. "You're so lucky that you weren't blown to pieces, too. Here, let's get these on, shall we?"

He was taken in a small bus with several other children to a country house in the middle of fields and woods. Having never lived in the country, this was an intriguing enough experience that he forgot for a time about his true circumstance. They slept four boys to a bedroom. The other boys were a bit older but nice enough, even if they did call him Shrimp. There were nurses to look after them, and a teacher came in the mornings to make sure they didn't fall behind in their schoolwork. She was delighted with Oliver. "What a bright little boy you are," she said. "I can tell you are going to go far."

There was plenty of good food, and they were encouraged to run around outside on fine days, exploring the countryside. Oliver's broken leg was still in plaster, so he couldn't run around to begin with, but he was encouraged to walk, to watch the football games and help with the animals. There were chickens and ducks, and the children took turns to feed them. That was exciting, if a little scary. There were sheep in a nearby field with baby lambs. Other fields contained cows, horses—all the things Oliver had looked forward to seeing when he was evacuated with his school. He wondered about his school now. Had many of his schoolmates been killed? He hadn't encountered any of them in hospital or here at the convalescent home. He wondered if he could ask to go back to his school, if it might even be nearby, but then he realized that it had been a private school. Someone must have paid for him to go there. Now there was nobody to pay for anything. Did he have any money at all? He wondered. If his grandfather's house had been bombed badly enough to kill all the people in it, then there was nothing left of it. But didn't grown-ups have money in banks? It was all too much to think about, and when he worried, the headaches returned.

So he let himself try to enjoy the moment. The cast was removed from his leg. He was given daily exercises to do, and eventually he could join in, playing football and rounders with the other kids. There were art and craft projects, being taken to see how cows are milked and even getting a ride on a horse.

If only I could stay here forever, it wouldn't be bad, he thought. But he knew from the constant turnover of children that he'd be moved out to make room for another wounded child as soon as he was quite healthy.

After class one morning, he heard his teacher talking with the lady in charge—a rather scary old woman called Miss Harland.

"He's such a bright little boy," the teacher said. "Amazingly well schooled considering his circumstances. Don't you think we could find a boarding school to take him? They give scholarships, after all."

"I'll certainly have the social worker look into it," the lady said. "For now, the best thing for him would be to go to a family that takes in evacuees. That way he'd stay out of London and harm's way and have a chance to fully recover."

"But he'd be attending a village school," the teacher insisted. "He's so much more advanced than the other children his age. I'd hate for that to be lost."

"He wouldn't exactly have had the best prospects in London, would he?" the lady said. "We'll do our best for him, within limits, of course. A safe place to live is the priority."

They moved away, leaving Oliver puzzled. Why wouldn't he have had good prospects in London? His mother had gone to university and was a teacher. His grandfather had been a teacher, too. Surely these were good things. But the trouble with being a child, he decided, was that nobody told you anything or asked you what you wanted. They always did what they thought was best for you, when perhaps it wasn't. Actually he had no objection against being put with a family in the country, living in a place like the one he was in now—maybe with farm animals, and his job might be to feed the chickens and collect the eggs—things he already knew how to do.

And so he waited to find out what was next, hoping, yet not really daring to hope, that it might be something good.

CHAPTER 17

Madeleine's training continued for the rest of the month. It wasn't really training—more like a weeding-out process, seeing which of the women might be suitable for future tasks. Some days they had physical activities: an obstacle course that involved crawling through a muddy tunnel, a race in which they had to carry heavy stones, a five-mile cross-country slog with a stream to be crossed. There were team-building days in which they had to plan how to cross a river using rope and a plank. Madeleine had done similar assignments with the Girl Guides at school and so was quite good at this. Portia was a natural leader. Other days they faced word puzzles, or even card games. Sometimes Madeleine noticed they were encouraged to cheat. She wondered if this was seen as a good or a bad thing. There were days when only French was allowed—their lectures were in French, they spoke French at the dinner table, they played a card game in French. Madeleine hadn't realized what a strain this would be after a year of speaking nothing but English.

Every now and then, she noticed that another woman was missing, presumably having failed some aspect of the course or having decided to quit. Nothing was ever said about the vanished ones, and an uneasy thought went through Madeleine's mind—that they had been hauled off somewhere, locked away so that they couldn't divulge anything. Then she reminded herself that this was England. A civilized country where things were done by the book. All the same, she realized she had an ongoing fear of failure—that she'd wind up doing mindless work in some ministry, unable to go home, unable to leave for the duration.

Most of the time they were so busy that she was able to keep thoughts of Olivier and Giles at bay. It was only at night, when she lay on her top bunk, listening to the rhythmic breathing of the others in the room, that memories swam into her mind: Olivier and Giles building a model together, laughing as they fed the ducks on the lake in the *bois*, and then Olivier's serious little face as he waved and went to board the train . . . Madeleine squeezed her eyes shut, trying to block out that memory.

At the end of the month, there was an interview by a board. Of five men and three women. Some of the members she recognized as her instructors, others were new. She was peppered with questions: Had she ever been sick in her life? Had an accident? How well did she tolerate pain? Had she ever been betrayed? What did she feel?

She thought of the time she smelled perfume on Giles's shirt. But he had always reassured her how much he loved her, so that wasn't really a betrayal, was it? Giles was just that type of man who needed women. She had come to accept it.

"Have you ever wanted revenge against someone?"

The question threw her, then she looked her interrogator squarely in the face. "Yes," she said. "My little son was killed in a bombing raid. I want revenge for him. That's why I'm here."

"So if you got a chance to kill Germans, you could do it?"

"I don't know," she said. "I'd like to think I could carry out whatever orders I was given. But I really can't tell you how brave I am because I haven't been tested yet. But I'd certainly like the chance to try."

She saw one member of the board nod at this, but then the officer in charge glanced down at the sheet of paper in front of him and said, "I believe your husband stayed on in France to work with the Resistance. Is that true?"

"I believe so," she said. "He stayed behind, and knowing the kind of man Giles is, I expected him to work to liberate his country. I haven't had any communication from him for a long time. I don't even know if he's still alive."

"So, Mrs Martin," the man continued, "if, in fact, your husband is still alive and you are sent on an assignment to France, having been given a different persona, and you happen to bump into him—do you think you could show no reaction and ignore him?"

Madeleine hesitated. "I hope I could, realizing that the fate of others would always depend on me."

"Could you betray him if necessary?" The question came from the far left of the table.

She looked up, startled. "For what reason?"

"If the lives of many others were at stake?"

Madeleine took a deep breath. "No, I don't think I could. I would rather surrender myself at that moment."

"Thank you, Mrs Martin," the spokesman in the middle said. "We need to have a little discussion, and we'll let you know."

Madeleine came out of the room. *I've wrecked my chances,* she thought. *But I had to be honest. I could never betray Giles. And he'd never betray me.*

She sat in the foyer, staring out at the peaceful country scene beyond. Then she got up and went outside, standing on the front steps and looking around. Everything was in bloom, the air smelled sweet, birds were chirping madly. It was England at its best, and she realized that if she was selected, she might be about to give it up, never to see it again. She didn't know whether she wanted to pass or fail at that moment. A job as a translator wouldn't be so bad, would it? Or a radio transcriber? But then she thought: *I'd just be existing, prolonging the grief and the meaninglessness of it all. Better to know that I was alive for a little while, even if it ended badly.*

"Mrs Martin?" the female officer called her. "You may come back in now."

Her heart was beating fast as she went back into the room.

"Well, Mrs Martin," the spokesman said. "We think you have what it takes. You are made of the right stuff. We're going to give you the chance to go on to the next stage of training."

"Oh, thank you." Relief flooded through her.

"We have to warn you, of course, that not all the applicants succeed. In fact almost half will not. It won't be anything to do with skills, or stamina. It will all come down to whether you can be trusted to do the job."

"Oh, I can be trusted, sir," she said. "I've been trustworthy all my life."

He gave her a sad smile. "I mean can you be trusted if someone is about to pull out your fingernails and asks you to name names? Do you have the grit to withstand that?"

She shuddered, having not really considered the thought of torture. "I don't think anybody could answer that question until they were faced with it."

"But you are prepared to go forwards, knowing there is a risk of torture, of rape, of death?"

Again she hesitated for a moment, then stood up straighter. "Yes, sir," she replied. "I am prepared to go forwards. I have to do something to make sure my son did not die in vain."

He stood and held out his hand. "Then we should say congratulations, although I fear it's a very broad interpretation of the term. You will wait at this facility when other women leave, and then you will be given your assignment briefing."

"Thank you, sir." She was escorted from the room.

"Nice girl," she heard one of them say. "Such a pity . . ."

Not quite knowing what to do next, she went back out into the grounds and walked amongst the bluebells. *Such beauty,* she thought. She had never really paused to appreciate beauty before. She had always been busy—at university, then bringing up a baby, then fleeing to England. Why had she not appreciated the Eiffel Tower, the trees in blossom up the Champs-Élysées, or even the Houses of Parliament, the view of the Thames . . . so many wonderful things all around her, taken for granted. She heard the chiming of a distant church clock and realized it was time for lunch. At least her appetite had returned. That was one good thing.

A strange scene greeted her at the dining table. Some women were in tears, being comforted by others.

"I don't know why I didn't make it," one was sobbing. "I did well on all the tests, didn't I?"

"They don't ever tell you," her comforter said. "They have their own set of rules. Maybe your French wasn't convincing enough. I don't know. Just think it's all for the best. You'll be put where you can do the most good."

Madeleine helped herself to more rabbit stew in silence. She didn't want the scrutiny of the other women, wondering why she had been selected when they had not. Marie-France pulled up a chair beside her.

"Have you had your selection committee yet?"

Madeleine nodded.

"And?"

"And I've been selected for the next stage."

"Me too!" Marie-France beamed. "Although I have to say that I wasn't thrilled to hear about the possibilities of torture. They made it all sound horribly real, didn't they?"

Madeleine nodded. "I hadn't really considered that before. I suppose I'm really naïve."

"But you're still going to go ahead, aren't you?"

"Oh, absolutely," Madeleine said. "And you?"

"Of course. Maybe we'll be sent together. That would be a lark, wouldn't it?"

"I don't suppose it would be much of a lark." Madeleine had to grin. "But I'd be glad to know you were nearby."

~

By the end of the day, they had learned that both Annie and Portia had passed the selection committee and they were all headed to the training facility together.

"Are we mad to be excited about this?" Portia said, as the four of them hugged in their room. "Do you think the Christians were dancing around when they heard they had been chosen to be sent to the lions?"

"But we'll be doing something," Marie-France said. "Something that might make a difference."

"And it won't be bloody boring, like working in the munitions factory," Annie said. "We'll know we're alive."

"Yes," Madeleine agreed with this. They would know they were alive. That was important. They had barely finished their celebration when Solange burst in without knocking. "I hear laughter in here," she said. She took in their faces. "You are celebrating? You were selected?"

"We were. All four of us," Portia replied. "How about you?"

"As if there was ever any question," she replied. "Who knows France better than I? I can blend right in, wherever they send me. Some of you others will be caught out, I know it." She gave a most Gallic shrug to show she didn't care. "I must go and pack. I expect we'll be leaving in the morning."

Four faces watched her as she made her exit.

"If we're caught and threatened with torture, I know one person I couldn't mind handing over to the Jerries," Annie said, making her roommates laugh.

CHAPTER 18

OLIVER

Surrey, June 1941

"Oliver, you're wanted." Oliver looked up from where he was squatting by the ornamental pond, feeding the goldfish. He liked the way they came to the surface, pursing those big lips as if giving him kisses. Jenny Brant stood there, hands on hips. She was a big, bossy girl and loved running errands for the staff.

Oliver stood up. Had he done anything wrong? He didn't think so. He had always been the sort of child who liked to obey the rules. "Who wants me?"

"Miss Harland. Go on. Don't keep her waiting."

Miss Harland. The lady in charge. The scary lady who barked orders if the children were too rowdy. He went slowly up the steps and knocked on the door of the lady's office.

"Come in!" came the imperious voice.

Oliver opened the door slowly and peered around it.

"Ah. Oliver. Come on in." She sounded quite cheerful. "Take a seat." She studied him. "Well, you are certainly looking a lot better than when you first came to us. And feeling better, too, I hope?"

"Yes, thank you," Oliver replied.

"So you've enjoyed your time with us?"

"Yes, I have," Oliver said. "It's been very nice."

"You have been a very brave boy," Miss Harland said. "I'm proud of you. Your mummy would have been very proud of you. You didn't give in to grief. You put your chin up and got on with life. Splendid. But I expect you're wondering what might happen next."

"I have been wondering," he said. "I mean, now I'm an orphan, I suppose. I don't have anywhere to go. So it will probably be an orphanage. Although I'd really like to stay with a family here in the country for now, just like the other evacuees."

"We had planned on something like that," Miss Harland said, "but a unique opportunity has just come up. The Australian government has offered to take in a ship full of children, to keep them safe until the war is over. I have put forward your name to be one of these children."

Oliver stared at her. "Australia? Did you say Australia?"

She smiled at his worried little face. "That's right. Such a lovely place. Lots of sunshine, good food. You'll grow up healthy and strong. And I think it will be out in the countryside, just like this. Maybe horses to ride. You'd like that, wouldn't you?"

"Yes, but Australia. It's awfully far away."

She gave him a sympathetic smile. "I don't mean to be cruel, but there isn't anything much for you here, is there? If you stayed, eventually it would have to be an orphanage, and they are not all very nice."

"So I'd be put with a family on a farm there?" His voice sounded slightly hopeful now.

"I'm not sure of the details yet, but the Australian government will make sure you are all well taken care of. Australia is keen to get more people settling there, you know. It's a big empty country, and you'll have so many opportunities when you grow up. Many more than here—even if we survive this war. But it's quite possible that the Germans will invade, and we will be in a very bad way here. You'll be out of it. Safe. That's good, isn't it?"

"Yes," Oliver said, but his brain was racing. Never see London again. Never see Paris again. Any of the places that had been familiar and fun. But then he wouldn't want to be here if the Germans invaded either.

"So Miss Everingham is going to take you shopping into Guildford and see if we can set you up with enough clothes. That will be fun, won't it?"

Oliver nodded. He really liked Miss Everingham and appreciated the interest she had shown in him, bringing him books she thought he might like to read, sharing an atlas with him to show where battles were now being fought. And she had fought for him, too, trying to get him into a good school. He waited for her in the front hall.

"Ready for an adventure?" she asked with her lovely, bright smile.

Oliver nodded and walked out beside her to where an old motor car was waiting.

"It just about goes," she said as she started it up. "I think it will get us to Guildford and back."

They drove out into a lane and passed through a village. Small children were playing on the village green, and there were ducks on the pond. Oliver watched the children with envy. When they were tired, they'd go home, and there would be food on the table and a nice warm fire and someone to tuck them into bed.

"So Miss Harland tells me you're to go to Australia?" his teacher said after a long moment of silence. "Are you excited about that?"

"I'm not sure," he said. "I mean, it's so far away. It's hard to imagine."

"I think it will be wonderful for you. I've a cousin in Australia. She loves it there. They go to the beach all the time, and on picnics, and it's always sunny. And lots of interesting animals, too: kangaroos, koalas. And birds—budgerigars, cockatoos. All flying wild."

"Really?" This did seem interesting.

"And after the war, whenever that will be, you can come back to England to attend university. You must make sure you continue your education, Oliver. You have a very good brain, and I'm sure you'll make something of yourself. Make your family proud, right?"

"I might be a teacher like my mummy and Grandpa," he said. "Or maybe an engineer. I like to build things."

"Splendid," she said, but she was frowning.

~

In Gammons, the big department store, they were able to find new socks, underwear, short-sleeved shirts and shorts for him to add to the donated clothes he had been given at the house.

"You'll need more summery clothes," Miss Everingham said, "but I expect they'll equip you properly when you get there."

They were about to go down in the lift when Oliver glanced to one side and stopped.

"Oh," he let out an involuntary gasp.

"What is it?"

"That toy dog. It's just like mine. I mean the one I used to have."

She looked at him with understanding. "Would you like a replacement? You might need a friend if you're going so far away."

"Oh no. I'm too old for that sort of thing," he said.

But she laughed. "Nobody is too old for a stuffed animal, Oliver." She picked up the dog, went over to the nearest counter, and paid for it, adding it into the carrier bag with the clothes.

"Our little secret," she said. "Nobody else needs to know."

"Thank you very much," Oliver said. "You have been very nice to me."

"I've enjoyed meeting you, Oliver. And if I had been in a position to adopt you myself, I would have done so. But alas, I'm a single woman with no home of her own, and I think Australia would be the better option right now. But will you write to me? I'll give you the proper address of the house."

"Of course I'll write. If they let me," he said.

"I shall be most interested to hear. You'll be taking an exciting sea journey. You'll see all sorts of interesting places. I look forward to hearing about them." She gave him a big smile as they pulled up outside the big house.

Oliver almost took her hand as they walked together to the front door, but then thought other children might see and decided against it.

He carried his new possessions to his bed.

"What you got there?" his roommate asked.

"Some clothes. I'm going to Australia."

"Lucky for some," the boy replied.

~

In the adults' common room, Miss Everingham sat lost in thought. Then she stood up and went through to Miss Harland's study.

"There is something about that boy that doesn't make sense," she said to Miss Harland. "He's supposed to be from a dockland family, and yet he speaks and acts like he is educated. Is it possible someone has made a mistake?"

"What sort of mistake?"

"Got the wrong person? If he was injured in a bombing raid, is it possible they mixed him up with someone else?"

"He answers to his name," Miss Harland said, frowning. "And nobody has made inquiries about him. It's not unheard of that a cultured family can live in reduced circumstances, is it?"

"I suppose not. I just wish . . ." But she left the rest of the sentence unspoken.

CHAPTER 19

The next morning a coach arrived to take Madeleine and the others back to London. The wording on the side was *Hanson's Fine Tours. Firms' outings, scenic drives, mystery tours.*

"This is a mystery tour, all right," Portia whispered to Madeleine. "None of us has any idea where we are going."

They joined the queue to board the bus and found seats. Madeleine could feel looks of resentment directed to herself and the others who had made the cut. *How silly,* she thought. *We are probably doing what nobody would wish to do.* But she understood, from expressed sentiments, that those who were French or had strong ties to France, like herself, wanted to do something to help liberate France from its oppressors.

The mood in the coach overall was a cheerful one as women discussed the food, the cross-country runs, the cold bedrooms. When the coach pulled up outside the same building in Whitehall, the same officer who had originally collected them stood with his clipboard by the front exit.

"From what I heard on the way here, you were quite happy to talk about what you had seen and done at a top secret facility," he said. "May I remind you that any such talk away from this bus can do serious harm to your country and can get you shot. From now on, you tell nobody where you have been or what you have done." He looked around at now-sombre faces. It was only just dawning on some of the women exactly what they might have ahead of them. "Now, when I call your name, you will collect your bags and leave the coach. You will wait on the pavement until you are escorted into the correct building."

He started reading off names. One by one, the women came down the aisle, some making last-minute quips to acquaintances. In the end, only eight were left: the four members of Madeleine's bedroom and four others, including Solange.

"Right, ladies," the officer said cheerfully. "You are off for the special ten-shilling tour, cream tea included. However, I leave you here. Your new tour guide will be waiting for you. I wish you all good luck." His expression said that he meant this. There was an element of compassion in his eyes.

The coach moved away. Some of the women on the pavement waved. They waved back. It all seemed so jolly and normal.

"Where do you think we'll be going now?" Annie leaned forward to ask Portia and Madeleine. "Out to the country again, I suppose?"

Instead they continued to drive through London. Up Park Lane, then up the Edgware Road.

"We're going north," Portia whispered. "That's interesting."

But the bus turned on to the Marylebone Road and then on to Baker Street, where it pulled up.

"Baker Street!" Annie exclaimed. "What on earth is on Baker Street?"

"Sherlock Holmes!" Madeleine said, turning round to the others with a smile. "Perhaps we're enlisting his help. Might be a good idea!"

Before she had finished talking, the coach door was opened by a rather shaggy young man in a tweed jacket. He looked like the sort of man one might find teaching mathematics at Cambridge, certainly out of place in the centre of London.

"Hello, ladies," the man said. "Welcome. You are expected. Now, if I could just have your names."

They gave them, one by one, and he ticked them off on a sheet he carried.

"And if you'd be good enough to show me your identity cards before you leave the bus?"

The women exchanged glances. He saw this. "One can't be too careful," he said. "You are entering a top secret facility."

They were led to an unassuming front door at Number 64. The house looked just the same as the others in the row—a respectable private residence, or maybe a solicitor's office. The man led them inside and then up a flight of narrow, uncarpeted stairs to an office at the back, looking out on to a narrow garden and the back gardens beyond.

"Take a seat," he said. "Someone will be with you shortly."

The room was basic in the extreme: wooden chairs around a table. Nothing on the walls except for a map of Europe. The women sat. Nobody said a word. They waited ten, maybe fifteen minutes. Then they heard brisk footsteps in the hallway outside, and a tall, pleasant-looking man in a well-cut suit came in.

"Sorry to keep you waiting, ladies," he said. His voice was upper-class and smooth. "That was Winston Churchill on the line. I thought it rather unwise to cut him short." He gave them a charming smile. "Welcome to the Baker Street Irregulars. I'm Gladwyn Jebb. I'm in charge of this little beanfeast, and I want to thank you for volunteering to help your country."

He took a seat at the far end of the table so that his head was now haloed by the incoming sunlight. "I'm sure you have already been made well aware of the dangerous nature of our work. You face a very real risk of capture, torture and death. You will find your training exhausting and emotionally draining, but everything we do is to try and keep you alive and well in the field. Also, as women, you will meet with considerable resistance from some of your male colleagues. There are plenty at all levels who believe that women should not be allowed to participate in this kind of operation. We believe quite the opposite. We are convinced that women make the best spies. They call no attention to themselves. They chat easily with local inhabitants. They can assume all kinds of low-level jobs, from waitress to shop assistant, thus becoming part of the community rapidly. And . . . they can flirt with the enemy, acquiring German boyfriends if necessary."

He paused and must have noticed an expression. "If this is repugnant to you, I quite understand. Not all women have the ability to cosy up to the enemy. Your wishes will be respected when we assign you. But that assignment is probably several months away. When you leave here, you will be sent to a series of training facilities around the country—or rather around Britain. You will learn self-defence, weapons use, unarmed combat, radio operation, signals, ciphers, disguises . . . you'll even learn burglary and how to pick locks. Quite useful after the war ends, I should imagine." He paused and chuckled. A couple of the women gave a nervous titter. "But one thing you should know: we would never send you into the field unprepared. By the time we are through with you, you'll be equipped to handle anything." He pressed his palms together, giving a little satisfactory clap. "Everybody in this room is destined for our French operation. May I suggest that you converse only in French after this, so that it becomes second nature. And I don't need to remind you of the Official Secrets Act you have signed. It is imperative that you give no hint—absolutely none—to anyone, anywhere, about what you are doing. Lives may be at stake. The integrity of our operation may be compromised. So any letters you write will be censored and should only include the broadest of statements. *Doing well. Food okay.* That sort of thing. *Work interesting,* if you like. But not *I am up in Scotland learning how to kill people.*"

This did make them laugh. He smiled, too. "So go through to the lounge. Take a rest, but make the most of your time. We have maps laid out on the tables. Study them as much as possible. Lunch will be served, and this evening you take the night train to Scotland."

He got up then and went around the table shaking hands. "I wish every one of you the very best," he said and left the room.

CHAPTER 20

Oliver

The next morning, one of the assistants helped Oliver to pack his suitcase. She said nothing when the new stuffed dog was squeezed in. After breakfast, he was taken to the front hall, where Miss Harland herself was waiting.

"All ready for the big adventure, then?" she asked.

Oliver tried to smile but found it too hard, so he nodded.

"Come along, then. Off we go." She went ahead of him out to the waiting motor car and helped him into the front seat beside her. They drove back to Guildford, where she parked the car at Guildford Station, then ushered him up on to a platform. A train was approaching from the other direction. Oliver froze in utter terror and went to flee. Miss Harland grabbed his arm. "What on earth's the matter?" she asked.

"Not a train. I can't go on a train," Oliver said. "I don't want to. Please don't make me."

"Oh, I see. Of course. You were bombed when you were on a train. I do understand, but we're quite safe here. We're out in the country. Nobody is going to bomb us here, I promise. And it's a lovely train ride to Southampton. You'll enjoy it. And I'm coming with you to the ship."

She was holding him in a firm grip so that he couldn't run away. Panic threatened to overwhelm him as she lifted him up into the carriage, then pushed him into a window seat. His heart was beating so loudly he was sure everyone could hear it.

"We can't give in to fear, Oliver," Miss Harland said. "If we give in to fear, then the enemy has won. That's what Hitler wants—to make us all so afraid that he can conquer us, and we don't want that, do we?"

Oliver shook his head.

"Here, have a sweetie." Miss Harland offered him a butterscotch. "Does wonders at calming the nerves."

Oliver took it and let the sweet taste spread through his mouth. Doors slammed. A whistle blew, and the train glided out of the station. Oliver kept his eyes tightly shut, trying to control his breathing.

"Oh look, Oliver, that girl is teaching her horse to jump," said the soft voice in his ear. He opened his eyes to see a girl riding a fat, round pony over tiny jumps. "I think that pony needs to go on a diet, don't you? Or he won't be able to jump any higher than that." She chuckled, and he found himself smiling, too.

After that he kept his eyes open. There were lots of farm animals in fields, large Shire horses pulling a plough, cottages with thatched roofs. The journey passed quite quickly with no incident, and they disembarked at Southampton. Oliver had crossed the Channel several times on the ferry boat that he considered a large ship, but when he saw the liner before him, his jaw dropped open. It was huge, impossibly large, like a whole floating city.

"That's the boat that will be taking you to Australia, Oliver," Miss Harland said. "Quite impressive, don't you think? And see the flag it's flying? It's American, so that is good news. The Germans will let it pass because the Americans are not part of the war. They are a neutral nation, so you'll be quite safe at sea."

It was just now dawning fully on Oliver that he was leaving England, leaving Europe, leaving everything he had known all his life and going far, far away. And there was nothing he could do to stop it. The only relative he could remember was Great-Aunt Janine in France, and he'd heard Mummy say that letters couldn't get to France any more now that the Germans were there. He couldn't think of anybody else he could appeal to, or even go to if he had a chance. Nobody would take him in.

"Come on now. We need to join the other children."

Miss Harland set off at a brisk pace, carrying his suitcase, so that he had to almost run to keep up. A group of maybe fifty children was waiting inside the terminal building. Some were older than Oliver, some younger. Some looked scared, others were larking around as if this was a good adventure.

"What's your name, dear?" a woman in charge asked him.

"Oliver Martin," he said.

She ran her hand down the list. "Oh yes. Jones. Oliver Martin. That's you. Good. Well, Oliver Martin, you're off on a wonderful adventure and to a new life. We wish you the very best."

"Well, goodbye Oliver," Miss Harland said. "I've enjoyed knowing you. I'm sure you'll do very well and be a credit to your parents." She shook his hand, then walked away. His last contact with England. He had to stop himself from running after her.

"Over here, dear." Another volunteer woman shepherded him over to the group. "We have to wait to board until everyone is here."

They waited. It was cold and windy in the half-open area, and Oliver shivered. His clothing had been chosen for a warmer climate. He thought wistfully of his nice striped cap and blue blazer with the crest on it. And the clothes he had worn in France—the soft wool overcoat and scarf for winter days when they walked in the bois and it had snowed and he had helped Papa make a snowman and they had thrown snowballs. Papa. Oliver considered him. So he wasn't alive any more. Grown-ups knew about things like that. A picture of his father's face came into his head: laughing. His father had laughed a lot. And swung him up on to his shoulders. And he had felt so happy and safe.

A whistle blew. "All right, children. Get into twos. Off we go. Straight up the gangway and on to the ship."

Oliver stepped into place beside a scared-looking little girl. He gave her a half smile.

"I don't want to go," she whispered to him. "Do you?"

"I don't think we have any choice," he said. "Come on. The boat will be fun."

They walked together up the gangplank and into a waiting area on the ship. There a man in uniform was in charge. "Hi, kids," he said in a strange, American accent. "Okay, let's get you to your cabins. When I point to you, you go with my steward. Got it?"

Small numbers of children were sent off, and then Oliver was pointed to. He found he was one of eight boys, all roughly his age or older. They followed the man in the white coat up two flights of stairs and then down a very long hallway.

"Here we are." The steward opened a door. "You four first." He selected three, plus Oliver. "In you go. Find yourself a bunk and a drawer in the dresser. Put your suitcases under the beds. Bathrooms are just down the hall to your right. There are several so you won't have to wait. But apart from the bathroom, no leaving the cabin, understand? It's too easy to get lost on a ship this size. So wait here. Get to know each other. And in about half an hour, I'll come and get you and take you to your first briefing."

He closed the door behind him. The cabin was small and very cramped. Two sets of bunks took up most of the space. There was a cupboard and a chest of drawers on one wall, but to Oliver's disappointment there was no porthole or window. They had an inside cabin.

"Bags I get a top bunk," one boy said.

"Me too."

Oliver was glad of this. He didn't fancy climbing up to a top bunk, especially if the sea was rough. He put his suitcase on a lower bunk.

"What's your name, kid?" the first boy asked him. He was chubby, with a round face with lots of freckles and reddish hair.

"Oliver," he answered.

"How old are you?"

"Eight."

"You're a shrimp for eight, aren't you? I think we'll call you Shrimp. I'm Joe. I'm nine. What about you blokes?"

"Danny," the other boy who had claimed a top bunk said. "I'm nine, too."

"And I'm Gabriel," the last boy said. Like Oliver, he was slight with big dark eyes.

"Gabriel? Are you Jewish?" Joe demanded.

"Yes." Gabriel stuck his chin out. "What's wrong with that?"

"Nothing, I suppose."

There was an awkward pause.

"We'd better unpack and put our suitcases away," Danny said, smoothing over the moment. "I'm looking forward to this trip, aren't you? And to Australia, too. It will be a lot better than eight of us crammed into two bedrooms and the lav out back."

"And the gasworks making the air stink," Joe agreed.

"And the smog," Gabriel said. "I've always had a bad chest. I get coughs every winter. And my mum said . . ." He paused. "But she's dead now, so it doesn't matter."

"I've always been an orphan," Joe said, more kindly now. "So I don't know what's like for you. What about you, Oliver?"

"My mum is dead, too. And all my family. I don't have anyone left."

"It's the same for all of us, ain't it?" Danny said. "No one wants us here. We'll be better off over in Australia."

They had finished unpacking by the time the steward returned for them. He led them up several flights of stairs to a room with big windows looking out on to the port. There another American officer gave them a talk about where they were allowed to go on the ship, what their days would be like and when they would eat. Then he led them on a tour, showing them their dining room, their playroom and their lifeboat stations in case of an emergency. They put on life jackets and had to do an emergency drill. Oliver found this rather alarming.

"Make sure you remember your lifeboat number," the crew member said.

Oliver thought the ship was so huge that his chances of finding the right deck and boat number were not good.

"Right," said the crew member. "We're going up to the top deck, and you can watch as we sail."

They followed him and came out on to the deck, where the wind was so stiff they had to hold on to the railings. Other passengers were up there and looked at the children with interest.

A loud blast from the ship's horn echoed out. Down on the dock, people were waving and shouting. Other people on the deck waved, too. Some of the children waved, although there was nobody for them to wave to. There was a churning noise of engines far below, and the great ship moved out from the dock. Gracefully it glided forward, the dock getting smaller and smaller behind it. Oliver felt very cold. His hands, clutching the rail, were icy, but he couldn't stop looking as the dock and the town and the countryside and England got smaller and smaller until it was just a line in the distance.

CHAPTER 21

Madeleine and the other women boarded the night train to Glasgow at Euston Station and were given a compartment to themselves. Thanks to a warning from the shaggy young man called Clive, who was to accompany them on the journey, they had bought food at the station. There was to be no dining car on the train. Madeleine ate her cheese and pickle sandwich but kept her packet of rich tea biscuits for the morning. The journey would take twelve hours. They had had a cup of tea at the station but managed to get bottles of pop for an early morning drink.

As the train pulled out of the station, Madeleine had a moment of panic. Oliver had been on a train like this, looking forward to going to the country, and then, in one instant, his life had been snuffed out. Had he realized what was happening? Had he suffered, or had he been killed before he even realized? A few weeks ago, she would not have minded if the same thing had happened to her. But now she had a renewed sense of purpose. She wanted to live, to make the Germans pay for what they had done to her son.

It was an uncomfortable night, eight of them sitting upright, the train rattling and shaking, the blinds drawn to comply with the blackout and only one anaemic light in the corridor outside. There were people standing in the corridor—mostly armed forces in uniform being transferred or going home on a brief leave. They talked and laughed and smoked, making sleep impossible.

At seven in the morning they arrived in Glasgow. Wearily they staggered along the platform. Clive joined them and treated them to a station breakfast—a stale iced bun and cup of tea, before they boarded another train and made another slow journey north. But this time it was daylight. The view from the windows was spectacular, past lakes and moors and high sweeping mountains until they came at last to Fort William. There they were met by a rickety old bus and proceeded westwards through increasingly wild and rugged country. They hardly passed a house for miles and then just the odd whitewashed stone cottage. Madeleine was feeling increasingly car sick as the bus navigated the windy roads, while belching out diesel fumes. Several of the women, including Annie beside her, were smoking. Her stomach groaned with hunger, and she munched on the last of the biscuits.

"How much longer, do you think?" Annie asked. "I feel like I'm going to be Uncle Dick."

"Uncle Dick?" Madeleine looked puzzled.

"Rhyming slang. Uncle Dick. Sick. Got it?" She laughed. "We used it a lot where I was living down the East End. I'll miss it. I don't suppose I'll ever use it again."

"After the war, you'll go back?" Madeleine shied away from fatalistic thoughts.

Annie shook her head. "Nah. You won't catch me going back there. I'll have useful skills by then. I'll get a job. Make something of myself. If I get through, that is."

"What would you like to do?"

Annie gave an embarrassed grin. "Don't laugh, but I'd really like to open a flower shop."

"Eliza Doolittle?" Madeleine asked.

"Who's she? Does she own one?"

"A person in a story," she said. "But she was a cockney girl who wanted to own a flower shop."

"And did she?"

"No, she married a rich man instead."

Annie made a face. "That won't be me. I'm staying away from getting married. I saw what my dad did to my mum." Then she looked out of the window. "Cor, look at that. It's the sea, isn't it?"

And it was. Cold grey waves were lapping at a nearby shore. They continued along a shoreline until ahead of them an austere grey stone house appeared on a bluff. The grounds around it, woods and lawns and formal gardens, were ringed with a high fence topped with barbed wire. The bus slowed, stopped at a wire-topped gate. A sentry checked the driver's papers, and the gate was opened. Annie looked at Madeleine as they drove through. "Feels a bit like going to the nick, doesn't it?"

Madeleine agreed that it did. There was no leaving this place without permission, that was clear. She wondered what they'd be doing there. Suddenly everything became all too real. She had volunteered for something highly dangerous, and now there was no way out. The bus drove up to the main house and stopped outside. Clive got out, went inside and then reappeared with a man wearing a big fisherman's jumper.

"Right, ladies. Out you come," he called in a tone that indicated he was used to commanding men. "You're at Arisaig now. This is where you will learn weapons and combat just like the men. You'll be training alongside the men, too, so don't expect any special treatment. You'll do what they do. Treated exactly the same, and I warn you it's going to be tough." He looked down the bus at solemn faces. "Any questions?"

"Yeah, how about a cup of tea and something to eat? We're starving," Annie said. The women laughed. The man smiled. "You'll be fed, don't worry. I'm Eric," he said. "First names from now on. Safer that way. We use all precautions here, and I can tell you that you were all heavily vetted before you came. But there's always the chance for a mole. So be on the lookout for anything that doesn't look quite right. Intuition is the best tool in our little game. When you're in the field, you'll find your hunches will keep you alive. So come on in. Dump your bags in the hall for now and go and get something to eat."

They stepped out into a bitter wind off the Irish Sea. Madeleine thought that the jerseys they'd been allocated wouldn't do much to keep them warm in weather like this. She wondered if the house would be equally cold and was pleased to find a glow of warmth as they filed in through the front door. Voices were coming from a room at the back. The women put down their suitcases, took off their coats and then went towards the sound. They entered a big, comfortable sitting room, with sofas and armchairs dotted around, a couple of low tables on which were a chess game and a half-finished game of cards. A fire was blazing in the enormous stone hearth. The walls were wood panelled and decorated with various sporting trophies: stags' heads, antlers.

"Well, hooray," said a voice from one of the sofas. "Help has arrived at last."

Madeleine now saw that several men were sprawled on the sofas, most of them smoking so that the air in the room, from the fire and the smoke, was hazy. The man sat up from his sprawled position. "Splendid. Just what we've been praying for. So be good girls and go and make us some tea before we die of thirst, would you?"

"I beg your pardon?" Solange said in her heavily accented English. "You want us to make you tea?"

The man's smile faltered. "Aren't you a contingent from the NAAFI or some other women's service come to cater for us? Make our beds? That kind of thing?"

"For your information, we are the new female recruits," Portia said. "Trainees just like you."

The men exchanged glances. "You can't be serious," one of them said. "They are not training women now, surely. Not sending women out into the field?"

"We are deadly serious," Portia said. "And we've been travelling all night and all day, so why don't you be good boys and make us a cup of tea?"

There was a stunned silence. The men shifted uneasily in their seats, glancing at each other and unsure what to do next. The first man who had spoken shook his head. "But that's absurd," he said. "This is the combat school. How do they expect you to tackle German soldiers? Wave a perfumed hanky at them?"

There was a general chuckle from the other men.

"I'll have you know that I was fencing champion at my school," Portia said.

This produced a laugh.

"I think you'll find that fencing little girls is not the same as facing the Gestapo," one of the men said. "They don't exactly play by the rules."

Marie-France took a step forward. "And I used to dance the can-can," she said. "I can kick really high, and believe me, I can bring any man to his knees."

"Anyway, we are here now," Solange said. "What do you British say? Like it or lump it? Now the first thing you can do is tell us how we can get something to eat. We have been travelling, and we are all very hungry."

"There's a small kitchen behind this room," one of the men said. "Tea-making stuff in there and also seems to be bread and jam. We got here yesterday, and they served us dinner and breakfast through in the dining room, so I presume there's a big kitchen with a proper staff somewhere."

"Right," Annie said, glancing at Madeleine, "I'm going to go and put the kettle on. And if you blokes want some tea as well, then one of you had bloody well better come and help."

"Oh, right." The man nearest the kitchen door got sheepishly to his feet.

"Good old Desmond," one of the men called after him. "He used to help his mummy serve afternoon tea at the vicarage."

"Useful skill, knowing how to serve tea," Desmond said. "And coffee. If you want to know, I worked in a café in Paris when I was a student. So I'll fit right in when we go to France."

The other men grinned uncomfortably. Madeleine took in this new dynamic. Whereas the women, on the whole, had been supportive of each other, the men were bluffing out their fear with bravado and insults. She should try and remember this.

~

Dinner that night was the usual wartime meal of stew composed mainly of vegetables followed by a stodgy pudding with a tiny dollop of custard.

"It's a pity we're not here in the autumn," one of the men commented. "We could practice our shooting skills on grouse and pheasant."

"Have any of you chaps had experience with shoots?" an upper-class lad asked. He was tall, lanky and looked absurdly boyish. "We used to have a shoot on the estate every year, so I've handled a shotgun since I could lift it."

"I don't think a shotgun is going to be much use when you have to silence an enemy sentry," came the comment.

"You don't want any kind of gun for that," another man said. "You'll need to slit his throat so he doesn't make a sound. I hear they have special little knives disguised as pens or that fit into the heel of your shoe. They've come up with brilliant things . . . I'm dying to try them out, aren't you?"

"Personally, I should choose chloroform," the older man at the end of the table said. "I went to medical school. Useful stuff, chloroform. Hold it over the nose for a couple of seconds, and they are out like a light."

Madeleine tried to eat her supper while she took in this easy discussion of methods of killing and disabling. Men took to it naturally. Would she ever have to slit a man's throat? Would she be able to do it if necessary? A fleeting panic gripped her. She should not be here. She would not be up to the task.

"I don't think we should talk like this at the dinner table," Desmond said. "I think we're upsetting the ladies."

"The ladies won't last ten minutes in the field if they are upset by talk of killing," the man who had first greeted them said. Madeleine had gathered by now that his name was Jack.

"You don't need to worry about us, *chéri*," a girl called Monique said. "At home in France I used to help my father slaughter pigs. I see the Germans in the same way—pigs, one slit across the throat—easy to slaughter if necessary."

The men looked down at their plates, rather stunned by this outburst.

"Well, I suppose we'll have to see how you ladies do on the course, won't we?" Jack said.

"Does anyone know what happens if we fail?" one of the women asked.

"You are driven off in a van and never seen again," one of the men said. There was laughter, but the man shook his head. "No, I mean it. They can't let you loose into society, so you're taken to a facility somewhere in the wilds of Scotland and held there."

"Like a prisoner?" the woman asked.

"Exactly."

"Are you sure about that?" Desmond asked.

"It's what I've heard. I was chatting to one of the instructors this morning."

"He was pulling your leg."

"I don't think so. I mean, letting us loose after what we have seen here is a great risk, isn't it?"

"So what do they do? Hold you prisoner for the duration, or do some sort of mind deprogramming? Wipe your memories? Turn you into a vegetable?"

Now there were looks of alarm from both men and women at the table.

"So you know the answer, don't you?" one of the men said. "You don't bloody well fail."

"Hey, old chap, watch your language in front of the women," the upper-class lad said.

The women now burst out laughing.

"Believe me, we can swear as well as you do, both in French and English," Solange said. "And I think you will find we do most things as well as you do. Some even better. Now, do they serve us coffee at the end of the meal here, in civilized fashion?"

Madeleine watched Solange with admiration. She was cool under pressure. She'd make a great spy. But what about the rest of them?

One of the men went in search of coffee and was told it would be coming shortly in the common room. So they moved through, and the men gallantly let the women sit on the sofas nearest the fire. Mugs of dark liquid were brought, with no milk or sugar. Solange took a sip and almost choked. "This is disgusting. What is it?"

The upper-class lad tried it. "It's Camp Coffee," he said. "Not coffee at all, but chicory. You pour it out of a bottle."

"Well, it is not drinkable," Solange said.

"I tell you what." Jack reached into a carrier bag beside him. "Since we're in Scotland, I suggest we add a wee dram to the coffee." And he produced a bottle of Scotch. He went around the room, adding a generous splash to each mug.

"Don't you want to save some for emergencies, old chap?" another of the men asked.

"I have a feeling we'll be able to get our hands on fresh supplies, if we butter up the cooks properly." Jack grinned. "One thing there is plenty of up here is whisky."

The warmth of the whisky spread through Madeleine's tired body. She battled against sleep and was glad when Annie got up and said, "I don't know about you lot, but I'm off to bed, if we're supposed to report at seven o'clock tomorrow morning."

Madeleine stood, and the other women followed.

"See, I told you they wouldn't last five minutes," Jack said with a chuckle. "One little drink and they are done for. Still, a couple of them aren't bad looking, are they? Who fancies their chances?"

Portia and Madeleine exchanged a look as they went up the stairs.

"Just let them try," Portia said. "I think they'll be in for a shock."

They were still chuckling as they entered the women's dormitory room.

CHAPTER 22

They were woken at six o'clock by either a cracked bell or a metal rod being banged on a rusty pipe. Either way the effect was not a smooth transition to consciousness. Madeleine sat up with a start, almost banging her head on the bunk above. This far north, it was already daylight at this hour, but the view outside the window was obscured by swirling white mist.

"Everyone up," called a loud male voice. "Outdoor clothes. Morning run."

"Bloody 'ell." Annie sat up in the bunk opposite. "Outdoor clothes—I don't think the jumpers they gave us were meant for this sort of weather."

"Neither were the gym shoes," Marie-France lamented.

They sat up, scrambled into clothing. One by one there was a hurried visit to the lavatory and a quick cleaning of teeth, then they went downstairs.

"Well done." It was Eric, the man they had met the night before, still wearing that big fisherman's jersey.

"Excuse me, sir," Portia said, "but the equipment they gave us isn't really suitable for runs in this weather. These shoes will be soaked through in minutes."

"You've got to learn to make the best of it, lassie," he said. "If we use you in the field, you won't always be wearing the right sort of clothing for an assignment. Go on. Off you go. Turn right—follow the red markers."

They came out into what was actually a soft rain that clung to eyelashes and soaked through a woollen jumper in minutes. The other four women came out right after them. Solange was wearing a mask. *How did she manage to get that?* Madeleine wondered. They set off, running over the smooth grass of the lawns, gasping in the cold air. After the lawn, it was through a stretch of woodland, then up a hillside of springy turf. The stitch in Madeleine's side made it hard to breathe, and she felt that she might pass out. Cloud swirled about them, parted to reveal a view of the sea below and then came together again, so that it was hard to spot the next marker. Annie and Solange went ahead, and the others followed, stumbling over tussocks and into rabbit holes. Then the way led down again, through another piece of woodland, and finally there was the house ahead of them. They put in a final sprint to the front door, where Eric was waiting. He glanced at his watch. "Twenty-five minutes. Not a bad time. Well done."

"Did the men come back ahead of us?" Madeleine asked.

"They were here a day ahead of you, and they did this yesterday morning," Eric said. "In pretty much the same time, if you want to know." And he gave an encouraging smile. "Now go on in to breakfast. Report at oh-eight hundred on the lawn."

The men were finishing their breakfast as the women came in.

"Oh, the orphans of the storm," Jack called out. "Surely they weren't mean enough to send you ladies out in the rain?"

"We did the same course as you," Solange said. "And in the same time, so we were told. Now, where is this breakfast?"

Breakfast consisted of a mug of sweet tea, a bowl of porridge, a slab of bread and jam. Madeleine had become used to the French habit of not eating much first thing in the morning, but today she finished everything, pleased with herself that she had completed the run. *I'm as fit as anyone else,* she thought. *As fit as these men.*

After breakfast they were back on the lawn for their first self-defence class. They learned how to block an assailant, how to release from a choke hold. All in all, the first day went well, and Madeleine began to feel that she could handle what they threw at her. Wind-proof jackets and stouter boots were delivered to them, but the boots felt heavy and gave them blisters, and the women all opted to keep wearing the gym shoes that could be washed and dried out overnight.

~

As the days progressed, they received their first lessons in unarmed combat: how to go for the enemy's eyes, how to break his nose so that his eyes watered and he couldn't see you. And then armed combat: efficient use of a knife, efficient killing with a blunt object, fending off the enemy if he had a knife, making an enemy release a gun. These courses made the future all too real. Madeleine questioned if she could really slam down a hand, break an arm, slit a throat, stab through the heart so that there was almost no tell-tale blood?

In bed at night, trying to get warm under the one rough army-blanket they were provided, she pondered these thoughts. A German soldier would probably be an ordinary man, conscripted into the army, who had no desire to fight or leave his safe home. Would she have the nerve to sneak up behind him and kill him? She consoled herself by reminding herself that not everybody would be sent as an operative: there would be couriers and radio operators and decipherers, all of which sounded harmless enough.

She realized that the whole object of this course was to break those who might be too frail. Up at dawn every day and some form of physical activity. There were increasingly arduous morning runs, and then the obstacle course was introduced. They had to run through a variety of terrains, to cross a swift-flowing stream, scramble up a scree-laden hillside, climb a wall by a rope ladder, scramble over a tree trunk and crawl under a fallen tree, wade through thick mud . . . It seemed never-ending.

I can't do this, a voice shouted in Madeleine's head, but she tried to shout it down. *I can do this. I've got to do this.* She was almost crying with exhaustion as she came to the mud. It was up to her knees, and every step required huge effort. When she stumbled forwards, hands grabbed at her and assisted her to the far side.

The men were quite surprised when the women returned, having completed the course. They did not realize that the women had helped each other—Annie climbing the wall first and then hauling up the others, Madeleine standing halfway across the swift-flowing stream to help others across and then being rescued after stumbling in the mud.

"What did you do, take a shortcut back?" one of the men asked.

"We did everything you did," Portia replied, "and did it bloody well, too."

Some of the men applauded. Even Jack was quiet for once.

But the days took their toll. One of the women and one of the men quit. They were driven away in a van, and the others wondered what would become of them. Strangely enough this was a great motivator to make sure they passed. There was something unnerving about watching the van go off and knowing that the occupants had not had a chance to say goodbye.

At the end of the month, they could all complete the morning run without gasping, and Madeleine had learned how to use jujitsu to throw a man who was attacking her. When the move worked and Jack landed on his back, it was one of her most satisfying moments. Their final challenge was to carry out a night-time commando raid, which entailed being dropped at the foot of a cliff by a small boat, scaling the cliff and overcoming the enemy soldiers at the top of it. It happened that an awful night had been chosen for it: the wind blew ferociously, and the sea loch was choppy and made landing a nightmare. They were sent in groups of eight: four men, four women. They were soaking wet from the waves as they tried to climb the cliff. Freezing-wet hands refused to grab on to ledges, and people slithered down again. Portia had done some mountain climbing when at school in Switzerland, and Madeleine followed her, her heart pounding as she looked down at the rocky shoreline. Marie-France discovered she had a fear of heights. The other women waited and talked her upward. One of the men lost his footing and fell, having to be evacuated in the small boat. At the top of the cliff, Madeleine's group overpowered the volunteer acting as the enemy. It felt immensely satisfying.

"We can bloody well do this," Annie shrieked for all to hear.

Eric met them for a final talk. They had done well, he said. But the secret was practice. All those moves should come like second nature, so that in the heat of an enemy confrontation they would not even have to think. Then he told them they had all passed and were being moved on to the next stage of their training. "And I hope you have all developed a head for heights," Eric called after them.

~

They were driven away from Arisaig in a coach, fourteen of them now, all feeling confident that they could handle any next challenge.

"What do you think he means by 'a head for heights'?" Marie-France asked. "That cliff was bad enough. I never thought I'd make it, but I did, thanks to you girls."

"I hope it's not scaling bigger cliffs," Madeleine answered.

"It can't be mountain climbing, or we'd be staying in the Highlands," Portia said. "Unless we're being taken to Wales. I did some challenging climbs on Mount Snowdon."

"Portia, is there anything you haven't done?" Marie-France asked her.

Portia shrugged. "I haven't been deep-sea diving. And I haven't killed anybody, yet."

This statement sent them all back to their own thoughts. Madeleine studied the other women. When they arrived at Arisaig, they had all been pale skinned, their hair in nice, neat waves, wearing lipstick, probably nylon stockings, too. Now they were freckled and tanned from so much exposure to sun and wind. Their hair was sun-bleached and wild, now held back with clips rather than in those perfect waves.

We're different people, Madeleine thought as the coach continued southwards, through Glasgow, through the lowlands and down into

England. They passed through Manchester. It was late in the day when they stopped outside what was clearly an RAF base. They could see the hangars, the planes covered in camouflage tarps, men marching. The sentry at the gate came forward to challenge the coach driver.

"New recruits from Arisaig," he said.

"Oh, right. Good luck, chaps." He grinned as the coach drove in and the barbed-wire festooned gate was shut behind them. They were shown to a barracks, told to put their things on a bed and then go for an evening meal. All night they were kept awake by the sound of planes taking off, rumbling with such vibration that everything in the room jangled.

It wasn't until the morning that they discovered why they were there. They were going to learn how to make a parachute jump.

CHAPTER 23

Of all the things they had been asked to do, the parachute jump was the most intimidating of all for Madeleine. She had learned the phrase "dropped behind enemy lines," but somehow she had imagined being put ashore in the small boat. It had never dawned on her that she'd literally be dropped from the sky, dangling from a parachute, an easy target for an enemy marksman. Unlike Marie-France, she did not have a fear of heights under normal circumstances. She had happily looked down from the top of the Eiffel Tower, and adrenaline had overcome fear as she climbed the cliff during the commando raid. But jumping out of a plane?

"Well, this is going to be a new experience, even for me," Portia said. She was the only one who looked sick and scared. "I wonder if we have some sort of training first, or they take us up and throw us out of a plane?"

"Shut up!" Marie-France burst out. "That's not even funny. I don't think I can do this. You saw what I was like on that cliff. I've never been in an aeroplane."

"You can't give up now," Madeleine said. "I'm terrified, too, but think of all we've gone through. Think of all the training we've had. What a waste if you quit now. And remember what they said about those who drop out? They are taken away and held somewhere in Scotland. Wouldn't that be worse than a few seconds jumping out of a plane?"

"But I wouldn't dare to jump. I'd just freeze, I know I would," Marie-France sounded close to tears.

"Don't worry, I'll give you a shove," Annie quipped.

The others laughed, but Marie-France did not. "You might have to. Because there's no other way I'm bloody well jumping out of a plane."

"You know what I'm thinking," Portia said. "The men will expect us to be terrified. Let's show them once again that we are as good as they are."

"Easy for you," Marie-France said. "You won't be peeing in your pants."

~

They ate a hearty breakfast, although Marie-France declared she was not going to eat anything as it would come straight back up again, and then they joined the other trainees, facing a rather terrifying RAF instructor.

"Now listen here, you people," he said. "I'm supposed to train you in a couple of days when it takes my men a couple of weeks to be ready for a jump. So I want complete concentration, every second. I'm going to do my best to make sure you hit the ground safely, although I understand that your drops are not like normal parachute jumps. To escape being detected by the enemy, your jump will be at considerably lower altitude—sometimes only three or four hundred feet. You're going to hit the ground pretty hard. So it's imperative you learn to land and roll perfectly, otherwise you are going to break your bloody necks."

Madeleine heard a small whimper of anxiety coming from Marie-France. She also felt her own stomach clench into a knot. After that, there was no more time for introspection or worry. They were taken into the gym, where they learned basic rolls, then to jump and roll, and practiced over and over. Madeleine had been a good gymnast at school, but some of the men had a hard time even mastering simple actions. They were taken to an outside area, where they had to climb to a platform, be attached to a harness and then jump on to mats below, landing and rolling correctly. Even this amount of contact with the ground was a shock to the system, and they were made to do it several times. They soon learned how easy it was to jar the whole body. One woman bit her tongue. One man twisted an ankle and was out of the rest of the training.

By the end of the day, they learned there was to be another component to add stress. The moment they landed, they had to learn how to bundle up yards of silk parachute, dig a hole with the small spade they carried and bury it. They repeated drills doing this in a wooded area, either hiding the parachute amid thick brambles or seeking out softer ground to bury it. That evening there was no conversation as they sat around the dinner table, trying to eat shepherd's pie and baked jam roll. When they collapsed into bed, the sound of the bombers taking off—the whole room shaking at their powerful roar—made it hard to sleep. Madeleine lay staring at the ceiling, wondering if she had made a huge mistake. She rattled off all the hardships she would encounter: being shot at and captured as she landed, breaking a leg as she landed, something she had seen was all too possible, interacting with the enemy, being captured and possibly tortured. Did she have the strength to handle what lay ahead? She got up and went over to the window, now covered in thick blackout material. She pulled this back a few inches and looked out. A moon was shining, outlining the silhouettes of the rows of huts and then picking up the glint of wings as the next flight of planes rose into the sky. It all seemed unreal. In fact, everything had seemed unreal since the awful news came—a bad dream from which there was no way out.

"Can't sleep?" said a voice behind her. She turned to see Portia standing there.

Madeleine sighed. "I'm asking myself if I'm up to what lies ahead. Do I have the gumption to handle it? I don't think I've been very good with pain. I'm not that brave . . ."

"Yes, you are," Portia said. "You're very brave. You had the worst news in the world, and you didn't give in. Other people would have retreated into their little private cave of misery, shut out the world and brooded. But you didn't. You want to do something to make a difference. I think it's wonderful. I admire you."

"But I can't tell you how scared I am," Madeleine said. "You seem to take everything in your stride as if it's all a big game. You're so confident and so damned good at everything, too."

"Darling, I have to tell you. I'm a good actress," Portia said. "Actually I'm as terrified as you. I don't know if I could handle torture. I'm particularly scared of being raped. I was once, you know. This chap after a party. He'd drunk too much. He took me for a walk, and then . . . you know. He forced himself on me. I didn't dare cry out because he was a fellow guest at the party and a respected man. I was only eighteen. I didn't know how to handle it. So I let him. And afterwards, every time he saw me, he gloated. He knew I wouldn't dare tell anyone."

"I'm so sorry," Madeleine said. "How awful for you."

"I survived," Portia said. "That's why we're going to be okay, you and I. We are natural survivors. Come on, let's get back to bed. We need all our strength for tomorrow."

She put a hand on Madeleine's shoulder and led her back across the room.

~

The morning dawned bright and clear, apart from a few puffy clouds that sailed across the horizon. Breakfast was cornflakes and a bacon sandwich. The absolute treat of real bacon boosted spirits as they were given their instructions. Each one was handed a flight coverall to put on. They were told they were going to make their first jump from a static balloon so they didn't have to worry about drifting into difficult terrain. When they landed, they were to take off the coveralls, gather up the parachute and bury both as quickly as possible. They'd be timed.

Then they each learned how to put on the parachute, how to pull the rip cord at exactly the right moment, waiting until they were clear of the plane. They rehearsed this, counting in unison before shouting, "Pull."

Nobody spoke as they were driven in the back of a military lorry out to a nearby field where an enormous balloon was waiting, tethered to the ground. The basket would hold three of them, plus an instructor and the balloon pilot. Wisely they did not ask for volunteers but pointed at three people. "You, you and you. In the basket."

Two men and Annie had been chosen. Annie shot her friends a sort of excited grin. "If I don't make it, you can have my chocolate ration," she called as she stepped through the little gate into the basket. The balloon was fired up, sending out a great burst of flame. The tethers were released, and it rose slowly into the air. Madeleine noticed that one tether still held it in place so that it rose directly above them. All the same, it seemed to be very high. There was a whistle, a shout to clear the area and one by one three small figures came out of the basket. Three parachutes opened and floated gently to the ground. All three landed safely, but one of the men allowed his parachute to collapse over him and had to fight his way free.

"That's what you don't want to do," their instructor barked. "Those added minutes could well cost you your life. Make sure you next lot don't make the same mistake."

Annie returned to them. "It was good," she said. "It feels like floating, and you have a lovely view all the way to the coast."

The balloon came down and was hauled back into place. Portia was called, plus another woman and man. She gave a thumbs up sign as she walked towards the balloon. Her jump went perfectly. Madeleine thought she looked as if she'd been doing it all her life. Then Madeleine was selected. There was a hiss of burning gas as they went up. The ground looked awfully far below with tiny figures staring up at them. They were told their jumping order. She was last. The man who was to go first sat with his feet over the edge. From behind him came the countdown. "GO!" was shouted. The man didn't move. He sat there, frozen. "Go," shouted the instructor again.

"I can't," the man whimpered.

Madeleine and a second man stood ready.

"Give him a push," barked the instructor. "And don't forget to pull your rip cord, or you're going to wind up as raspberry jam."

Madeleine felt frozen herself. Could she push another man to his possible death? Then she saw her fellow trainee step forward. "Out you go, old chap," he said. "See you at the bottom."

The man pitched out, and a few seconds later the parachute opened. The second man followed. Madeleine sat there, hearing her countdown. She took a deep breath and hurled herself into space. For a moment she was falling, the ground coming up to meet her. "Pull the cord" shouted through her mind. She did, was jerked upwards and floated towards the ground. It rushed up to meet her faster than she had expected. She braced, felt the jarring impact, rolled and got to her feet as the parachute collapsed behind her.

"Nicely done," the instructor said. "Quickly now. Release and bury."

She still felt wobbly on her feet as she scooped up yards of parachute, found a spot, put together her shovel and started digging.

When she rejoined the group, she found that Marie-France was already on her way up with the next batch of recruits. Madeleine watched her float down, disengage flawlessly and bury her parachute quickly.

"You did it." The three friends greeted her as she staggered back towards them.

"Don't talk to me," Marie-France said. "I've got to throw up."

That afternoon they were taken up in an aeroplane to do their second jump in true conditions. It wasn't as bad as they expected, and that evening they all went to the officers' mess for a beer.

"So it's on to somewhere else tomorrow," one of the men said. "I wonder what they are going to throw at us this time?"

"Couldn't be worse than what we've already been through," Jack said jauntily.

"Famous last words," came a comment from the other side of the bar.

CHAPTER 24

OLIVER

Australia

"Oliver, wake up! You've got to come and see the Heads!"

Oliver came back to consciousness like a diver emerging from deep sea. Come and see the heads? Images of disembodied heads floated through his mind—heads on pikes in the Middle Ages, shrunken heads in cannibal territory. Before his brain could make sense of the words, he was shaken awake and opened his eyes to see Timmy Henderson, his bunkmate, standing over him.

"Come on. Before it's too late." He yanked the bedclothes off Oliver and flung his jacket at him.

"Where are we going?" Oliver sat up, reaching for his shoes.

"On deck, of course. You can see land. We're almost there. The others are already up on deck."

Oliver was now fully awake. He pulled on his jacket, tied his shoes, and stumbled along the corridor after Timmy. Up one flight of stairs they went, then another and another. At last they emerged, gasping on to the deck. Warm, moist air blew in their faces. Seagulls wheeled overhead, and before them was land. After six weeks at sea, Oliver felt like crying. Not that it had been all bad. In fact it had been quite a lark for all the children. They had been allowed free range of their class of the ship. There had been no attempt at lessons. They had learned to play deck quoits, and the meals had been interesting. Since it was an American ship, they had been introduced to hamburgers, which the boys declared were "wizard" and "spiffing." What's more, they had called at interesting ports along the way: because of the threat of enemy ships and submarines who might not honour a neutral ship, they had travelled the length of the Atlantic Ocean, instead of the shorter route through the Suez Canal. They had called at Senegal, Cape Town, around the Cape of Good Hope to Port Elizabeth. After that it had been Ceylon and down to Perth, Adelaide, Melbourne and finally Sydney. They had not been allowed ashore at any of the ports, but it had been interesting to look down from the deck to see life going on in foreign cities and to have new and interesting foods brought on board. They had tried avocado pears and coconuts, pineapples and mangoes.

The first part of the trip, on the Atlantic, had been rough, and everyone had been seasick, but after the cape it had been smooth sailing, the weather mild. The fresh sea air and good food had made them all bigger and stronger. Oliver felt a vague sense of optimism that life would not be bleak forever and this new world might be okay.

"See, what did I tell you?" Timmy demanded in his high voice. "Look. We're going to pass through the Heads."

Oliver saw now that there was an opening between rocky headlands, and the ship was now approaching this gap. They steamed through, close enough to see people waving from the clifftops. And then they were in a smooth inlet. Wooded slopes came down to beaches. Red-roofed houses perched above the water. They passed marinas full of yachts. A ferry passed them, tooting its horn. Pleasure craft came alongside to welcome them into port. And there, ahead of them, was Sydney, with its tall buildings and its famous bridge spanning the harbour. Oliver thought it was the most beautiful sight he'd ever seen.

"It's going to be all right, isn't it?" he said to no one in particular.

The boys were sent back to their cabin to pack their things and wait to be taken ashore. It seemed to take a long while, and Oliver was annoyed that they didn't have a porthole so he could watch the ship docking. At last a steward came for them, telling them to follow him. They joined other children assembled in a lounge, waiting. Other passengers disembarked. Oliver began to feel hungry. They hadn't had breakfast or even a cup of tea.

After a long wait, a man wearing a uniform came to them. "G'day, kids. Had a good trip?" he asked, giving them a friendly smile. "Ready for the next part of your adventure? Right. All follow me as we go ashore. No dawdling. We don't want to lose anyone along the way."

He spoke with a strange accent. Oliver picked up his suitcase and joined the line going down the stairs, along the gangplank on to the dock below. There were several adults waiting for them, each holding lists in their hands.

"When your name is called, go over and stand beside the person who called you," one of the women instructed. "Staying here in Sydney we've Mike Johnson, Anne Black, Fred Holt, Timothy Henderson . . ."

"That's me," Timmy said, giving Oliver a nudge. "Nice meeting you, Ollie." And off he went.

Another woman read out a list, and more children went with her.

"I presume the rest will be yours, sister?" the woman in charge said, and a nun nodded, holding up her list. "You children come with me," she said. "The bus is waiting for us outside the port. All together now. Quick march."

Oliver fell into line, looking back at the woman on the dock to make sure this was all right. He hadn't quite liked the tone of the nun they were following. They marched through a terminal building and out on to the street, where a bus was waiting.

"When I call your name, you get onboard," the nun instructed. "Leave your suitcases for the driver to put in the luggage compartment."

"Where are we going, miss?" a girl asked.

"I'm not a miss, I'm sister," the nun said. "Sister Elizabeth Ann. You'll do well to remember that. And we are going to the Ferndale Farm Orphanage, which my order runs. Now, no more questions, no more dallying. Prescott, Jake."

A bigger boy Oliver had met on the boat stepped up into the bus.

"Merriman, Marjorie. Denton, Michael. Jones, Oliver." She paused, glaring. "Jones?"

There was no answer.

"Oliver Martin Jones? Are you here?"

Oliver stepped forward. "My name's Oliver Martin, not Jones."

"Oliver Martin Jones. That's what it says here. If you're being smart with me, young man . . ."

"No, miss." Oliver shook his head. "I'm not trying to be smart. My name's not Jones. It's just Oliver Martin. There must be some mistake."

"So we've a clerical error." She waved a dismissive hand in his direction. "It happens from time to time. Poor handwriting that's illegible. No matter, Oliver Martin, or whoever you are. It's all the same to me what you are called. Up you go. Get on the bus."

Oliver climbed the three steps on to the bus, but he looked back to see if anyone else was around. He was still battling with the profound sense that something was wrong. He should not be on this bus going with the unpleasant nun. Maybe he shouldn't be in Australia at all. But there was nobody to appeal to. Nobody to tell.

CHAPTER 25

The coach continued southwards to another country house. It was hard to tell where they were, as all road signs had been removed, but Madeleine decided, from the length of the journey and from the terrain, that they must be not too far from London. From the towers on the hill above, she concluded it was a radio station, and this proved to be true. At their first briefing, they were told that they were going to learn everything there was to know about radios. How to assemble one, take one apart, operate one, conceal one, send and receive messages. Radio messages could come through innocently as part of a BBC broadcast, or they could be sent and received in code. The instructor asked who was familiar with Morse code. A few hands were raised. Madeleine had studied it briefly for one of her Girl Guide badges but had long forgotten it.

"Morse code may well be your one lifeline," the speaker said. "Your one chance to save your skin. If you are captured or want to communicate when speech is impossible, you tap out your message. You will each be given the Morse alphabet at the end of this lecture. Study it hard, keep studying so that it becomes second nature. There will be tests along the way."

Then followed a few intense days of hands-on work—building radios from parts, taking them apart again rapidly—and mental work, using Morse telegraph, learning cyphers, decoding enemy messages. There was so much information that Madeleine felt her head reeling. She fell asleep with Morse code echoing through her dreams. At the end of the course, there was a test. She passed, but not brilliantly. And after the test an interview.

"Mrs Martin, we have been debating how we can use you. You are clearly not as manually dexterous as some of your fellows. We don't see you as a radio operator or as a demolition specialist. So there seems to be no point in your continuing here . . ."

Madeleine's mouth dropped open. "You're not failing me, are you? You're not booting me out of the programme, because I've worked hard and I want—"

"Nobody said we were booting you out of anything," the man replied smoothly. "We want to make sure we use people where they are best suited. We have noted that you don't seem to possess the killer instinct, so it would be wrong to send you into some kind of commando or undercover attack situation. However, you have displayed grit and a cool head. It has been noted you get along well with people, you are not antagonistic, you are observant. We will probably be using you as a courier. How does that sound?"

"I think I can handle that well, sir," Madeleine said.

"Let's hope you can." He nodded. "Some of your fellows will now be heading off to explosives and weapons training. Some will stay here for more radio experience. You will go straight to HQ, where you will learn how to be a spy." When she couldn't resist an incredulous grin, he went on. "Not only things like disguises, how to lose a tail. Our chaps have developed all sorts of ingenious little gadgets to make life interesting and to keep you safe. Should be fascinating."

Madeleine had to agree that this sounded more useful than learning how to blow up bridges, and she was glad that she had not been selected to send rapid Morse code messages. When she met up with the others, she found that Annie had been selected to be a radio specialist and was staying on, while Solange was going off to the weapons and explosives training with most of the men.

"Blimey, who'd have thought that I'd be the one who passed the radio aptitude tests," Annie said, chuckling. "I'll miss my old mates. I hope you don't get sent abroad before I'm finished."

"And then there were three," Portia commented as she, Marie-France and Madeleine were taken on in the back of an army lorry, along with Desmond, the former doctor, and another of the men, who introduced himself as Michel and was clearly French. They sat on hard planks along the sides, not able to see where they were going, and the trip seemed never-ending. Madeleine began to feel car sick as they swerved around corners. From what they could see out of the back of the lorry, they were going through country lanes, no signs of a city.

"How much longer, do you think?" Marie-France whispered. "I'm dying for a pee."

"Me too," Desmond agreed. "A pee and a cup of tea. We must be close to the south coast by now. It seems we've been heading due south, judging by the position of the sun."

"We could tap on the cab and ask them to stop," Michel suggested.

They tried this, but either the cab was too noisy or the driver chose to ignore the signals.

"So what do you think we'll be doing now?" Desmond asked.

"I was told learning to be a spy, whatever that means," Madeleine said. "At least it won't be climbing up cliffs and those awful obstacle courses, one hopes."

"Hold on, we're stopping." The doctor leaned as far as he could, pulling back the canvas that covered most of the rear of the lorry. "I think we might have arrived."

They could hear voices, the sound of a rusty gate swinging open, the crunch of gravel as they started up a driveway. Flowering shrubs and manicured garden stretched on either side. *Another country house,* Madeleine thought. But then they stopped. A soldier came around and released the canvas cover. "Out you come," he said. "Not a bad billet you've got here. All right for some."

One by one they climbed down, stretching out stiff limbs, and looked around.

"Mon Dieu!" Michel exclaimed.

Madeleine was taking in the house before them. Not a country house this time but a huge grey stone building with a turret on one side and beyond it the ruins of an abbey. Portia's face lit up. "I know where we are," she said. "This is Beaulieu." She pronounced it *Bew-lee*. "It's the home of the Montagues. I came here to a dance once. How frightfully jolly."

A man in officer's uniform had come out of the front door at their arrival. "Names, please?" He checked them against his list. "All present and correct. Come on in."

They followed him into the house, standing in an impressive timbered entryway.

"Right," he said. "I'm Captain Stanton. I will be part of the team that is to train you in the noble art of spying." He waited while they gave nervous smiles. "You've learned the physical side of what you need to survive. This will be the final stage—the mental and psychological preparation. Go upstairs now. Find yourselves rooms on the second floor, have a wander about the grounds and get to know where the various cottages are. That's where some of your specialty classes will be held. Dinner at seven in the dining room."

"Well, I must say this is a bit more civilized," Portia said as they went up the stairs. "Dinner at seven. Not supper at six or grub when you can get it. Wine and candlelight, do you think?"

The bedrooms had once been for servants, that was clear. Each contained a narrow iron bed, a couple of hooks on the back of the door, and a chair. They quickly located the lavatory and bathroom and took turns to clean off the grime of the journey. The tour of the house and the grounds followed. It was a warm summer evening. Pigeons were cooing in the trees. The breeze wafted the scents of jasmine and roses. Ducks rose from a lake. It was all so peaceful and remote that it was easy to forget for a few minutes that there was a war on.

"Golly, I hope we can stay here for a while, don't you?" Portia said. "I wonder how long we can draw out our training? Excuse me, sir, could you go over that bit again?" She laughed.

"Then they'd fail you and you'd be hauled off to the north of Scotland," Marie-France said. "I don't know about you, but I'm itching to get going—sent over to France, I mean. I think we've been training long enough. I want to do my part."

"You're not afraid?" Madeleine heard her own uncertainty in her voice.

"Of course I'm afraid. I don't even know how good I'll be at this. Sometimes I wonder why I even thought it was a good idea to volunteer," Marie-France said. "But the longer we have to think about it, the worse it gets. I wish they'd shipped us out that first week when we were all keen."

"We'd have been useless," Portia said. "Think of how many skills we've developed. We can disarm a man, use a radio, send messages in Morse code . . . we're invincible."

"Gosh, I hope you're right," Madeleine said. "I don't feel very invincible myself."

It was funny, Madeleine thought as she went to bed that night, but she had almost forgotten what they were training for. The object of all this—the parachute jump into occupied France, the spying on the enemy—was suddenly very real again.

~

The next morning they met for their first briefing from a Major Walcott and were told that from now on things got serious. They were all destined for France, so all conversation would be in French from now on. Their first task was to meet with an adviser and create a persona for themselves—it should be a person they could easily identify with, someone who would have a good reason to appear suddenly in a town or neighbourhood. Think of any skills you have, they were told. Any particular affinity for a place. Madeleine went away and thought. She decided on Minette Giron. Minette because that was Giles's mother's name. She had a secret reason for wanting it. If Giles was still alive, if she was operating anywhere near him, he might be curious to see who had his mother's name. She decided Minette was a quiet, studious type. She had met her husband at the Sorbonne, then worked in a bookshop in Paris while he was a schoolteacher. They had no children. Her husband, Jacques, had been killed fighting for the French army during the invasion, and she was finding it hard to cope with her grief. Now she wanted to be out of the city and to move nearer to her family.

This was approved. She was taken to one of the cottages, where she was outfitted with suitable clothing. She worked in a bookshop, so she wasn't ever particularly fashionable. Good, sensible clothes and shoes, well-worn. Her hair was now quite long, and she was shown how to roll it in the French way. She was given books. She would volunteer at a local library if there was one. From now on, she was to be Minette at all times.

Then came lessons on disguise, given by a former actor at the Old Vic. Forget about false moustaches, they were told. It was the little things—a different walk, a different hairstyle, a little powder on the hair to make it look grey, a little tape under the hairline to alter the eyebrows. They practiced these. They were rather fun. So were the lessons on burglary, given by an ex-convict. They learned how to pick a lock, how to make an impression of a key using Plasticine. They practiced how to tail someone and how to lose a tail on them. They were taken into the nearest market town and had to follow a person, then escape when they were being followed. Again this felt like a big game until they were reminded of the seriousness of what they were about to do.

Their instructors took pains to remind them of this, whenever they could. One morning Madeleine was crossing the courtyard when someone behind her called out, "Hey, Madeleine."

She turned round and was struck with a resounding slap across the face. She recoiled in horror, her hand to her stinging cheek. Her instructor stood there. "You just signed your death warrant, young lady," he said. "You make one slip like that, and they'll catch you. You are to be on your guard every second, even with people who seem to be harmless and friendly. Do you understand that?"

"Oui, monsieur," she replied.

~

Classes continued: how to make and use invisible inks, how to hide things inside other objects, how to set signals to notify when it was safe and when it was not. They were shown a cigarette packet containing, amongst real cigarettes, a false one with miniature tools. A pencil containing a map and compass where the eraser should be. The maps were made of parachute silk and could be rolled into something as small as a hollowed cigarette. It was all rather clever and wonderful, and Madeleine wondered if she'd ever have to use any of them. She was equipped with items especially for her: a hollowed-out book, a little jewellery box with a false lid, a powder compact that could be used not only for signalling on a sunny day but which also had a space behind the mirror to hide daily cyphers or messages to be delivered.

All went well until there was a stumbling block: they had to practice receiving and delivering messages. The radio operator gave them the message, and they had to take it to a contact whom they would recognize by some previously given clue. As they came out of the building, Madeleine was handed a bicycle. She looked up in horror. "I can't ride a *bicyclette*," she said.

"You're the one person in the world who has never had a bicycle?"

Madeleine shook her head. "I've never learned. I went to boarding school really young, and when I lived in London and Paris, I didn't need a bike."

"Then you'd better learn quickly," came the response. "Here, Holden. Take her around until she's comfortable on it."

So she spent an embarrassing afternoon wobbling around the estate while a soldier ran behind, holding on to her saddle. At last he let her go, and she wobbled away, successfully. After that, she had to practice every day until she could handle it smoothly in all weathers.

After they had been there for a while, they were joined by Annie and some of the men, straight from their radio training.

"What's it like here?" Annie asked.

"Well, for one thing, you'd better not be caught speaking English," Madeleine said. "It's only French from now on. But everything is quite fascinating—disguises, clever little implements to pick locks. It all seems quite unreal, like a *Boy's Own* comic."

"Sounds good. I can't wait to get at it," Annie said in perfect French. It was interesting that her English was pure cockney but her French sounded quite refined.

As they were heading for the dining room, Portia said, "I wonder when Solange will join us? At least she'll be in her element here, probably correcting my grammar all the time."

Annie frowned. "Haven't you heard? She got booted out."

"She did?"

"She attacked an officer."

"What?" Madeleine stared at her.

"Yes, they were doing weapons drills, and the trainers were deliberately trying to make them get rattled and see if they could still shoot straight. And one of them said something about the French and how they weren't worth fighting for . . . It was all carefully designed, of course. And Solange struck him with the butt of her rifle. So they decided she could not be trusted to control her anger and would be a liability."

"So she's gone?"

"Where the others are, I suppose. Locked away for the rest of the war. I pity the others."

"I'm sorry for her," Madeleine said. "She was so keen to go to her country and do something brave."

"But they were right," Portia said. "She would have been a liability. Can you imagine if she'd heard Germans talking in a disparaging way about the French, about how they were going to rape a particular French girl? She'd give herself away and risk a whole network."

Madeleine nodded. It was true. In France they would not just be responsible for themselves but for anyone they worked with.

~

The end was getting closer. They were briefed on the situation in France today—what they needed to know about rationing rules, how to use ration cards, how to avoid the Germans, how to behave if they had to interact with them. It was impressed upon them how easy it was to slip up. They were told of one operative who went into a café and asked for a café au lait. This alerted the enemy, and he was captured. With milk in such short supply, all coffee was now served black in cafés and had been for some time.

At last came the psychological classes: how to handle living a secret life under surveillance, how to interact with the enemy and what do if brought in for interrogation. "How to resist torture," the instructor said. He looked around the room. "For most of us, we can't. When the pain becomes bad enough, we give in. Pulling out fingernails and toenails is a favourite. Have you ever had anything wedged under a fingernail? It's unbearable, isn't it? And burning—burning with cigarettes to soften you up. Or burning with a poker or an iron. And for the women there is always the threat of sexual violence. Maybe for the men, too. Who knows? A lot of the German secret police are smart and well-versed in psychology. They'll work out quickly your weakest point and what can break you. So you may decide to give them enough of what they want to know before the torture starts. As long as you don't betray a network or turn in your fellows. And if it looks as if they've got you and they are going to get every ounce of information out of you, we equip you with the final chance: on your jacket there is a button that contains a cyanide capsule. A quick and relatively painless death. Preferable to a lingering one in a German prison camp."

He paused. There was now complete silence in the room. Nobody looked up, each one staring in front of them, lost in their own thoughts.

"Even now, at this stage, you don't have to go," the instructor said gently. "Nobody is being forced into this. The dangers are very real. I won't deny that your chances of survival are not great. The decision is yours alone. If you change your mind in the middle of the night, come and tell me, and by morning you'll be out of here and gone. No need to explain or say goodbye." He looked around the room. Nobody said anything. But the next morning they were not entirely surprised to find that Desmond had left. He had always seemed like such a gentle sort of man.

Later that week Madeleine was sound asleep in the middle of the night when she was woken with a crash. Bright light shone in her face. Shadowy figures stood over her.

"Aufwachen! Aufstehen! Raus mit dir!" screamed a voice as she was dragged to her feet. Men in Nazi uniform grabbed her and dragged her down the hall, shoving her into what seemed to be a cupboard. The light continued to shine in her face. "Name?" a voice barked.

"What is your name?" he repeated in French.

"M—Minette Giron," Madeleine realized how she had almost given herself away.

"Do you speak German?"

"No, monsieur."

"What about English?"

"No, monsieur, only French."

"And what are you doing here? Why did you come to this town?"

"My husband was killed. I was afraid to be in Paris alone," she said. "I used to have a relative here, so I know this place. It seemed safe. I thought I could get a job here."

"As what?"

"I used to work in a bookshop, but now I deliver shoes for the shoe repairman."

"And sometimes you deliver other things, too?"

"Yes, monsieur. Sometimes I deliver flowers, or even pastries a couple of times."

"You know what I mean. I mean messages. From the enemy."

"No, monsieur. Not true. I am a simple woman. I just want to be left alone, that's all."

"We will search your room, and if we find anything, it will be very bad for you. But I can make it easy on you, if you just tell us what we want to know . . ."

"I have nothing to tell, monsieur. On my honour, I have nothing . . ."

"Enough," said one of the men in English now. He took off the German cap. "Well done, Minette. You handled it well. But I presume you realized we were only acting."

"Not at first. I wasn't fully awake. But then I did realize . . . That didn't make it any less frightening."

"No. So stay alert. Practice bracing yourself mentally. What will you say if this happens? Think of ways to wriggle out of it. Practice saying them, over and over. Because the next time it will be real."

Still shaking, Madeleine went back to bed.

CHAPTER 26

Oliver

Australia

The bus drove the children down a wide main street past shops and banks and theatres. After London and the war, it was amazing to look at bakeries full of pastries, people sitting in cafés or queueing up for the cinema. Oliver was interested to see that women were wearing furs and men were in overcoats. He had been told that Australia was a warm country, with lovely beaches and picnics and horse riding. It hadn't occurred to him that here, in July, it was the middle of winter—not bleak by European standards but still cool enough for a coat at times.

The bus came to a halt outside a large train station. "Follow me, children," the nun said. "Get in twos. We're going out to the farm by train now. Quickly. Out you get. Pick up your bags and go to line up."

The children scrambled for the exit. Oliver located his suitcase, then he looked around.

"You—stand next to that boy."

A bigger boy was placed next to Oliver. Oliver's heart was pounding. This had happened to him before. He had lined up next to Gerald Hopkins, and they had marched into the station, and lots more kids came as they waited for the train, and then . . . And then it was blank. He did not remember the bomb at all. He could not even remember where he was sitting or who he was sitting next to. But he remembered something was not right. Something had been worrying him and still lurked on the fringes of his consciousness now. Something that had been reawakened today when that nun had called him Jones.

He had no more time to ponder this as they were marched briskly into the station. The nun showed the man at the barrier their tickets, and they went on to the platform. No train had come in, and they stood there.

"Now remember, on the train, you find a seat and you sit quietly. No larking about. You are to be a credit to your new home."

At that moment the train came in. The other children surged forward, propelling him towards an open door. This had happened before. He remembered his feeling of panic as he was swept into the train because something had been wrong then. Was it the wrong train? Should he not have got on? But at that moment, a firm grip grabbed his shoulder. "No dilly-dallying, I said. On you go." And he was shoved into the compartment.

As the train pulled out of the station, they were handed a biscuit and an orange each. The orange was such a huge treat that Oliver forgot his panic. He stared at it with longing before he dared to peel it. He had not seen an orange since the start of the war. He savoured the juice running down his chin and saw that other children had the same enraptured look on their faces.

The train passed grimy streets, not unlike the London slums, except that the houses here had balconies made of attractive wrought ironwork, which made them look more elegant than their London counterparts. But the children who played in the street outside were just as grubby as London street kids, and the washing that hung on lines was just the same. But the outer suburbs were attractive: red-roofed bungalows, surrounded by lovely lawns, trees, flowering shrubs. Oliver tried to work out if they were going north, south, east or west by the position of the sun. It seemed as if they were going inland, away from the coast and those wonderful beaches he had seen.

The suburbs were left behind and replaced with market gardens, small farms, glimpses of a river. They came to a halt at a town called

Parramatta. The children around Oliver made fun of the name, chanting it over and over until the nun frowned at them. After Parramatta it was mainly countryside with little farmhouses, surrounded by verandas, and with roofs no longer tiled but made out of sheets of corrugated iron. Each had a pond nearby. Some had cows and sheep in pastures and lines of unfamiliar blue-green trees with delicate leaves. They crossed a river, and almost imperceptibly, the train began to climb. Now they passed through groves of the new and different trees, then plunged into a tunnel.

"We are ascending to the Blue Mountains," the nun said. "We will pass some fine resorts. People come here for their health."

Oliver looked out of the window for signs of mountains but couldn't see any. Just many more of the trees, whose strange, sharp scent now wafted in through the windows. At last they stopped at a station called Katoomba. Lots of people disembarked. The train continued onwards—more tunnels, more trees, more cuttings through yellow rock—and finally stopped again.

"We get out here, children. Gather up your things," the nun said.

Oliver climbed down to the platform, breathing in fresh and scented air. Then he saw the name of the station and stared in amazement. It was called Blackheath. He had come halfway around the world to a place with the same name as his English home. He felt the irony of it bitterly. If he was really in the true Blackheath, there would be Mummy and Grandpa and Eleanor and his toys in his bedroom and the heath to walk on. This place looked quite nice, but it felt so different and remote, reminding him exactly how far from home he was. As he stood on the platform, looking around, a flock of brilliant pink parrots wheeled and landed on the lawn outside the station, making a racket of loud squawking cries. The boy sitting next to him nudged Oliver.

"Like a ruddy zoo, ain't it?" the boy said.

"Come along, children. Follow me. The transport is waiting," the sister said. They marched behind her to see an old farm lorry, open aired, with bench seats along both sides. The children crammed on to these, with their luggage piled between their feet. The nun sat in the cab at the front, next to the driver, and off they went. Outside the little town the road climbed, then wound down to the next valley, zigzagging and turning until all the children felt sick. When one vomited, others followed, and Oliver swallowed back his own need to throw up. At last the winding road smoothed out, and they were in dry countryside of yellow grass. Suddenly one of the children gave a shout. He pointed into the distance where a line of kangaroos were bounding with unbelievably long strides. They seemed like magical creatures, half flying as they moved with incredible speed through the landscape and were lost in a grove of dusty trees. The paved road became a dirt track, and they bounced over ruts with red dirt blowing up behind them. After a few miles of this, they came to a fence, a gateway with the words *Ferndale Children's Farm*.

Ahead were several long, low buildings. All were made of wood and had corrugated iron roofs. A veranda ran the length of the main building, where the lorry came to a halt. The children climbed out one by one as three more nuns and several older children came out to greet them.

"And what happened here?" one of the nuns asked as she looked at a small girl with vomit down her front. The nun had a thin, bony face with a long nose, and Oliver immediately thought of the witch in the Hansel and Gretel book.

"I threw up, miss," the girl said. "It was the road. It went round lots of corners."

"I am not miss. I am Sister Jerome," the nun boomed out. "Were you children not raised to be good Catholics?" She took a step towards the girl. "You threw up? On your clothing? You must learn to control yourself better," the nun said sharply. "What a dirty little girl you are. You're a disgrace. Take that coat off and leave it here, then go and wash yourself immediately."

The little girl looked around fearfully, not sure where to go.

"I'll take her." A big, cow-like girl stepped forward. "Come on, you. I'll clean you up." Her expression was not friendly.

"The rest of you pay attention." The nun who had spoken now addressed the rest of them, a hard gaze sweeping over the group. "You are now in the care of the Sisters of St Agnes. Our aim is to turn you into good citizens, able to make a useful contribution to this new and growing country. You will work hard and obey orders, and disobedience will not be tolerated. I am Sister Jerome. This is Sister Margaret. And Sister John Mark. You have already met Sister Elizabeth Ann. When you address us, you will say, 'Yes, sister.' Is that clear?"

"Yes, sister," came the chanted answer.

"Right. These are our monitors who will be supervising you. Edith just went with that dirty child. She supervises the girls' dormitory. Rusty is in charge of the younger boys. Dan is in charge of the older boys. Now, everyone leave your luggage here. Go to your new dormitories and get changed. We all wear the same uniform here. No preferential treatment."

Oliver went over to the big boy called Rusty. He didn't look too bad. He had red hair, cut in a shaggy fashion that indicated he might have done it himself.

"Come on, follow me." He gave them an encouraging grin.

"What about our bags?" Oliver asked. "My stuff is in there."

The big boy laughed. "You won't see those again, mate."

Oliver thought of the new dog that Miss Everingham had bought him, of the new clothes that had been given to him before he took the ship.

"What happens to them?" he asked.

"I reckon they sell them," the big boy muttered, looking around to see if anyone had heard him. "You only get to wear the uniform from now on."

They reached a second building—a long hut with a tin roof. Inside were at least twenty iron beds, each with a pillow and sheet. At the bottom of each bed was a neat pile of khaki clothing.

"Go on. Get changed," Rusty said, "Or you'll miss your tea. They don't wait for us."

The boys scrambled to take off their clothes. Oliver found the pile contained shorts, an open-necked shirt and a thick wool cardigan. There was a spare vest and underpants. No socks.

"What happens when we want to change our socks?" he asked.

"Take a look at my feet, Squirt," Rusty said.

Oliver looked down. The boy was not wearing shoes.

"We go barefoot here. You won't see shoes again, I can promise you that." He gave the boys a commiserating smile. "You'll soon get used to it. Just do what you're told and keep your head down. Don't complain. Don't make waves, and you'll be right."

The boys took off their clothes and put on the shorts and shirts and also the cardigans, as a cold wind had sprung up.

"Is it always as cold as this?" one boy asked. "I thought they said Australia was a hot country."

Rusty laughed. "It's the middle of winter, Squirt. Don't you know anything? The seasons are upside down here. We're at the bottom of the world . . . and that's what it feels like. Living at the bottom of the world."

~

A bell clanged somewhere outside.

"Right, you boys. Now we march over to the dining hall. Line up. Let's go."

Oliver fell into line with the others, conscious of the cold concrete floor on his bare feet. He had never been barefoot publicly before, except once in the sand on a beach. Once outside the hut, he realized the coarse gravel was painful to walk on, and he noticed the other new boys hobbling and wincing, too. Rusty, however, strode out as if this way of walking was quite natural.

Oliver saw that the buildings stood around a dusty central square with a Union Jack on a flagpole. In the centre of the square, he also noticed a small girl standing on a stool, holding up some kind of white cloth that flew out in the evening breeze. Some kind of flag ceremony, he wondered, although he associated white flags with surrender.

"What's she doing?" Oliver asked Rusty, who was walking beside him.

"Oh, her? She wet the bed last night. If you do that, you have to wash out the sheet and then hold it up to dry all day, and if it's not dry by evening, you have to sleep on a wet sheet that night. I don't recommend it," he added.

Oliver stared at the small girl's face. He could tell she was trying to be stoic, but her eyes were a picture of misery. She could only have been four or five at the most. Hadn't he wet the bed at times when he was that age? He remembered the cold, hard face of Sister Jerome. Rusty looked back at the boys trying to walk over the gravel. "Come on, you lot, or there will be nothing left to eat." The boys tried to walk faster as they reached the long, low wooden building with its corrugated iron roof. "Okay. In you go. No talking. Find a place at the tables."

The boys went into the building. Two long tables stretched the length of it, and at these other boys and girls were standing. They observed the newcomers with interest. Some of the boys and girls looked quite grown up, others even younger than Oliver. He took a place next to the boy he had been following and waited. On the table in front of them were slabs of bread spread with a thin coating of butter and jam. They continued to wait. Nobody sat. Nobody spoke. Oliver's stomach growled at the thought of that bread. Why couldn't they sit and eat?

At last the door at the far end opened, and Sister Jerome came in. She looked around the room with an expression of utter distaste. "Before we start the meal, I'm afraid to tell you that there are punishments to be handed out: Marilyn Grove. Step forward."

A skinny little girl with long straggly hair came out, head down.

"I am told that you were shirking today when you were supposed to be weeding. Is that right?"

"I wasn't feeling very well, sister. I felt dizzy. I needed to sit down." The girl's voice was scarcely more than a whisper.

"You weren't feeling well? Did you go to the infirmary at the correct time this morning?"

"No, sister. I was feeling all right then."

"So it was the thought of good, honest hard work that made you feel ill, was it?"

"No, sister. I just came over all funny."

"All funny, eh? Well, you won't find this very funny, missy. You'll go straight to your dormitory now, with no tea. You'll get on your knees and recite a dozen Hail Marys and ask the Blessed Virgin for forgiveness. You'll stay on your knees until the other children come to bed. And if it happens again, the punishment will be worse. Off you go."

The little girl walked away, head still hanging. Oliver longed to rush over to her and comfort her.

"And now for something more serious that was reported to me. Frank Bell?"

An older boy—round faced, chubby—came forward, shuffling his feet slowly. "And what did you do, Frank Bell? Go on. Tell all the children what you were caught doing?"

"I took a piece of lamington, sister."

"A piece of lamington that was supposed to be for the sisters' tea," Sister Jerome said. "You deprived one of the sisters of a small treat she was looking forward to—a treat to make up for dedicating her life to the service of others in this godforsaken part of the world so far from her home. What have you got to say for yourself?"

"I'm sorry, sister. I was just so hungry. We didn't get much breakfast . . ."

"I'm afraid you're going to be even hungrier, Frank. It's the sin bin for you this time, and I can't tell you for how long. I may even forget about you. Take him there, Sister Margaret."

"Oh no, sister." The boy seemed to melt, shaking in fear. "I'm scared of the dark. Please don't put me in there. I'll work really hard tomorrow, I promise. I'll do everything you say. Just not in there."

"Take him away, sister," Sister Jerome's voice rang out.

Oliver saw the younger sister's face. He could tell she didn't like being part of this. *So at least there is one nice nun,* he thought. He could hear the sobs as the boy was taken away.

"Now, after that unpleasantness, we shall say grace," Sister Jerome said. "And we welcome a new batch of orphans from England. Make sure you explain all the rules to them. We don't want them to be punished unnecessarily, do we?" Then she said a long grace. The children crossed themselves.

"You may eat."

Benches were pulled out with a loud scraping sound. The children clambered on to them and grabbed at the piles of bread, stuffing it into their mouths. Oliver managed to get the last piece. The boy he had travelled with, who sat beside him, was looking around, realizing that all the bread had gone.

"I didn't get any," he said.

"You have to be quicker, mate," one of the big boys replied through a full mouth. "You'll soon learn."

Oliver ate his bread. He felt he should share with the other newcomer and wrestled with his conscience while he ate. It was spread with margarine, not butter, but he was so hungry it didn't matter. Beside his plate was a beaker of what looked like milk. He drank it and found it had been watered down.

"What time is supper?" he asked the boy sitting on his other side.

"Supper?" the boy laughed. "This is it, mate. No more food until tomorrow morning. You're not exactly overfed here, I can tell you."

"And what's the sin bin?"

The boy lowered his voice, looking around to see if anyone was listening. "It's this little building, see. No windows, and it's outside, so it gets really hot in the summer and really cold in winter, and there are all kinds of insects—spiders, ants—and it's too small to lie down or stretch your legs out, so you have to sit on the dirt floor as best you can.

They leave kids in there for days sometimes." He leaned closer. "Kids have died in there before now."

Oliver stared at him, digesting this, wondering if the boy was making it up just to scare the newcomer. But he seemed earnest enough. "How long have you been here?" Oliver asked.

"I got here a couple of months ago," he said. "I came from an orphanage in London. I'm Charlie, by the way."

"I'm Oliver. Nice to meet you, Charlie."

Charlie studied him. "You don't sound like the usual type. You talk posh. What happened?"

"My family was killed in the bombing," Oliver said. "Only I think they might have made a mistake because they got my name wrong."

"Oh, that's too bad," Charlie said. "Don't worry. We look out for each other here. If you're a good sort, the other kids will take care of you. Keep you from getting into trouble."

"What about that poor boy today? The one who stole the cake."

"Well, that was ruddy stupid, wasn't it?" Charlie said. "I mean, you don't touch food meant for the nuns. They like their food. You should see how much they eat." He gave Oliver a knowing grin.

"So what about that girl who didn't do the weeding? Do we all have chores?"

"We all work, mate," Charlie said. "Up at dawn. Out in the fields mainly for the boys, or in the laundry or kitchen for the girls."

"What about school? Don't we have lessons?"

"We have to, by law," Charlie said. "So a teacher comes out to us a couple of times a week and makes sure we know how to read and write enough that the nuns don't get into trouble. But what they really teach us here is how to be good farmhands and kitchen maids. And when we get old enough, they apprentice us to a farmer somewhere." He leaned closer. "What we think they do is sell us to a farmer. The girls go into domestic service."

Oliver was feeling bleak despair. He saw a life of no love, no books, no education and no hope stretching ahead of him. And he made a vow. Somehow he had to get out of it.

CHAPTER 27

It was a time of waiting, holding breath. Madeleine had finished her training and was wondering what would happen next. Some of the men had already left, apparently heading for France, but the women stayed. It seemed there was a hold-up in their plans—members of Parliament objecting to using women in the field as operatives. Winston Churchill was all for it, so it was likely to pass, but in the meantime hers was not an unpleasant life. They stayed at Beaulieu, speaking French, practicing skills, keeping fit, but also enjoying good meals by wartime standards and taking long walks around the grounds. The weather, in late July, was glorious, and they sunbathed on the lawns until they were hauled in and scolded.

"Would Minette Giron sunbathe with few clothes on? I don't think so. It's fine to have a tanned face and arms, but don't risk the rest of you." The trainer looked at the group with sympathy. "Remember, it's often one small slip that gives someone away. A local person saying, 'Wait. That doesn't make sense. She can't be from here.' And then you're done for."

"Do you think we should look on local people as the enemy?" Portia said. "Will they not be on our side?"

"By and large, yes," the trainer agreed. "But there are those who would sell their grandmother for a shilling, also those who would like to stay on the good side of the Germans in return for being allowed to do business, those who are really hungry and would do more for extra food . . ." He put his hands together. "In times of war, people do not behave according to a normal code of conduct. Some will display extraordinary bravery, beyond what you'd expect of them. Others extraordinary greed, or cowardice or depravity. The war brings out the best or the worst in all of us."

They were permitted to write a final letter. Madeleine wrote hers to her father and Eleanor, telling them absolutely nothing about what she had done but hoping they were well and assuring them she was still healthy and physically fit. She tried to feel remorse that she might never see her father again, but she realized he was one of those upper-class English boys who go to boarding school at an early age and learn to shut off all emotions. He had cared for her, she knew that, but he had never really loved her in the way she wanted to be loved—the way her mother had loved her, and Giles and Olivier. Dear little Olivier, who would hug her fiercely and say, "I love you, Maman."

She paused, thinking of Giles now, her heart quickening with excitement. Was it possible he was still alive, in hiding, and she might see him one day?

~

It wasn't until July had turned into August that they were summoned again. By then the prospect of being parachuted into France seemed like a fairy story, something that wasn't really about to happen.

"Right." It was Major Walcott himself who addressed them this time. "The balloon is about to go up. We've been given permission to deploy a test group of women to France. So do your best to stay alive, won't you? The future of our operation will depend on it."

"I think we'd do our best to stay alive anyway," Portia said, evoking a nervous chuckle from the other women.

"Our first assignment," Walcott said slowly, "will be in Paris itself. We've just lost an operative there. He made a small mistake—he looked the wrong way when crossing a road. He jumped back in time and wasn't hit, but somebody saw. And somebody told the Germans. And he's been shipped off to a concentration camp. So we need someone to take his place, and a woman seems like the ideal candidate."

Madeleine took a deep breath before saying, "I used to live in Paris. I think I'd be useful there. I know my way around. I know the métro, and I wouldn't look the wrong way."

Walcott eyed her critically. "Thank you, Minette. But the objection to that is the very thing that makes you useful. You presumably still have friends in Paris. Do you have relatives? Your husband's relatives?"

"I have an elderly great-aunt," Madeleine said. "I don't even know if she's still alive. I haven't heard anything for a while."

"But you were in contact with her when you lived there?"

"Oh yes. We had Sunday lunch together every week."

Walcott shook his head. "Which would make you too much of a risk, I fear. I know Paris is a big city, but the chance of someone recognizing you is there. Someone who knows who you really are. So I think I must say no."

There was a silence in the room, then Marie-France said, "Send me. I lived there before. I know lots of people, but I could go as myself. People would expect to see me in the neighbourhood of Pigalle. Nobody would question it. I could say I left the city when the Nazis invaded but I missed it so much I've come back. I could probably even get my old job back, at the Moulin Rouge. Not sure I'd be up to dancing, as I'm out of practice, but I could wait tables, and maybe entertain Nazi officers, serve them drinks . . ."

Walcott frowned, tapping his pencil on the table as he thought. "I do see the value of that," he said, "but also the risks. Not just for yourself, but for this whole operation. If the Germans wanted to know where you had been while you were out of the city, if you had happened to tell anyone you were going back to Ireland, if they got the full details of this operation while you were being tortured . . ."

"Ah, well that's the clever part," Marie-France said. "Ireland, you see. I'd say I went back to Ireland. People wouldn't know I meant Northern Ireland, so a part of Great Britain. They'd think Ireland, which is neutral. So I'm no threat to anybody, right?"

"You do have a point there," he said. "Let me discuss this with my colleagues and get back to you. But in the meantime, we've an assignment in the town of Fontainebleau. Do any of you know it?"

"I've been there," Madeleine said. "We went several times during the hot summers. I remember once we had a picnic in the forest. My husband grew up in that region. It's very lovely."

"And very useful," Walcott said. "The Germans have taken over the great palace and are using it as a regional headquarters. On one side of the town is the River Seine, with its barge traffic coming up towards Paris, and on the other side is one of the major routes south. We have local people observing those, and we need a courier to run messages and a radio operator to share news with us." He paused. "I was thinking of you, Minette, and you, Colette." He looked at Madeleine and then at Annie, who had chosen Colette because it was her favourite cousin's name.

"Very good, sir," Annie said. "I'm anxious to get going and start being useful."

"I'm willing to go, too," Madeleine said. "I'd be especially happy to be working with a friend."

"That was our thought precisely. You girls seem to have got along splendidly and formed quite a friendship. That is valuable in time of war. So I'd like to send you together."

"Hey, what about me?" Portia demanded. "I don't want to be left behind. Can't you use me in the same situation?"

The major frowned again. "We have plans to send you to Rouen, in the north. It's an industrial city, and we need better eyes and ears there, looking out for a possible invasion threat."

Madeleine could see the disappointment in Portia's face.

There were three other women in the room, and one of them spoke up. "I know Rouen," she said. "I lived there as a child. Send me. Let Portia—I mean Jeanette—stay with her friends."

The major stroked his chin. "That sounds like a good idea, Françoise. And your cover story will fit well there. But as for using Jeanette in Fontainebleau . . ." He paused. "There is an active Resistance presence in the area, keeping the Germans on edge. We could use a go-between, but the question would be how we could explain three new women in a small town. Minette, we have your cover story, and it fits perfectly. Just the sort of place you would come to if you wanted to get out of Paris. Colette, since you will be confined to a room with a radio for part of the time, we need a good reason for your presence."

"She could have been ill. Tuberculosis? Something like that, and her doctor advised she needed to get out of the city to country air," one of the women offered.

"Something like that," the major agreed.

"Wait a minute," Annie said. "I need to work, don't I? How else am I going to pay room and board?"

"Me too?" Madeleine asked.

"We have Minette covered," the major said. "She will be renting a room from the shoe repairman. He's taking on all sorts of handyman jobs. She will make deliveries for him, and also for the bakery next door. Of course they won't pay enough to live on, but we'll set you up with enough cash to get you started."

"I've been a waitress," Annie said. "That might be a good job for me—you hear a lot when you are waiting tables."

"That sounds like a good idea. We'll ask our contact in town if there is a café where they could be persuaded to take you on. And we've a suitable room for you, up in an attic. The house belongs to a schoolmaster. On our side. Easy to put up an aerial for the radio."

"This shoe repairman, is he also on our side?" Madeleine asked.

"He is."

"So you can't use me?" Portia looked at her friends.

"Not at this moment. Let us think how we can bring you into the region without alerting anyone."

So that was that. Portia was devastated to be left behind. She watched Madeleine and Annie studying the maps of Fontainebleau, circling safe houses and drop-off points for messages. Then these same maps were reproduced into squares of silk, so flimsy that they fitted into the lid of a powder compact. The women were equipped with other vital equipment: the cigarette packet with the false cigarette containing miniature tools, a piece of Plasticine for making impressions of keys or hiding small objects, a pair of shoes with a hollowed heel, a pencil with a compass where the eraser should be. They packed these in the small suitcase they were given. Annie would also be transporting a radio and cypher book. Their contacts would have bicycles ready. The object was to land in a field near the forest, bury the parachutes, make for the station at Bois-le-Roi, a small village near the landing site, and take the train into town during daylight hours and at different times.

They received a final briefing. They were told that all communication would be from Uncle Francis or Oncle Francois when necessary. If the message did not say that, it was not genuine. Ration books were given to them with the right coupons removed from them and updates on current rations. Newspaper headlines from the last week. Updated German movements.

"This is the best we can do," Walcott said. "We won't be completely au fait with the situation until you girls are on the ground and reporting in daily."

A night with a full moon and good weather was fixed for the drop.

"But won't that make it easier for the enemy to spot us?" Annie asked. "I don't like the thought of dangling there while they have all the time in the world to aim their guns at me."

The major smiled. "It is an added risk," he said, "but the pilot has to be able to see the landing site and know exactly where he is so that you don't land on the grounds of Fontainebleau Palace in the middle of the Germans." He gave her a little nod. "Don't worry. These chaps are experienced at making safe drops by now. You'll be fine. And if anything goes wrong with the equipment . . . if the parachute with your luggage gets blown off course, leave it and go into hiding as agreed. Our people who set up the drop site will retrieve it for you. The important thing is not to be seen on that first occasion."

Madeleine was staring down at her hands, trying not to let her face show any emotion. It was now all too real. She pictured landing to find herself surrounded by Germans, being marched to the secret police, tortured . . . Could she really not give away her friends if that happened? Just how brave could she be? And then she told herself she was brave. She had endured the greatest torture of all—knowing she had lost her son and yet still carrying on and wanting to do something.

~

On their last day in England, the four women walked together on the grounds. A cuckoo was calling from the woods, the fresh scent of new-mown grass wafted towards them, as well as the tang of a distant bonfire. The view across the lake was breathtaking. A flight of ducks came in to land. Madeleine looked at everything as if seeing it for the last time. She thought she had never seen anything so lovely and tried to imprint it all on her memory. And she thought, *Olivier would have loved this.* She had tried to stop herself from thinking about him because the memories were so painful. *How will I handle Fontainebleau,* she worried, *when I'll remember that picnic and Olivier trying to climb the boulder and Giles helping him up to the top?*

"This time tomorrow you'll be at your new digs in Fontainebleau," Portia said, interrupting her thoughts. They were speaking English as a last special treat. "And I'll be here. I wonder if they don't really want to use me because I didn't grow up speaking French and they think I'll be a liability."

"Nonsense, your French is as good as mine," Madeleine said. "They just aren't sure where to place you yet. I do wish they'd send you with us. It won't be the same without you there. You're always the brave and clever one."

"Oh no I'm not," Portia said. "I've been terrified most of the time. I just didn't want to show it. I think you're all the brave ones."

"Well, good luck. We'll be praying for you," Marie-France said.

"So any news on when you are going?" Madeleine asked.

"They are still working on a safe place for me to lodge," Marie-France said. "Apparently the man who was captured spilled too many beans, and a lot of people were rounded up and sent off to camps. So naturally there isn't a great deal of interest in housing a new operative." She shrugged. "I hope it's soon. It's the waiting that's the worst, isn't it?"

"Waiting and thinking and not knowing," Annie said. "Drives you round the ruddy bend."

"It's been smashing knowing you," Portia said. "I've never felt this close to anyone in my life. You're like the sisters I didn't have."

"I feel the same," Madeleine said. "I never really had close friends at school. They were mostly richer than me, and all they wanted to do was to marry well. They didn't like me because I wanted to read and study and I was a teacher's pet. I had good friends in college, but they are long since married with families. And I had nice neighbours in Paris but nobody I was really close to."

"When this is all over and we're back in England, we'll all meet up again and have a bloody good blowout at a restaurant," Annie said.

"That's an interesting point," Marie-France said, frowning. "They haven't mentioned how they plan to extract us if they want to get us out."

There was silence as they digested this.

"They can't know ahead of time because they don't know what conditions will be like," Madeleine said, trying to sound cheerful. "We can always make our way down to the *zone libre* where things are still controlled by the French government. I'm sure it's easier down there—fewer Germans. And at the very worst, we try to get over the Pyrenees into Spain and then Portugal."

"Can you see yourself doing that with no money and no contacts?" Portia asked.

"There will be local resistance groups. I'm sure we'd get help if we needed it."

"Famous last words," Annie said.

CHAPTER 28

It was the night of the full moon. Madeleine and Annie said their goodbyes under the watchful eye of their trainers. Everyone appeared stoic and cheerful. "Well, good luck, ladies." Hands were shaken. Madeleine was glad that outsiders were present because she feared too much emotion might be shown if she and Annie hugged Marie-France and Portia. But she did notice tears bright in Portia's eyes. She left the building without looking back.

The women were driven away through the darkness, not knowing where they were heading. Near the Channel, Madeleine supposed, so that the flight would not be too long. They came to what looked like an ordinary working farm, only to discover it contained an airstrip amongst the trees.

"You girls are in luck tonight," the RAF officer who greeted them said. "We've just got in a new Westland Lysander. You know what that means, don't you?"

"No, what?" Annie asked.

The RAF chap looked smug. "It's a tiny plane with great mobility. It can touch down and turn around in 150 yards."

"Touch down?" Madeleine tried to process this. "Then we don't have to . . ."

"No parachutes needed. Wizard, eh? And you can travel in your street clothes. No coveralls needed. But it's lucky you're both light. It can really only take one or two passengers with their gear. That's the annoying part. No heavy payloads."

They walked out to the airstrip. In the moonlight the silhouette of the plane did look awfully small—almost like a toy. They climbed in and were shown how to buckle themselves into rudimentary seats in the tiny, cramped cabin. The door was slammed shut. The engine revved up, shaking the entire plane, then it rumbled forwards and was airborne. Complete darkness lay below them, not a single light showing, but soon they saw moonlight glinting on water, the dark shapes of ships. They were crossing the Channel. Nobody spoke. In fact it was too loud in the tiny cabin to speak without shouting, and both women were wrapped in their own thoughts. Madeleine counted the minutes. They must be approaching the French coast by now. She held her breath, waiting for German artillery to target them, but heard nothing.

"They must have gone to bed early tonight," the pilot called back to them, as if reading her thoughts. "Or they think one plane by itself is not worth worrying about. On the other hand, they may be tracking us to find out where we plan to land. You never know how they think. But the good thing with most Germans is they obey orders—they are not trained for independent thinking."

They flew on. It was impossible to tell where they were from the darkness below. Sometimes they could make out the square shapes of houses within a town or village, but mostly it was fields and woods. And suddenly a bright strip of moonlight on a river. It was cold in the cabin, which was good as it kept them alert.

"We should be getting close now," the pilot called back. "So grab your stuff and be ready to bail out the moment I give the order. You throw your bags ahead of you, you jump out and you run like hell into the trees. Make sure you get out of my way because I'll be turning and taking off again."

"How will you know where to land?" Annie peered down into blackness.

"If all goes according to plan, they know we're coming, and they'll light the landing strip for us," the pilot shouted back.

"Who is 'they'? Do we already have men on the ground there?"

"No, it will be Resistance blokes. At least we hope it will be. These planes are so new we haven't tried this here. I've done a couple of landings nearer the Channel but not this far inland. And not south of Paris. Hello—here we are!" He sounded jubilant.

Madeleine peered out and saw tiny pinpoints of light ahead of them. The plane dived steeply, and they saw two lines of lights. Then they were flying in between tall trees. The landing strip was so narrow that the wings were almost touching the trees on either side. The lights turned out to be flares, glowing red beside them. Wheels bounced over grass. While the plane was still moving, the door was opened and hands reached in.

"Give me your bags," said a deep French voice. The women handed them to him. "Now your hands. Quickly." Madeleine grabbed his hand and was jerked out of the plane, stumbling forwards as she made contact with the ground. She hauled herself to her feet.

"Now run. Into the trees."

"But the bags?"

"Already there."

The plane was already turning as they ran. They heard the engine rev up again. It raced past the flares, and a dark shape rose into the moonlight. The flares were extinguished, and they found themselves in complete darkness.

"This way." A torch, partially shaded, was shone, and they followed a dark shape into the forest.

"Alors," said the French voice. "We've done our part. You're on your own. You have your instructions, *non*?"

"We do," Annie replied. "How far is it to Bois-le-Roi?"

"About two kilometres. Not far. That direction."

"Thank you," Annie said. "We'll wait in the forest until morning."

"I wish you good luck and good hunting," the man said. He held out a gloved hand, shook theirs, then melted into the forest. They never saw his face.

"Well, here we are," Annie whispered to Madeleine. "Now we just have to find a safe spot to wait until it gets light and then locate the railway line."

Madeleine drew the small torch from her pocket and shone it around rapidly. "There is a patch of ferns over there," she said. "They should give us cover if we need it."

"It went rather smoothly, don't you think?" Annie asked. "Amazing."

"Don't speak too soon," Madeleine said in a whisper. "We have no idea how close to a settlement we are. I remember Fontainebleau Forest. It goes on for miles. I hope he's right about the two kilometres and we don't have too far to walk tomorrow, especially you carrying that radio."

"It's not too bad in the rucksack," Annie said, hoisting it on to her shoulder.

They made for the ferns and lay down amongst them. Madeleine tried to sleep, but every nerve was taut, and every stirring of the night breeze jerked her awake. An owl hooted as it sat in a nearby tree. At last there was a hint of dawn in the night sky. They could make out the vague shapes of trees.

"We should get moving." She nudged Annie.

Annie stirred, opening her eyes. "Is it morning?"

"You were asleep?"

"What else was there to do?" Annie sat up and smoothed down her hair. "I'd welcome a cup of coffee, wouldn't you?"

"Not me. I don't like it black, and remember, there's no milk in cafés these days."

They were about to get to their feet when they heard sounds. A dog barking.

"Get down." Madeleine pulled Annie back into the ferns. To her horror she heard the sounds coming closer. The barking louder. And suddenly the dog was standing over them. They could feel its warm breath on them, its panting loud in their ears.

"What's this, then?" said a man's voice. A French voice.

They sat up, staring up at a man with a gun and a large hound.

"Oh monsieur, you terrified us," Annie said, sitting up. "My sister and I had to leave Paris because where we were living was so dangerous, and we're making for our aunt's house in Moret-sur-Loing—do you know it? Have we still far to go?"

"You came on foot?" he asked. Now they could see he was an older man, still strong and upright but with a grey moustache and bags under his eyes.

"We started in the train, but there were German soldiers in our compartment, and they were fresh with us, so we got out at Bois-le-Roi and decided to walk the rest of the way," Annie said. "But we got lost and it got dark, so we felt safer here. Now we'll go back to the Bois-le-Roi station and continue our journey, hopefully in safety."

"Those damned Germans. Always making trouble of one sort or another," he growled. "Well, at least you have not strayed too far from the station. There is the good path up ahead. I'd invite you back to my house for something to eat, but I don't think you want to go in the wrong direction. And my dog is anxious to get to work."

"What work does he do?" Annie asked.

"We're out hunting rabbits," the old man said. "How else does one get meat these days? And old Louis here, he has a good nose for finding game. Rabbits, squirrels. Anything for the pot so my wife can make a stew."

"We wish you good hunting, monsieur," Annie said.

"And you too, ladies." He tipped his old felt hat to them and whistled for the dog to follow him.

The two women got to their feet. "You were amazing," Madeleine said. "I can see you're going to be good at this. You think on your feet. So convincing."

Annie grinned. "I was good at lying when I was a kid. I could make my mother believe anything. Who thought it would come in handy in later life? But I don't think he was fooled for a minute. He knew who we are."

"He did?"

"When I wished him good hunting, he replied, 'You too,' didn't he? He suspected we were Resistance of some sort, but he was on our side." She brushed down her coat. "Well, we've had good luck so far. Let's hope it holds up. Ready to make for the station?"

Madeleine picked up her suitcase as Annie hoisted the rucksack on to her shoulders. She found she could hardly put one foot in front of the other. The terror of that dog coming closer and then standing over them was still too real, as well as the horrible realization that Annie had done all the talking. She had not dared to say a word in French, in case something sounded wrong. As they walked, she remembered Giles when she first met him at the university. "You speak French like a professor or an elderly nun," he had said. She had taken for granted that eight years of living with him in Paris had brought her language up to date, but what if there was something still not right? If so, she'd have to refine her cover story to say that she grew up with relatives in the south—in the Pays Basque, maybe where the locals spoke a mixture of French and the Basque language. Yes. That was a good idea. Nobody around Fontainebleau would know what a Basque accent sounded like. She hurried to catch up with Annie, who was already striding out ahead.

CHAPTER 29

The first houses of the small town became visible through the trees. They spotted a road but decided to remain hidden within the forest for as long as possible. The plan was that Annie should take an early train and get settled first and that Madeleine should follow later. It might look suspicious if they arrived in Fontainebleau at the same time.

The sun came up, flooding the forest with light. Madeleine looked down at her watch, already set to French time. "It's almost seven."

"I can't catch a train before eight. That wouldn't look right," Annie said. "Here. Have a square of chocolate. I saved some for emergencies."

She handed Madeleine a small piece of a Cadbury's bar. Madeleine took it, savouring the flavour.

From their hiding place, they noticed men going to work on bicycles, a woman driving two goats, and then they heard the bright voices of children going to school.

"I think it's all right to go now, don't you?" Annie asked.

Madeleine nodded. "Well, good luck, *mon amie*," she said in French, examining her accent as the words came out. "Next time we meet, I won't know you."

"Good luck to you, too," Annie said. "We're going to be bloody good at this," she added in English, then stepped out on to the road and towards the train station.

~

The next hours of waiting felt like an eternity. Madeleine's stomach growled with hunger. She stayed well back from any view of the road, hidden amongst thick foliage. Sunlight filtered through the leafy canopy, between the ancient oaks and beeches. It was all so tranquil. She leaned against the trunk of a great tree and dozed off—awaking with her heart pounding that she might have been asleep for hours and anybody could have seen her. But her watch told her that it was only just ten o'clock—a perfect time to enter Fontainebleau and find her digs. She brushed herself down, adjusted her hat, put on her gloves and changed the gym shoes she had travelled in for a pair of smart but well-worn court shoes. Now she should look like a respectable but impoverished widow and former employee of a bookshop.

She waited until there was no traffic of any kind before she stepped out on to the road. Nobody gave her a second look as she went up to the ticket office and bought a one-way to Fontainebleau.

"The ten thirty may be running a bit late today," the ticket clerk said. "They had trouble on the line last night, I hear. Someone tried to lay explosives. I wish those damned Resistance people would leave well enough alone. No use really, like a mosquito stinging the backside of a bear. Only makes him grumpy. All it does is make the Boche clamp down on us even harder, deprive us of more things. Is it like that where you have come from?"

"Oh, I've come from Paris," she said. "I got a ride in a lorry this far. But things are bad there. They keep cutting our rations, and the Germans are patrolling everywhere."

"Curse the Germans." He spat. "You're wise to get out, madame."

She thanked him for the ticket and went on to the platform, letting out a sigh of relief. She had survived her first encounter. It was going to be all right.

CHAPTER 30

The train stopped at two more stations before arriving at Fontainebleau-Avon. Madeleine came out of the station and asked another passenger the way into town. That would be a natural thing for a stranger, she decided.

"The town centre?" the woman asked.

"I think so. I'm looking for the shop of Monsieur Henri Dumas. I believe it's on the rue Saint-Honoré? Do you know it?"

The woman grinned. "Ah, so you need items mended. Don't we all. M. Dumas has never been so popular. You'll probably have to wait patiently until he can get to you. Well, you're heading in the right direction, but you've a long walk ahead of you. It's on the other side of the town, past the central *place* and the château." She leaned closer. "You've probably heard that the Germans have taken over the château. The good God knows what damage they might have done to that beautiful place. Their military vehicles are stationed all over the lovely lawns. It's a crying shame."

Madeleine nodded. She hadn't realized she'd be living so close to the German headquarters, but she managed a pleasant smile.

"There used to be a bus all the time, but now it's only once or twice a day because nobody can get any petrol. So keep going along this road until you find the rue Grande. Follow that until you come into the very centre with all the shops, then turn right on to the rue de France. That way you don't have to walk past the château. It's always best to stay well away from the Germans, especially when one is young and pretty like you."

"Thank you, madame." Madeleine held out her hand to the other woman. "Let's see what miracle Monsieur Dumas can do for me, shall we?" And she set off along the straight highway, still very much at the edge of town with smallholdings, a garage, what looked like a factory. The day had become very warm, with the sun now beating down and no shade along the street. The suitcase felt heavier and heavier, and Madeleine sensed the sweat trickling down inside her blouse. She wanted to stop and take off her jacket, but then she'd have to carry it as well as the bag.

At last she came to a row of houses, a couple of shops, and turned on to the rue Grande. It was lined with pleasant cream-coloured stone buildings, decorated with wrought iron balconies. This was clearly the main shopping street, although some of the shops now had shutters covering their front windows. She looked longingly at a little café and was tempted to sit with a coffee and baguette, but that might mean she'd have to explain the suitcase, and that probably wasn't wise. So she went on until, before her, she could see a fountain, a small square and beyond it the lovely cream-coloured lines of the château. German sentries were standing outside the wrought iron gates, and there were two military vehicles parked nearby. She felt a sigh of relief as she turned up on to the rue de France and did not have to walk past them. They might have enquired why she was carrying a suitcase.

Madeleine didn't feel she could walk much further by the time she came to the rue Saint-Honoré. It was lined with attractive yellow stone houses, some with white shutters, none very tall. Amongst them were a few shops, and she walked on until she came to a sign: *H. Dumas. Shoe repairs.* A bell jangled as she opened the front door. A dapper older man wearing a bow tie over a clean white shirt was standing at the counter, serving a customer. He looked up as Madeleine came in. "I'll be with you in a moment, madame."

He finished writing a ticket, then handed it to the woman at the counter. "That will be twenty francs. These should be ready by next week, Madame Dupont."

"Next week? How is my husband supposed to go to work when he has no shoes?"

M. Dumas shrugged. "I regret, madame, that I am overwhelmed with work. I only have two hands, you see, and everyone wants everything mended. I will be as quick as I can, I promise you. And I'll deliver it out to you."

The woman shrugged. "Ah well. If that's the best you can do . . ." And she left, giving a curt nod to Madeleine.

"And for you, madame? How may I assist?" he asked.

"I am Madame—Giron," Madeleine said. A flicker of alarm went through her. She had almost said Martin. "You were expecting me, monsieur? I was told you have a room for rent, and I've come from Paris."

"Ah yes. Of course. Madame Giron. We've been expecting you. You are welcome, and I, as you see, will welcome the help around here. I'm run off my feet." He picked up the big pair of well-worn boots from the counter and placed them on a shelf behind him. "I used to repair shoes—a pleasant occupation for an older man. Now I mend saddles and horses' equipment. The farmers have gone back to horses now that there is no diesel for tractors. But I also mend bags and suitcases, I solder kettles and pans, I even stitch leather patches on jacket sleeves. Jack of all trades, that's what I've become. And my wife repairs the clothing. She even darns the socks." He shook his head with a sad smile. "Make do and mend. That's what we're told, isn't it?"

Madeleine could see that he was going to be a talker and wondered if that was dangerous. Might he let slip that he had a strange woman staying with him? And who that woman really was? Did he know that? Was it better that he didn't know? But someone in London had selected him, so he must be reliable, surely . . .

He went over to the door and turned around the sign that read *OPEN*. "Come this way, and I'll show you your room." He picked up her suitcase, led her down a narrow hallway and then up a flight of wooden stairs. The room was at the back of the house and looked on to a small garden, planted with rows of vegetables. From the open window came the sounds of chickens clucking. The room looked simple but clean and inviting, with a white coverlet on the bed, some embroidered pillows, a small armchair and a table with a crucifix on a lace mat. On the wall was a print of a Monet painting of sailboats.

"It's very nice, thank you," Madeleine said, hearing her voice sounding strange to her. "I'm sure I'll be most comfortable here."

He nodded.

"And the matter of rent?" Madeleine went on. "I should like to pay what is fair, but I don't have much since my husband was killed and it's impossible to get work in Paris."

"I understand," he said. "As I just mentioned, we could do with help. You do the shopping for my wife so she can get on with the mending. You deliver the items when I've fixed them, and maybe I teach you how to do various tasks as well. You give us your ration card, and we'll call it even—is that fair?"

"That sounds perfect, monsieur. I am so grateful to have found you."

"Not at all. My wife will welcome the company of another woman. Our son and grandchildren are down in Lyons, and that's in the zone libre so we don't see them any more." He gave a little nod. "I expect you could do with a cup of coffee? Although when I say coffee, that is a euphemism these days, is it not? It's more chicory than anything else. But it's hot and refreshing after your long walk from the station." He moved out of the room. "Bathroom on your right, only there is not always hot water. Toilet beside it." He smiled again. "You're lucky. Until a few years ago, the toilet and bath were out behind the house. My wife's father died, and with the money he left us, we put in an indoor bathroom. Such a luxury. Most neighbours do not have one yet."

He started down the stairs. "Claudine?" he called. "We have a visitor. Is there coffee?"

Madeleine hurriedly took off her jacket, then followed him to the back of the house and into a big, sunny kitchen, looking out on to the garden. There was the smell of something herby cooking. Madame Dumas was standing at the stove and looked up expectantly as they came in. Madeleine immediately thought of the nursery rhyme of Jack Sprat, who could eat no fat, and his wife could eat no lean, because she was a big woman and he such a small, spare man. But she beamed at Madeleine. "Well, here you are, madame," she said. "I hope you will be comfortable."

"Oh yes, I'm sure I shall. It's a lovely little room."

"It was our son's." She paused, looking as if she wanted to say more about him, then went on, "Sit down, my dear."

A cup of hot dark liquid was put in front of her as well as a piece of baguette.

"We still have jam, thanks to what I put away before the invasion," Madame Dumas said, "but alas no butter. Only that filthy margarine when we can get it. And meat? It's as if every animal has vanished from the earth. Of course we hear that those German swine live well enough. But Henri keeps the garden growing, and we have the chickens until the Germans find those, so we shall not starve."

"I'll bring you my ration card, madame," Madeleine said.

"No hurry. Eat first. You must be hungry, leaving the city so early this morning. How are things there?"

"Not good," Madeleine said. "Food is already scarce. Everyone is afraid."

She spread a thin layer of jam on the piece of bread. At least it was good and fresh, as she remembered bread in France.

"As soon as you've finished, I've got work for you today," M. Dumas said. "A delivery they are waiting for. Do you know your way around Fontainebleau?"

"No, monsieur. I have only been here once before. My husband and I took a picnic here before the war."

"Don't worry. I have a street plan for you. And one of the surroundings, too. Sometimes we have to make deliveries quite far afield—to a farm if it's equipment they need."

"You have a bicycle I can use, monsieur?" she asked.

"I do. An old bone-rattler, I'm afraid, and the tires are not so good, but we make do with what we have. And of course I'm used to patching up bicycle tires now." He gave a sad little shrug. "I must get back to work. There will be a line out in front by now, I don't doubt."

He left, and Madeleine heard the bell jangle as a customer came in. She finished her bread and coffee, then went upstairs, changed into sensible shoes again, washed her face and brushed her hair. She stood for a moment, studying herself in the mirror. She certainly seemed to have fallen on her feet with this nice couple. Now she would worry that she might put them into danger.

Her first delivery was to a farm close to the Seine. Madeleine studied the map before setting off, carrying a mended bridle in the bicycle basket. The day had become extremely hot, and the bicycle was indeed old and hard to pedal. Also some of the streets were cobbled, making it hard to control. Madeleine knew she must not fall off—that would attract attention. Surely every person in this town knew how to ride a bicycle. There were certainly enough of them in the streets. She managed to make it safely back to the road leading out of town, past the station and then out into the countryside. She saw the wide sweep of river ahead of her and stopped for a moment, studying it with interest. It was somewhere along this bank that a fisherman would be passing messages, describing what river traffic was going north and south. She couldn't see him now but guessed he was a little further upriver. She mounted the bicycle again and headed for the bridge over the river.

As she approached it, she saw it was manned by Germans. She got off the bike and wheeled it forwards, her heart beating very fast.

"Identity card, *Fräulein*," one of them said.

Madeleine opened her purse and handed it to him. He seemed to study it for a long time.

"It says you live in Paris," he said. His French was rudimentary.

"I do, normally," she replied, speaking slowly so that he understood. "I have come to stay with friends for a few months. It is not agreeable in the city in hot weather. And I help a friend with his deliveries."

"Deliveries, eh?" The German moved closer. "And what might you be delivering?"

He pulled back the piece of cloth that covered the basket.

"A bridle for a horse on the other side of the river," she said. "My friend mends broken equipment."

The German took out the bridle, examined it, then nodded and put the cover back over it. "Very well. On your way, Fräulein."

Madeleine cycled on, over the span of the bridge. Water flowed swiftly beneath her. It took a while before she could breathe properly again. But then she felt euphoric. She had survived her first encounter with Germans.

~

Madeleine did not see Annie for the next two days. She wondered how to get in touch with her without arousing suspicion. They had not discussed this. She knew Annie's address, but it would not be a good idea to go there. But she could not collect any information until a radio was up and working. Instead she made several deliveries around the town and did some shopping for Madame Dumas. At each place she was greeted with curiosity and had to explain that she was visiting for a few months because her building in Paris was in such bad shape and life there so difficult. She was met with sympathy.

"We have heard how horrible it is now in the city," the woman behind the counter in the grocer's shop said. "Is it true you are on such short rations there? There are even queues for bread?"

"It's quite true, all of it," Madeleine replied.

"Then you should stay out here, madame. It is more agreeable than the city, and we still have the food we grow."

Madeleine came out of the shop feeling the warmth of acceptance. But reality hit her when a German lorry rumbled past, and she realized that she could well be putting fellow citizens in danger.

~

On the third day she was loading up the bicycle, preparing to make deliveries, when Annie came into the shop.

"Monsieur, I am looking for a miracle," she said, going up to the counter. "These old shoes, I wanted to throw them away, but today one must hold on to everything, *n'est-ce pas*? Are they beyond hope?" And she handed him a pair of well-worn court shoes.

M. Dumas examined them, making tut-tutting noises. "Why have you let them go so long, mademoiselle?" he asked.

"It was not I, monsieur," Annie said. "I have inherited them from my dead great-aunt, but my own shoes are in not much better condition."

"I will do what I can," M. Dumas said, "but I cannot guarantee that they can be made wearable again. Please write your name and address on the card, and my assistant will deliver them when they are ready. I will only charge you twenty francs, which is my usual fee, and we will hope for the best, *oui*?"

Annie reached into her purse and handed him a twenty-franc note.

"I will be on my way, monsieur," Madeleine said, wheeling the bicycle towards the door. Annie seemed to notice her for the first time.

"Bonjour, madame," she said, then she frowned. "Don't I know you? You look familiar to me. Are you from Paris, by any chance?"

"I am," Madeleine said.

Annie waved her hands excitedly. "Did you ever eat at a bistro near the Porte d'Auteuil? Chez Marcel? On the corner of rue Michel Ange?"

"Why yes. We lived just down the street from it. My husband and I had a glass of wine there sometimes."

"See. I knew it. I never forget a face." Annie waved an excited finger at her. "I was the waitress at Chez Marcel. People don't remember the waitress, but I do remember your hair. It's striking. I commented on the colour. So unusual."

"How amazing!" Madeleine said. "What a small world it is. Are you living here now?"

"For the summer," Annie said. "I have been quite sick. My doctor said I should get out of the city for the sake of my lungs. So I have found a room with an elderly gentleman—a schoolmaster. Monsieur Gustave."

"Ah, Monsieur Gustave," Monsieur Dumas interrupted. "A fine gentleman. He retired from his position at the lycée several years ago, but now, with no young men to teach the students there, he has gone back to work, and he has turned seventy. We old men are all in demand again, it seems." And he laughed.

"If you can rescue those shoes, I will be in eternal gratitude, monsieur," Annie said.

"I can't work miracles, mademoiselle, but I will do my best." He gave a gracious little bow.

"I should be on my way," Madeleine said, unsure what to say next. "It was nice meeting you, madame."

"It's mademoiselle," Annie said. "Not lucky enough to have found a good man yet." She looked back at Monsieur Dumas and gave a shrug. "One can always live in hope, no?"

Madeleine opened the door and steered her bike through it. "I won't be long, Monsieur Dumas," she said.

"No hurry, my dear. Take your time," he called after her.

"I should be on my way, too," Annie said, rushing to help Madeleine hold the door open. "I need to find a job. I can't sit idle all day." She followed Madeleine out of the door. "Have you moved here from Paris now, madame?" she asked.

"Like you, only recently. I'm not sure how long I'll stay, but I find it most agreeable here, don't you?"

They passed two women on the pavement. Madeleine wheeled her bicycle beside Annie until they came to a deserted part of the street.

"I'm glad to see you," Madeleine said when they were alone in the street. It had become second nature to converse in French now, and anyway she would not have dared to use English. "I was wondering how to get in touch with you."

"I was lucky that the woman next door was throwing out these old shoes." Annie grinned. "I snapped them up as an excuse to come. How is it?"

"They are very nice. I'm quite comfortable."

"Me too. The schoolmaster is extremely welcoming. I've volunteered to cook for him. He does not eat well since his wife died."

"Does he know who you are, do you think?"

Annie shrugged. "He didn't say, and I'm not going to enlighten him. It's better that they know nothing, so if they are brought in for questioning, they can't give anyone away."

They passed an open window. Music was coming from a radio programme.

"And the special baggage you brought with you?" Madeleine lowered her voice, just in case someone was listening at that window.

Annie leaned closer, her voice to almost a whisper. "All set up in my attic room. Once I tell them I have established contact with you, I will be ready to send and receive. And you will be delivering my messages. We have to hook up with the local Resistance group, let them know we are here and operational."

More people were approaching—a mother with two young children and a baby in a buggy.

"When I have a chance to chat with Uncle Francis, he'll tell me how we can help out," Annie said in normal tones, using the code name for their contact in England.

Madeleine nodded. "And if I want to get in touch with you, what do you suggest?"

Annie glanced around quickly. There was now a man with a small dog on a leash walking past on the other side.

"Let us go and sit in the plaza," she said. "Enjoy the sunshine on a nice bench—unless you are in a big hurry?"

"No, I have a little time, and I'd enjoy talking to someone who lived in Paris."

Madeleine wheeled the bicycle beside her until they found a bench. It felt strange sitting so near to the German presence, but there was nobody close enough to hear their conversation. Annie took out a pack of Gauloises and offered it to Madeleine. Madeleine shook her head.

"You still don't smoke? How do you calm your nerves, then?"

"I tried it in college but never liked it," Madeleine said. "I must be the only person who doesn't smoke here."

"It will save you money." Annie grinned. "So this is how you get in contact with me. There is a big leafy shrub by Monsieur Gustave's front path. I don't know what it is. I've never been a gardener, but it's thick enough to do the trick. Tuck a message into it. I will check it several times a day. I can easily retrieve a note from it without arousing suspicion, and it will only take a second for you to slip the message in where it can't be seen."

"A little risky," Madeleine said. "What if someone was looking out of a window?"

"The good thing is that the house is at the edge of the forest. On the road towards Barbizon. So there are no houses opposite and not many pedestrians passing, thank God. Also I plan to get a job as quickly as possible. The best thing would be a waitress in a café. Then you could come in, have a coffee, leave your message for me under your saucer and I'll pick it up."

"Yes, that would be sensible." Madeleine stood up. "And if you want to leave messages for me?"

"I'll try to find enough old things to be mended, and if not, I'll be on the lookout for you as you come through town. Until you can set up a safe site to drop off messages, that is."

Madeleine nodded. "I must be on my way, mademoiselle. Might one know your name?"

"It's Colette," Annie said, "Colette Bonet. And yours?"

"Minette. Minette Giron."

Annie shook her hand. "Delighted to make your acquaintance, Madame Giron. We Parisians must stick together, no?"

Madeleine stood up, righting the bicycle. "I must be on my way. I've deliveries to complete. I hope I see you again sometime, Mademoiselle Bonet."

She wheeled the bicycle away as two Germans headed towards them, eyeing the young women with interest.

"My regards to your husband," Annie called after her. Madeleine wondered why until it dawned on her that she was indicating to the Germans that they were off-limits.

As she went on her way, the bicycle bumping over cobbles, she was amazed how civilized it all was, how smoothly it had all gone. Had they been worrying over nothing after all?

CHAPTER 31

OLIVER

Australia

It didn't take Oliver long to fit into life at Ferndale Children's Farm. To learn that if you didn't fit in and obey all the rules, punishment was waiting. Up at dawn. Cold water wash. Prayers in the central square. Then breakfast, which was either porridge or bread and jam. After breakfast there were supposed to be lessons, but the lessons were of the most basic kind: reciting times tables, copying words from the blackboard. Sometimes there was a geography lesson, and they were taught how England ruled most of the world but how badly it had behaved towards Ireland (which was where the sisters came from).

By mid-morning they were out in the fields, assigned to weeding, planting, harvesting according to the crops. By lunchtime Oliver's stomach was growling with hunger, and he couldn't wait for the bell that summoned them all back to the dining hall. Lunch was usually a big stew with some sort of meat but mainly vegetables. Sometimes there was a steamed pudding, too. After lunch there was a rest time on their beds, then out in the fields again, although some days there was football or cricket as a treat.

Oliver was quick to learn that if you did the smallest thing wrong, there would be a punishment. Sometimes it was something simple, like no tea. Other times it was the strap, administered across the bottom, in front of the whole school. Oliver was a quick learner, but he knocked over his milk one day, in his hurry to grab a piece of bread. He was marched up to Sister Jerome at the front of the room.

"Wasting valuable food, were you?" she asked.

"It was an accident, sister," he said, not daring to look at her. "I'm sorry."

"Well, since you've been no trouble before, I'll accept your apology," she said. "But if it happens again, you're going to be very sorry, I can promise you."

Oliver went away, giving a big sigh of relief.

He had been there a few days when he found there were chickens. He went to Sister Elizabeth Ann. "Please sister," he said. "I see we've got chickens, so I wondered if you need anyone to help take care of them."

She eyed him as if he were an insect on her foot. "Trying to get out of good hard work, are you, Jones?"

"Oh no, sister. It's just I've worked with chickens before, so I thought I might be useful."

She was frowning at him. "You're a strange one, Jones. Not like the other boys. How are you settling in? Are they giving you a hard time because you're different?"

"Oh no, sister. I think the other boys are looking out for me," he said. "They're really nice."

He didn't mention that twice someone had tried to steal his slice of bread and once his blanket, but Charlie—big and strong for his age—had intervened and taught the thief a lesson.

Sister Elizabeth Ann stared at him long and hard, then she said, "Well, we can give you a trial with the chickens. But make sure no eggs get broken, or there will be trouble."

News got around quickly that Oliver was now going to be assigned to the chickens. As he got ready for bed that night, he found himself surrounded by bigger boys.

"So you're trying to worm out of proper work, are you, Squirt?"

"Oh no," Oliver said. "It's just that I took care of chickens when I was at the convalescent home after I'd been hurt in the bombing. I thought I might do something useful, you know."

"Sucking up to sister, eh?" One of them pushed him.

"Hey, you, keep your hands off." Charlie stepped between the boy and Oliver. "Or you'll have me to deal with."

"I should be scared of you?" The boy smirked.

"I came from a pretty rough orphanage in the East End of London. I know how to fight dirty if I need to. I broke a boy's nose once. But give the kid a chance, eh? I don't see you volunteering to take care of chickens."

"Me?" The bigger boy laughed. "Worst job in the world. All those flies. Drives you mad. You'll soon find out, Squirt. Those flies get in your mouth, your eyes, your ears, your nose. All over you. Rather you than me."

Oliver now realized he might have made a mistake. He had thought that the boy taunting him was making it up about the flies. There were always flies around when they worked in the fields—a nuisance, but not unbearable. But as he walked into the chicken run on that first morning, he saw a boy wearing what he thought was a black jacket. This was strange as their uniform was entirely khaki. Then he realized that the boy's back was covered in flies—covered so densely that it seemed entirely black. Oliver swallowed hard. Then he didn't swallow again as the flies descended on his face.

The bigger boy in charge noticed him. "Come to help, have you? Well, good luck there if you don't have a hat."

Oliver noticed that the boy was wearing a broad-brimmed hat to which corks on strings had been tied. He gestured to it. "See the corks? They swing around and keep the flies off."

"Where do you get a hat?" Oliver asked. "Do the sisters supply us with one?"

"Supply us? Are you stupid?" The boy laughed. "They don't give us nothing. No, I tell you what I did—on visitors' day this bloke wanted to see the chickens, so I told him about the flies, and he brought me a hat. Nice of him, wasn't it?"

"Visitors' day?"

The big boy nodded. "Once a month they open this place to the public. Oh, my word, you should see it. You wouldn't recognize it. You'd think we were all having a bonzer time here. Paradise." He laughed bitterly. "Well, come on. Eggs to collect. Only for heaven's sake don't break one. There will be hell to pay."

Oliver followed him into the hen house, brushing flies from his face as he reached in to collect eggs. Flies crawled over his face, into his ears. He flailed his arms in panic.

"Won't do any good, kid," the big boy said. "Too many of 'em."

Oliver got through the chores, wondering how he could tell Sister Elizabeth Ann that he'd made a mistake and wanted to go back to field work. He did not think this would go down well. What he'd have to do is what Archie, the bigger boy, had done. Appeal to an outsider for a hat and corks on strings.

The next week was his first visitors' day. The children were up early, fed a good breakfast of beans and tomatoes on toast and then inspected to see that their uniforms and persons were clean. After breakfast they went out into the central yard to find that a seesaw and merry-go-round had miraculously appeared, as had a cricket pitch on the lawn beyond. There were toys in the common room, too. Stuffed animals on their beds. Oliver noticed that one of these stuffed animals was his beloved new dog, given to him by Miss Everingham. He longed to take it and hide it but knew this was impossible.

At eleven o'clock the first guests arrived, a busload of them. Children were lined up and sang for the visitors. Older kids took the visitors on a tour of the farm while the younger ones were encouraged to play on the equipment or with the balls. Oliver watched the visitors with longing. How could he tell them what life was really like here? Then he realized that he was now an orphan. Perhaps life was this bad for orphans everywhere. He had no chance to go anywhere near the chickens, but he enjoyed the unaccustomed ham and salad served for lunch. The moment the visitors had gone, the toys and equipment were all removed. His dog hidden away until the next time.

~

Life went back to normal. He tried to get out to the chickens as early as possible, when the flies were not so bad. He also learned to drape his shirt over his head, although his back burned in the sun. One day Archie sent him in with a full tray of eggs. Oliver walked slowly and steadily, balancing the tray carefully. He crossed the yard as Archie opened the gate for him. Then suddenly, as he took a breath, a fly flew into his mouth. Instinctively he reacted, the tray teetered and the eggs cascaded to the ground.

He tried to apologize to the sisters, telling them about the flies and how one flew into his mouth, but he could see it wasn't going to do any good. At tea that day he was called out.

"This boy, Oliver Jones, was so clumsy that he dropped a whole tray of our precious eggs—eggs we need to sell to be able to buy food to feed you. So if you're all feeling a bit hungry next week, you can thank Oliver for depriving you. And you, Oliver, can have time to reflect on your selfish behaviour in the sin bin. Take him away, Edith."

"No, sister. It was an accident. I told you," Oliver called out, but the big girl's nails dug into his forearm as he was hauled off across the yard and out to a small outhouse standing alone in the middle of a patch of bare earth. Edith opened the door and pushed him in. "Have fun," she said. "Let's hope they don't forget about you." And the door was shut to almost complete darkness. The only light came through the cracks in the wood. It was about three feet square with a dirt floor that smelled where previous occupants had urinated. Oliver wondered what he was supposed to do for a toilet and saw a bucket in one corner. Was this to pee in, or was there water in it? He bent down to examine it and recoiled at the smell. Definitely not drinking water. Panic started to set in. What if they didn't come for him for days? Something ran over his foot, and he jumped back, his heart pounding. He had heard all about the poisonous snakes and spiders in Australia. Would they come if he screamed? If he was dying? He didn't think so. Nobody cared.

He squatted down, leaning his back against the warm wood. Somehow he had to get out of this place. He tried the walls one at a time for a potentially loose plank, but they all seemed solidly in place. He wondered, if he stood on the bucket, could he reach the roof that seemed to be made of corrugated iron? He stood until he could stand no more and then sat carefully on the earth, hoping not to disturb any creature that lived there. His heart was beating so loudly he was sure his heartbeat must have been echoing from the sides of his prison. Hours seemed to pass. He sensed daylight fading outside, and despair overcame him. He had nowhere to run, nowhere to go . . . but a face swam into his consciousness, the sweet, kind face of Miss Everingham. "Write to me," she had said, and she had bought him a toy dog. If he could write to her and tell her the way things were here, maybe she'd find a way to save him.

He was just drifting into uneasy sleep, leaning against the rough wood of the structure, when he heard a sound. Cold air blew in as the door was opened. Oliver scrambled to his feet.

"Shh," said a voice. "Don't make a noise. I've come to get you out."

Oliver saw the big, lumbering shape of Charlie outlined against the starry sky.

"Won't I get in trouble if they find me gone?"

"Better than starving to death in here, isn't it?" Charlie said. "Come on. If you like, you can share my bed, and in the morning we'll put you back in this dump, and they'll never know."

"Really?" Oliver said. "You'd do this for me? Why are you being so kind?"

"Cos I grew up in an orphanage," Charlie said. "We learned to look out for each other. It's us against them, ain't it? Come on, Squirt. Let's go."

Oliver tiptoed beside him to the barracks and was hidden under the blanket in Charlie's bed. He fell asleep with the comforting warmth of the bigger boy beside him. In the morning they crept out at the first sign of dawn. Oliver pretended to be asleep when Edith came for him.

"Learned your lesson, have you, stupid?" she said.

"Oh yes," Oliver replied. "I've learned a lot."

CHAPTER 32

Annie wasted no time in finding herself a job. She managed, or contrived, to bump into Madeleine as she cycled down the rue Grande.

"I wanted you to know I've been hired, madame," she said. "By the café on the corner, facing the château. You can't miss it."

"Wonderful. Congratulations. So I will know where to find you."

"Exactly," Annie said. "I won't be anything as glamorous as a waitress—dishwasher and general cleaner is what they need right now, but it may lead to something better. Besides"—she lowered her voice, moving slightly closer—"the sink is at the kitchen window at the back of the property. It opens on to an alleyway with dustbins. It should be easy enough for you to pass a message to me, or vice versa. And if I'm not at the sink, I'll put a flowerpot on the window ledge. You can leave a message under it."

"Right," Madeleine said. She looked around before lowering her voice. "Have you made contact yet?"

Annie nodded.

"And the people we need to do business with?"

"Will contact us, that's what I was told. But your fisherman is already operating, and the sooner you visit him, the better. A lot of traffic is going past unhindered."

She stepped aside as people were approaching. "I'll see you around town, no doubt, madame." She gave a friendly wave and walked off. Madeleine watched her with admiration. She was sure Annie was enjoying every moment of this. *I've got to learn not to be worried,* she told herself. She finished her deliveries, did some shopping for Madame Dumas and then returned to the shoemaker.

"Is there anything else you require right now, monsieur?" she asked.

"Not at the moment. How nice that you have struck up an acquaintance with a fellow Parisienne."

"Yes. She seems quite agreeable," Madeleine said. "Not an educated woman, but . . ."

"Education is not everything. At this time of strife, one needs solid friends," he said.

Madeleine tried not to look at him. Was he indicating that he knew why she was there and who Annie was? "Indeed one does," she said.

For lunch they ate green beans in olive oil, radishes and coarse homemade bread.

"Heaven knows what we are going to have tonight," Madame Dumas said. "There's no meat to be had again. I suppose it will have to be an egg, although the chickens are not laying well in this hot weather."

Madeleine seized the opportunity. "Are there fish to be had in the Seine?"

Madame shrugged. "I suppose so. One would need a fishing license, and who has the time to stand and fish all day? It is for old men."

"I am an old man, and I do not have the time to fish," Monsieur Dumas said.

"I'll ride out that way this afternoon and see if anyone has fish for sale, if you like."

"By all means, but I think it will be a waste of time. However, if you wish to ride through the heat of the day, it is your choice. Me, I have to get back to work. There are three million items waiting to be mended."

"When you have a moment, perhaps you can teach me some of the simpler ways of mending things," Madeleine said. "I know I should never be able to do the fine work on shoes, but perhaps mending leather reins, or soldering the handle of pot—I could perhaps do those."

"I bet you could." He looked absurdly pleased. "Well let's make a moment to teach you, shall we?"

Madeleine got on the bicycle and rode in the direction of the river. It was indeed a hot afternoon, and she regretted her eagerness to find the fisherman. He was nowhere to be seen near the bridge, but she followed the left bank towards the little commune of Samois-sur-Seine and saw a rustic bridge going across to an island. The island looked shady and appealing, so she decided to take a rest and watch the river. As she wheeled her bike across, she spotted an old man, lying propped against a massive oak tree. He opened his eyes as she came past.

"It's certainly hot enough today, isn't it?" she said.

"August heat is the worst, isn't it?" he replied. "Even the fish are sleeping and not interested in my bait."

She noticed the rod propped against the trunk and a fishing basket beside it. "You are a fisherman?" she asked, trying to sound casual.

"I am a man who fishes, unlike the disciples of our good Lord," he replied. "I do not fish for my living but because it gives me an excuse to sit doing nothing all day instead of helping my wife around the house."

Madeleine chuckled. She had no idea whether he was *the* fisherman, her eyes and ears on the river, or a man who liked to fish.

"Do you happen to have any fish for sale?" she asked.

"For sale?" He gave an apologetic shrug. "Madame, I can scarcely catch enough fish to satisfy the hunger of my wife and myself. However . . . should I ever have an extra fish, I should be happy to share it with you."

"You are very kind, monsieur," she said. "I know people who would welcome a fish dinner."

He nodded. "It's a pity you weren't here yesterday," he said. "You hear about the one that got away, but this really was the one that got away. A big, ugly brute, armour plated like a sturgeon—didn't even look at my bait, travelling south fast. Too bad. One doesn't see many fish like that one."

"As you say, too bad, monsieur. I'd be interested to know if you ever see such a spectacular fish again."

"So you are interested in fish, madame?"

"I am. Fascinating creatures. I like watching them swim."

"Personally I like catching and eating them." He chuckled, then lay back against the tree, closing his eyes.

"*Bon après-midi,* monsieur," Madeleine said, wishing him a good afternoon. "And good fishing."

She wheeled the bicycle off the island and set off back in the direction of Fontainebleau, scarcely containing her excitement. When she came to a deserted stretch of road, she paused, took a tiny scrap of paper from her pocket and wrote on it, *German armaments spotted yesterday, heading south on Seine.*

Then she rode to Annie's house, stuffed the folded scrap into the shrub by the entrance and went on her way without being noticed. First mission accomplished, she thought, and it went so smoothly.

~

Madeleine didn't go near Annie's café for a few days, giving Annie time to get settled and into a routine, and she had nothing more to report from the fisherman, except for a real catfish, which Madame Dumas welcomed as if it were gold. Madeleine understood there was another spy who lived beside the main road going south, but he had been sick and in hospital, so she waited for word that he was home again. But no word came. She also waited to hear how to contact the local Resistance but heard nothing. It was August, summer holidays, steaming-hot days. People swam at the edge of the Seine, no doubt driving the fish away. They stood in the fountains. They basked in the shade in the forest or sat on the grass of parks. Madeleine took the opportunity to familiarize herself with all the roads leading out of the town. Old memories resurfaced. She found the forest a fascinating place, with its giant boulders set amongst the trees, rearing up in weird shapes so that in the dappled shade they looked like prehistoric creatures. She was admiring one of these, wondering if it was the one that Giles had climbed with Olivier, and tempted to see if she could climb to the top, when a woman came up beside her.

"Are you going to give it a try?" she asked. "Or don't you have the nerve?"

Madeleine turned to look at her. She was youngish, of striking appearance, with long black hair, upturned dark eyes and a gash of red lips. Those eyes were appraising Madeleine.

"The nerve I have," Madeleine said, "but maybe not the skill. I've never climbed anything in my life, except up to the upper bunk."

"You need the right shoes," the other woman said. "And really strong fingers to grip on to the ledges. I have been climbing here all my life. Let me show you." She started up what looked like the smooth vertical face of a boulder, moving with ease and grace until she was twelve feet above Madeleine. "Now you try," she called down. "See that crack there? Put your foot on the ledge and your fingers into the crack and pull yourself up."

Madeleine was about to refuse, but she got a sense that she was somehow being tested and this encounter was important. She followed directions until she emerged triumphant at the top, sitting down beside the woman, who nodded, grudgingly. "You have the fitness," she said, "and the will."

"For what?" Madeleine asked, still playing the innocent.

"For whatever is needed to survive this war," the woman said. She held out a hand. "I'm Jacqueline. And you are?"

"Minette." She shook Jacqueline's hand.

"I'm glad you are here, Minette," Jacqueline said. "We have been out of communication with London for too long. I see you have taken over visiting the river. That's important. We can't be seen there, of course. Too well known. So if you see anything we should know about, you tell us as well as London, agreed?"

Around them the forest was silent apart from the chatter of a squirrel in the treetops. No breeze stirred the great trees. "I have no idea what you are talking about," Madeleine said.

"Good. It's good to be cautious, but if I tell you that we, too, have received a communication from your Uncle Francis?"

"Oh, from Uncle Francis. How is he?"

"Worried, of course. He fears the Germans will not leave the zone libre alone and will move south to take over the whole of France. They are already moving troops in that direction, are they not?"

"So I understand," Madeleine replied.

"If we can find out about them soon enough, we can make sure the payloads don't reach their destination," Jacqueline said. "We have a team of saboteurs coming into the area in the next weeks. They will be able to disable German vehicles stationed at Fontainebleau, syphon off their petrol, and disrupt any convoy going down by road. And pass on the word about barges carrying German supplies, too."

"I'll do my best," Madeleine said. "How do I contact you?"

"Let me ask, are you religious?"

"Religious?" Madeleine reacted to the question, then shook her head. "I was baptized a Catholic and attended Mass with my mother and later with my husband, but I can't say I've attended for a while. Why do you ask?"

"It might be a good idea to become religious again," Jacqueline said. "You passed a wayside shrine on the route here. Did you notice it?"

"Not really."

"One of those little houses with a statue of Our Lady. People leave flowers and sometimes prayer requests. You should stop and pray at it every time you pass from now on. And if you have a message for us, you tuck it behind the statue of Our Lady. I'll make sure there is a candle in a blue glass candleholder amongst the other candles. When you have a message, place this candle where it is visible at the very front."

Madeleine nodded. "That's a good idea."

"And you should also make it a practice to visit the church—Saint-Louis, the big church near the château. Kneel. Say a prayer. Be seen. If we need to communicate and for some reason you cannot leave the town to go to the shrine, you can do the same thing. The candle in the blue glass holder. We'll make sure there is one. You put it in front of the statue of Our Lady, and leave any message inside the hymn book at the far end of the back pew in the side chapel on the left."

Madeleine nodded again. "Do you live in the town?"

"Not any longer. Too dangerous. We move from place to place, but we do have a safe house in the forest if we need to vanish in a hurry," Jacqueline said. "I'll draw a map for you, as you may need to use it yourself if things get hot. Do you have a handkerchief?"

"Yes." Madeleine drew it out of her pocket, again unsure what the other woman wanted.

Jacqueline took it. "Ah, good. It's plain, not a stupid lacy one. And unused. Even better."

She spread it out on the surface of the rock and started to draw. "After the crossroads, the road comes around a bend. A path goes off to the right. Head due north. You have a compass, yes? More boulders. Keep to the left of them . . ." As she spoke, she drew on the white linen until she had finished a map, ending in a small hut, well away from any road. "Tuck this into your knickers as you ride home, in case you are stopped. Memorize it, then wash the handkerchief. The ink will wash out."

"Presumably I should not think of coming to this safe house unless it is a real emergency?" Madeleine asked.

"Absolutely not. It would be putting us all at risk." She gave Madeleine another appraising look. "Frankly the less you know, the better. I am not at all happy to be working with the English—especially untrained women like yourself—but the orders come from our regional boss, and so I obey."

"I can assure you we were well trained," Madeleine said.

"Really? You know how to kill a man silently?"

"I do," Madeleine said.

"But could you do it? Do it without thinking twice?"

"I hope so, if it was necessary," Madeleine said, "but I won't know until I'm put to the test."

"You delicate English ladies," Jacqueline said, shaking her head. "What can you know? Your country is not occupied. You have not really suffered like us."

Madeleine stared her down. "I'll have you know I had to leave my home and my husband. I don't even know if he is still alive. Probably not, as I have heard nothing from him for ages. And in London we endured night after night of bombing," she said. "What's worse, my son—my only child, my little boy—was killed by a bomb, so don't ever tell me I have not suffered enough."

"I'm sorry," Jacqueline said quietly. "I misspoke. Maybe you are up to the job after all."

CHAPTER 33

Oliver

Australia

Days turned into weeks for Oliver—days, weeks with no end in sight. No escape. Some days were not so bad. Charlie had become a real mate, sticking up for him when he might have been bullied. He was funny, too, with that quick cockney sense of humour.

"See that boy over there?" He nudged Oliver. Oliver looked. "His name's Isaiah. Do you know why?"

Oliver shook his head.

"Because one eye's 'igher than the other." And he burst out laughing. Oliver laughed, too. It felt strange to smile, as if his mouth had been frozen into a hard line for so long. Charlie assumed the role of his protector and always managed to show up if one of the bigger children was giving Oliver a hard time. Another bright spot was when the schoolmaster, Mr Baxter, came out from the town to give them lessons twice a week. He noticed Oliver right away, the bright boy whose hand shot up when he asked a question. At the end of the session one day he called Oliver over to him.

"How are you settling in, young man?"

"All right, I suppose," Oliver muttered. "I miss my school. We don't learn much here."

"You went to a good school?"

Oliver nodded. "St Mark's, in London."

"St Mark's, eh? What did you like there?"

"Everything. I liked geography, and there were lots of books to read. There's almost no books here."

Mr Baxter studied him with interest. "You read well, do you?"

"Oh yes," Oliver said.

"What sort of books did you enjoy?"

Oliver frowned, trying to remember. It already seemed like a dream-life, so far away. "Well. *Winnie-the-Pooh*. That was funny. And Enid Blyton. I like her books. My grandpa read *Swallows and Amazons* to me."

"It's terrific." The schoolmaster smiled. "How about I bring some books out for you to read, if you like?"

"Really? That would be smashing." Oliver beamed.

Mr Baxter went away frowning. Oliver was so different from most of the children. Surely there had been some relative in England, money for a boarding school, so that he shouldn't have had to come to this place?

Oliver was having similar thoughts. There had to be a way to escape, he thought. There must be somewhere better than this. He wrestled with the nagging thought that he should not be here. He didn't belong. One day, lying on his bed for the afternoon rest, Oliver had a brilliant idea: he thought of Miss Everingham. "Write to me," she had said, and given him her address. That piece of paper had been taken from him with all his other belongings when he arrived, but he thought he knew it by heart. Now all he needed was writing paper. He didn't think the sisters would let him write to anyone, so he didn't ask them. Instead, when he was having a lesson with Mr Baxter, he tore a page from his notebook, as carefully as he could so that the sisters would not see and accuse him of wasting paper.

He finished his work ahead of his classmates and wrote carefully,

Dear Miss Everingham:

I am at a place in Australia called Ferndale Children's Farm. It's not very nice. The nuns are horrible and make us work in

the fields. I think I'm here by mistake cos they got my name wrong. Can you do something for me? I'm not sure what cos I got no family left but you were so nice to me.

Oliver Martin.

He folded the letter, and at the end of the class he approached Mr Baxter.

"I wrote a letter to a lady who took care of me after the bombing," he said. "I don't have an envelope or a stamp. Could you send it for me?"

"Of course," Mr Baxter said. "I'd be happy to. You have her address?"

"I think I remember it. I've written it at the top," Oliver said.

The schoolmaster read it, frowned, but said nothing. "Don't worry," he said. "I'll mail it for you."

On his way out, he stopped by the sisters' office and saw Sister Margaret doing the accounts. "That boy, Oliver Jones. There is something about him. Are we sure he has no family left in England?"

"Jones? He's a strange one, isn't he?" the nun replied, frowning. "But they only send us the ones with no family, so where else could he go? Orphanage in England? Would that be better for him? I don't think so."

"No, I suppose not," Mr Baxter said. He didn't mention the letter but went home and mailed it.

~

Oliver felt a new blossoming of hope. Miss Everingham would get his letter, and something would happen. Someone would come to get him. It would be all right. In the meantime, he now had an ally. Mr Baxter brought him books. He tried to give him extra coaching in maths. He left an atlas for the common room. Oliver studied it, running his finger along the route they had taken from England. So far away. It was going to take ages for that letter to reach Miss Everingham. But he'd wait patiently.

~

The letter finally reached the convalescent home near Guildford. (Oliver had spelled it Gilford).

The secretary who received it stared at the name on the envelope. "Miss Everingham—who is she?"

"Oh, she was the teacher assigned to us for a while," the director said. "Nice woman."

"There's a letter here, addressed to her. Can we forward it?"

The director shrugged. "She left to join up. I don't know if she went to the army or air force. I believe the latter. But I don't know how we'd find her. Is it important?"

The secretary opened the letter. "It's from some child. It seems to say he doesn't like his new school very much."

The director looked up, smiling. "Well, there's not much we can do about that, is there?"

And the letter was dropped into the wastepaper basket.

CHAPTER 34

It was August fifteenth, the Feast of the Assumption, one of the most important religious holidays of the year in France. Madeleine had followed advice and attended Mass almost daily, getting nods of approval from the older women. She found the simple service oddly comforting—the murmur of the priest's voice as he faced the altar, the sweet chime of the altar bells at the consecration, the serene faces of the statues in the side chapels, the coloured light from stained glass windows dancing in pools on the stone floor. It felt like a place that war could not touch, although she found it hard to believe. Even harder to pray.

"Well, here I am, God," she would mutter. "I don't know if you are there or if you can hear me. I don't even know if I want to ask you to keep me safe. But if Giles is still alive, then please watch over him."

On this holiday she went with Monsieur and Madame Dumas to the parish church of Saint-Louis. The church was packed with what seemed to be the whole town. Everyone was dressed in what finery they owned. Afterwards there were tables and chairs set up in the square beside the church. Families brought food and wine, and there was a festival atmosphere. A brass band played. Children danced and ran around with balloons and ice lollies. Madeleine watched, trying to join in the excitement of the day, but suddenly she spotted a young boy with glasses, a boy who reminded her of Olivier. This son was alive. He hugged his mother and made her laugh. She looked away hastily.

A few German soldiers stood watching but did not interfere.

"Just like the good old days," Madame Dumas muttered to Madeleine, "only of course there would have been a pig to roast, plenty of good food and wine and the best cakes for those called Marie, whose name day it is. Now we feast on radishes and maize!"

Madeleine spotted Annie, who was with Monsieur Gustave, the schoolmaster. They exchanged a polite greeting as Annie settled the elderly man on a bench. From the way he studied Madeleine, she suspected he knew who she was. As the afternoon wore on, impromptu songs and dances sprang up. There was the traditional song for young girls called Marie and some small, simple cakes. Then, as it got dark, a small bonfire was lit.

"They wouldn't let us have one for Bastille Day," a man near Madeleine said. "But they didn't say anything about the Feast of Our Lady. Even the Boche don't dare go against Our Lady!"

People gathered around the fire, and suddenly someone started singing "La Marseillaise." Everyone joined in. The sounds rose, filling the warm night air. As it died away, someone shouted, "Look, there's another bonfire at the château—just like the old days."

People started heading towards the château. But they had hardly taken a few steps when there was an explosion, followed by another and another. A man came rushing into the square. "A whole line of German lorries has just gone up!" he shouted. Everyone cheered. But even before the cheering died away, German soldiers arrived in force, their weapons drawn.

"Nobody move!" shouted a commanding voice, and a man, clearly the officer in charge, stepped out in front of the armed men.

"You think this is amusing, do you?" he said in remarkably good French. "You think you can hurt us with your pathetic attempts? So you have destroyed a few of our vehicles. But don't worry. We have many more. And until they arrive, we will requisition every car and van from this town for our use. Also, there will be no more petrol coupons. You will just have to walk. Too bad. And maybe you will learn to respect your conquerors." He turned back to the troops behind him and issued a command in German.

"Hold out your hands, palms up," the officer commanded. "Everybody. Men, women and children."

Madeleine glanced at Madame Dumas and complied. Soldiers came around, bent to sniff her palms, then went on.

"What do they want?" she whispered.

Madame Dumas shrugged.

Suddenly one of the soldiers gave a shout. "Here, Captain."

And a man was dragged forward. "So we have found the culprit?" the officer said.

"What do you mean? I was here at the church all day," the man said. "I never left this place all evening. I have plenty of witnesses who drank wine with me."

"Then how come you have the smell of petrol on your hands?" the officer said.

"I used some kerosene to start the bonfire," he said. "Ask them. Ask everyone."

"And they will assuredly lie for you," the officer said. "Take him away. Tomorrow you will see what the consequences are of defying the German army."

"But I didn't . . . ," the man shouted, struggling to free himself as two soldiers grabbed his arms and tried to lead him away. "I was here. Ask them. Ask my wife. Ask my mother-in-law. They saw me. Let go of me. I didn't do anything . . ."

His voice grew fainter as he was dragged down the street away from the crowd.

"Everybody go home! This instant. Anyone who remains on the street will be arrested." The order was barked, and the crowd dispersed, hastily gathering up picnic supplies and rugs, looking over their shoulders at the bayonets and guns. Madame Dumas took Madeleine's arm.

"That we should live to see this day," she muttered. "That was Thomas Bardot. A good man. With a wife and family. What will become of him?"

"Perhaps they will let him go when he can prove his innocence," Madeleine said, although in her heart she didn't believe this.

In the morning German armoured cars drove through the town, loudspeakers blaring out, commanding everyone to assemble outside the château at nine o'clock. Madeleine and the Dumases joined the stream of people, finding themselves packed into the plaza and forced to stand in the sun. After what seemed like an eternity, the man who had been arrested was brought out. He was blindfolded, and could barely stagger forward, propped up by two guards. Madeleine could only imagine what had been done to him. Had he been tortured to get a confession? She felt sick. The prisoner was tied to the railings outside the château. His head slumped forwards, as if he was only semi-conscious. Eight soldiers marched out of the gates and took up positions. It was only then that Madeleine realized they were a firing squad. A command was given. Shots rang out. The man slumped forward, suspended by his wrists against the railing as blood dripped into the sand. There were gasps and cries from the crowd, a woman's scream.

"You may now go home." The officer walked over to the man's body, kicked it, then turned back. "Except those of you who wish to claim this corpse. Remove it immediately And let this be a lesson to those who wish to oppose the might of the German army."

As they left with the other townspeople, Madeleine caught a glimpse of Annie and the schoolmaster. Annie's face was ashen. Madeleine was sure Annie had just realized, as she had, too, what they were up against and what might happen to them if they were caught. She was also trying to come to terms with her own role here: if she passed along a message to the Resistance and they used her information to destroy German equipment, bomb a railway line, steal ammunition, ordinary people like that poor man would be punished instead. How could that be right? How could she justify what she was doing?

She tried to tell herself that it was a war. She was part of a force fighting the opposing army. Soldiers had to kill the enemy every day without wondering if the man they were mowing down was an ordinary, decent bloke who didn't want to be there. A man with a home and a family, just like them. That's just how it was. And if you thought too much, you'd go mad.

~

After the sabotage of the German lorries, there was increased German presence in the town. Madeleine was stopped almost daily as she went to make her deliveries. As her basket only contained a pair of well-worn boots or a repaired harness, she was waved on. But she now moved with a sense of danger in the air at all times. She worried about Annie and her radio. She now worried about putting the old fisherman at risk, although their conversations would always seem completely harmless to an outsider, and she did occasionally manage to buy a fish from him. There was still no report from the cottage on the main road, for which she found herself grateful. If nobody reported a German convoy going past, she would not be responsible for any sabotage and German retribution—although she realized this was her mission.

~

She saw nothing of Jacqueline, but the slips of paper she left at the shrine disappeared. There were no more acts of sabotage at the German base. In fact, life became a smooth and comfortable routine as summer turned to autumn, the weather turned chilly and a carpet of leaves lined the forest floor. Occasionally she would bump into Annie. If nobody was around, they'd exchange a few words.

"How long do you think we're here for?" Annie asked when they passed on the street and found themselves alone.

"I've no idea," Madeleine replied. "They didn't say."

"You're right. There was no mention of getting us out."

"We seem to be okay so far," Madeleine said. "Apart from that horrible day when the lorries were blown up and that poor man was shot . . ."

"Which scared the daylights out of me," Annie muttered. "Until then, I hadn't somehow thought it was real."

"I felt the same," Madeleine agreed.

"I even wonder if we're doing any good," Annie said. "I mean, I send messages to London. I get messages, and you deliver them, but nothing that's going to change the direction of the war. I keep asking myself if this is all for nothing."

"I hope not," Madeleine said. "To tell you the truth, I felt terrible when that man was executed. I wondered if any message I passed along would lead to more innocent people being killed."

"I felt the same." Annie nodded. "I wish we could meet more often. It's the loneliness that's hard. Being stuck here with nobody to talk to."

Madeleine nodded with understanding. "We can't risk it, can we? Nothing that links us."

"You're right," Annie said. "Bloody Germans."

They went on their way, Madeleine now concerned that Annie might be about to crack. Then one morning, as she knelt to pray at early Mass, she was conscious of a woman watching her—kneeling off at a side pew, her face invisible beneath the scarf that covered her head. Not Jacqueline, she decided. Jacqueline was taller and bonier. Maybe just someone who had noticed her coming to Mass on a daily basis. But when others went up to communion, this woman slid into place beside her. Madeleine looked up sharply and found herself staring at Portia's face.

CHAPTER 35

"What are you doing here?" she whispered in French, sliding her hand across to grab Portia's. "Did they send you to help us?"

"Wait until after Mass," Portia whispered back.

The last communicant returned to her pew. The priest said the final prayer and blessing, and the congregation filed out. Portia stood and went over to one of the statues in a side chapel, standing in front of it in devotion. Madeleine followed her when the church had emptied out.

"I had to come," Portia said, still keeping her voice low.

"Keep speaking French, just in case," Madeleine warned.

Portia nodded. "Sorry. You're right." She gave a big sigh. "I didn't know where else to go. I've been sitting in this church since before daybreak. I didn't know where to find you, but I hoped I'd bump into you on the street, or at least find someone who knew you or Annie, but I didn't want to be seen before the shops opened. That would look suspicious."

Madeleine saw the alarm in Portia's eyes. "What happened?"

"I was to be sent to Chartres," she said "All arranged. Myself and Jack—remember him? We were to set up a cell there—near the main road leading south to Bordeaux. We came in on the new little plane that can land and take off, so we didn't need to parachute—lucky we didn't, or I'd be dead, too." She moved towards a dark corner of the church, standing in front of a statue of an unknown saint. Madeleine followed. Portia crossed herself. "They were waiting for us."

"Yes, I know. We had the same thing. People darted out of the trees, grabbed our bags and helped us."

"No. I mean the Germans," Portia said. "The message must have been intercepted, or somebody betrayed us. There was a line of little lights in the darkness. We landed. Someone hauled me out, and then suddenly gunfire broke out all around us. The man helping me was shot. Jack was shot as he got out of the plane. He yelled, 'Run!' to me. I ran into the trees and hid. They kept firing at the plane, but it somehow managed to take off again. I don't know if it was badly damaged or could make it home. I couldn't see. All I could see was men in uniform with guns and bodies lying on the ground. So I didn't know what to do."

Madeleine put out a hand and rested it on Portia's.

"Come on," she said. "Let's go and get a cup of coffee at the café where Annie works."

"Do you think it's safe? Safe for you, I mean?"

"I don't think anyone would be looking for you here. They wouldn't know exactly who London would send, would they? So you're my friend from Paris, visiting for a day. How nice."

She took Portia's arm and led her out of the church. The town was starting to come to life, with shopkeepers hauling up blinds and opening shutters. There were several people sitting in the café. Madeleine took a table outside and ordered coffee and bread. The owner greeted her as a regular.

"Going to be a fine day, madame. You have a visitor?"

"Yes. A friend from Paris. I haven't seen her in ages."

"Are you staying long, madame?" he asked Portia.

"No, she's just here for the day, unfortunately," Madeleine said for her. "I'm dying to find out what conditions are like there now."

"Bad, from what we hear," the café owner said.

Portia nodded. "Very bad," she said.

"I'll get the coffee." He went.

Portia let out a sigh. "I almost couldn't remember how to speak French," she said. "After all that training, my mouth wouldn't work."

"That happened to me when I first arrived," Madeleine said. "Annie was brilliant. She chatted as if there was no problem."

"Where is she now?"

"She works here, at this café. I expect we'll see her. I just hope she's not too surprised." She smiled as the owner placed a carafe of coffee, two cups and a plate of bread and jam on the table.

"Now tell me." She lowered her voice.

"I didn't know where to go," Portia said. "If they knew we were coming, clearly I couldn't proceed as planned. I had to assume there wasn't a safe house for me in Chartres. At first I thought I might go up to Paris and find Marie-France, but I thought that might be more dangerous. I knew you and Annie were here, and I thought you'd at least be able to send a message to London to let them know and they could tell me what I should do next." Then she shook her head. "But I don't want to put you in danger. Maybe I acted too hastily. Frankly I panicked. I thought I'd be calm and efficient, but I wasn't. It was all so sudden and so horrible. Poor Jack. I never liked him, but to see him fall dead like that . . ."

Madeleine nodded. "I can't take you home with me," she said. "I wouldn't want to put the family in any more risk. But there is a safe house in the forest that the Resistance uses. I'll take you there. And Annie can get in touch with London to . . ."

As she was speaking, Annie came out of the kitchen to clear away dishes from the other outside table. She nodded to Madeleine. "Bonjour, madame," she said.

Then she saw Portia. She started in surprise, knocking over a glass and just managing to grab it before it rolled on to the pavement.

"This is my friend, Madame Jeanette Renoir," Madeleine said. "She's visiting for the day from Paris."

"Very nice for you, madame," Annie said. "I hope you enjoy your visit."

She went on putting dirty dishes into a tray and carried them back to the kitchen. Madeleine took out a piece of paper and wrote on it, folded it small and put it into her saucer with the cup on top of it.

When Annie came out again, Madeleine called her over. "You can take this cup. I've finished with it," she said.

"Very good, madame." Annie picked up the cup and went away with it.

Portia watched in admiration. "You are good at this."

"We've had practice," she said. "Now, let's get you out to the forest before too many people notice you, just in case."

She wheeled her bicycle home with Portia walking beside her, then took her in to introduce her to Monsieur Dumas.

"A friend is visiting from Paris," she said. "She has come to pick chestnuts in the forest. You know how hard it is to get food in the city."

"Of course. I've heard. Welcome, madame." He gave a little bow.

"Thank you." Portia's voice still sounded taut.

"I wondered if you need me to make any deliveries at this moment or if I could walk with her for a while," Madeleine said.

"Nothing to deliver before noon," he said. "Go and enjoy yourselves. And Madame would not say no to some chestnuts herself if you find them. Nor to hazelnuts."

"I'll do my best," Madeleine said.

They came out together. Madeleine wheeled her bike beside Portia. "I'm afraid we've quite a long walk," she said.

"I don't mind," Portia said. "I have nothing to carry, except for this small bag, which luckily I was wearing slung across me when I came out of the plane. Otherwise I'd have no identity card, no money, nothing. As it was, I was able to keep walking cross country in the dark until I found a train station and caught an early train towards Paris, then changed to come here. That should have put anyone off the scent if they were indeed looking for me, shouldn't it?"

"It should," Madeleine said. "With any luck, they don't even know you are a woman."

They walked in companionable silence along the deserted road.

"You don't see much traffic here?" Portia asked.

"The Germans took all the motor vehicles," Madeleine said. "The Resistance blew up their lorries, so they paid us back by removing our means of transportation—except bicycles, luckily. I make the deliveries for Monsieur Dumas. It gives me a perfect excuse to be going all over the place. Every time I'm stopped, I have a pair of old shoes in my basket. Or a horse bridle." She smiled.

They continued on. At the wayside shrine, they paused. Madeleine stared at it, then continued. "This is how we communicate with the Resistance," she said. "If the blue candleholder is at the front, there is a message for me. I place it at the front if I have one for them, and the actual slip of paper is behind the statue of Our Lady."

"It all sounds so simple," Portia said.

"Until that message and my information gets someone shot. I haven't quite come to terms with that."

They continued along the deserted road. As they walked, she was observing trees. Then she gave a grunt of satisfaction. "We take this path," she said and turned on to a slim bridle path between trees. "I had to memorize the map," she said. "I hope I've got it right."

The path led them around another group of great boulders, appearing like crouching creatures in the dappled light. Some of the trees were now almost bare, others glowed with yellow and brown leaves, and a carpet of leaves now covered the path, allowing them to move silently. At last they came to a small clearing with yet another group of boulders. Behind the biggest boulder was what looked like a woodcutter's hut—a primitive building made of slats of wood.

"This is it," Madeleine said. She walked up to the door and tapped on it. "It's Minette," she called. "I've a message from Uncle Francis."

The door opened slowly. "Are you alone?" asked a man's voice.

"I've brought Jeanette with me from Uncle Francis. She needs a place to stay," Madeleine said.

"Entrez, alors."

Madeleine stepped into a small dark room. It was primitive in the extreme with a rustic wooden table on which sat a candle, a loaf of bread and an almost empty bottle of wine. In the corner was a small cast iron stove. She only had a second to take this in before the man shut the door behind them, leaving them in murky half darkness.

"I hope you weren't followed," the man said.

"No. You're quite safe," Madeleine said, and turned to face him. Even in twilight of the room, she recognized him instantly and gave a gasp at the same moment as he recognized her.

"Madeleine? Is it you? It is you," he said.

She took in the familiar face, the unruly hair. "Giles! I can't believe it."

She burst into a great sob as his arms came around her.

CHAPTER 36

For a long moment they stood locked together, not speaking. Then he released her and stood staring incredulously. "What are you doing here? Did you come to find me? Are you mad?" There was fear and anger in his voice now.

"I didn't know where you were," she said. "I didn't even know if you were alive. I hadn't heard in ages . . . But I was sent here by the British secret service. I had no idea you were anywhere near."

"This is my territory," he said. "I'm in charge. You know I grew up near here, so it made sense. But you—why on earth did you allow the English to send you here to this hellhole? How can you risk your life like this? Who is taking care of our boy?"

"I volunteered," Madeleine said. "I volunteered because of Olivier." She paused, taking a deep breath before she said, "He's dead, Giles. He was killed by a bomb."

"Ollie is dead?" All the anger faded from his face to be replaced with disbelief and bleak despair. "A bomb?"

She nodded. "I wanted to protect him. His school was being evacuated to the country for safety. I let him go, and his train was bombed." She could hardly finish the sentence.

"His train was bombed?" He repeated the words, frowning as if trying to comprehend a foreign language. "Oh no. How does one even . . ." He left the words hanging. "And now you put yourself in harm's way?"

"I was so angry, Giles. I had to do something. I volunteered for this. I trained as a courier, and I've been here a couple of months now. I've been passing messages to Jacqueline."

"So you've met Jacqueline?" he asked.

She nodded.

"How strange. She mentioned an Englishwoman, and I had no idea . . ." He glanced to a door on his right. "She's asleep at the moment. She was out all night. We blew up a train."

"Near here?"

"No. Closer to Paris. At the goods yard at Melun." He seemed to notice Portia, who had been standing motionless by the door until now. "I'm sorry. We've been ignoring your friend. My apologies, madame. As you can see, I know this lady from before the war. I was surprised and shocked to meet her here."

"He's my husband," Madeleine said. "I didn't even know he was alive. It's a miracle." She turned back to Giles. "Portia arrived last night from England. She was supposed to set up a cell in Chartres, but there must have been a leak, and they were betrayed. The Germans were waiting for them, and everyone else was killed. She came here to find me. Can you hide her until the radio operator can get instructions from England?"

"Of course." He nodded. "I am Pierre." He emphasized the name, perhaps realizing Madeleine had called him Giles. "You are?"

"Jeanette," Portia said.

"You are French?"

"No. English. But I went to school in Switzerland."

He smiled. "Ah, that explains the strange accent. You are not a Parisienne, that is clear. So. You stay here for now, and we will see what we can do."

"Thank you," Portia said. "I am truly grateful. I was really afraid that . . ."

"I must be getting back." Madeleine stared at Giles, taking in every detail of his face.

"Where are you staying?"

"In the town. I live with the shoe repairman, and I make his deliveries. That gives me a good excuse to be out and about on a bicycle. I said I'd be back by noon."

She moved towards the door. "Good luck, Jeanette. Let me know what they decide for you." She looked at Giles. "Will I see you again?"

"I can't say," he said. "It may be wiser not to. I'm not normally here. We operate mainly further north where supplies come in from Germany. But I'll try . . . I want to keep you safe."

Madeleine nodded, too overwhelmed with emotion to speak.

"Goodbye then, my darling," she said. She took his face in her hands and kissed him gently on the lips. Giles gave a little moan, grabbed her shoulders and crushed her to him, kissing her with abandon.

They didn't hear the door open behind them. They were not conscious of anything or anyone until a voice said loudly, "Pierre? What is going on?"

Jacqueline stood there, her eyes flashing dangerously.

Giles broke apart from Madeleine. "Oh, Jacqueline. You are awake. An amazing thing has happened. I have just found my wife."

"Your wife?" Jacqueline was still glaring.

"I had no idea she was in France. She had no idea I was operating near here. It's like a small miracle, don't you think?"

"I think it's dangerous," Jacqueline said. "No attachments, that's what we're told. Certainly no close relationships. You need to get her out of here before she puts us all at risk."

"I can do my job," Madeleine said. "I am just overwhelmed with joy at knowing he's still alive. All this time I didn't hear, I didn't know . . ."

"I never knew you were married," Jacqueline said, giving Giles a questioning stare.

Madeleine watched her and suddenly knew with absolute certainty that she and Giles had been sleeping together. "As you just said, our personal lives should be kept private," she replied coldly. She reached out and touched Giles's arm. "*Au revoir, mon amour.* Stay safe. And if I don't see you again, then after the war is over."

"After the war is over, I will come and find you," he said simply.

Madeleine let herself out of the cottage before anyone could see her crying. She was heading for home before she remembered that she needed to find some nuts to bring to Madame Dumas. Luckily she came upon a chestnut tree and filled her bicycle basket with enough to make the old woman happy.

~

Knowing Giles was nearby changed everything. Whereas before she had felt fatalistic about her assignment, not really caring if she lived or died, now she had an overwhelming desire to live, and to keep Giles alive, too. She tried not to think about Jacqueline and the surge of white-hot jealousy she felt. She could understand that a man like Giles would have sought out a willing woman at a time like this, but the thought of Jacqueline lying in his arms was unbearable. Would he continue the relationship, knowing that his wife was now nearby? Would she even see him again?

She tried to suppress these feelings, but she also worried about Portia. Was Portia really up to the job? She had panicked and fled and appeared really distraught. Would they want to bring her back to England or send her somewhere else in France? Madeleine tried to wait patiently to find out. She made a point of only seeking out Annie if it was really important. But this time Annie found her. She saw Annie waiting as she came out of church. They greeted each other politely, exchanged words about the weather, then Annie fell into step beside her.

"It's all arranged for Jeanette," she said. "She will take the place of the man who was our observer on the highway south. He's had a stroke and been in hospital until now. He's coming home and will need someone to look after him. Portia will be his long-lost niece, and also our observer."

"Isn't that risky?" Madeleine whispered.

Annie shook her head. "He can't speak at the moment. And he's a bit gaga. She's had some nursing training, so she'll do fine."

"Yes," Madeleine said, feeling relieved that Portia was going to be given an assignment she could handle. And it gave her an excuse to go to the safe house and maybe see Giles again. "I'll deliver the message right away."

It was a blustery autumn day with clouds heavy with the promise of rain as she battled the wind and rode into the forest. She passed only one farmer returning home with horse and cart, who remarked that the weather was about to take a turn for the worse. She had hardly taken a few steps into the forest when the storm broke. Stinging rain drenched her in seconds. She was cold, miserable and out of breath by the time she located the little wooden structure and knocked on the door with the correct code. For a while nobody came. She knocked again, louder this time, worried that nobody was home, that something might have happened and the house had been discovered.

At last the door opened to reveal Giles, dressed only in singlet and underpants, clearly having just awoken from sleep.

"Oh, it's you," she said, gazing at him with delight and longing.

"Come in." He was smiling, running his fingers through ruffled curls. "Welcome to my humble abode."

"I'm sorry. I disturbed you," she said, feeling strangely polite with a man she knew so well.

He grinned. "Rather a rough night last night," he said. "We were supposed to raid a van full of weapons. We got the wrong van and had to get away in a hurry."

"I wish you didn't have to do this," she said.

"I wish it, too, but someone has to," he said. "We can't let these bastards take over our country without a fight. The army caved in too soon. The government caved in. It's only up to us now. It may be useless, but we have to keep on trying."

"Yes," she said. "We have to keep on trying."

"But you—look at you. You're soaked. Come in. Take your wet things off. The stove is working. You can dry them."

She did as she was told, conscious of his presence. She wondered if Jacqueline was still asleep in the back room. An image of the two of them, lying together, came into her head, and she batted it away angrily. She wanted to ask him but didn't want to know.

"I've made some coffee, or at least what pretends to be coffee," he said and poured her a cup. "So what are you doing here? It must be important or you'd not have risked it."

"I have instructions for Jeanette," she said. "They came by radio this morning. Is she still here?"

He shook his head. "Jacqueline took her away to somewhere more suitable. Another safe house with a little more comfort." He smiled at her. Madeleine had forgotten how devastating his smile was.

"London has found a place for her. The cottage on the highway south where there used to be an old man. He's had a stroke and can't talk or move. She's going to be his nurse and also keep a lookout for us."

"Excellent. We've really missed having an observer there. Convoys going south and nobody sees them. You know they plan to occupy the whole of France soon—no more zone libre. It will all be German territory. We have to slow that down as much as possible." He reached for a hook on the wall and took a towel. "Here, dry your hair." He came over to her, put the towel over her head and rubbed vigorously. "It's shorter than it used to be. I liked it long, the way it brushed over your shoulders . . ." His hand traced the curve of her bare shoulder. "God, Maddie, I've missed you." He kissed her shoulder, running his hands over her body. Then she was in his arms and somehow he half carried her through to the bedroom and they were making love as if there was nobody else in the world.

Afterwards they lay silent, their limbs entwined, their hearts beating together. Madeleine felt it was the most perfect moment of her life. *I will remember this forever,* she thought.

"I should go," she said. "I can't be away too long."

"You were sheltering from the storm under a big tree," Giles said. "You couldn't be expected to cycle home in this sort of rain."

"You're right."

He rolled over, and she rested her head against him, feeling the protection of his arm around her.

"We probably shouldn't see each other again," he said. "I don't want to risk compromising you, or you me, for that matter. And I probably won't be using this house again. They try to move us around so there is less likelihood of being recognized. We've more to do on the roads from the east—German supplies coming to Paris." He sat up suddenly. "I wish I could arrange to get you home first. Back to England, I mean."

"But I'm needed here."

He stroked her shoulder. "I could work so much better if I knew you were safe. This is a horrible business, Maddie. If they catch you, God knows what they'll do to you."

Madeleine shuddered. "I know that. They made it quite clear during training what might happen to us."

"You're very brave. I knew when I first met you that you had spunk, but I hadn't realized how strong you could be."

"I have to do it, for Olivier," she said. "He meant everything to me."

"And me too," Giles said. "Now I shall happily slit more German throats knowing I'm doing it for my son."

"Have you heard from your mother since the war began? Is she all right?"

"As you remember, my mother and I don't exactly chat very much. I know that her château was taken over by Germans and she has to live in the gardener's cottage. It's not far from here, of course. I saw her once. Not a smile or a hug or any indication that she was glad to see me. So I stay away. I'll never understand her. She has nobody in the world, but she doesn't want the one person who might have loved her. And anyway, I would not want to put her in danger by being associated with me. Your father is still alive?"

"Yes, but rather frail, I'm afraid. Eleanor looks after him quite well, but both of them drink too much. And they are still in London with bombs dropping all the time."

Giles nodded. "You'd better go," he said. He stood up, pulling her to her feet. "I won't forget today."

"Neither will I," she said.

"It's been lonely. I've thought about you so often. I wanted to write. I wasn't allowed to."

"You've had Jacqueline," she said, surprised at herself for daring to say it out loud.

He laughed. "Jacqueline? I'd say half the men between here and Paris have had Jacqueline. Yes, she's a warm and willing body. That's all." He paused. "But good at what she does. A fierce fighter for our cause. She'll take good care of your little friend." He took her face in his hands. "You are my one true love," he said. "From the moment I first met you, I knew we were meant for each other. We will be together again one day if we can get through this moment of hell."

Madeleine nodded, afraid she might cry. She put on her still damp clothing, took one long last look at Giles, then went out into the storm.

CHAPTER 37

Oliver

Australia

Every day Oliver waited in hope for a letter back from Miss Everingham. After several months, that hope began to fade. Either she had not received his letter or she simply didn't care. It looked as if he was stuck here, stuck forever in a nightmare of work, punishment, chickens, no love.

Christmas was approaching. With it, came the hot weather. The flies became unbearable. Oliver had asked Mr Baxter if he had any spare corks at home. When he explained why he wanted them, that he wanted to construct himself some kind of hat with corks around it to keep the flies at bay, the teacher had responded by bringing him a hat with a net on it. Oliver had almost wept at the sight of it. It made life bearable again.

At Ferndale the children were decorating for Christmas. They were given strips of coloured paper and instructed to make paper chains. It was a pleasant occupation, sitting gluing long chains together. Charlie, ever the tease, made a garland and then dropped it over Oliver's head. "King Oliver," he said. "Or are you the mayor?"

Oliver stared at him, his mouth open.

"What's wrong?" Charlie was still smiling. "Don't you like being king?"

Oliver could hardly breathe. All he was seeing was another bigger boy standing over him and putting something over his head like that.

"We should swap labels. Bit of a giggle." And he had taken something from Oliver and put . . . Oliver frowned, trying to remember . . .

And put another label on a string over Oliver's head. Suddenly he gave a little cry. He heard the voice clearly. "We've got the same name." Oliver Martin Jones. And then . . . then the train had come in, and the children had all rushed to get on, and . . . he never got his own label back!

"I was right," he shouted to Charlie. "It wasn't me. He took my label."

Charlie stared as if Oliver had gone crazy. But Oliver headed for the door. "I have to tell the sisters. I'm not supposed to be here. I knew it."

He ran across the courtyard, knocked on Sister Elizabeth Ann's door and burst in, panting.

"Sister, I've remembered," he said. "Charlie put this chain over my head, and it came back to me. My name's not Jones. I knew it wasn't. It's Oliver Martin."

Sister Elizabeth Ann was frowning.

"Actually it's not even Oliver Martin. I'm really French. It's Olivier Martin."

She smiled now. "Oh yes? Really French, are you? You always have given yourself big ideas, haven't you?"

"But I am French."

"And you speak the language?"

"Bien sûr. Je suis né à Paris. J'y ai vécu jusqu'au début de la guerre," he said, rattling off the French words. *I was born in Paris, and I lived there until the war.*

The frown deepened. She said nothing.

"There was a mix-up at the station, see?" Oliver said. "This big boy—his name was Oliver Martin Jones, and he said we had the same name and we should trade labels for a lark. I didn't want to, but he was bigger, and he took mine off and put his on me instead. And then the train came in and I lost him. And the train was bombed, and I was knocked out and in hospital for a long while, and I didn't remember. I just knew something was wrong, but now it's all come back to me."

"I see." Sister Elizabeth Ann stared at him, long and hard. "And what do you want me to do?"

"See if I still have family in England? See if I'm here by mistake."

"Very well."

Oliver walked out elated. There was a chance his family was alive, that he'd go home and Mummy would be there, and Grandpa, and he'd go back to St Mark's.

When he had gone, Sister Elizabeth Ann met with her fellow sisters. "It does seem as if there was a mix-up and this child was right. The question is—what do we do about it?"

"What can we do?" Sister Jerome said. "If the child's family is found, and he is released, he'll give an account of this place. Probably an exaggerated account. The authorities will come and inspect. What we see as healthy outdoor activity they may choose to call child labour. They may shut us down—send us back to Ireland. We can't let that happen, can we?"

"But that poor child," Sister Margaret said. "If there is a chance he still has family, are we right to deny him that?"

"Do you want to be sent back to Ireland, Sister?" Sister Jerome asked. "I seem to remember you came from a most unhappy background there. You were so glad to enter the order, to get away. And do I need to remind you that you took a vow of obedience?"

"No, sister." The younger nun hung her head.

"And we've devoted our lives to these children," Sister Elizabeth Ann said angrily. "Yes, we are strict and make them work, but we are preparing them for their hard lives ahead."

"But you can see how our methods could be misinterpreted," Sister Jerome said.

"What are you suggesting?"

"After a suitable amount of time, we tell the child that no relative has been found and it doesn't matter what his name is, he still belongs here."

She looked around at the other sisters, who nodded.

CHAPTER 38

Madeleine didn't see Giles again. She realized he was right that any contact might put them both in harm's way. Portia moved into the little house on the main road, and they arranged where to leave messages if Madeleine was not able to bicycle that far out of town. She seemed to relish the job and didn't mind taking care of the stroke victim in the back room.

"I'm just glad to be doing something useful," she said to Madeleine. "He's a dear old man with no relatives nearby. What would have happened to him if I hadn't shown up?"

Autumn turned to winter. The first snowfall made riding a bike hard, and it became too cold for the old fisherman to stand by the river for long. In the house, the challenge was to stay warm. There was a coal ration but no coal to be had. Madeleine went out into the forest to search for fallen wood, but as everyone else in Fontainebleau had the same idea, it was hard to come by. She had learned to go out at first light after a big storm, in the hope that a branch might have been blown down overnight. On days when it snowed hard and they did not want to light the stove too early, they stayed in bed, huddled under comforters.

Food was also a problem. The shelves at the local stores were almost bare. The bread ration was halved. There was no meat apart from the odd piece of offal. The only things still growing in the garden were cabbages and turnips. The chickens had stopped laying. Monsieur Dumas killed one of them, the oldest, and Madame made a huge pot of stock, so that cabbage or turnip soup was their daily main meal.

"I don't know how long we can go on like this," Madame said with a sigh. "The Germans clearly mean to starve us to death. If we kill more chickens, what will we do for eggs next year?"

Next year. Madeleine considered this. She had never known how long their assignment in France was to be, but she hadn't imagined it would stretch on for years. Not that she felt in any immediate danger. With the winter storms, there had not been much to report. She had not heard of any cases of local sabotage, until at Christmas time a lorry carrying food supplies for the Germans was hijacked and the food distributed secretly to local inhabitants. The German commandant was furious and made it clear that any person caught with meat or other foodstuffs destined for his army would be shot immediately. This caused everyone to turn any meat they received into stews, casseroles or pies so it was not readily identifiable. No culprits were identified, and nobody was shot.

The one piece of encouraging news around the same time was that the Americans had entered the war. Maybe they would make a difference, people muttered. In the last war it was the arrival of the Americans that brought about the armistice. Otherwise there was little to cheer about, and little news filtered through now that newspapers only carried what the occupiers wanted people to know. Most battles were far away. There was fighting in North Africa, where the Allies were gaining the upper hand, and in Russia, but Britain had still not been conquered. That was the one small ray of hope during dark days when Madeleine lay curled up in bed.

On Christmas Eve, she went to midnight Mass with Monsieur and Madame Dumas. The church was packed. The whole town was there, and they sang the sweet old carols: "Noël nouvelet" and "Il est né le divin enfant," reminding her sharply of Christmases past—her mother singing the same sweet songs . . . and later Christmas with Giles and Olivier, his delight in his Meccano set and his tricycle and the roast goose shared with Great-Aunt Janine. Aunt Janine. Madeleine sighed. She had thought of her many times. Was she still alive? How was she getting enough to eat? She wished she could write, but of course she couldn't.

They came home to what counted as the Christmas feast: no bûche de Noël this year—the Christmas log made of rolled cake and rich butter frosting. There was no butter to be had. No sugar either. But Madame had made a terrine out of the small piece of ham from the hijacked lorry, and they drank a glass of brandy with it, toasting each other.

Then Madame Dumas handed Madeleine a parcel wrapped in brown paper. "It is not right that Christmas should pass without any presents," she said.

"Oh, but I have nothing to give you." Madeleine's cheeks flushed. "I wanted to, but . . ."

She opened the package, and it was a fur jacket.

"Oh." Madeleine put her hands to her face. "I can't take this. It's lovely."

Madame Dumas smiled. "It was my mother's. I never wear it but kept it for sentimental reasons. My husband and I worried that you did not have warm enough clothing with you for when you are out in the elements. Now you can wear this under your raincoat."

"I don't know how to thank you." Madeleine hugged her impulsively.

Now Madame Dumas blushed. "You are a sweet girl. Like a daughter to us."

And immediately the warmth of the scene exploded into tiny shards. They thought of her as a daughter, and she was bringing them into danger.

~

The next morning they slept late. For the Christmas meal, Monsieur had killed another chicken. "Don't worry about it," he had said. "We'll find someone with a cockerel next spring and hatch some fertilized eggs for the next generation. It's more important that we eat now."

They sat down to a midday meal of roast chicken, roast potatoes and root vegetables. It tasted like the best meal Madeleine had ever eaten. After it the old couple retired for a rest. Madeleine was about to do the same when there was a tap at the front door. She opened it. "I'm sorry. We are closed today," she said. But it was Annie standing there, a package in her arms.

"Merry Christmas," she said in French. "I was thinking about Portia, stuck out there all alone with only the old man who can't speak. I thought we should visit her and take her some cheer. I've half a duck here and a bottle of wine. Shall we go?"

"Is this wise?" Madeleine asked. "We could be seen."

"So what? It's Christmas Day. We are visiting a neighbour with food and wine. Isn't that a normal thing to do?"

Madeleine nodded. "I suppose," she said cautiously.

"Come on. Even the Germans take Christmas Day off from killing people, I'm sure."

Madeleine smiled. "Let me get my new jacket, and we'll go." She left a note to say she had gone to pay a Christmas visit on a sick neighbour and would be back. She put on the new jacket, savouring the warmth, and they set off. Annie had a bicycle, too, and they rode together over the snowy surface of the road. It had snowed the day before, and the trees in the forest sparkled like magic. Portia was amazed and delighted to see them. But also cautious. "He's asleep at the moment, but if he wakes and hears voices?"

"We are neighbours bringing you Christmas cheer," Annie said. "And see what we have brought." She produced the duck and the bottle of wine and put them on the kitchen table. Portia's eyes opened wider. "Mon Dieu, it is a feast," she said. "All we've had is a vegetable casserole and a small sliver of cheese. As soon as spring comes, I'll get the garden going again so we can produce more vegetables, and see if we can get some chickens, too, although I'm told the Germans take them all."

They sat together at the kitchen table and shared the bounty. Portia raised a glass. "To good friends and old times," she said. "May we be celebrating again together one day in happier circumstances."

They clinked glasses, each savouring the moment. Then they rode home again before darkness fell.

~

Winter gradually gave way to spring. Snow melted, leaving paths muddy and treacherous. Madeleine bicycled out to visit Portia or the fisherman and came back with news of German convoys going south. She left messages tucked behind the statue, as always. The messages disappeared, but she didn't run into any members of the Resistance. There were no new acts of sabotage at the château, and some days it was hard to believe that she was a spy in the middle of a war.

Then one day after Mass, she stopped off at the café. She had not received any radio messages from Annie for several days.

"Sorry, I am short-staffed," the café owner said. "Colette has not shown up for work for two days now. She might be ill, but she sends no message."

Madeleine tried to drink her coffee, showing no signs of alarm, but immediately afterwards she rode fast to Annie's address on the road out of the town. She knocked on the front door, but there was no reply. As she stood on the front path, contemplating, a woman came out of the house opposite. "A big black car came in the middle of the night," she said. "They took someone away. I couldn't see who."

Madeleine's heart started racing. They had come for Annie, which might mean they also knew about her. And the radio? Had they found the radio in the attic? She had to go and see. She went around to the back of the house and peeped into windows. The kitchen table was laid for a meal. There was a half-eaten piece of bread on one of the plates, and two bowls of something. A meal that had been interrupted. She tried the back door, and it opened. Taking a deep breath she went inside. The house lay in silence apart from the deep ticktock of a grandfather clock in the hallway.

"Monsieur Gustave?" she called. "Are you there?"

There was no answer. She tiptoed up the first flight of stairs, checking the bedrooms, but they were empty. Then she went up the second flight to the attic rooms. There were two doors leading off a small, uncarpeted landing. The first door led to what was clearly a storage room. Boxes and old furniture piled high. She tried the second one. This seemed more likely. It had no layer of dust, for one thing. Someone had used it recently, and there was a table below a window cut into the slanting room. Madeleine took a step inside and tiptoed towards the table. The radio would be hidden somewhere near . . .

"Are you looking for something, Fräulein?" The voice behind her made her heart leap out of her chest. She spun around. A man was sitting in a small armchair behind the door. He was slim, with fine cheekbones, light hair and light eyes and wearing a black overcoat.

"I was looking for the lady who lives here," she said. "I went to the café this morning as usual and was told she had not shown up for work. I stopped by to see if she was sick and I could help in any way."

"How noble of you," he replied. "And you thought you'd find her up here, hiding under the table in the attic, did you?"

"I was merely checking the whole house," she said. "There was nobody in the bedrooms so I couldn't imagine what had happened."

He was smiling, as if he found this amusing. "I was planning to come and look for you," he said. "But you have saved me the trouble."

"Why would you want to find me?" Madeleine demanded. "I am simply a woman who makes deliveries for a shoe repairman. And I met the lady who lives here at the café. That's all."

"We know exactly who you are, Fräulein," he said in perfect English. "We have your friend from London in custody. We have taken over her radio and enjoyed getting messages from your friends in England. And now you have walked into our parlour, right? Isn't that what the spider said to the fly in your children's rhyme?"

Madeleine tried not to let her distress show. "You have made a mistake, monsieur," she said. "I am Minette Giron, a widow from Paris. I came here after my husband, Jacques, died. I do not understand much English."

This made the German laugh. "No, no, my dear lady. We checked. There was no Jacques Giron who was killed in action. No Minette who lived at your address. We don't know your real name yet, but you will tell us. You will tell us a great many things, I hope." He stood up. He was tall and wearing some kind of black uniform under the greatcoat. "You will come with me now. I think you and I need to have a little chat, don't you?"

"I can't go with you now," she said, still in French. "My employer, Monsieur Dumas, expects me back to make the next delivery. He will wonder what has happened to me."

"He will soon find out, when we bring him in as well," the officer said.

"No!" she blurted out, realizing as she said it that she had made a mistake. She had reacted to something said in English. She could have kicked herself. Stupid.

"You do not wish us to question your employer?" he said, smiling gently now. "To punish him for harbouring a foreign spy?"

"He knows nothing," Madeleine said, still keeping up the charade of answering in French. "I merely rented a room from him and started helping him with his repair service. He is a good man."

"If you don't want him punished, you had better cooperate fully," the man said. "You will come with me now." He took her arm and led her out of the room and propelled her down the first flight of stairs. As they descended the second, he shouted something in German. The front door was opened, and a man in an ordinary German army uniform appeared. Madeleine's captor barked another order. The soldier clicked his heels. "*Jawohl,* Herr Geller." He disappeared out of the front door again.

"Let's go. No fuss now, or we will shoot you on the spot." The man now identified as Herr Geller forced her down the second flight. They came out on to the street, where a big, low Mercedes was now idling. The soldier stood beside it. He opened the back door. Madeleine felt herself propelled towards it, as if in a trance. She could feel Herr Geller's fingers digging into her arm. She was trying to make her brain work, looking around the street, wondering if she could give a message to anyone to tell Monsieur Dumas. But people had mysteriously disappeared at the sight of the soldiers. There was no one within shouting distance.

"After you, my dear."

Madeleine glanced around for a second. If she broke free and ran, what chance would she have? Two German soldiers would quickly catch and overpower her. They might just shoot her. Besides, her legs didn't want to obey her. Before she could react sensibly, she was forced into the back seat of the vehicle. Herr Geller climbed in beside her. The soldiers took the front seat, and the doors were closed. The engine started, and the vehicle began to move, gliding forwards with little sound. So this was it—the moment she had dreaded all this time. She was in the custody of the Gestapo.

CHAPTER 39

They were driving north, Madeleine decided, away from Fontainebleau. She had expected to be taken to the château, but they were on the road leaving the town, heading into the forest. She watched the trees go past, the car moving from dappled shade into sunlight. She wondered if she was being taken to headquarters in Paris or merely into the forest to be shot? But no, they wanted information from her, she was sure. She wondered how much Annie had told them. What had they done to her, because clearly she must have betrayed Madeleine? She wondered about Portia. Did they know about her? Had they brought her in yet? Was there any way to warn her? She tried to think clearly, working out what she would say, how much she could give away to make them satisfied. She tried not to think about what they might do to her. She remembered giving birth to Olivier—had she been good at withstanding pain? Probably not. She had yelled, she remembered. She had even cursed Giles.

As they travelled along the narrow road, not a word was spoken. She was conscious of the slim, meticulous man beside her but wouldn't allow herself to glance once in his direction. He was smoking a cigarette, and the smoke made her eyes prickle. Instead she stared out of the window, marvelling at how attractive the forest looked. Gradually trees gave way to open countryside, houses, the beginnings of a town. They came to the Seine and crossed by a bridge, first to an island and then into a town. Madeleine noticed incongruous things—swans on the Seine, gliding easily along, the tall towers of a Romanesque church, a pleasant town centre, similar to Fontainebleau, with yellow stone buildings with blue shutters, a square with a garden in the middle. A sign said, *The best cakes in Melun*, revealing where they were. Melun. The next town up the river from Fontainebleau. She waited to see if they would drive through it and continue on to Paris, but instead they came to a halt outside what had probably been the town hall. Now a long Nazi flag hung from an upstairs window. The car door was opened. Her captor stepped out first, came around and offered her a hand to help her from the back seat. It was such a strange gesture of kindness that she began to have hope.

"This way, my dear," he said, and led her up the steps and into the building. Once inside they were met by other men, one also in the black uniform. Herr Geller exchanged a few words in German, then gave a command to one of the soldiers.

"Follow me," he said in French. She glanced around. Armed guards standing by the front doors, several other armed men in the room. No chance to run. She followed, along a marble hallway, down a flight of steps. She was now entering a basement. At the bottom she was greeted by a stout middle-aged woman, wearing what looked like a matron's dress.

"In here," she said in French and opened a door. Madeleine stepped into a small square room. No windows. No furniture apart from a bench along one wall. A naked light bulb hung from the ceiling.

"Take off your coat and shoes," the woman commanded. Madeleine did it.

"Now your other clothing." Feeling horribly vulnerable, Madeleine removed her skirt and jumper. Did the woman mean all her clothes? Was she to be naked?

"You may keep on the undergarments," the woman said and proceeded to pat her down very thoroughly. Satisfied, she nodded. "Give me your watch and purse. You will wait here until they are ready for you." And she left. Madeleine sat on the bench, trying to think clearly. She went through every detail of her training. What was she going to tell them? And if they started to torture her, how long could she hold out? Suddenly she remembered they had taken away her raincoat—the coat with a special button on it, containing the suicide pill. No way to escape from what lay ahead. She sat, trying to control her breathing. The room felt horribly cold and damp, and she shivered in her silky under-slip. Minutes passed. Then hours. Nobody came. She felt an urgent need to urinate and found there was a bucket under the bench. But she didn't want to give them the satisfaction of seeing that she used it. Were they actually spying on her? At last she could hold it no longer and had to pull out the bucket. The smell of urine now hovered in the room. The smell of fear. As soon as they came for her, they would know she was afraid.

Hunger gnawed at her stomach. She wished she had asked for some bread to go with her coffee that morning. How long ago that seemed now—another world, another universe. Her mouth now felt dry. She lay on the bench and tried to sleep. At last a door opened, and Herr Geller came in. He was smoking a slim cigarette again.

"Not very comfortable accommodation," he said. "I must apologize. Now I hope you've had time to think about things and be a good girl and cooperate. Your friend with the radio has already told us most of what we want to know, but you can corroborate her story. Now, your real name please."

"Minette Giron," she said.

For a moment, anger flashed across his face, then he controlled himself. "I do hope you are not going to be stupid," he said. "I am a civilized man. I like to do things in a civilized fashion. Others here are not so restrained. I can assure you that you can either talk to me now or tell them everything later. I don't think you can have any idea what if feels like to have your fingernails removed, one by one. Or to be burned with a poker. Burns are most painful, are they not? Even small burns like this." He moved across and touched the cigarette end against her bare thigh. Madeleine gasped, tried not to cry out or even show pain, but she felt tears spurting from her eyes as he kept it there, watching her face. "Now think of a poker, straight from the fire," he said. "On which part of you will they choose to employ it?" He was smiling again, enjoying this. He removed the cigarette. Madeleine felt her leg continue to burn.

"I must confess that you are an attractive woman. I quite desire you myself." He ran a finger down her front, tracing the outline of her breast. "But I am not a selfish man. I like to share. I have soldiers here who have not been with a woman in months or years. They would welcome the chance . . ."

All the time he spoke he was watching her face. She fought to stay calm. Then he laughed. "I, of course, might enjoy watching. So you see, my dear, there are many fine options waiting for you. And all of them will vanish if you just tell us what we want to know."

"I have nothing much to tell," Madeleine said. "I was recruited because I had lived in Paris and my mother was half-French. But I did not do well in my training at either cyphers or radio operation, so they decided to use me as a courier. I took messages that came by radio from London, and I left them in places to be picked up by other operatives I never met. That's all I did, I assure you."

"You never met other operatives? I find that strange. A cell is usually composed of several people—observers, courier, radio operator and the liaison with the local Resistance. I hardly think it was worth their while putting you here if you never met anybody."

"I had to leave messages in code that the radio operator had written in various places for the Resistance to pick up."

"Ah yes. The Resistance. They have been quite active around here, an ongoing nuisance of small sabotage—telephone lines cut, vehicles disabled—which makes me think you may have been helpful to them. And yet you say you never met them. I find that hard to believe. And you had no contact with observers? Strange. Very well. If you insist. I will leave you now. And next time I come, you will remember some names, or I will have to take you to another room that is not quite as pleasant as this one. Your choice entirely."

~

He left Madeleine alone again. She had no idea what time it was, whether it was day or night. The light bulb bathed the room in glaring light. She heard no sound from the outside world. The burn continued to throb. Finally the door was opened, and the woman who had taken her clothing came in. She brought a bowl of some meagre soup and a piece of bread. "We don't want you passing out on them before they get any information, do we?" she said in a matter-of-fact way.

"You are French," Madeleine said. "Why do you do this?"

A brief spasm of pain crossed the woman's face. "I need to feed my family," she said and left the room hurriedly.

Madeleine turned to the soup. It looked and smelled like cabbage water with a couple of cabbage leaves floating in it. But it was warm, and she dipped the bread into it, savouring each mouthful. She still found it hard to believe this was happening to her. It would only be a matter of time before they killed her, she was sure. If only she still had the cyanide pill, she could have ended it now. That seemed like a wonderful idea at this moment—if she died, she would be with Olivier again. Would there be a heaven, and would Maman be there, and her dear son? And if there wasn't, at least she'd be out of misery.

She realized her fear was that she would betray Giles, or Portia, or the old fisherman. Her thoughts turned to Annie, and to Monsieur Gustave. They must have taken him, too, as he wasn't in his house. Was Annie here in this building? Tentatively she tapped on her wall, using Annie's Morse identifier. She tried it again. Very faintly she heard the reply. "Here. Didn't crack." Then Annie tapped, "Stay strong."

"God bless," Madeleine tapped back.

She lay down, not sure if she should try to sleep or not. She remembered the drill when they had seized her in the middle of the night. But weariness overtook her. She began to hallucinate, seeing things floating before her eyes, until ultimately she dozed. Again she had no idea how long she had slept and what time it was, but the matron returned with a piece of bread and a beaker of water. She used some of the water to splash on her face before drinking the rest. The bread was stale and hard to swallow. But at least she was awake and ready for them when they came.

At last she heard the sound of boots outside her door. It was flung open. Several soldiers stood there. "You will come with us," one of them said in English.

They marched her along a narrow hallway. Pipes ran overhead. It was quite dark apart from an occasional light bulb. At the end of the hall, she was thrust into a big bright room. She blinked in the strong light, and the first thing she saw was Annie, being dragged across the floor like a broken doll. Her face was bruised almost beyond recognition. Her mouth hung open. One eye was swollen shut. Madeleine could smell burned flesh. She recoiled in horror.

As she passed, Annie raised her head. "Didn't tell . . . ," she said. Her head slumped forwards again as Madeleine was propelled towards where Herr Geller was sitting in a leather chair, a cigarette in his fingers. He looked pleased to see her.

"Time for our little chat," he said. "I do hope you've thought this through and you're going to cooperate. Your foolish friend. It took a lot to break her, but break her we did, in the end. Now she will be sent to Ravensbrück. Do you know it? A concentration camp for women like you. Not a pleasant place, I am told. But where are my manners? Do take a seat." He motioned to the upright chair across from him. She sat, shivering, even though the room was rather warm.

"So, let's begin again. You were sent from England to be a spy for the enemy, correct?"

"Not a spy. A messenger."

"Same thing. And you were placed with a Monsieur Dumas—a man who has a supposed repair business, which gives him the opportunity to deliver messages as well as shoes. Is he part of the Resistance, do you know? Or just a stupidly loyal Frenchman?"

"Monsieur Dumas knows nothing of this," Madeleine said angrily. "They are just a kind couple who made me welcome in their house."

"And didn't wonder why a young woman arrives out of the blue and goes off on a bicycle here and there? And maybe receives messages from other strange women?"

"I told them I no longer felt safe in Paris. They were kind to me, but no messages were ever delivered to the house. They knew nothing."

"If we bring them in, I wonder if they will tell us a different tale?"

"No!" Madeleine shouted the word. It echoed from the bare walls. "They know nothing of what I did. They are an old couple. Please . . . don't put them through this. They have nothing to tell you."

"You, on the other hand," Herr Geller said slowly, "have plenty to tell me if you choose. So if you want me to leave your landlord alone, give me names. Your contacts. Who watched traffic on the Seine? Who watched traffic on the road south?"

"I don't know," Madeleine said. "It was all set up so that we never met. I rode out and found messages in a hollow tree. I passed on those messages."

"You passed on those messages, to the Resistance."

"Yes. I left messages behind a statue in the wayside shrine."

"And you never met a member of the Resistance?"

"No."

"So how did they know whether to trust you? I understand they are very picky about who they trust, as we have set traps for them before. I am quite sure they would not have accepted messages from an unknown person. So I ask you again, what were the names of the members of the Resistance you dealt with? And where did they have a hideout nearby? We know they did, because several times they vanished into the forest and were not found."

"I know nothing of this," she said. "I told you. I left messages at the shrine. That's all."

"Dear me, you are proving as stupidly stubborn as your friend," he said. "I did admire her bravery, but it was useless in the end."

"If she told you everything you wanted to know, you don't need to hear it from me," Madeleine said. Scoring a point against this man made her feel more powerful.

"All the same, we shall enjoy hearing it from you. And the one thing she didn't know was the names of the Resistance contacts. These we need. Those you are going to give us now." He snapped his fingers. Two soldiers stepped forward, grabbed both of Madeleine's arms and took her over to the wall, holding her up against it. Her legs didn't seem to want to support her. Herr Geller walked slowly over to the stove in the corner. He opened the front and removed a poker. It glowed red with heat. In fact, she could feel the heat from it as he came towards her.

"Tell him!" screamed a voice inside her head. "Tell him Jacqueline. Jacqueline. Her name is Jacqueline!"

But she couldn't. If Jacqueline in turn was tortured, she'd give them Giles. Madeleine heard herself give a whimper. The heat from the poker was now intense.

"Now you are going to tell me, aren't you?" Herr Geller said. "The names of your contacts and the names of those in the Resistance and where we might find them."

"I know no names." She managed to get out the words.

"Of course you do. And bravery won't help you, you know. Once we've broken you, you'll go to Ravensbrück with that other pathetic female. Or we may just shoot you here. As we choose."

If they were going to kill her anyway, perhaps she could hold on, she told herself. Eventually she'd faint. Eventually . . . After how long, though?

Suddenly there was a knock at the door, and a soldier came in. "Sorry to interrupt, Herr Geller," he said, "But this just arrived. Herr Harzmann thought you should see it immediately."

He handed a note to Herr Geller, who put the poker carefully back in the stove before turning to the note. As he read it, Madeleine watched his expression change, from confusion to incredulity, almost amusement. He folded it again and looked up. "Well, well," he said. "I have here a letter from a man who claims to be the head of the local Resistance cell. He is stating that if we let you go, he will surrender to us. Isn't that touching? You two must have had quite a fling for him to exchange his life for yours."

"He's my husband," Madeleine said angrily. "The father of my child. And I won't accept. I won't let him do this."

"So noble." Herr Geller shook his head. "But you have no say in the matter. Of course we'd rather have him than you. You, my dear, are small potatoes, as they say. He is valuable. If we can take down an entire Resistance cell, we can have peace and quiet for a while. So I shall reply that we'll be delighted to do the exchange."

"How will we know that you'll keep your word? That you won't kill both of us?"

"My dear, I am a man of honour," he said. "I come from an old family. If this husband of yours shows up, I guarantee that you will not be harmed or killed or sent to a concentration camp. There, does that satisfy you?"

"How can it satisfy me to lose the man I love?" she demanded. "I would willingly give my life in exchange for his."

Herr Geller nodded to the soldiers. "Take her back to her cell. We'll see if the brave husband actually goes through with this before anything else happens to her."

And Madeleine was led away.

CHAPTER 40

More endless waiting, sitting on the hard plank, staring at four blank walls. No sounds came through from the outside world. She was no longer conscious of hunger or thirst, just a deep dread in the pit of her stomach. Giles was going to turn himself in, and he'd be tortured and killed. To have found him again had been a miracle, hope in her darkest hours. And now he was to be taken from her forever. She closed her eyes, trying to shut out the pain. If only there was something she could do to prevent it, some kind of miracle in which the Resistance swooped in to rescue them both. But this was war: there were no happy endings. She realized that only too well. And so she waited. She tried to pass the time by reciting every poem she had ever learned in school. When she got to Browning's "Oh, to be in England Now That April's Here," she felt tears trickling down her cheek.

I shouldn't have come here, she told herself. *What have I achieved by being here? All that's happened is that my beloved husband is going to die, and it's my fault.* Black despair engulfed her.

At last she heard the sound of the key turning in the lock, and Herr Geller came in. "You will be pleased to know that the man you love has arrived, as he promised," he said. "When he has told us what we need to know, you will be removed from this place. Until then . . ." He shrugged, closed the door and left.

More endless hours, half dozing, hallucinations and great waves of guilt. She tried not to imagine what they were doing to Giles. He would not give in without a fight, she knew. Another bowl of cabbage soup and a piece of bread was brought to her. They had not changed the bucket under the plank, and the room now stank. She was still in her satin slip and trembled uncontrollably. She tapped Annie's call sign but there was no returning tap. Annie had gone, either to the concentration camp, or she was dead. There was nobody.

She curled in a ball and must have dozed off to sleep because she woke with a start when she heard the key in the lock again. Two German soldiers came in. "Come," one of them said. She stood up, feeling dizzy from lack of substantive food, and found it hard to walk. He grabbed her forearm and led her out of the room, this time towards the stairs.

"I can't go up there. I'm not dressed," she retorted.

"Up!" Clearly his French was limited.

She climbed the stairs, blinking as she came to daylight. The sun was streaming in through an open front door. An early morning sun. Was she being released? Soldiers marched beside her out of the front door, down the steps. In the square beyond, a crowd had gathered. She shrank back, arms crossed, conscious of her near nakedness. She was marched forwards relentlessly, her bare feet reacting to the cobbles, and she saw that one part of the square was cordoned off and Herr Geller was standing in front of the crowd. People were staring at her with looks of surprise and pity. One woman took off her own shawl and darted forward. "Here, my dear," she said. "You should not have to be seen like this." Madeleine gave her a grateful smile and draped it around her. The men came to a halt at the front of the crowd. Herr Geller nodded in approval.

"Now we can proceed," he said. "Bring out the prisoner."

And Giles was brought out. He walked erect and proudly between lines of soldiers, although he was barefoot and wearing only an undershirt and trousers. He stared straight ahead until he saw Madeleine.

"You shouldn't have done this," she shouted to him. "You're more valuable than me. I didn't want it. I tried to refuse . . ."

"Hush, mon amour," he said. "It's all right. Don't worry. You are going to be free. That's all that matters. Go back to England. Lead a happy life."

"How can I when you're the only thing I love? I love you so much."

"And I love you."

There were murmurs from the crowd as some of them overheard this.

"Let him go, you bastards!" a voice shouted.

"You'll regret this. We won't forget," another called. Soldiers searched for the speakers.

"I'm so sorry," she said. He was almost close enough to touch now. She shook herself free from her escort and ran to him. "It shouldn't have to end this way. It's not right. I would have done anything to stop them . . ."

"I'm sorry, too," he said. "I'm afraid it was Jacqueline. She betrayed you. Jealousy, I think, not realizing that by giving you up she'd also condemned me."

"I love you so much." Tears were now streaming down her cheek.

"I love you, too, my darling one." His eyes, also full of tears, held hers with great longing.

"Goodbye." She tried to embrace him but was jerked back.

"We'll meet again in heaven," he said. "I'll wait for you."

"There is no heaven," she wanted to say but stopped herself. *Let Giles have one hope,* she decided as he was led past her.

Herr Geller stepped forwards as Giles was marched before the crowd. "This man has committed acts of atrocity and vandalism against the German army," he said. "Let him be a lesson to any of you who think they might want to follow in his footsteps. Anyone who defies us will pay the price."

As he spoke, Giles was tied to a post, and a soldier produced a blindfold.

"Take that away," Giles snapped. "I want my wife's face to be the last thing I see."

Again there was an angry murmur from the crowd.

"Remember your promise, Geller," Giles called out. "You let her go."

Herr Geller walked over to him and said something in a low voice that the crowd could not hear. Giles reacted with a roar of anger, struggling like an animal against his bonds. "You promised, you swine."

They could not hear Geller's answer, but he was smiling. A line of soldiers now took up position, kneeling with guns pointed at Giles.

"I curse you to hell for this, Geller," he shouted. "You and your family. May you rot in hell and." He went to say something more, but Geller raised his hand. "Fire," he shouted, and Giles slumped forward, blood spurting from his chest.

CHAPTER 41

An angry murmur ran around the crowd. Madeleine put her hand to her mouth so that she didn't scream or vomit. She couldn't take her eyes away from Giles's body, hanging there with a small trail of blood running across the dais. *This cannot be real,* she told herself.

"Now go home," Geller shouted, "and remember to tell any friends who think that the Resistance is a good idea what will happen to them. Go. Go. My men have orders to shoot anyone who lingers."

The crowd dispersed. Madeleine stood there, still overwhelmed with horror and grief, with her army escort on either side. Herr Geller came up to her. "Bring my car," he commanded, and one of the soldiers ran off.

The car arrived. Herr Geller opened the back door. "Get in," he said.

Madeleine obeyed. He climbed in beside her. The car glided off.

"Where are you taking me?" she asked. "Can I have my clothes back, since I'm to be released?"

"We will find you some new clothes, if you are a good girl," he said. "You are coming with me, back to the château where I am staying. It's quite pleasant there. You'll like it."

"What?" She spun to face him. "You promised my husband that I would be released. You gave your word."

He was smiling again, that cruel, tight-lipped smile. "No, actually I promised that you wouldn't be harmed and you wouldn't be sent to a concentration camp. I am abiding by that promise. But you see, I have been rather lonely here in France. Such a cold and lonely bed. And I find you quite desirable."

"That's what you told Giles before you killed him," she said, staring at him in horror. "He gave his life for nothing. You are a despicable man."

He put one hand on her knee and ran it up her thigh. "I rather hope you'll come to like me after a while."

"I'd rather die," she said.

He laughed. "I do like a spirited woman. But you see, my dear, you will not have a chance to die. I intend to keep you alive and well for as long as I find you pleasurable."

The car drove out of the town, into the countryside. Madeleine stared out of the window, trying to remember everything they passed. She was going to escape. She was not going to let this vile man win. At last they turned in through an impressive brick gateway and up a gravel drive to a handsome grey stone building, set amid attractive grounds. Herr Geller got out and went ahead into the house. He returned, motioning that the two soldiers should bring Madeleine in. They held a tight grip on her as they half dragged her out of the car and in through the front door to a marble-tiled foyer. A curved flight of marble stairs ascended on the right, and she was marched up those. The wall was covered in old family portraits—men on horseback, men with curly wigs who stared down at her, their gazes mocking her helplessness. Then along a long hallway, adorned with more paintings and in through a door at the far end. It was a pleasant room with a high moulded ceiling, a four-poster bed in the middle, an enormous wardrobe on one wall, two upholstered chairs by a fireplace, which was not lit, a dressing table with mirror.

"Well, here we are," Herr Geller said. "An agreeable room, is it not? A lovely view over the grounds." He closed the door, leaving just the two of them alone. "Now, I hope you're going to be sensible. You might even come to enjoy it. I am told I'm rather good at it."

As he spoke, he came towards her and pulled down the strap of her slip. Madeleine was frozen in revulsion. She tried to think of self-defence classes in Scotland. Could she kill him? Escape through a window?

She sensed he'd rather enjoy a fight, overpowering her, forcing her to submit. And so she stood. Never taking his eyes off her face for one second, he released the second strap, then the brassiere beneath it and the panties, until she was standing there naked. All the time he had the ghost of a smile on his face. She stood like a statue. *I am made of stone,* she told herself. *I am white marble.* He grunted with impatience as he threw her on to the bed with great force. She turned her face away as he raped her.

"Such a nice little body," he said as he got up. "Until tonight then, *ma petite*. And don't think of doing anything foolish because there will be a guard watching you at all times." He blew her a kiss as he left.

~

Day followed day. Night followed night. She searched the room thoroughly, but there was nothing she could use as a weapon. A guard sat outside her door. The windows only opened a few inches. She tried to see if there was any way she could hang herself, but the ceiling was too high. Off the bedroom was a small bathroom with a toilet and washbasin. Again there was a small window, but too small to climb through. She even checked the chimney—hadn't they put small boys up chimneys during Victorian times? But this one was narrow, and she could not even see daylight at the top.

The irony was that during the daytime her life was not unpleasant. Good meals were brought up to her—the Germans still had butter, meat, cheese, rich sauces. The guard sat with her as she ate, then removed the cutlery. She was never given a knife. Herr Geller brought up a book from the library and offered to replace it when she had read it. He was polite and charming to her, which only infuriated her even more. He also smelled faintly of eau de cologne. At night, when he had finished with her, he left to go to another bedroom, presumably not wanting to risk her smothering him in his sleep.

During the day she sat by the window, looking out, hoping against hope to attract the attention of a gardener, someone who might show her sympathy. But she realized they would think her complicit—she would be a German whore, to be despised. She thought a lot about Annie and wondered if she was still alive. Poor, brave Annie, who hadn't betrayed her, even under terrible torture. Would she also be sent to Ravensbrück when Herr Geller tired of her? She wondered. She thought of Portia. Had she managed to escape, or had the Germans captured her, too? And the lovely old couple, Monsieur and Madame Dumas—had they been punished for harbouring her? Not knowing drove her mad.

Then one day she heard voices down below. Two people were walking towards the château. She heard a woman's imperious voice: "I don't care what they have told you. I know I am no longer in charge, and I am forced to live in my gardener's cottage. It's still my garden, and they are not digging it up!"

A tall, distinguished woman with grey hair was walking beside a man Madeleine had seen before—one of the gardeners. Madeleine watched her with growing excitement. There was something about her . . . Surely she recognized her: it was Giles's mother. She was in the château where he was born.

CHAPTER 42

Suddenly Madeleine had renewed hope. If only she could get a message to Giles's mother, perhaps she would help. She was well aware that Giles and his mother had long been estranged. She had not wanted to see her daughter-in-law or her grandson, so perhaps she wouldn't care if Madeleine was imprisoned by a German gestapo agent. But just maybe . . .

She watched every day when and where Giles's mother took her walk. She was passionate about her garden, that was for sure. She personally trimmed roses, weeded beds, picked flowers. Madeleine couldn't see from her window where the gardener's cottage was that she now had to live in. She wondered if she dared shout out to her as she passed, but the guards might hear, and maybe she'd be moved to a less pleasant room. Or chained up.

Slowly she formulated a plan. She would let Geller think she had come to accept her fate. She would be docile and even smile a little. Then maybe he'd give her more freedom—a walk in the grounds, perhaps? But she had no outdoor clothing. He had brought her a robe, a couple of negligées, fluffy slippers, but nothing that could be worn outside. She wouldn't get far in a feather-trimmed robe. If only she could write a note and lob it down on to the gravel when her mother-in-law walked past. But she had no writing materials. Pens were sharp.

"So you are coming to enjoy it after all," Herr Geller said as he left her the next night. "I knew you would." He put on his purple silk robe and left her. As always she rushed straight to the bathroom and washed as thoroughly as she could. The next morning she searched the room to see if there was anything she could throw down to attract her mother-in-law's attention. The great wardrobe was empty, except for spare towels on the top shelf. All the drawers in the dressing table had been cleared out, except for some handkerchiefs and a couple of face cloths. But amid the handkerchiefs she found a lavender sachet and, in the far corner of a drawer, a tiny vial of perfume—the sort of thing that would be handed out at Printemps. She thought both might be useful, although she was not sure how. Then one lunchtime she was served pickled beetroot. She realized the significance instantly, scooped some off the plate when the guard wasn't looking. He had grown more relaxed, or was it lazy, by now and hardly ever watched her. She stood up. "Sorry. Bathroom." He didn't speak much French. He nodded.

She rushed to the bathroom and deposited the beetroot in her tooth mug. She added a little water, washed the red stain from her hand, flushed the toilet and came back, giving her guard a little smile. After he had gone, she tried writing with her fingernail on one of the pages of her current book. It wasn't successful. She tried the end of her toothbrush, then the tip of her comb. Finally she broke off one of the teeth of the comb. This might just work. Next she managed to unpick one end of the lavender sachet. Finally she found an almost clean page at the end of a chapter in the book and tore it out. On it she wrote: *Help. G's wife. Here. Prison* . . . She folded the paper and stuffed it inside the lavender sachet.

That afternoon she waited until Giles's mother came past, then reached out of the window and tossed down the perfume vial. She saw Madame Martin react with surprise as it landed in front of her, pick it up, then look up in Madeleine's direction. Madeleine stood at the window and waved. Her mother-in-law frowned. Taking a deep breath Madeleine tossed out the lavender sachet. Madame Martin picked this up and continued on her walk as if nothing had happened. Now all Madeleine could do was to hope.

Evening turned to night. Herr Geller was in a good mood. "You'll be pleased to know that the whole local cell of Resistance has now been rounded up," he said. "No more Resistance nonsense in this part of the country. I may be moving south soon. One gathers that Resistance fighters are growing brazen near Bordeaux, and there is work to be done with the French Jews. We've finally been given the order to round them all up and deport them. About damned time!"

Madeleine tried not to let her disgust show on her face. "But some of them have lived in France for generations. It's their home."

"I'm sure rats feel at home in your cellar," he said. "It doesn't mean they have any right to be there, and of course you exterminate them." And he pulled her towards him.

If he was moving south, would he take her with him? She wondered. She didn't think he'd just let her go. But tonight he was unusually chatty. "Tell me where you come from," he said.

"I was born and grew up in London," she replied. "My mother was half-French and spoke to me in that language until she died when I was ten. Then I was sent to boarding school. I went to Paris to study and met my husband. I lived there until the war."

"Do you miss England? I spent an agreeable year at Cambridge," he said.

"I miss my former life," she said with a shrug. "My family."

"I am also far from home," he said. "I am from Bohemia, actually—the German ethnic part of Czechoslovakia that our Führer has now reclaimed for the Reich. But I miss my family, too. I have not seen them for three years now."

"I have no family to miss any more," she said flatly. "You killed my husband and my son."

"Perhaps you will have more sons," he said, giving her a knowing look as he stroked her knee. She had to hide her desire to kill him and not let him see how this statement had terrified her. *Soon,* she thought. *I must escape before it's too late.* She prayed Giles's mother would come through. She had, after all, picked up the lavender sachet, but that was probably just because she was intrigued.

The next afternoon Madeleine waited by the window. At last Madame Martin came, wearing a big hat today. She did not look up but walked past slowly. When she came level with Madeleine's window, she called out loudly to her gardener, standing still long enough for Madeleine to see that on top of her hat she had pasted two words: *Ce soir.* This evening.

Madeleine could scarcely contain her excitement. She had to be ready. She put on undergarments, a slip and the robe. The slippers would be no use as she could not run in them. Her evening meal was brought. She tried to conceal the fork, but her guard was attentive and whisked the plate away as soon as she had finished eating. She drank the red wine to give herself courage, then went to watch at the window. She had no idea what an elderly woman could do and was terrified that Herr Geller would return before any plan could be put into place.

Just as it was getting dark, she heard voices: a man's voice. "Stop, madame. You may not enter. You may not go . . ."

"This is my house, whatever you may think, and you can't stop me!" Madame Martin's voice, loud and clear, coming up the stairs.

"No, madame! You may not."

"I just want to find my spare glasses, that's all. Glasses, you know. *Brille.* I know I left them here in a drawer somewhere. I've broken my only glasses, and I can't see properly without them. Would you want an old woman not to be able to see?"

"But I have my orders . . ."

"You can come with me, if you are frightened I might do something wrong. They are in the blue bedroom, I'm sure."

The voices passed her door.

"Come back, madame, or I will have to . . ."

Madeleine opened her door an inch or two. Her guard was gone after her mother-in-law. She was going to dash down the stairs, but another thought came to her. She opened her door wide, then ran back and hid in the wardrobe.

It only took a moment until she heard loud shouts in German. They had noticed she had gone. Boots clattered down the stairs. Madeleine came out and glanced around. Giles's mother was standing at the top of the stairs. "Quick," she whispered. "Go that way. Servant's stair. Hide in the uniform cupboard. Wait till it's dark."

Madeleine flashed her a grateful smile, sped down the hall and opened the door to the servant's staircase—a narrow stone stair that wound down to a dingy hallway. The only light came from a window at the end. Cooking smells wafted towards her. Onions frying. Off to her right, she could hear sounds of pots clattering coming from the kitchen. She tried one door. Broom cupboard. Another: butler's pantry. Then she spotted uniforms hanging from a bar across a whole cupboard. She squeezed in behind them, wrapping a dark cape over her head and draping a black maid's dress over her feet so they wouldn't be seen. She waited, holding her breath. She worried about Giles's mother. Would she be punished for her role in this?

Nobody came for a long while, then Herr Geller's voice, close by: "You saw nothing? She didn't come this way? You didn't see her run past?"

"Oh my honour, monsieur, I saw nobody. No one has come this way. I'd have seen if she tried to escape through the back door."

A door was opened and slammed shut. Then her door. She was sure he'd hear the beating of her heart. A mere second, and it was slammed shut again.

"Keep searching the grounds. She can't have got far. She has no clothes or shoes. Put out the alert for her."

And the voices died away. She heard the clatter of washing-up, the cook's heavy tread as she went past, presumably going up to bed. When all had been silent for a long while, she opened the cupboard door cautiously, listened, then crept out. She snatched one of the uniforms, pulled the black cape around her as she opened the back door and hugged the wall of the château until she spotted the shape of a cottage, off on the other side of a kitchen garden. A light glowed in a window—a single candle. She crept past rows of beans and peas, keeping low all the time, then through an orchard, trying to move silently from tree to tree. Up in the house she saw lights still burning. Maybe they were searching for her, room by room. And guarding the main gate. She made a final desperate dash to the cottage door, tapped gently and heard the bolt being retracted.

"Well done," said the distinguished-looking lady. "Quick, inside. You'd better go up to the attic tonight. They've already searched once, but they may do so again." She indicated a stepladder. Madeleine climbed, pushing open a small trapdoor. Up there a mattress had been laid on the floor, and there was a jug of water and bread and salami beside it.

"You'll be safe enough," Giles's mother said. She studied Madeleine, staring up at her. Then she climbed up beside her with remarkable agility. "I can't believe it is you, of all people. We were told the officer had brought a French tart to live with him."

"I was an undercover agent, sent from London. I was arrested. They were going to torture and kill me, but Giles gave himself up instead."

"Giles is still in this region?"

"He was. He's dead now. They shot him."

"They shot my son?"

Madeleine nodded.

"I had no idea he was still close by. I was stupid. And now he's dead."

"He gave himself up so that they would let me go." Madeleine fought back tears. "But they didn't let me go. That awful man brought me here instead as his mistress. I've been trying to come up with a way to escape and I saw you, and I hoped against hope that you'd want to help me."

"My dear." Giles's mother reached out to touch her hand, "I am so sorry. What an ordeal. But let's not risk talking any more tonight. Put down the trapdoor. I'll hide the ladder and they won't ever suspect."

Madeleine did as she was told. She lay down and fell asleep. Early in the morning she heard muffled voices: Madame Martin's shrill, "You've already disturbed me once. Do you think I'd want to hide a tart who goes with Germans? I am a true Frenchwoman."

She heard movements down below. And then a door slamming. She sat up. Light came in between the slats of the roof. Birdsong was deafening, a pigeon sitting right above her. She drank some water and splashed more on her face. Soon after, her mother-in-law appeared on the stepladder, bringing up coffee, a boiled egg, bread and cherries.

"I think it would be wise to stay here for a few days," she said. "They will tire of looking here and naturally assume that you have got away."

"I don't want to put you in danger," Madeleine said. "I feel so guilty about Giles. I didn't want to accept when he volunteered to take my place, but they wouldn't listen to me."

"He must have loved you very much to sacrifice his life for you."

"He did. He sent Olivier and me to England when France was invaded."

"But you left your son and came back to be with your husband?"

Madeleine shook her head. "Our son was killed in the bombing. I felt so angry I had to do something. I volunteered to go undercover in France, and by chance I was sent here. I didn't even know Giles was still alive. I hadn't heard anything for a long while. It was like a dream to see him again. And then . . ." Tears trickled down her cheek.

"I'm so sorry, my dear. I always thought my son would turn out to be a no-good like his father. But it seems he was an honourable man."

"He was a wonderful man," Madeleine said angrily. "He really wanted to do good in the world. I wish you'd known him better. And Olivier. I wish you'd known your grandson. Such a delightful little boy—so curious and wise."

"I did see him a couple of times," the older woman said. "I came up to Paris. I watched your apartment. I saw you pushing him in a pram, and later, I saw him riding a tricycle as you went for your walk in the bois."

"Why didn't you come and speak to us? Giles so wanted you to know his family."

"I was going to, but stupid pride, I suppose. And now it's too late. I have nobody."

"You have me," Madeleine said. "After all this is over, maybe we can become properly acquainted?"

"Maybe," Madame Martin said.

CHAPTER 43

Madeleine stayed hidden in the attic for a week. Giles's mother brought her food and news. "I eat quite well," she said. "My cook, who now has to cook for those German swine, makes sure I get some of their food. And she also says they think you'll be making for the coast. There are reports of your having been seen in the forest, and even one that you've been picked up by a plane. It might be possible to move on. Where had you planned to go?"

"I have no idea," Madeleine said. "Herr Geller told me he had rounded up all the Resistance fighters in the area, so I'd have no one to help me. I need to contact London, but I don't know how. I do have a friend who was sent to Paris. Maybe if I could reach her . . ."

"I could keep hiding you here," Giles's mother said. "But it would be a boring life for you, and a risky one. Who knows how long those monsters will stay?" She shook her head. "I am also told that they have started to round up Jews, even here in France—can you imagine? It is lucky that my husband left me and went off to Monte Carlo, or he'd be rounded up with the rest of them. My son also, I suppose." She sighed. "I was a silly woman. I was lured by a handsome face and smooth-talking personality. My family was furious, but luckily I was the only child and inherited this property. Giles would have inherited from me. This would have been your home . . . such a waste. So many mistakes." She took Madeleine's hand. "I do not wish to make another one. I will help you get away."

"I'm not sure how," Madeleine said. "Isn't there a wall around the estate? And the front gate is guarded?"

"There is also a little door under the ivy." Her mother-in-law smiled. "Giles used to use it when he climbed out of the window to go and visit his forbidden friends. He thought I didn't know, but of course I did. I can give you my bicycle."

"I can't take that. But then how would you get around?"

"I don't really need to go anywhere, and if necessary I can borrow the gardener's. I don't think you should try to travel by public transportation. They will be checking identity cards, and I take it you no longer have yours. That will make it difficult." She paused, staring out past Madeleine. "But I do have an idea. I know an old man who transports wine up the Seine on his barge. In the good old days when we were still a producing winery, we shipped casks to Paris with him. I presume he still comes past. It was always twice a month, on the first and the fifteenth. He ties up for the night, just north of here, before going into Paris the next morning."

Madeleine nodded.

"So you use my bicycle to get as far as the river, then hide it amongst the bushes beside the towpath. I'll see if the gardener's boy can retrieve it for me. You'll be able to identify the barge—it's a small one, not like the monsters that go past now. And it will have wine casks on board. I'll give you a letter for Monsieur Gaucher—he's an old man with a red face and not much hair. If he agrees to hide you, he'll take you right into the centre of Paris."

"That would be wonderful," Madeleine said.

"I wonder?" Madame Martin said. "It will be like entering the lion's den. They say the place is crawling with Boche."

"Nobody will be looking for me there," Madeleine said. "The one problem will be no identity card and ration book. If I can find Marie-France, she may be able to help. But I have to get away from here first without being spotted. Surely I'll be recognized?"

"Go at night, and we'll work on some sort of disguise for you. Let me see what I can do."

Later that day Giles's mother returned, a triumphant smile on her face. "Look what I have," she said. She unfolded a big bundle. "I went to my house and told them there were items of clothing I needed desperately from my storeroom. I told them they could accompany me if they wished. So they let me go up, and I found some things that might be useful." She held up a dress, a cloak, an old-fashioned cloche hat, a pair of old-fashioned shoes, a tub of talcum powder and a small box. "We'll disguise you as an old woman," she said. "Nobody pays any attention to old ladies. See, the hat comes over your face. We'll powder your hair to make it grey, and I've brought the make-up we used to use when we put on theatricals long ago. We'll give you some wrinkles."

"You're amazing," Madeleine said. "This should be perfect."

Madame Martin gave a tired smile. "My dear, this is the first time I've felt alive in ages. It's so good to be doing something useful and to know that I am getting the better of those vile men."

They waited until the fifteenth of the month. That evening they worked on Madeleine's make-up and hair. She dressed in the garments, which were a little too large but covered her nicely. She looked suitably old and worn. Madame Martin served her a good supper and drew her a map of the area, then gave her a purse with money in it. "It's not much, but it will get you on your way," she said. "I'm afraid I no longer have what I used to. The estate has been let go—all my servants taken away except for my old gardener and cook."

"I can't take your money," Madeleine said. "You've been more than kind. You've risked your life, just like your son did."

"You must let me make it up to you. I regret all those lost years, and I am appalled at what you have been through."

"I'll come back, if I make it through the war," Madeleine said.

"I'd like that." Giles's mother gave her a long look, as if trying to memorize her face. "And I want to give you something else. You don't have a ration card, but I understand there is a thriving black market in Paris. Take this—" And she handed Madeleine a small leather box.

Madeleine opened it, saw the sparkle of diamonds inside, gasped and looked up sharply. "I can't take this, it's lovely. And it's yours."

Madame Martin shrugged. "When will I ever wear it again? And who knows, those Germans will probably loot the place when they leave. I'd rather you had it than they did."

At two o'clock in the morning, Madeleine crept out of the front door. Madame Martin led her around the estate to a wooded area, where she had previously left the bicycle. Then she searched the wall, pulling back a curtain of ivy to reveal a small door. It opened with a creak.

"Go with God, my dear," she said and hugged Madeleine.

"And God be with you, too, until we meet again," Madeleine said, fighting back tears. She wheeled the bicycle to the road and pedalled away. There was a rising moon that gave just enough light so that she didn't have to use the headlamp. It wasn't easy bicycling in cumbersome clothing, but she met nothing on the road and passed few houses until before her she heard the rushing and gurgling of the river and located the towpath. She found a good place to stow the bicycle in a thicket of elder bushes, then positioned herself behind a big willow tree. Cold, dank air rose from the river. Madeleine hugged her knees to herself, trying to keep warm. It was hard to believe that she had escaped. That she was free. Hours passed. She heard the hoot of an owl, the sound of a distant vehicle. She thought of Giles's mother and the extraordinary turn of events that had made them into allies after all this time. Would she be all right? Perhaps they'd punish her for Madeleine's escape. She crouched, worrying, until the first streaks of daylight appeared in the sky. She smoothed down her clothing, adjusted her hat and took a deep breath as she walked along the bank, slowly and hobbling a little like an old lady. Several barges were tied up there, and she heard shouts of bargemen, but they paid no attention to her. At last she spotted the smaller barge with wine barrels on board, and an old man already making ready to cast off. She hurried forward, realizing how close she had come to missing him.

"Bonjour monsieur," she called.

"Madame?"

She handed him the letter. "From an old friend. Madame Martin from the château."

"Ah, my old friend, Madame Martin. It is a long time since I have transported any wine for her. How is she?"

"She suffers at the hands of the Germans. They have taken over the château. She lives in the gardener's cottage."

The old man shook his head. "Such a terrible time for all of us. Last time they stopped me and confiscated the best barrels—said my papers were not in order, but of course they wanted the good wine. And what could I do? Hand it over to them or be shot?"

He read the letter, looking first at the paper, and then at Madeleine. After a long pause he said, "Very well. Come on board." He held out his hand to her. She stepped on board just as there was a popping sound, and a German motorcycle and sidecar came up the bank towards them.

"Quick. Inside. I'll cast off," he said. She lowered herself into the tiny cabin as the noise of the motorcycle grew louder.

"You!" a German voice shouted. "You have the correct papers? Permission for this route?"

"Of course I do. I come this way regularly," the old man replied.

"And the woman?"

"My wife comes with me this time," he shouted. "She does not trust me to be in Paris on my own, knowing my reputation with the ladies." And he laughed loudly.

She heard the chug chug of the diesel motor revving up as they pulled away from the dock and the splash of water against the hull.

"I've escaped," she told herself.

It was early evening when they docked in the city of Paris. They had come all the way to Paris without incident. They went through several locks, which Madeleine found fascinating as the sides rose beside them. Some of them were guarded by German soldiers, but they were not questioned or detained. As they approached the city, she retreated back into the cabin and only caught glimpses of the buildings on the Île de la Cité and then the Eiffel Tower as they passed. Then she heard the engine revving and they were coming into port. As she looked out she saw they were not far beyond the Eiffel Tower.

"We stay here for the night," he said. "It should be close enough to the city centre that you can get where you need to go."

Madeleine thanked him profusely as he helped her ashore. "Anything for a member of the Resistance," he said, "And for a relative of the lady at the château. I wish you good luck, madame."

And Madeleine walked up the steps, trying to decide where she was. On the right bank, not far from the Bois de Boulogne and the part of the city where she had lived. As soon as she recognized a street name, she headed for the nearest métro station. In this mainly residential part of the city, the streets seemed quite deserted. She lingered by the station, watching other people taking the métro. No identity cards seemed to be required so she risked taking the train rather than walking all the way to Pigalle. She came up to a lively scene. There was the sound of jazz music, laughter, singing. Prostitutes were in evidence, lingering on corners. Then she saw that those occupying the bars were German soldiers and hurried a safe distance away to the trees that ran down the median of the boulevard before making her way to the Moulin Rouge.

"Madame?" The ticket taker looked at her with curiosity, and she realized that she still looked like an old woman.

"I am wondering if my niece still works here," she said. "Marie-France?"

"Marie-France?" the man in the booth said, shaking his head. "Then you can't have heard. The Germans took her away. We don't know what happened to her."

"Oh no, how very sad. Poor girl. What had she done?"

He shrugged. "How would I know? Those Germans don't give reasons, do they? One minute she was here, and the next day she'd gone. That's all I can tell you. We haven't seen her in months."

Madeleine came away feeling sick and despairing. Marie-France also taken. Her one contact. What could she do now with no identity card and nowhere to go? Then she reminded herself she did have somewhere she could hide out until she made a decision. If Tante Janine was still alive . . . Was it too late to call on her that night? It wasn't even nine o'clock. Worth risking it. She went to the Pigalle Métro station and studied the map. No easy way of getting to the Marais from here. The journey would involve at least two changes to the Place de la Bastille. She tried to recall the map of Paris in her head. She was not far from the Gare du Nord, and other métro lines. She found the station easily and stood looking at it with longing. Before the war she'd taken the train to Calais from here, then the boat back to England. So simple. She had never thought twice about it. Now it was an impossible dream. But again the métro was complicated. Instead she found herself on the boulevard de Magenta—a straight shot to the Place de la Bastille. There must be buses. She found a bus stop and stood there. The street was now deserted. No vehicles passed, no pedestrians either. At last a man came towards her, wearing some kind of uniform. "Excuse me, monsieur," she said, "but do you know how often the buses come?"

He stared at her incredulously. "They do not run after curfew, madame. You should be home by now—you know that."

"Oh, curfew. Of course. I had forgotten how late it was," she said, exaggerating her old-woman persona. "How silly of me. I was visiting my friend and we quite forgot the time. I must go home right away. Thank you, monsieur."

"You'd better hurry. If a German patrol sees you, they shoot on sight."

Her heart pounding, she headed off under his watchful gaze. How near she had come to making a mistake. If he was an informer and told the Germans . . . She dodged into an alleyway between buildings. All was in darkness. She bumped into a rubbish bin, grabbing the lid before it clattered down. A dog barked nearby. She hurried on and came out to what seemed like a small park. In the light of a rising moon she could make out trees, a park bench. She heaved a sigh of relief and positioned herself behind a large tree. With any luck she'd be safe until morning. But two nights in a row were beginning to tell. She fought off sleep but finally curled up on the grass and slept.

Awaking at first light, she was conscious of city noises—a radio blaring out through an opened window, the smell of bread baking. She sat up, her neck stiff from its awkward position, and recoiled in horror. Where she was lying was in complete view of the building behind. Anyone could have seen her from a window. Hurriedly she scrambled in between trees, taking time to spruce herself up. There was a drinking fountain on a gravel path, and she used this to wash her face, removing the last of the make-up. *Breakfast at a café first,* she thought, remembering not to ask for milk with her coffee. She retraced her steps through the alleyway and came back to the boulevard de Magenta. It was an attractive boulevard, lined with trees that had just come into leaf, and she walked for some time, conscious that the shoes she had been given didn't fit well, until she saw a waiter cleaning off tables and chairs outside a café.

"Are you open yet, monsieur?" she asked. "Or am I too early?"

He eyed her with interest. She realized the outdated clothes no longer matched her features. "I just came from the Gare du Nord," she said. "I had to leave my town. Too dangerous—Allied bombing, you know."

He nodded. "If we're not bombed by one side, then it's the other. Sit, madame. The coffee is brewing. And the bread should have been delivered by now."

With hot coffee and warm bread in her stomach, she continued on her way. She stood at a bus stop, observing other people. Yes, they still bought tokens from the nearby tabac. She bought one, too, and boarded the next bus, getting off at the Place de la Bastille. From there it was a short walk to Tante Janine. Madeleine tried to calm her breathing as she stood outside. The name was still on the plate beside the bank of bells. *Du Bois.* She pressed the bell. There was no answer. Fighting off despair, she was wondering what to do next when the front door opened and a man came out—a middle-aged man dressed in a business suit. The only thing strange about his outfit was that he wore a big yellow star stitched to it.

"Excuse me, monsieur," she said, stepping forwards before he could close the door again, "but do you live here?"

"Of course," he said tersely, eyeing her maybe for a beggar.

"I have come to visit my great-aunt, Mademoiselle du Bois. Is she still alive? I rang her bell, but she doesn't answer."

He shrugged. "She has become deaf of late. And I know she sleeps a lot. My wife takes her a bowl of soup when she makes some. The old lady has not been doing well."

"That's why I've come," Madeleine said. "I've come to take care of her."

"Very kind of you. Go on up. You'll have to rap loudly on the door, or she won't hear."

As Madeleine was about to enter, he called after her, "I'm afraid the elevator is not operating. You'll have to walk."

Madeleine took a deep breath before attempting the four flights and was feeling rather dizzy when she reached Tante Janine's landing. She stood a while, catching her breath before rapping on the door. At first there was no answer. She tried again. Then a feeble voice said, "Who is it? What do you want?"

"Tante Janine, it is I, Madeleine," she said. "Can I come in?"

The door opened a few inches, and a tiny, fragile face peered out, blinked, then said, "It is you! My dear child. What on earth are you doing here?"

Madeleine stepped into the apartment and shut the door, going into the sitting room before she spoke. "I'm sorry to come like this, but I've just escaped from captivity, and I had nowhere to go."

"Captivity?"

"The Germans."

"But you were safe in England, surely?"

"I was. Then Olivier was killed, and I thought Giles was dead, and life didn't matter any more. So I volunteered to be trained as a spy. I've been in Fontainebleau for almost a year. I was a courier, taking messages to the Resistance. Then we were betrayed and . . ." She stopped, unable to go on. She was aware now that Great-Aunt Janine was in her nightdress and looked horribly old and thin.

"You poor child. Sit down. I'll make you some tea."

"No, it's all right. I stopped at a café on my way here. My big problem is that I have no identity card and no ration book. The Germans took everything from me. I won't stay long . . . just until I can figure out what to do, where to go."

"Of course you must stay for as long as you want," the old lady said, "but there is a little problem—the food ration. For people my age the government decree is eight hundred calories a day—a few beans, a piece of bread . . ."

"That's not possible. They are starving you."

"That is the idea, I'm sure. Get rid of the old people, make everyone else weak enough so they comply." She shrugged. "The nice lady downstairs sometimes brings me a bowl of soup. A Jewish couple—Dreyfus. The poor man lost his job as bank manager because Jews are no longer allowed to work. He goes out every morning, but I don't know what he does with himself. Sometimes he goes into the bois and manages to catch a rabbit or a pigeon. Otherwise there is no meat, and my ration wouldn't be enough anyway."

"I'll have to see what I can do," Madeleine said. "Of course I can't take any of your food. But I do have a little money and maybe something to barter with on the black market."

"My child, isn't that a risk?"

"We have to take risks, Tante. It's the only way to survive. But if you don't mind, I'd love to take a bath and get out of these clothes. The Germans took everything from me. I borrowed these from Giles's mother . . ."

"You've seen Giles's mother? I thought they were estranged."

"I was held a prisoner in her château. It's now occupied by Germans, and she is made to live in the gardener's cottage. But she helped me escape. She risked a lot for me."

"She obviously felt badly for you. And so she should—cutting you off all those years. Foolish snobbery."

Madeleine had to smile. In spite of everything, her great-aunt still had her feisty personality.

"You'll have to hurry with the bath," Great-Aunt Janine said. "They turn off the water at nine o'clock. And we seldom have electricity. I take it the lift was not working?"

"It wasn't."

The old lady nodded. "Life has become very hard. I can't manage the stairs, so I have no way of getting food or anything unless someone helps me. The people in the building have been kind, but they, too, suffer. Especially the Jewish families."

"It's horrible," Madeleine said. "I hear they are starting to round up Jews and deport them."

"We live in a time of great evil," Great-Aunt Janine said.

CHAPTER 44

Once she had bathed and rested, Madeleine tried to formulate a plan. Without an identity card and ration book, she couldn't do much. She had been given an identity card at the beginning of the war, before they fled to England. Could she possibly go to the town hall and say she had lost hers and needed a new one? But she was no longer at her old address. They'd want to know where she had been. Could she lie and say they had escaped to the south but then the Italians invaded and she decided to come back? It might just work, but it would be an awful risk. If the Gestapo had found out Giles's true name, they'd know hers.

She was able to put off this worry for a while because Tante Janine had not left her apartment for a couple of weeks. She still had stamps unused on her ration card. Madeleine went with it to the local grocer.

"Mademoiselle du Bois?" he asked, eyeing Madeleine suspiciously. "This is her card."

"It is. I'm her niece, and I'm now taking care of her. She can't manage the stairs, and our lift doesn't work."

"Ah, I see. Poor old thing. She was not looking well last time she was in here."

"She's starving," Madeleine said. "The food ration is not enough."

"I know. What can I do?" He shrugged. "What about your ration? If you add the two together."

Madeleine decided to take a risk. "I was arrested by the Germans. They took everything from me." She saw the concern on his face and went on, "But I do have a little money and I understand that things can be acquired through the black market?"

"I wouldn't know anything about that, madame," he said stiffly. "But for your aunt, let me see what I can do. A tin of sardines—nourishing. Some lentils. A little flour. No sugar, unfortunately. Coffee—no problem now that it's not the real thing. I'm afraid that's about it. I think the greengrocer across the street has some potatoes today. You'd better hurry over there."

She paid and had the ration card stamped, then went across the street and was given three potatoes and a small head of cabbage.

"No onions?" she asked.

The greengrocer looked at her incredulously. "Where have you been? We haven't seen an onion in months."

Madeleine shrugged. "I'm sorry. I just arrived from the country to take care of my relative. People there grow their own onions."

"They should bring some to Paris," he said. "They'd make a fortune on the black market." He paused, then added, "Not that I know anything about that, of course."

As she walked back, Madeleine realized something was troubling her. It wasn't just the lack of city noise—no more hooting of traffic, no more shouts of vendors. Suddenly she realized—pigeons. There were no more pigeons. They had all been eaten.

The supplies made a lentil and cabbage soup, and Madeleine served her aunt sardines on toast, making the tin last three days. *If I could get a job,* she thought, *perhaps they'd feed me there and I wouldn't have to take any of Tante Janine's food.* But how to get a job with no identity card? Every excursion into the streets was fraught with danger. The Germans were a constant presence, stopping people and demanding papers whenever they felt like it. Madeleine tried to pinpoint the times of patrols and sneaked out early in the morning when the shops were just opening. One day she dared to go to the fashionable area around the boulevard Haussmann until she found a jeweller's shop and showed the brooch to the owner. He nodded. "It's a fine piece, madame. Unfortunately I can't buy it from you." When he saw her disappointment he shrugged. "Who would buy it? Who has money for luxuries in a war? Only the German officers, and they don't come in here because I'm Jewish. Any day now and they will take my shop away from me, I know it." He leaned across the counter. "But you could try the pawnbroker over in Montparnasse. His name is Rosenberg. He's a good man. You can trust him. If he's still in business, that is."

Madeleine took the métro across the Seine to the Gare Montparnasse and found the address. As she approached the shop, the door was opened abruptly and two German soldiers came out, half dragging a small, grey-haired man between them. "Where are you taking me? I've done nothing wrong!" he shouted. "I can't leave my shop open like this. It will be looted in no time."

"You're going where you belong," one of the Germans said. "With all the other Jews."

"My wife—let me tell my wife. She'll worry . . ." The words were cut off as he was bundled into the back of a van. Madeleine came away sickened. So it had begun. She feared for the Jewish families in her building. She hurried home and banged on the door of the Dreyfus apartment. Madame Dreyfus opened it. Madeleine told her what she had seen. "Do you have somewhere you can go?" she asked.

Madame Dreyfus stared at her, white-faced. "We have a cousin in Marseilles. Do you think it will be any better there?"

"I don't know. At least it's in the zone libre. Not run by Germans yet. Or perhaps you could cross the Pyrenees to Spain?"

"My dear, the Spaniards hate us as much as anybody. We have nowhere to go. We are sitting ducks."

If only I had a contact here, I could get them forged papers, Madeleine thought. But then she added, *and forged papers for me too so that I'd be safe when I went out.*

A few nights later there was a tap on the door. Madeleine had just helped her great-aunt into bed and was settling down to listen to the radio—not that there was any more real news, only propaganda and pro-German songs. She went to the door. "Who is it?" she asked.

"Madame Dreyfus," came the voice. Madeleine opened the door. The woman stood there in outdoor clothes. Madeleine stood aside for her to come into the apartment and closed the door.

"We've come to say goodbye," she said. "We have decided to get away while we still can. My husband thinks we should head for the Alps. We used to have lovely skiing holidays in Chamonix. We are taking the night train. Maybe the Germans won't bother to come that high up, and we could perhaps cross into Switzerland." She gave a big sigh. "At least it's better than sitting here, waiting for doom to fall."

Madeleine nodded. "I wish you all the luck in the world," she said. "Of course I won't mention to anyone that you have gone."

"That was what I was going request," Madame Dreyfus said. "Not everyone in this building feels the way you do. If you could go into our apartment—turn on the radio, walk around, talk loudly as if you are speaking to my husband . . . maybe we could hide our escape for a while, until we are safely away."

"Of course," Madeleine said. "Is there anything else I can do?"

"Nothing." Madame Dreyfus sighed. "Nothing anyone can do. We are all helpless, are we not? But please take what food remains in our pantry. Help yourself to any of the clothes I am leaving. Anything you like. I doubt we'll be coming back for quite a while, if ever."

"Do you own your apartment?"

"Oh yes. We've owned it for years. But who knows, maybe the Germans will confiscate that, too."

"Maybe we should rent it out to a suitable person," Madeleine said. "If the Germans come and it's occupied by a good Aryan, they'll not be interested."

"Yes. That would be a good idea." Madame Dreyfus nodded. "Would you do that for us? Find a good tenant?"

"I will. And I'll keep the rent money safely for you."

"Take it for yourself, my dear." She sighed again. "Money is not the problem. We have plenty. But it does no good."

"All the same, I'll keep your rent money for you," Madeleine said. "I'll only use some if I really have to."

"You are a kind person." Madame Dreyfus wiped an eye. "If only everyone in the world was kind. How lovely it would be."

She handed Madeleine a bunch of keys. Then she tiptoed down the stairs.

~

In the morning Madeleine went down to the Dreyfuses' apartment and let herself in. She turned on the radio, made some coffee, walked around. She tried not to feel delighted that there was food in the pantry. Various tins of tomatoes, herring in wine sauce, jars of matzo balls, jars of pickled beets, as well as rice, split peas, spaghetti. There was even one jar of preserved fruit. She carried the prizes upstairs, and they were on the table when her aunt woke up.

"It's Christmas in summer!" she exclaimed. "We are not going to starve for a while."

~

In the next few days she set about packing all the Dreyfuses' personal items away so that the apartment could be rented. She put everything in the smallest bedroom and then locked the door. Madame had said she could help herself to clothes, and she certainly needed them, so she took essentials. There was even a fur coat. She hesitated to take it but thought that her great-aunt might need it if there was no power next winter. She paused, reflecting on this. She was already planning for next winter with Tante Janine. Should she not be trying to get back to England? Then she decided she had done her duty. Nobody had come to rescue her. It was now time to survive, and besides, her aunt would die without her.

Madeleine set about renting out the Dreyfuses' apartment, at a rent that was low for such a building. A good tenant was found—a woman who worked in a bank and who knew Monsieur Dreyfus. "Such a pleasant man," she said. "It's unthinkable the way they are treating people just because of their race. Inhuman."

So there was money coming in, enough food for now, but there was still the matter of the ration and identity cards. Madeleine took risks and ventured out into the nearby countryside, coming back with whatever she could forage: dandelions, elderberries, blackberries. But nothing nourishing. No protein. The tins were almost gone. Tante Janine seemed listless. "Don't worry about me, my dear," she said. "I've lived a good life. Maybe it's time to go."

"Don't say that. You're all I've got," Madeleine said, looking at her with concern.

~

As Madeleine became more friendly with Mademoiselle Deschamps downstairs, she confided what had happened to her and that she had no identity papers. One day Mademoiselle Deschamps came home from the bank with a triumphant look on her face. "See what I have." She put identity and ration cards on the table.

"But what are these?" Madeleine asked.

"A customer came into the bank today and said her sister had passed away. She wondered what she should do with her papers. So I said I'd take care of them. And I thought of you. So here you are: you are now Michelle Rambert. At least you can get food now."

Madeleine studied the cards in wonder. "She lived out at Clichy," she said. "Does that mean I'd have to shop out there?"

"As long as you have the stamps, the shopkeepers won't care," she said. "You tell them you're visiting a relative."

"I don't know how to thank you," Madeleine said.

"You've done me a good turn. You've let me rent an apartment I couldn't normally afford. The only problem would be if the Germans took you in and checked on your identity. Otherwise I think you're safe," Mademoiselle Deschamps said. Madeleine hoped she was right.

As summer turned to autumn, she went foraging again and came back with mushrooms and then nuts. Autumn turned to winter—a bitter winter with snow and ice. Madeleine wrapped the old woman in the fur coat and made her hot soups, but she seemed to grow weaker every day. They celebrated Christmas with an egg each and turnip soup. And one of her aunt's last bottles of wine. The old lady raised her glass in a toast. "I want to thank you for all you have done for me," she said. "Without you, I would have died, starving, cold, lonely. You have made my last months happy ones."

"We'll get you through this, Tante Janine," Madeleine said. "Maybe the tide is turning soon."

The old lady shook her head. "I want you to know that I have left everything to you. This apartment will be yours. I don't have much in the bank, but enough to set you up after the war, if you choose to stay here and not go home to England."

"After the war?" Madeleine shook her head. "Who knows when that will be . . . if that will ever be."

"Hitler can't live forever," Tante Janine said. "All empires fail eventually."

"The Roman one lasted three hundred years," Madeleine pointed out.

Aunt Janine laughed. "Such a pessimist," she said.

CHAPTER 45

Great-Aunt Janine died at the end of January. It was a peaceful death, quietly slipping away, not wanting to eat or drink and then sleeping and one morning not waking up. Madeleine was glad she was at the old woman's side. She wept, not for Tante Janine, but for herself—her last connection to her mother gone, another person she loved gone.

Madeleine continued to live in the apartment, although she couldn't officially claim it as hers with no proof of identity. She decided to try and get a job. She remembered the Shakespeare and Company bookshop from before the war. She had always loved to browse there and bring home English books. Working in a place like that would be heaven . . . She set off, hoping she might get a job there. But to her disappointment the shop was boarded up. *Fermé* said the large notice. It looked as if it had been closed for a long time. As she turned away a man came towards the shop. He stopped, stared at the boarded-up windows and gave a sigh. Then, to her amazement, he muttered, "Bugger."

Madeleine went over to him. "You're English," she said.

He stared nervously. "Does it show?"

"You said bugger."

"Oh dear. I've got to watch that, haven't I?" Then he stared at her, frowning. "Don't I know you?"

Impetuously she took his arm. "I'm so glad to see you again, dear cousin," she said in French. "Come on. Let's go for a walk along the Seine."

"Along the Seine? But it's freezing."

"That's a good thing. Nobody will be about." She steered him to the river and down the steps to the path that ran beneath the bridges. Snow lay in the shadows. It was icy underfoot.

"What are you doing here?" she asked as soon as she detected they were quite alone.

"I can't tell you that."

"You can't have been in Paris long. No Englishman would still be here unless there was a very good reason."

"You could be a German informer with a good British accent," he said.

She laughed. "You're right. I could. But I'm not."

They walked on.

"You don't happen to have an Uncle Francis, do you?" she asked.

His face lit up. "I knew I'd seen you before, but I couldn't put two and two together. I used to be at the radio and cyphers training centre. You were there, weren't you?"

She frowned. "You weren't one of my classmates."

"No, I was one of the instructors. I taught you how to dismantle a radio."

"I wasn't very good at that," she admitted. "How amazing. But what are you doing here, then? I'd have thought your other job was valuable enough."

He glanced around. Out on the Seine a lone barge headed for the coast. "We've designed a new radio. Much smaller and lighter. Easy to carry around so we can broadcast from different places and make it harder for the Germans to locate a signal. I've been sent to replace radios and show the operators how to use them."

"I hope you had some training first," Madeleine said. "This place is not exactly a piece of cake."

"You're not operating here, are you?" he asked. "You're not on my list."

"I was a courier in Fontainebleau," she said. "Then we were betrayed and captured. I managed to escape."

"I say, that's rather clever of you. Well done." He tossed off the words as if congratulating her for winning a tennis match.

She frowned. "I was lucky. I had help. But others working with me were killed or shipped off to a prison camp in Germany—which is essentially the same thing."

"But they didn't torture you, then? We've been given dire warnings . . ."

"They torture everyone," she said, "in ways that will cause the most pain."

"Oh crikey."

He was rather loveable, Madeleine thought. Like a Labrador puppy, carefree, wanting to please. Quite wrong for this assignment. She feared for him.

"Do you have to stay long?"

"Just until I've got the new radios in place. Then they come to pick me up."

"So you're in touch with London, then?"

"Oh, rather."

"Can you tell them about me? I haven't been in communication since I escaped. They probably think I'm dead, but I had no way . . ."

"Of course I will. Can you write down your name and identifier code?"

"I'll tell you them, but I'm not writing anything down. You could be captured as soon as we part company."

"Oh, right." She repeated the information. He nodded. "Got it. Madeleine. Nice name. I'm Simon. And how do I find you when I hear back from home?"

"Where are you staying?"

"Not too far from here. Near the Sorbonne. Close to the digs I had when I was a student there."

"I was a student, too," she said. "I met my husband there."

"Oh, you're married." He looked absurdly disappointed.

"A widow. My husband was shot by a firing squad when I was captured."

"Crikey, I'm so sorry."

"It's war. That's how it is. So for God's sake be careful. I hope you realize now that muttering 'bugger' under your breath might have cost your life?"

"I do now."

"You can't let your guard down ever. You can't trust anyone except your actual contacts with the proper code. I'm sure they've told you little things like not ordering milk with your coffee and looking the right way when you cross the street?"

"Yes, they did tell me all that."

"And curfew. You need to be inside before curfew. They shoot on sight."

He nodded. "It's all right. I don't need to go out at night."

"What is your cover story?"

He grinned. "I'm an electrician. Etienne Barbour. I've got a bag with a hidden compartment for the radio and a good selection of tools on top. I make my calls when everyone is going to work in the morning or coming home in the afternoon so I'm just one more worker."

"That's good. So you asked how to contact me? I'll give you my address. Just make sure you're not being followed first. The name on the doorbell is du Bois. Give four sharp short rings and I'll come down."

"Splendid. You could always fly out with me, when I'm picked up again."

"That would be wonderful. It's been hard being stuck here, not knowing when my false ID will be discovered."

They came to another flight of steps leading up from the Seine. "I should be getting back," she said.

"I say, you wouldn't fancy a coffee first, would you? I know there are some splendid coffee shops around here."

Madeleine hesitated, then said, "Of course. Why not."

They found a coffee shop on Saint-Germain, and Madeleine realized it was the first place she had gone to with Giles. She gave a little gasp.

"What's wrong?" he asked.

"This café was the first place I went with my husband when we were both students at the Sorbonne. He picked me up during a lecture. He was quite fresh." She smiled at the memory.

"So you married and lived in France?"

"We did. On the other side of Paris, near the Bois de Boulogne."

"And had any children?"

"A son. He was killed. That was what made me join this stupid endeavour. And then my husband. I've lost everyone. I won't know what to do with myself any more if I get back home to England."

"You have no one at home?"

"My father and stepmother. It would be good to see them again."

~

A few days later the doorbell rang four sharp times at eight a.m. Madeleine went down to find Simon standing there, dressed in typical Parisian workman's clothes, carrying a tool bag.

"Electrician, madame."

"Thank you for coming, monsieur," she said. "There is something wrong. I smelled burning when I turned on the electric fire. And if I can't have that in winter, how will I keep warm?"

"Let me take a look, madame," he said. His French was surprisingly good. The lift was working for once, and they stood together in silence as it rose. Once inside the door, he looked around. "Nice digs," he said. "The rent must be high."

"I inherited this place from my great-aunt. My mother's family was French."

He went over to the window, looked out, then let the blinds fall again. "I have news. They can extract you on February the tenth. If I'm finished by then, I can come, too. So I have instructions for you . . ."

He opened the bag, removed the tools, then lifted out a second lining. From this came a piece of paper. All the details. The password for the local Resistance. "You'll meet him in a café." Madeleine scanned the sheet. Train from Montparnasse. Get out at Millemont. Café de la Paix—Café of Peace. That was ironic. Glass of wine at five o'clock. Gaston would come. She'd recognize him by the blue scarf. He'd take her to the pick-up site.

It all sounded so easy.

"I'll be there," she said. "Thank you."

"They were amazed," he said. "They thought they'd lost you."

For the first time in ages, she allowed herself to hope, to picture England, home.

He hesitated. "I should go."

"No, you have to fix my electricity, remember?"

"Oh yes."

"I'll make us both some coffee."

They sat at her kitchen table and chatted. He told her about his family in Devon. His father, who was a gentleman farmer and wanted him to take over the farm some day. Cambridge and the Sorbonne. "I didn't quite know what to do when the war broke out. But I've always been good at crosswords and things, and I like designing things, so I was recruited rather quickly."

"How old are you?" she asked.

"Twenty-five."

"You're ridiculously young. I'm over thirty."

"Age doesn't matter, does it?" He paused, cleared his throat. "When I get back, may I come and visit you?"

She paused, then said, "If you like."

He beamed as if she had given him a present.

CHAPTER 46

For the rest of the month she tried to put everything in order without giving away that she might be leaving. The rent paid into a new account at her tenant's bank. Deciding what to take with her: obviously she could only take a small bag, so she took a few photographs of her mother as a child, of Tante Janine, her few pieces of good jewellery plus the brooch from her mother-in-law she'd never needed to pawn. And on February the tenth she locked up the apartment and set off as arranged. All went smoothly. The train left on time. A German soldier sat opposite her in the carriage and gave her a friendly smile.

"You go to visit someone?" he asked.

"My brother. He's working in Rouen," she said.

"Ah. Your brother. You have a sweetheart?"

"I lost my husband recently," she said. "Too soon to think about sweethearts."

He nodded as if he understood. "I lost my mother this year. In a bombing raid," he said. "War is stupid, is it not?"

She looked at him as if she was seeing him as a person for the first time. *Not all Germans are monsters,* she thought. The soldiers did what they were told. They hated to be away from home. They grieved lost relatives, and they didn't want war.

Alighting at the right station, she made for the Café de la Paix, finding a table in the window. She ordered a glass of wine and a bowl of stew. Better to be fortified. She ate the meal, sipped the wine and waited. Five o'clock came. No Gaston. Five fifteen. She began to be alarmed. Then, at five thirty, he sauntered in, the blue scarf flung casually around his throat. "Yvonne—there you are! I'm sorry if I kept you waiting!" he said, pulling her to her feet and kissing her on both cheeks. "How is what's-his-name again?"

"You mean Jean-Louis. Don't tell me you've really forgotten."

Code words had been exchanged. All was well.

"Come on. The family is waiting. Let's go."

Madeleine paid and they left.

"Sorry," he said. "A German convoy was going down the road. I had to wait."

"But the landing site tonight?"

"Should be fine," he said. "There's enough moon. We'll only need a few lights." He glanced at her. "So you're going back to England? But you are French, no?"

"Half," she said. "I'm half-French." And she hadn't realized this before. Half of her did belong in France. Maybe after the war, one day, she would return.

They waited in a forested area. It was bitterly cold, and a few snowflakes fluttered down.

"I hope it's not going to snow," she said. "What happens if the moon is hidden?"

"It will be all right," he said. "Don't worry."

"Will anyone be joining me?" she asked.

"Not that I know of. Supplies will be arriving. Guns and ammunition for us."

So Simon was not coming with her. She felt disappointed.

Just after midnight, they heard the drone of an approaching plane.

"Be ready," Gaston commanded.

A small black shape swooped down from the sky, landed, slowed. A door opened and bags were flung out.

"Now!" Gaston commanded. She sprinted forward. Hands yanked her aboard as the plane kept on moving. It swung into a tight turn. The engine revved up, and they soared into the night. Madeleine found she had been holding her breath, waiting for the shots to ring out as she sprinted forwards, waiting for the plane to be struck, and then suddenly she looked down and there was the Channel below them, moonlight glinting on water, the dark shapes of ships. And the English coast ahead.

"Looks like we made it this time," the pilot said with a chuckle. "Better than last week when we nearly had a wing shot off."

Madeleine didn't know whether to laugh or cry. After years of holding back emotion, fighting against fear and dread and grief, the wealth of emotions now flooded to the surface. She put a hand to her mouth as tears trickled down her cheeks.

Back in England she was given a hero's welcome she didn't feel she deserved. She was sent to a lovely country house for debriefing. There was discussion on whether she should be sent back to France. She looked at the calm faces with horror. Had they any idea what it was like to face a torturer? To see your husband shot? To be raped night after night?

"I'm sorry, but I just can't do it," she said. "And frankly I don't think what I did was worth a human life, or more than one human life."

So it was agreed that she'd be posted to headquarters. On returning to London, she went to find her father and stepmother, only to discover the house had been sold. Neighbours only knew they had moved out of London to somewhere in the country. She didn't have time to try to locate them with a war still going on. She took a bedsit in London and was posted to intelligence gathering. It was challenging and disheartening at times, and she grew more and more angry. So many agents lost and often for so little worth. She searched and found Annie and Marie-France had both been taken to Ravensbrück. Portia's name did not appear anywhere. So there was a chance she was still safe. And then she came across Simon Boddington. Shot trying to escape after only a few weeks in France. This was almost too much to bear. Why was everyone she cared about taken from her? She wondered what the point of going on living was.

CHAPTER 47

Paris was liberated in August of 1944. The war was coming to an end, and Madeleine wondered what she would do with herself. The agency had made it clear that there would no longer be any high-level jobs for women once the men returned from service. She could train to be a typist. No thank you. She couldn't imagine going back to teaching—all those bright young faces. How could she ever inspire the next generation when she walked under a black cloud? How could she see other people's sons alive and well when Olivier had been taken from her? The Germans surrendered. There was great rejoicing, street parties, kissing strangers. She knew she should feel relief, but she found it hard to feel anything.

London was a place of rubble and blackened shells. There was still little food to be had. People walked around like ghosts, hollow eyed and painfully thin. Madeleine knew she should trace her father and stepmother and found them eventually living in a tiny cottage in Kent—her father now pathetically weak and frail, her stepmother bitter and belligerent. She obviously didn't care a hoot about her father, she was told, or she would have been to visit them more, helped them with the move.

"You didn't even bother to write," Eleanor said. "I expect you were being well fed, working for the government, while we were close to starving."

And she couldn't tell them what she had been doing.

~

During her last days on the job, news began to trickle in from the Continent. Annie and Marie-France both dead at Ravensbrück. Annie had died just days before the camp was liberated. Madeleine fought back tears of anger. And then one piece of good news. Portia came home. She looked just as she had done when Madeleine last saw her: fresh faced, bright eyed.

"I can't believe it's you," she said, hugging Madeleine fiercely. "You don't know how many times I've thought about you and wondered if you were safe."

"I escaped and hid out in Paris," Madeleine said. "What about you?"

"I was lucky," Portia said. "I was tipped off that they'd arrested Annie and you. So I thought I'd better get away while I could. I had no way of contacting England, so I made for Switzerland. I'd been to school there for years, so I knew it well. I climbed one side of a mountain in France and came down in Switzerland. They let me stay. I've had quite a pleasant time, actually. Felt rather guilty, of course, but what else could I have done?"

Madeleine fought back a rush of resentment. Portia had spent the war in Switzerland while the rest of them had suffered and died. "Nothing, really. There was nobody left near Fontainebleau. If they'd captured you, you'd be dead, too."

"So how did you survive?"

Madeleine told her, trying to sound matter-of-fact. Portia stared, open-mouthed.

"How awful for you. Poor Giles. Gosh, what a love you two must have had for him to do that. And that vile Herr Geller. I hope he gets his just deserts now."

"I've tried not to think about him," Madeleine said.

"Look, Madeleine. I'm going to my family home," Portia said. "Why don't you come with me? You'd love it. Beautiful grounds, good food. We're celebrating Daddy coming home safe and sound from the POW camp, and my brother surviving as a fighter pilot. Rather miraculous, actually. So our home would be just the sort of place to recuperate and try to forget."

"Thank you," Madeleine said. "I'd like to visit sometime, but I have things I have to do first. I promised my mother-in-law that I'd help her get her château back in working order when the Germans left. She was so good to me. She took a tremendous risk, so I owe it to her."

"Sometime you should do something for yourself," Portia said. "Do come soon."

It was tempting. But she had made a promise. She continued working until the end of 1945, closing the books on the various agents who had not come home. She was let go just before Christmas and went to join Portia at her parents' palatial home. But it had been a mistake. To be surrounded by people laughing, eating, drinking as if there had never been a war was more than she could bear. She made an excuse and left as soon as possible.

CHAPTER 48

Oliver

Australia, 1945

For Oliver, day followed day. Month followed month. Year followed year. When he was called into Sister Jerome's office and informed that no relatives could be found for him, he had finally given up hope. He did his chores, tried not to make mistakes and wondered if it was worth staying alive. His bright part of the week was when Mr Baxter came. He had many children to teach and only a couple of hours to do it, so he couldn't spend much time with Oliver, but he did try to leave him books—not just novels but books on various subjects. Oliver had to avoid seeming too keen or risk being seen as the teacher's pet. It was not wise to make enemies when you needed all the friends you could get for back-up.

News of the German surrender was greeted with joy in Australia. There were street parties. Local people brought treats out to Ferndale. The students were invited to join the town picnic. It was strange and wonderful to be amongst ordinary families, to watch other children being hugged, little ones sitting on parents' laps, bigger girls dancing with their dads. Oliver met Mr Baxter and was introduced to his wife and his son, home from the army.

"How old are you, Oliver?" Mrs Baxter asked.

"Twelve," he replied.

"My husband tells me you are a good student," she said. "I'm wondering if we couldn't get you into the boarding school that Jamie went to. I know they give scholarships. You need more than that place offers you."

"That would be wonderful," Oliver said.

~

A few weeks later Mr Baxter came out to Ferndale with exciting news. He went to see Sister Elizabeth Ann. "I've been in touch with the boarding school my son attended. I told them about Oliver Martin and that he is gifted academically. They are prepared to offer him a scholarship to the school. He can return to you during his holidays if that's all right?"

"It is not all right," Sister Elizabeth Ann snapped. "We treat all our children equally. We can't have one getting above himself. What will all the others think if he's given preferential treatment they can't have? The child is an orphan with no family to support him. He needs to remember his place in life."

"But if he is capable of more? If he could become a doctor or a scientist? Would you deny him that?" Mr Baxter fought to control his anger at the woman's implacable face.

"As I said, Mr Baxter, all of our children are treated equally. There can be no favouritism. Oliver is no different from any other orphan in our care. Now good day to you. You'd be wise not to mention this again."

Oliver heard nothing more about the chance to go to a real school and assumed they had not wanted him. Nobody else did, after all.

He did, however, have one friend. Charlie had become his protector and now became a real mate. With Charlie's encouragement, they undertook small and risky things—managing to steal a little extra food or introducing a poisonous redback spider into the nuns' dormitory. Oliver was horrified at first, as someone who had always obeyed the rules, but he soon realized the sense of power and fun this gave him in an otherwise drab life.

Charlie was not the brightest of boys but was a keen observer. One day he dragged Oliver aside as they were walking out to the fields.

"You know that little kid, the new one who was cheeky to the nuns?"

"Freddie? Was that his name?"

Charlie nodded, looking around before he murmured. "He tried to run away. They caught him and brought him back and put him in the sin bin."

"Poor kid."

"No, it's worse than that," Charlie whispered. "I reckon he died. They left him in there all day yesterday, and you know how hot it was, and he had no water. Anyway, I heard something during the night. I crept out to see, and I saw two of the nuns digging, out in that patch of scrub. I reckon they were burying him."

"Crikey," Oliver said.

"Something's going to happen to us one day," Charlie said. "We ought to try and run away."

"Like Freddie. And be caught, and punished?" He shook his head. "Besides, where would we run to? We've no money and nowhere to go."

"Anywhere would be better than this. I'm big for my age. I could get a job. I could say you're my little brother."

"I'd like to get away, Charlie. Do you think Mr Baxter would help us?"

"He likes you," Charlie said. "But whether he'd go that far. He'd lose his job teaching, wouldn't he? And if he betrayed us to the nuns—well, it would be the sin bin." He straightened up and moved apart from Oliver.

"You, boy, have you picked up your spade yet?"

"Just going, sister," Charlie said. He shot a look at Oliver. "Anyway, think about it. And be alert. We must take any chance we get."

CHAPTER 49

Madeleine had to wait until February of 1946 before she was able to travel to France. Having been paid her back wages and her demobilization money, she had enough to survive for now, but wondered how she would continue to live. There were no jobs for women, it seemed. They were all supposed to marry, become homemakers and have babies. She was not allowed to take any money out of the country, and she hoped her French bank account had not been touched.

On St Valentine's Day, Madeleine crossed the Channel to Paris. The city had begun to emerge from the deprivations of the war. The cafés were bustling with life, there was food in the shops again, there was music and laughter. It all felt so unreal. Her tenant had only recently moved out of the Dreyfuses' old apartment and had kept it in perfect shape. The rent money had created a healthy balance in the bank, which rightfully belonged to the Dreyfuses should they return. Madeleine started to make enquiries about them, going to a hotel in the Marais where news of survivors was posted on a board. Paris was gradually emerging from the horrors of war. News was just emerging of the fate of so many Jewish neighbours and friends. All dead. All gone. Nobody returning to tell the tale. That would have been Giles, she realized. She would have lost him anyway. But then, miraculously, the Dreyfuses did return. They looked like living skeletons, but they had both survived the horrors of the camp. When they found that Madeleine had kept their apartment for them and the rent had accumulated in the bank account, Madame Dreyfus wept. "You are a good woman. God will surely reward you," she said.

Madeleine did not say she thought it unlikely that God even cared about her, if He existed. She did not linger in Paris, having submitted all the necessary documents for probate of her aunt's will, but caught the train first to Fontainebleau to check on the Dumases. The gates to the château were open, the grounds deserted, the beautiful lawns torn up and the flower beds empty. Such a sorry sight. Madeleine hardly dared to breathe as she walked up the rue Saint-Honoré, then found the little shop boarded up.

"Oh," she said, putting her hand to her mouth. So the Germans had come for them after all. Those sweet people. She blinked back tears, looking up to see a woman emerging from a nearby house.

"Monsieur and Madame Dumas?" she asked. "What happened to them?"

"They have gone, madame," the woman said. "Gone to their son in Lyons. I hear he has a fine house and will take care of them in their old age."

"Oh, that is good news." The woman stared at her, frowning. "I remember you," she said. "You worked for him."

"I did, until I was taken by the Germans," Madeleine said.

"Mon Dieu. You were lucky to survive," the woman said.

"Very lucky. I owe a debt to the woman who helped me escape. I'm on my way to visit her now."

She set off for Melun and the château. She found her mother-in-law still living in the gardener's cottage. Madame Martin seemed to have aged tremendously during the time they had been apart. They hugged fiercely.

"You survived. I am so proud of you," Madame Martin said.

"Thanks to you. I worried about you. I was afraid they'd punish you for my escape. And now I've come to help you put the château back to rights as I said I would."

The older woman's face clouded. "My dear, I fear it is beyond my power. When the Germans left, they took or destroyed everything. I don't have the money to make everything right. And anyway I can't find workers. Nobody wants to be a servant any more, and as for the vineyard—I can't pay what the big new wineries are paying. So I must leave it to crumble, I suppose."

"But I'll help," Madeleine said. "And see—I've brought you something."

She held out the box with the brooch in it. "I didn't need it after all. Maybe it can help pay for restoration."

They went around the château. It was a grim sight. Paintings had been slashed, wallpaper torn down, furniture smashed. "They took everything of value," Madame Martin said.

Madeleine studied her—the once proud face now looking hopeless and resigned. She made a quick decision. "Listen, I have a nice apartment in Paris," Madeleine said. "Why don't you come and live with me there for a while, until we can sort out what can be done to the château? There must be government grants we can apply for. Your son was a hero of the Resistance. That should count for something."

"The son I rejected." She shook her head. "You should reap the benefit of his death."

"I don't need anything. I'd rather help you."

They returned to Paris and to the apartment. At first Madame Martin seemed remote and resigned, a mere shadow of the strength she had shown, but as she and Madeleine threw themselves into the task of getting the place spruced up, she began to show more interest in life. They went together to government departments and battled red tape for grants and pensions, and Madeleine was glad to see her fighting spirit and will to live returning. In fact she felt her own spark of interest coming back to life. They went out to bistros. They laughed at silly movies. And they went to the château to bring back furnishings to decorate the apartment. *Yes,* she thought. *I could live here.*

Then one day when she was at the town hall, wanting to find out if probate had been granted for Tante Janine's will, she passed a man wearing British military uniform. They stopped, recognizing each other at the same moment.

"Madame Martin!"

"Uncle Francis, I presume. How good to see you. What are you doing here?"

"I'm part of the war crimes commission," Major Walcott said. "Getting all the facts to prosecute Nazi atrocities and preventing the local people from killing collaborators. Some poor girls who were dragged off to be German prostitutes are now having their heads shaved or even being strung up."

Madeleine shuddered. *That could have been me.*

The major paused, considering, then said, "It's most fortuitous that I've found you, because I've been thinking about you. What are you doing with yourself these days?"

"Nothing much. I want to help my mother-in-law restore her château, but I fear it will take a long time."

"I might have a job for you," he said. "Can I take you to dinner tonight? At the Ritz?"

She smiled. "I've never had dinner at the Ritz. I'd be delighted."

That evening they sat together under glittering chandeliers. White tablecloths. Oysters and champagne. Duck breast. It was hard to believe there had ever been a war. Such a contrast to the bleak conditions still existing in London, she thought.

"I remember your file clearly," he said. "You were captured by a certain Gestapo agent called Karl Geller?"

She nodded, trying not to shudder.

"A vile specimen if ever there was one," he said. "He moved south through France rounding up Jews and Resistance members. He had whole villages executed for hiding a Resistance fighter. He put so many Jewish children crammed into a cattle car that they all perished."

"Do we know where he is now?"

Walcott shrugged. "Vanished. No trace of him, except . . . you know that Australia has been opening its doors to boatloads of European refugees. They have to work in agriculture to begin with, wherever the government sends them. We suspect that some former high-ranking

Nazis have taken advantage of this to change their identity and escape amongst the Eastern Europeans."

"And Geller is amongst them?" She felt a chill run through her.

He took out his wallet and unfolded a piece of newspaper. It was a picture of a group of men, holding axes, standing beside a fallen tree.

"We have people working with us in Australia. Someone sent me this," he said.

He handed it to her. She studied it hard, then shook her head. "I don't see Karl Geller," she said.

"We believe that these men may have had plastic surgery done to change their appearance. That's why it's so hard to trace them. But this man"—he pointed at the photograph—"is called Karol Voyzek, and his papers say he's a Czech citizen who was drafted into the German army against his will."

"Geller told me he grew up in the German part of Czechoslovakia," she said, now studying the photograph with more interest. "The build is the same, but this man's hair is darker."

"Dyed?"

"And I don't think I see the resemblance in his face."

"As I said. A clever doctor can do wonders with plastic surgery. The moustache helps, too." He looked up. "Tell me, did he have a scar?"

"He had one down the side of his cheek. From a duel when he was in a fraternity. He was proud of it."

"The surgeon may have been able to remove it partially, but probably not completely."

Then she remembered. "He did have another scar. On his shoulder. He was injured in a car accident and had stitches." She paused, frowning. "Why are you telling me this?"

"Because you're the one person who might be able to identify him. He may look different, but he can't change his eyes. If he looked at you, you'd know."

She stared then. "You want me to go to Australia and find him?"

"Would you do it?"

She hesitated, considering. Her terror at facing Geller again fought with her desire to see him brought to justice. But her mother-in-law was counting on her.

"I'm sorry. My obligation now is to my mother-in-law. I want to put the past behind me."

"Very well," he said. "I can't force you, of course. I have to respect your decision, but if you change your mind . . ." And he handed her his card.

When she went back to the flat, her mother-in-law was sitting with a small leather-bound book in front of her. "Look what I discovered," she said and opened the book. Madeleine saw the photo of a small child, sitting on a rug in a garden, holding up a toy car. For a moment she thought it was Olivier, but then she realized it was Giles. She sat beside her mother-in-law and turned page after page. Giles making his first communion, Giles playing football, skiing, always laughing, always challenging the camera with that defiant smile of his. Madeleine felt a little sob come to her throat.

"He loved life so much," she said. "It's so unfair."

"Yes," her mother-in-law agreed. "So unfair. But you and I are alive, my dear. We must find a way to carry on. So did you have a pleasant dinner with your friend?"

Madeleine recounted what had occurred. The older woman looked horrified. "But of course you must go."

"But what about you? I want to help you with the château."

Madame Martin took Madeleine's hand. "My dear, I fear I am way down anybody's list for rebuilding. So many people have a greater need. Besides, what does a woman like me need with all those rooms? Don't worry about me." She looked at Madeleine long and hard. "I think you need to do this—for yourself and for my son." And she put the book into Madeleine's hands.

Then Madeleine remembered what Portia had said: "Sometime you should do something for yourself."

"Maybe you're right," she said. "If I'm the only one who can identify him, I can't let him get away, can I?"

"That's the spirit," Madame Martin said. "I will take care of the apartment for you. I may even find a job. I am not completely ancient yet, you know."

Madeleine looked at her mother-in-law's face and impulsively hugged her. Madame Martin reacted with surprise to the hug, then her arms came around Madeleine. "God go with you, my dear," she whispered.

"Good." Major Walcott smiled when she contacted him again. "I'll arrange a passage for you out of Southampton on a liner called the *New Australia*. Recently refitted. All expenses paid, of course."

"A ship? Doesn't that take a long time?"

"It does, but it's impossible to find an air ticket at the moment. None of the airlines are properly up and working yet. Look upon it as a holiday—good food and seeing the world."

"A holiday?" She had an absurd desire to laugh.

CHAPTER 50

As Madeleine returned to London, she felt both excited and scared. She wondered if she could do this again. It had been so nice to live a quiet and safe life. Restoring a château would be something constructive and healing. But if Karl Geller had escaped and she was the only person who could find him, how could she not go to Australia?

At headquarters in London, she was given a cover story—she'd be writing a piece for a women's magazine on New Australians. She'd visit the various lumber camps and take pictures. She had a crash course in developing photographs. Then she was given items she would need: a good camera and a gun—a Colt revolver. She stared at it.

"I'd be allowed to shoot him?"

"Only to defend yourself. I don't think he'll come quietly."

"No." She put the revolver into her bag. "Will there be a problem with me bringing it into the country?"

The officer smiled. "Put it amongst your most intimate items in your suitcase. Nobody will go through that too thoroughly."

Her bags were packed. She boarded the liner with excitement and anticipation. She found the ship full of hopeful migrants and would be sharing a cabin with three other women: one going to join her fiancé in Melbourne, another a war widow going to join her brother and a third an unmarried office girl, fed up with the stifling, depressing conditions in England.

"I'm hoping to snag a rugged sheep farmer," she told Madeleine. "Tanned and lots of muscles. How about you?"

Madeleine shook her head. "I can't think about marrying again. I loved my husband. I miss him every day."

They were all intrigued that she wrote for a women's magazine.

"I love the knitting patterns in your magazine," Brenda, the widow, said. They treated her like a celebrity, which she found amusing. They were pleasant enough company, even if they were not educated women, but she found that she didn't want to get close to them. They were too much of a reminder of the special close relationship she had known with Annie and Marie-France and Portia. She couldn't risk that feeling of loss again. So they thought she was a bit snooty and left her alone.

There was plenty to do on the ship, and Madeleine tried to make the most of the entertainment. She played deck games, enjoyed good meals, and as the ship moved south and into the Mediterranean, she swam in the ship's pool. They stopped at fascinating ports—Marseilles, Rome, Malta, Cairo, through the Suez Canal, Ceylon and then Perth, Adelaide, Melbourne and finally Sydney. The whole journey took six weeks, and Madeleine was sorry when it came to an end. It was the first time she had been completely free in years. She had felt the layers of stress and worry and grief gradually starting to melt. She had even danced with some of the ship's officers, realizing that she could now let a man hold her without being overcome with fear and revulsion.

At last they docked in Sydney. She stepped ashore and was met by a contact of Major Walcott. His name was Bruce, and he was young and enthusiastic with red hair and freckles. He took her to a hotel with a view over the harbour, and during the next days he was a good host, giving her tours of Sydney and the surrounding countryside. After the drabness of the war, the sights and sounds were almost overwhelming: the bright sunlight, the blue ocean, the golden beaches dotted with tanned and healthy people, extravagant meals that everyone took for granted—ice cream and milkshakes, lamb chops, oysters, and big slabs of steak. After a few days, Bruce took her to a government building where she was given a map of the highland areas of New South Wales with the various lumber camps circled.

"You should take the train up to the Blue Mountains," Bruce said. "After that we'll have to play it by ear. There is no public transportation where you are going. It's back o' Bourke, as we say here. We'll have to see about getting you a car and a driver."

She went to the *Sydney Morning Herald*, where the original article had been published, and met with the journalist and the photographer. Neither could remember exactly which lumber camps had produced which photographs. They had visited many. But the photographer was sure that this one was not too far south—on the far side of the Blue Mountains, not the Snowies. That would at least cut down the amount of travel. It was agreed that she'd take the train to Katoomba—the tourist centre of the Blue Mountains, and a car would be arranged for her from there for a week or two. It was only as she was escorted to the train station that Bruce said to her, "We haven't talked about the real reason you are here. We do know what you've been sent to do: You're hunting Nazis—one Nazi in particular. And officially I'm not allowed to help you. I'm sure you're quite aware that these are dangerous men. They may no longer be armed, but they would do anything not to be caught. Are you armed?"

She nodded. "I have a revolver."

"Make sure you keep it loaded, and carry it at all times. And I'm afraid you'll be out of communication with the rest of the world. It's the Bush. Nobody around for miles. So if you find this man, don't do anything heroic. Walk away. Go to where you can telephone us, and we'll come and get him. He may try to escape, but he can't get far. Nobody gets far in that sort of terrain. And also there will be Aussie blokes working at that lumber camp, too. Ask them for help if you need to. They won't take kindly to a Nazi under their noses."

Madeleine nodded. Until now the reality of what she was about to do had not hit her. When she thought of confronting Geller, she felt sick. There was a good chance he'd kill her first. But she wasn't backing out now. She packed a small bag, leaving her bigger suitcase at the hotel then was driven to the station.

"Good luck." Bruce shook her hand. As the train pulled out, the whole adventure felt quite unreal. Could she do this? Would she really recognize him? She tried to quieten her nerves by staring out of the window. City gave way to suburbs with attractive, red-roofed bungalows, to market gardens and small farms. They stopped in Parramatta, a small country town, then almost imperceptibly the track began to rise. Several more hamlets, fields with crops or sheep, stands of eucalyptus trees, until after two hours they pulled into Katoomba Station. Madeleine climbed down and stood breathing the amazing mountain air, tinged with the strong scent of eucalyptus. She looked around her, expecting to see peaks like the Alps but all she saw was a forest of grey-green eucalyptus, stretching on all sides. There were several small wooden-built hotels near the train station, and she checked into one of these.

"I thought this was supposed to be a mountain resort," she said. "I don't see any mountains."

The proprietress, a buxom woman with wisps of hair escaping from a grey bun, laughed loudly. "Well, you see, love, our mountains are different here. Straight out from pommy land, are you? Well, our mountains go down, not up. Walk out to the Three Sisters, and you'll see what I mean."

Madeleine settled herself into a small clean room, then left the hotel and followed the sign to the lookout. As she approached the lookout point, she gasped with amazement. Below her the land fell sharply away, dropping in sheer cliffs to a valley far below. She was indeed on a mountain top. The Three Sisters were rocky outcrops that loomed over the valley. She was conscious of the utter silence that rose to greet her. Then the cry of a strange bird echoed from the cliffs. And to her delight a flock of white cockatoos wheeled, screeching below her.

This is a magical place, she thought. She decided not to meet up with her car until the next day but to enjoy her surroundings. As she walked through forested paths that the locals referred to as "the Bush," she heard so much new and different birdsong: one sounded like a person playing a flute, another like ting of a small bell and a third . . . "What was that?" she asked a couple who were standing nearby.

"That was a whip bird," the man answered. "Sounds just like the crack of a whip, doesn't it?"

Madeleine walked as if enchanted. Since the war, this was the first time that she'd felt pure joy. *I could live here,* she thought. *I believe I could heal if I lived here.* She arrived back at the hotel to find a man sitting on a bench outside, waiting for her.

"Mrs Martin?" he asked, standing up. She noticed he was tall and lean with dark hair that was greying slightly at the sides, and dark eyes. "I am Tony. I'm to be your driver. The car is ready when you wish to leave."

"Oh, hello Tony," she said uneasily. He looked different from what she had expected. He was dressed in a crisp white shirt, open at the neck, but his face was not bronzed like the other Australians. In fact he looked pale and drawn. It was hard to tell his age. Maybe forty, she thought. And he spoke with an accent she couldn't quite define. "I thought I might spend the rest of today getting to know the area," she said, "and we can set off in the morning."

"Very good," he said.

She frowned now. "You're a New Australian, too?" she asked.

He nodded. "I am. I have only been here a month or two."

"You're German?" She identified the trace of an accent, setting off alarm bells in her head.

"I was born in that country," he said, "but my parents moved to South Africa when I was a child."

"And you've left South Africa for here?" she asked, still wary. "Why would you do that? Isn't it supposed to be a lovely place?"

"I don't agree with the politics," he said. "So I understand you wish to visit lumber camps, yes?"

"I do," she replied. "I've been sent by my magazine to do an article on New Australians, especially men. It's a women's magazine and

Australia is anxious to have more women immigrate. So they've told me lots of pictures of brawny men in their undershirts." She chuckled.

"Oh, you'll find plenty of those to the east of here," he said. "Lumber is big business these days. So many new houses to build. Very well. I will pick you up at eight tomorrow morning. And I should warn you, the Bush roads are not paved. It will be all dirt from here. You'll be in a Jeep, which can handle the road bonzer, but you'll still get bumped around a lot. Maybe borrow a pillow from the hotel?" He smiled as he spoke, and the smile made him look younger. *He has suffered,* Madeleine realized suddenly, recognizing her own face in his.

At five o'clock she was summoned for tea, and, expecting to find tea and cakes, she was confronted by a huge plate of roast lamb with all the trimmings. Her stomach was still not used to eating large meals, and she had to apologize when she couldn't finish it. Afterwards came treacle pudding and custard, again delightful but too filling. That night she lay with her window open, listening to the rustle of leaves, a distant laugh and the sigh of the mountain breeze. All so peaceful, and yet not far from here might be a man who had willingly sent thousands to their death.

CHAPTER 51

The next morning Madeleine was confronted with a plate of steak and eggs for her breakfast.

"Heavens, I'll get fat if I stay here long," she said, laughingly to the proprietress.

The woman looked confused. "It's just our normal breakfast," she said. "Don't you eat like that at home now that the war is over?"

Madeleine shook her head. "Everything is still on ration. We rarely see meat."

"My word," the woman said, "the men round here wouldn't go for it if you didn't feed them their meat. I reckon you'd be wise to stay out here then, not go back to Blighty."

"I may well," Madeleine replied.

Tony was waiting outside with an ex-army Jeep. She climbed in and they set off. They decided to tackle the lumber camps to the south first and then work their way northward. Tony was pleasant to chat with, although chatting was at a minimum after they left the paved road. It was too easy to risk biting a tongue. They drove through unbroken forest. Eucalyptus leaves painted dappled shade on the track ahead while a great plume of orange dust rose up behind them. Once several wallabies bounded across the track ahead of them, to Madeleine's delight.

At the first of the camps, Madeleine was greeted with great interest, a woman being a rarity. The men laughed and joked with her, begging her to stay, offering to marry her. They thought it was a great idea for their pictures to appear in a women's magazine back home (which was how many of them referred to England) and hoped it would send out more women to Australia. Madeleine felt guilty for deceiving them. *Perhaps I will submit the pictures to a magazine when I return,* she thought. Then she added, *If I return.*

At each of the camps there were New Australians, most of them only speaking a few words of English. From Greece. From Romania. From Yugoslavia.

"Anyone here from Czechoslovakia?" she asked. They shook their heads. She noticed Tony looking at her with interest.

"Why particularly Czechoslovakia?" he asked as they finished taking pictures and drove on.

"Oh, I met someone in Sydney who had a cousin working in one of the camps," she lied easily.

Tony nodded and didn't say more. They visited two more camps but came away empty-handed. Darkness had fallen as they made it back to Katoomba. Madeleine showered, washing off the coating of dust, ate a hearty supper and fell asleep. The next day was a repeat. More camps, more men, an enthusiastic greeting but no luck. At the last camp of the day, there were some men from Czechoslovakia, but they were big burly peasants, not speaking much English, and they did not know a Karol Voyzek.

Tony had heard her mention him, and again she could feel his eyes studying her. She began to have an odd feeling. Was it a coincidence that her driver was a German? She wondered if she could request a new driver but decided to give it one more day and to observe him more closely. *If he really was one of them, he'd find a way to dispose of me miles from anywhere,* she thought. Not a comforting feeling, but until now he had been most solicitous, helping her across difficult terrain, warning her when there was a snake on the path.

On their third day, they came to a camp in great uproar.

"Sorry we can't talk to you now," the foreman said. "One of the boys has hurt himself bad. Tree branch fell on his leg. He's got a nasty open wound. We're trying to find a way to get him to hospital."

"Would you allow me to see him?" Tony asked. "Maybe I can help."

"You're a doctor?"

Tony shook his head. "Not in Australia. Back in my country I was a doctor, but I have to resit all my exams if I wish to practice here. But I have treated many men in bad conditions. So if you want me to take a look at your bloke, I can."

"Right. Anything's better than nothing," the foreman said. "It's up this way."

Tony turned back to Madeleine. "I'm sorry if I hold you up, but I must help this man," he said.

She nodded. They set off up a steep incline. Madeleine followed, wanting, but not wanting to see what happened. A group of men were standing around a person lying there. Madeleine could see he looked so young, not more than a boy.

"We managed to get the bloody thing off him," one of them called as the foreman approached.

"I've brought the next best thing to a doctor," the foreman called.

Tony didn't hesitate but dropped to his knees, examining the boy. His face was ashen white, and he was clearly in a lot of pain. Madeleine saw his leg, then looked away.

"That's a nasty wound," Tony said. "We must get him to hospital, or he may lose the leg. But I will clean it up and stop the bleeding."

"We've no way of getting him to a hospital," the foreman said. "The truck doesn't come until next Monday. I've put out a call on the radio, but so far no luck."

"No worries. We will take him," Tony said. He looked up at the foreman. "Bring me some alcohol and any clean cloth I can use as packing and bandages."

The foreman winced. "You won't find much clean stuff around here. We all sweat a lot, and the stuff only goes to the laundry once a week."

"Then we have to use this." Tony stripped down to his undershirt, borrowed a knife and ripped his own white shirt into pieces. He went to work on the boy, who screamed in pain.

"I'm sorry. I have to remove the fragments of bone and get the dirt out of the wound," Tony said. "I will be as gentle as I can."

After an hour the wound was packed and bandaged, and the boy was loaded on to the back of the Jeep. It was only then that Tony turned to Madeleine. "I'm sorry if this has spoiled your day, but infection will set in if we don't take him. Would you rather stay here, and I will come back for you?"

"No. I'll come with you. You might need help."

"Very good. I'm not sure how far we are from the nearest hospital. There will be a field unit in a town called Oberon, and the flying doctor can come for him there if they think it is necessary."

Madeleine nodded. "I'll sit next to him in the back to hold him steady." She climbed in and positioned herself beside the boy. "What's your name?" she asked.

"Billy, miss," he said.

"Don't worry, Billy, you're in good hands," she said.

"But if I lose my leg, who's going to take care of the family?" he asked.

"It's going to be all right." She took his hand, and he gripped hers desperately.

They bumped off up the track, Tony driving as smoothly and slowly as possible. Madeleine held the boy, trying to keep him stable. It seemed to take an eternity until they reached the small town and the boy was carried into a low whitewashed building with a veranda around it.

"Well, we've done our bit," Tony said, blinking as he came out into the sunlight. "Thank you for your help."

"I didn't do much," she said.

"You kept him hopeful and let him know you cared. That was important," he said. Then he studied her face. "You look almost as white as he did. I think we should find the pub and get you a brandy."

The town only had one hospital, but five pubs. Tony escorted her to the ladies' lounge, telling her that women were not allowed in with the men. He sat her down with a glass of brandy in front of her. "They did not want to serve a man who was not wearing a shirt but only an undershirt," he said, smiling at her. "I explained what had happened, and then they wouldn't let me pay. Get that down you. You'll feel better," he said.

She drank it, feeling the fiery warmth spreading through her body.

"Better?" he asked.

She nodded.

"I'm sorry I've ruined your day. I'll try to do better tomorrow, but I think we should get you back to the hotel now and not try to do more."

"All right." He was right, she thought. She didn't feel like confronting another camp.

"It's getting chilly," she said, looking at his thin torso in only an undershirt. "I've a cardigan. I could drape that around you."

He laughed. "I'd never live it down if word got out. I'd rather freeze."

As they drove away, she finally asked him: "You're really a doctor?"

"I was," he said. "In Australia they do not acknowledge foreign qualifications, so I would have to retake all my exams. So for now I am a driver."

Madeleine frowned. "But then why leave South Africa? I presume that's where your qualifications were from?"

"No. Unfortunately I studied in Germany," he said. "My father felt it was a superior degree. He was also a doctor who had studied at Freiburg University. So as a dutiful son I went to study there also. A very nice place. I liked it. But I made a stupid mistake. I assumed that I was safe."

"Safe?" She turned to stare at him.

"I am half-Jewish. My father is a Jew. I thought this would not matter. I was a doctor. A valuable man. But I was interned before the war started. Then I was packed off to be a doctor in one of the camps. I treated living skeletons, only to have them sent to the gas chambers the next week."

Without thinking she put her hand over his. "I'm so sorry. It must have been unbearable. I lost two friends in a concentration camp."

He turned to her with surprise. "You had Jewish friends in Europe?"

"No. Two British girls. They were working undercover as spies," she said. "They were both captured and sent to Ravensbrück. Neither survived."

"Ah," he said. "So you came to Australia to get away from the wounds of the past?"

She made a sudden decision. "I came to Australia to hunt down a Nazi who tortured me."

"You were also a spy in Europe?"

She nodded. "I was a courier in France," she said.

He stopped the Jeep and sat staring at her. "I thought there was something—something that connected us. I believe I can trust you to tell you something—I am here on the same mission. I've been working for a secret Jewish organization—trying to bring those who wanted to wipe us from the face of the Earth to justice. I was sent here to follow up on a hunch that several high-ranking Nazis have come to Australia, managing to pass as refugees from Eastern and Southern European countries. In particular a man called Heinrich Siedler—a big chubby brute of a man. He ran the camp where I was forced to work. I would like to catch him. He was the most sadistic bastard you can imagine. He actually smiled while he did unspeakable things to small children."

"You think he's in this region?"

"We have reason to believe so. I have already checked out many refugee camps further south. I am working my way north."

"So you only took the job as driver because I wanted to visit the camps?"

He smiled. "Actually it was arranged that I should drive you around. There is not officially assistance from the Australian government, but their secret service has been more than cooperative."

"Gosh," Madeleine said, "I feel so much better knowing I have an ally. Is Tony your real name?"

"It's Anton," he said. "Anton Rosenauer."

"And I'm Madeleine."

He held out his hand to her. "I'm very glad to meet you, Madeleine."

They drove back to Katoomba, reaching it as the sun sank out to the plains of the West.

"Well, here we are." Tony stopped the Jeep and went around to help her out.

"Would you like to have dinner with me?" he asked.

"Won't it raise eyebrows to have dinner with the driver?" she asked.

"Australia's the land of equality. A chimney sweep can have dinner with the prime minister here."

"In that case I'd love to," she said.

Over dinner at a local restaurant overlooking the valley, she told him about Olivier and Giles and her life in France. He was a good listener. He didn't interrupt but let her talk.

"These are wounds that will take a long time to heal, if ever," he said. "Will you feel better if we do locate this Nazi of yours?"

"If I can get him sent back to Germany to stand trial, absolutely. I'll think I've avenged my husband's death."

"Your husband was in the Resistance, then?"

"He was."

"But he was caught?"

"No," she said. "He volunteered himself in exchange for me. I didn't want him to. But he wouldn't listen. If he hadn't given himself up, I'd be dead instead of him. I owe this to him."

"So he was killed instead of you?"

She took a deep breath. "Geller promised I'd go free. He lied. The moment Giles was shot by the firing squad Geller hauled me off to a nearby château where he was living. He kept me a prisoner there, and every night he . . ." She put her hand to her mouth, embarrassed by the sudden overwhelming emotion. Tony reached across and took her hand.

"But you survived. You got away. And now he is the hunted one, hiding out, fearful. Now he has no power over you."

Her eyes met his. "That's right. He has no power over me."

After dinner Tony escorted her back to her hotel.

"I think this was the first evening I have enjoyed in many years," she said to him.

"I feel the same way. It is as if I am emerging from a dark tunnel, and now perhaps I can see some light ahead."

"Yes." She stood staring at him. "Some light ahead."

CHAPTER 52

OLIVER

Australia, 1946

"Hey, Oliver." Charlie grabbed his friend's arm and dragged him away from the other children.

"What?"

"I just heard them talking about me. Them sisters." He pulled Oliver close to him. "You know I'm turning fourteen, don't you? They are planning to send me to a sheep station. Jerome said they've got a good offer for me. Only it's miles from anywhere. Back o' Bourke. I know because Jerome said, 'How do you expect us to get him to you? We don't own a plane, you know.'"

"A plane?"

Charlie nodded. "And then apparently the station owner said that if she put me on the train and I got off at Cook, they'd send somebody out for me. Cook? You know where that is, don't you? Middle of nowhere. I'll be stuck as a bloody slave in the middle of nowhere."

"Tell them you don't want to go."

"Are you stupid?" Charlie demanded. "They don't listen to us. They'll get a tidy sum for a boy like me."

"So what can you do?"

He leaned down and whispered in Oliver's ear. "I'm going to run away while I've still got a chance. Want to come with me?"

"Where would we go?"

Charlie shrugged. "Anywhere. Far away from here. Maybe we'll make for Sydney. You want to come?"

Oliver hesitated.

"If you don't, it will be your turn next. How old are you now?"

"Thirteen."

"Well then. Next year it will be you sold to some farmer with no way out. Come on. Say you'll do it."

"All right. When?"

"There's a moon. I say we go in the middle of the night. Make for the hills."

But they found, on the next night of full moon, that the door to their dormitory had been locked. Maybe the sisters suspected something. They had their spies everywhere, after all.

"So what do we do now?" Oliver whispered.

"In a few days we'll be harvesting the peaches in the far orchard. We try to work as far from the others as possible. Then we wait for a chance, and we run for it."

Oliver nodded. They worked, side by side, knocking down peaches with the long pole, sometimes with a smaller child up in the tree. Then their chance came: a little girl, climbing down from the tree, slipped and fell to the ground, letting out a loud shriek that made everyone look up from their tasks. The monitor ran over to her. Charlie nodded to Oliver. They darted from tree to tree until before them was the fence. Charlie scrambled over and hauled Oliver after him. Another farm was ahead. They ran through a field of hay. A dog barked. They kept running. They reached a track and kept going. Behind them they heard a whistle blown, raised voices, the sound of a motor car starting up. A cloud of dust behind them indicated that someone was driving after them. They kept running. The first strands of bush—the forest of gum trees that covered the rising hillside like a coat of grey-green fur—were ahead of them. They put on a final spurt and plunged into the first of the trees as the sound of a motor car drew closer.

~

The two boys ran through the forest, their breath coming in ragged gasps. Their feet crunched on dry gum leaves, a cloud of yellow dust rose up behind them and the scent of eucalyptus hung heavy in the air. At last they could run no more and paused, panting like animals against a towering blue gum tree.

"Do you think we've lost 'em?" Oliver asked.

Charlie looked around. They both held their breath, listening. But the forest around them was silent, apart from the stirring of gum leaves high in the trees and the distant tinging-call of bell bird.

"Reckon we have," Charlie said, and the boys exchanged a grin.

"Now what do we do?"

"Now we head for Sydney."

"What do we do when we get there?"

Another grin. "We lie about our ages and get a job. Plenty of work around, I hear. Or maybe we get a job on a sheep station or market garden outside Sydney. Anywhere far enough away so they don't find us."

"Don't you want to try and get back to England?" Oliver looked at his companion wistfully.

Charlie shook his head. "Nah. Nothing for me there now. Family all gone. And from what we hear, things are bad there—not enough to eat, houses all destroyed in the bombing. And nothing for you either, right?"

Oliver paused, thinking. "I suppose not."

"Anyway"—Charlie grinned—"you'd need money to get to England, so you'll have to find a job first. So we make for Sydney."

"Do you know the way?" Oliver asked. He took off his glasses, wiped them on his shirt, then wiped sweat from his brow with a grimy hand, leaving a streak of yellow dust across his face.

"I reckon it's probably due east from here," Charlie said. "We can get our direction from the sun. We want to stay away from roads cos they'll be out looking for us. The only bad thing is if we stay away from the roads, we'll have to find a way across the Blue Mountains. That will be a bit of a bummer."

"We have to find a way through the mountains?" Oliver sounded nervous. He glanced at the land that sloped gently ahead of them. "That's not going to be easy, is it?"

"We'll find a way. I reckon we just head east and hope to find a way through."

Oliver shook his head. "That's just the point, isn't it? You can't find a way through them. I read a book. The early settlers tried to find a way inland from Sydney, and they all died trying. Cos there's no way through. All blind valleys with steep sides."

"There must be a way through, cos we came by train when we got here, and it didn't go through long tunnels."

"That's right." Oliver nodded with enthusiasm. "Cos eventually they discovered the only way to cross the mountains was over the top of the ridges. That's where the train and the road go. It was all in this book and it had a map. And I traced the map, see. It's on my handkerchief!" And he produced it from his pocket. "So we won't get entirely lost, I don't think."

"You know what, Squirt? You're pretty sharp, aren't you? I'm glad I took you along with me."

"But how are we going to get to Sydney if we have to avoid the road?" Oliver tried not to sound as scared as he felt.

"We'll have to follow the same route but try to avoid people—unless we can find a decent bloke who'll give us a lift. That would be the best, wouldn't it?"

Oliver nodded. He didn't remember actually seeing any mountains when he had come to the farm. He was picturing mountains like the Alps—with steep sides and snow on top—the sort you had to climb with pickaxes. He certainly hadn't seen those. Above their heads a kookaburra burst into what sounded like hysterical laughter, making them both jump. He looked around. The forest, with its endless gum trees, seemed to go on forever. They had been running since before dawn and had already eaten the bits of bread they had managed to hide in their pockets. His mouth felt parched in the dry air. "We need to find a stream. I'm dying for a drink."

"So am I," Charlie confessed. "And I'm ruddy hungry, too."

Oliver nudged him, laughing. "Sister Jerome would have washed out your mouth with soap for saying a swear word."

"Too right." Charlie laughed, too. "And now we can say what we like, think what we like. Do what we like. We're finally free, do you realize that?"

"Yeah. Finally free." But free for what? he wanted to add.

They pushed on, up the hillside, finding no stream before nightfall. It was cold the moment the sun went down, and they huddled together like puppies.

"If we don't find water today, we've had it," Charlie said as they rose with the dawn.

"There are waterfalls up in the mountains. I saw them on the map." Oliver drew out his handkerchief and consulted it. "I think if we keep heading more northeast, we'll find a road and a stream."

"I bloody hope so," Charlie said. "My mouth feels like sandpaper. I wish we could have sneaked an orange with us."

"Me too. I'm trying to think what the Abbos eat when they're out in the Bush. I know about witchetty grubs, but they're up in Northern Territory."

"We should be able to catch a rabbit or a bird. Then we could drink its blood."

"Ewww."

"Better than nothing." Charlie gave him a playful slap. "I've got the catapult I made. Let's see what we can do."

After a while the forest thinned into an area already cleared for lumber. A flock of budgerigars, hundreds of them, had landed on the dry grass in a moving mass of green and blue. The big boy nudged the other, silently got out his catapult and aimed. The air echoed with their shrill little cries as they rose into the air. The big boy tore off his shirt, ran forwards and flailed, knocking a bird to the ground. He pounced on it.

"Got it!"

Oliver saw the tiny bird struggling, its beak open in terror. "No. Let it go. We shouldn't kill anything."

Charlie turned on him. "What's wrong with you? The early settlers killed kangaroos and wallabies, didn't they? And we certainly ate plenty of rabbit at the farm." He put a big finger over the bird's throat and the life went from its eyes. Oliver blinked but said nothing.

"Now, if we could make a fire, we could roast it. Just like chicken."

Oliver took off his spectacles. "I bet I can make a fire. I read about this. You get dry grass and wood, and we'll make one in this patch of bare earth."

When a small mound was piled up, Oliver held his spectacles so that the sun's rays were magnified on to kindling. It took a while, but at last the grass began to smoke. A small flame flickered. He looked amazed and delighted as he dropped the burning grass into the pile of wood.

"I read about it in a book. I never knew if it would work."

"You and your ruddy books. Teacher's pet, that's what you were."

Oliver shrugged. "I can't help it if I like to know things. The teacher wanted to help me get into a good school, but they wouldn't let him."

"Of course not. They wouldn't collect the bounty on you, would they?" He laughed, holding out his hands to the fire that now leapt up towards the clear sky. "We'll use this stick and singe off the feathers first. Then we'll roast it."

Oliver nodded. Now having forgotten the horror of killing a bird and thinking only of meat. Suddenly a wind rose, sweeping up from the flatlands below. It snatched at glowing embers, blowing them into dry grass. The grass ignited.

"We have to put that out before it gets away," Charlie shouted, rushing over to beat at the grass with a fallen branch, while Oliver tried to kick earth over it. But the wind was stronger now. As they stomped on it, the fire ran the length of the clearing. It caught dead leaves. It sparkled up the side of a trunk and the whole tree exploded like a torch.

"Crikey!" Oliver yelled. "Now we've done it."

CHAPTER 53

It was Friday.

"No sense in visiting any of the camps over the weekend," Tony told her. "The men all try to find a way to get into the nearest town and drink themselves silly for a couple of days."

"We're running out of camps to visit around here, aren't we?" she said. "Maybe we should try further north?"

He nodded. "Maybe out past Mount Victoria. There's a camp beyond Hampton."

"All right."

Madeleine collected a picnic lunch, and they set off, following the main highway east, past Blackheath, which made her nostalgic. "I grew up in Blackheath," she said. "This one looks quite different."

"I think all the places have British names, don't they?" Tony said. "People came here but wanted to remember their homeland. Funny, really, as most of them came to escape from a life that wasn't satisfactory."

They continued through the mountains, sometimes dipping down before rising sharply again. They passed waterfalls that cascaded from steep-sided cliffs, and crossed mountain streams. Flocks of bright birds—the pink ones were galahs, she was told—provided bursts of colour in the otherwise grey-green of the eucalyptus trees. Then they left the paved road and took a dirt track that zigzagged down into a valley until they came to the lumber camp. They met the foreman, who was intrigued when Madeleine told him her reason for visiting.

"Our photos in a women's magazine? My word. This will make the blokes get cleaned up. They might even shave."

He laughed. "You'll have to wait until they all get in from the Bush, but sit yourselves down in the shade and make yourselves comfy."

"Do you have any Czech immigrants here?" she asked, casually. "I've heard there were some in this region."

"Too right. We've got a mob of them. Seven or eight, isn't it, Willy?" He turned to the young man who was with him.

"That's right." The other man nodded. "Good workers they are, too. And sober. Don't get themselves drunk every Saturday night like the Aussie boys. That's one of them, coming in now. Hey Vlad, get over here. Lady wants to meet you."

Madeleine's heart raced, but then she saw a giant of a man, brawny, tanned, walk over to them. "Yes, boss? What you want?"

"This lady asked if we've any Czech workers."

"That is my country," the man said. "And we have more of my countrymen."

"He's a good bloke, Vlad." The foreman thumped him on the back. "Not a bad check, are you?" And he laughed at his own joke, which the other man clearly didn't get.

"You don't happen to have a Karol Voyzek, do you?" She fought to keep her voice even.

"Old Christmas, you mean?" The foreman laughed. "Yeah, we've got him. Miserable bastard if you ask me. Not good fun, like old Vlad here. Keeps himself to himself. Doesn't go into town with the rest of them."

"Is he around right now?" She realized that he'd be at a disadvantage if the other men were present.

The big man shook his head. "He went off with his mates, didn't he? They finished early today so they buggered off." Madeleine noticed he had picked up swearing.

"That's right," the foreman said. "He and a couple of other blokes are doing up this abandoned cabin, couple of miles away. They go out there at weekends—don't go into town on the booze like the rest of the blokes. I don't know what they get up to out there. I know they hunt wallabies. They bring us a carcass sometimes. Makes a good stew, wallaby meat."

"New Australians are allowed to have guns?" Tony asked.

"My word no," the foreman said. "It would be bow and arrow, or they'd trap the animal."

A small sigh of relief escaped Madeleine. No guns. And she had the Colt, loaded.

"We might take a run out and visit them, then," she said. "That would make a good human interest story—how the New Australians are making themselves at home. How do we find this cabin?"

"You drive another mile or so past thc camp, then you'll see a small track that goes off to the right. Follow it another mile or so. It dead-ends at the old cabin, so you can't miss it."

They thanked him and set off, neither saying anything but feeling the tension. Madeleine found she was half hoping that Karol Voyzek would not turn out to be Geller. She still wasn't sure what she'd say to him if she met him. But she was glad to have Tony beside her. At least she wouldn't have to face him alone.

Oliver

Oliver stared in horror as the flames licked up the mountainside, thick smoke curled and the crackling sound turned into roaring.

"What are we going to do?" he asked.

"Get away from here quickly so they can't pin it on us."

"But they'll know. They'll find us. We can't go up into the mountains any more, can we? It's all on fire. We're sitting ducks."

Charlie nodded. "We need somewhere to hide out until this is all over. We wait here until dark, and then we see if we can find an abandoned shed or something."

"All right." Oliver nodded. He didn't think this was likely. He felt sick and scared. He had seen what punishments the smallest infractions had received. He couldn't imagine what terrible fate awaited them when they were returned to Ferndale. He glanced up at the fire, now going from strength to strength as it engulfed the hill ahead of them. Might it not be better to die here? Get it over with?

Suddenly he had an idea. "Hey, Charlie. I know where we might be able to go. But we have to wait until dark."

~

Tony and Madeleine continued along the forest road until they spotted the narrow track going off to their left. Tony slowed to a halt, suddenly alert. "I smell smoke," he said. "There's a fire somewhere."

"It's probably just a bonfire or someone barbecuing," Madeleine replied.

Tony shook his head. "Out here you learn to take fire really seriously. If these trees catch alight, you won't believe how fast it spreads. It's the oil in the eucalyptus, you see. They just explode into flame. And the fire can leap across whole valleys at once."

"I don't see any smoke yet," she said. "Do you think we should not go on?"

"I'd hate to be so close and then not find out the truth," he said. "No, I reckon we are all right. The wind isn't too strong today."

The track wound through thick forest until they came around a bend, and there was the cabin before them, nestled in a hollow surrounded by towering paperbark trees. Smoke was rising from the chimney.

"That must have been the fire you smelled," she said.

"Maybe." Tony didn't sound convinced. He turned off the engine. "What do you want to do?"

"Why don't I start off alone?" she said. "Maybe it's best if they don't know you are with me."

He nodded. "I'll turn the motor around so that we can make a fast getaway if we have to, but I'll stay within reach." He took her hand. "Good luck. Don't do anything too brave or silly, all right? If it's him, walk away. We'll go and report them."

She nodded, trying to control her breathing before she climbed out of the Jeep and walked forwards with determined strides. She knocked at the front door. Almost instantly it was flung open. The man who stood there had an unmistakably Germanic look to him. He was big, blond and had that air of arrogance she had seen so often during the war.

"Hello, little lady," he said. "I thought I heard a car. What a surprise. What are you doing out here? Are you lost?"

"I'm a reporter from a magazine in England," she said, trying to sound enthusiastic and confident. "I was told at the lumber camp that some of the New Australians had made themselves at home in this old cabin. So I thought it would make a good story for our readers. Which country are you from?"

"I am from Romania," he said, his eyes holding hers.

"Romania—fancy," she said. She remembered Tony describing the big brute of a man. This could well be the camp commandant.

"You are here with friends from your country?" she asked.

"My mates are from Czechoslovakia and from Yugoslavia. Do you want to come in?"

"Thank you. Kind of you." He opened the door and she stepped into the gloom of the small main room. A stove was burning in a corner. There was a crude central table and two men sat at this, drinking something from beakers. They both stood up as she came in.

"Look what I have found," the first man said. "This lady is from an English magazine. She wants to interview us. Maybe take our picture. Amusing, *ja*?"

One of the men—thin, scrawny—watched her, his eyes darting nervously. The other was staring at Madeleine. He had knocked over his beaker when he stood up but didn't seem to notice brown liquid dripping on to the dirt floor. He had dark hair and a bushy dark moustache, but Uncle Francis had been right. The eyes that looked at her had recognized her at the same moment she recognized him.

I should walk away now, she thought. *I can identify him. He can't get far.* Almost imperceptibly, she moved towards the half-open door. Would Geller go along with the pretence? She wondered.

"So you came alone, little lady?" the big blond one asked. He was smiling.

She felt the thrill of fear. They were not planning to let her go. Tony was nearby, outside. If she screamed, he'd come to her aid, but she was determined to bluff this out. Then the man known as Karol Voyzek came around the table towards her. She saw a mixture of wariness and amusement in those eyes.

"You missed me after all, did you, Minette? You've come all this way across the world to find me again? I am touched."

The big man asked a quick question in German. Geller replied. A rapid exchange followed.

"Of course I know her. My former mistress," he said in English. "I'm pleased to see you alive and well, Minette. Were you really looking for me, or is this just a happy coincidence?"

"Oh no." She found her voice and her determination. "I came to find you, Geller. To make sure you don't escape justice."

"I'm afraid you are hopelessly naïve, my dear," he said. "May I point out that we are three strong men and you are one small woman. You don't expect to leave here alive, do you? I assure you it will be easy to dispose of your body in the Bush and nobody will ever know."

"Not quite as naïve as you think," she said. "You see, I have one thing that you don't."

She reached into her purse and brought out the Colt. "I'm going to leave you now, radio your position and have the authorities come for you."

"I don't think so." Geller started towards her. "Do you even know how to use that thing?"

"Don't come any closer, or I shoot." She sounded braver than she felt. The gun seemed heavy in her hand. Dare I? she was asking.

Then Geller laughed.

"Last warning," she said. "Stay exactly where you are."

The big man, standing to her left, took a step towards her. She fired. Aim for the knees, she had learned at her training camp. She had never done it on a living target, but the man let out a yell of pain and dropped to the floor. Karl Geller froze, a look of amazement, or was it admiration, on his face.

"So you do know. But we will make you pay for this. It is a long time since we tortured somebody, but I don't think we have forgotten how."

The big man was still groaning, rocking on the floor and shouting out German curses. The third man looked green.

She took a step back, now halfway through the door, conscious of the warmth of the sun on her back. Tony would be nearby.

"You're going to stay exactly where you are," she said. "Next time I shoot to kill."

Suddenly Geller rushed at her. She fired again. She was too close to aim for the legs, but the bullet went through his shoulder. The force of it made him recoil, almost losing his footing. As he righted himself, blood staining the front of his shirt, she turned and ran. Tony and the Jeep were right there, the engine running. She half flung herself inside as Geller staggered out of the front door.

"You can't get away, you bitch," he shouted. "We'll catch you and run you off the road."

Tony gunned the engine, and they left a cloud of yellow dust as they surged up the track.

"Don't worry," he said. "They won't follow us. I did a little operation to their car. I removed the rotor from the distributor. It won't start."

"You're brilliant," she said.

"And you are amazing," he replied. "I heard everything. Did you kill one of them?"

"That wasn't my mandate," she said. "I shot the big one in the knee. I know where I would like to have shot Geller, but he rushed at me, so he got it in the shoulder."

Tony looked at her and burst out laughing. "Madeleine Martin, you are a formidable force."

They drove up the hillside until they reached the main track. Tony paused, looking around. Then he said, "See? I was right about the smoke. There is fire down below in that valley. I wonder which way we should take? If it comes up the hillside ahead of us, we may be trapped."

"But surely it's still far away?" She stared down at the pall of smoke that hung below them. In the distance she could now hear crackling and an occasional muffled explosion.

"What's that?"

"That's the gum trees bursting into flame. The oil is so volatile. We need to get a move on."

He turned back towards the lumber camp. A wind had sprung up. Embers were now floating up towards them. The fire was racing up the hill. They came around a corner only to find that a tongue of fire had outrun them. Ahead of them the forest was already burning.

"Christ," he said. "I can't turn around here. We'll have to risk it and drive through."

"Through the fire?"

"By the time I've reversed and managed to find a place to turn around, we could find ourselves trapped. We have to go on." He glanced into the back seat. "Grab the picnic blanket and put it over you. Keep your head down. Try to breathe as little as possible."

"What about you?"

"I'm going to drive really fast."

The Jeep shot forward, bouncing over ruts so violently that Madeleine had to cling on for dear life. Trees were now burning on either side of them. Acrid smoke made her cough. She was conscious of the flames licking out towards them as they shot past. The heat was intense. Embers landed on them, and she tried to brush them off. Then ahead she could see trees blackened and smouldering but no longer actively burning. They were almost through. She sat up.

"We're going to make it," she said.

At that moment there came a great cracking sound, and a huge branch fell from a smouldering tree.

"Look out!" Tony yelled. He gunned the engine and tried to swerve as the branch crashed on to the Jeep. As Madeleine flung herself sideways, she was conscious of a side branch, sticking out at an angle, coming at her. And she knew no more.

CHAPTER 54

Madeleine opened her eyes to see stripes of sunlight on a white wall. She frowned, trying to remember where she was. There was the smell, vaguely familiar. She sniffed again, and immediately an image of her mother came into her head. "Don't cry. Maman will make it all better for you, but it may sting a little so be brave."

Dettol, she said out loud. She had fallen and skinned her knee, and Maman had cleaned it with something that made it sting. And she had once done the same for Olivier.

Outside the window came the call of a strange bird—the one that sounded like a badly played flute. Gradually she put the pieces together. Birds. Australia. Looking for something . . . a man. A gun . . . fire. She tried to sit up, but the world swung around, and she lay back again. She had found Karl Geller and she had shot him and there had been a fire and the great branch had fallen on their car.

"Tony!" she said the name out loud. Had the branch landed on Tony?

A door opened. "Oh, you're awake. That is good news. Did you call, my dear?" The woman was in starched white nurse's uniform. The room, the smell and the sight now had a name: hospital.

"The man I was with in the car—what happened to him?"

"Mr Rosenauer? He's doing well." The nurse came over and with efficient fingers took Madeleine's pulse. "Only a few minor burns and scrapes, but the man is hero. Do you know he must have carried you for a mile to the lumber camp? The car was destroyed." She let Madeleine's arm rest again. "Now you've had a nasty concussion. Don't try to move. Doctor will want to see you. But I expect you're hungry. You've been in and out of consciousness for two days now. I'll bring you a cup of tea."

She left again. Madeleine lay back, watching that sunlight dancing on the wall through the Venetian blinds. She felt strangely content. When the door opened again, she expected to see the nurse with the teacup, but instead it was Tony. He came over to her and stood looking with compassion and relief. "How are you feeling?" He perched on the bed beside her, touching her arm gently.

"My head still hurts," she said.

"Well, it would. You're a lucky woman, Mrs Martin. The roll bar of the Jeep took the worst of the impact. If the branch had landed on you, you wouldn't be here to tell the tale. You should see what the Jeep looked like. Flattened like a pancake."

Madeleine shuddered. "It missed you?"

"By about an inch. I must lead a charmed life, or perhaps the devil doesn't want me."

"Don't say that." She reached out and took his hand. "You saved my life. I'm told you're a hero."

He shrugged, embarrassed. "I couldn't just leave you there."

Suddenly she remembered. "The Nazis. Geller? What . . ."

"All dead. Burned to a crisp trying to flee. Which is only just. It pays for those poor souls who ended up in the crematoriums at the camps."

"Was the big man your Heinrich Siedler."

"They are waiting for dental records, but I'm pretty sure he was."

"So you've completed your assignment. What will you do now? Go back to Europe or South Africa?"

"I may have more Nazis to hunt here. In any case, I think I'll stay."

"But your folks in South Africa?"

"My dad died a couple of years ago. I didn't have a chance to see him. He died not knowing if I was alive or dead. And my mum—she married again. To a bloke I'm not fond of. So I don't have any great desire to rush home. Besides, I like it here."

"So do I," she said.

He looked at her, went to say something, then stood up. "You should rest."

The doctor visited, told her she was not to think about going anywhere for a week. The next day she was allowed to sit in a rocking chair on the veranda. It was cool and pleasant with a view of the hills, including a large streak of black where the fire had been. She learned the lumber camp had been spared and no more buildings had been threatened. The nurse brought out a newspaper. "Details of your fire, if you want to read," she said and put it beside Madeleine.

Madeleine picked it up, not sure she wanted to focus on small print yet. *Fire Spares Settlements* was the headline. Then halfway down the page was a lesser headline. *No Sign Yet of Missing Boys.* She read on: *Charlie Stubbs, 14, and Oliver Jones, 13, two orphans from Ferndale Children's Farm, have now been missing for a week. It is feared that they were making for the mountains and were overtaken by the fire. Sister Jerome commented that . . .*

Madeleine stopped. Beside the headline was a grainy photograph: two boys standing together, the bigger one grinning, but the younger one, a slim, dark-haired boy with round spectacles, looking at the world with serious eyes. Madeleine let out a little cry. Instantly Tony, who had been sitting further down the veranda, leapt up. "What's wrong?"

She pointed at the newspaper. "That boy. I think it's my son."

The local policeman was summoned, and she learned about the sisters who took in British orphans. Tony borrowed a car and drove her to see the orphanage. It was a long way out of town, towards the first hills. As they drove up the track from the gate, Madeleine was surprised to see children working in the fields.

"Look at that," she said to Tony.

"I expect it's good for them to be out in the fresh air," he replied.

"But look—that little mite can't be more than six or seven and he's lugging that big sack. That can't be right."

As they approached the buildings, Madeleine had a sinking feeling in the pit of her stomach. Children working in the fields, far from anywhere . . .

A tall girl came out at the sound of the car, and quickly ran back inside. Almost immediately a nun came out. Her grey habit flapped out in the breeze, and the face that stared from beneath the wimple was not friendly.

"What do you want?" she asked. "It is usually required to get permission to visit, as an unexpected visitor disturbs the children in their daily routines."

"Like working in the fields?" Madeleine asked.

The sister's stone-like face showed no sign of annoyance. "We grow our own crops. We only receive very limited funding here, and the children are proud to be contributing to their well-being. And it's a healthy activity. What can I do for you?"

Madeleine showed her the newspaper cutting. "This boy. I think he may be my son."

"Your son? All the children who come to us are orphans."

"There might have been a mistake. A mix-up. It was war. We were told he had been killed, but it looks so much like him. And his name was Olivier—French. Olivier Martin. He was born in Paris. But he changed it to Oliver Martin when we came to England. But not Jones. That wasn't his last name, which makes we think that . . ."

The sister now had gone quite pale. Madeleine was suddenly sure she had touched on a nerve, that the sister did know something. She became defiant, even belligerent. "The child came to us as an orphan. We were told none of them had families, or naturally we would have searched. I don't know what made him run off like that. He was normally such a good, quiet little boy. It must have been that Charlie's influence. He was always a bad lot . . . No, I've no idea where they might be headed. We sent a search party out for them, but if they were trying to cross the mountains, they'd never make it from here. There's no way across except where the road and railway go. And then there was the fire. If you really are his mother, I'm so very sorry."

Madeleine drove away with Tony beside her. "I can't believe that I was that close only to find Olivier has just been lost. Surely no universe could be that cruel."

"Don't give up hope." Tony squeezed her hand. "Boys are resourceful creatures. We'll spread the word that you're here and you're looking for him."

She gave details to the police, to the newspaper and the local radio station. Volunteer search parties were renewed, but all Madeleine could do was to sit on the veranda waiting, hoping, dreading . . . She tried to shut the image from her mind of the fire, racing up the hill towards two little boys who tried to outrun it, to hide, to find refuge. She was dozing in the afternoon shade when Tony woke her gently. "There is someone to see you, Madeleine."

A middle-aged man in an open-necked shirt and khaki shorts was standing behind Tony. He wore heavy spectacles and had a worried look about him. Bad news, she thought. He's come to bring me bad news. She sat up abruptly, causing the world to swing round again.

"You have news of my son?"

"I'm Fred Baxter. I was Oliver's schoolmaster," he said. "Such a bright boy. So much promise. I tried to persuade the nuns to let me get him a scholarship to a boarding school, but they refused."

"Why would they do that, Mr Baxter?"

He shook his head. "That farm is an awful place. In my mind it should be shut down, but most people think the nuns are saints. They manage a good image, but those poor kids . . ." He shook his head. "I do what I can when I go out there to teach. But your son, Mrs Martin—can you tell me more about your son?"

She told him everything she could remember. He nodded, then said, "I think I can take you to someone who might help you."

"Really? You think he's still alive and I might find him?"

"I think it's highly possible."

She stood up, wobbled and had to grasp the chair arm. She turned to Tony. "Will you come with us?"

"Of course." He helped her down the steps and into an old Ford car. They drove through the little town to a pleasant bungalow on the far side. It had a white fence around a lawn and flower beds. Two large dogs came bounding up at the sound of the car.

"Down, you brutes," Mr Baxter said good-naturedly. He opened the gate for Madeleine and Tony to go through and then led them into the house.

"Margie, I've visitors. Put the tea on," he called as he ushered them into a living room with well-worn furniture and bookcases around the walls.

"Take a seat, and tell me again what you remember of this boy of yours . . ."

Madeleine talked of the flat in Paris, Olivier riding his tricycle in the Bois de Boulogne and loving his Meccano set. She related going to England, the new school. A small sound from the doorway made her look up. A boy was standing there, a slightly built boy with dark hair that flopped across his forehead and dark, serious eyes that blinked through round glasses. He was staring at her as if he was seeing a ghost. Then he said, in a small voice, "Mum?"

And Madeleine, who had been so brave, so stoic for so long, opened her arms as he came tentatively towards her and enveloped him in a hug, her body shaking with sobs. "My little boy," she gasped. "It's my little boy."

They stood, her little boy now almost her own height, their arms wrapped around each other, both crying now.

"I thought you were dead," he said when they could speak again. "They told me my family all died in the Blitz."

"They told me YOU were dead," she replied.

"There was a mix-up. I swapped labels," he said. When they were finally sitting down, side by side, with a cup of tea, Oliver explained the labels and how he hadn't remembered until too late.

"But why didn't you tell the sisters, my darling?" she asked.

"I did. They wouldn't listen. They didn't care," he said.

"All these years—" She stroked tears from his cheek. "All these years taken from us."

Oliver glanced at Tony. "Where's Papa? Is he still alive?"

She shook her head. "He died, a hero of the Resistance in France. You'd be very proud of him."

Oliver nodded seriously. "I always thought he'd do something like that. He was that sort of person, wasn't he?"

"Yes. He was." She actually smiled at his memory.

There followed a lot of explaining—how she came to be in Australia, who Tony was. How he had saved her life. At the mention of the fire, Oliver frowned. "Will I be in big trouble for starting that fire? We didn't mean to. We were hiding in the woods, and Charlie caught a bird, and we lit a fire to cook it. Then suddenly the wind came up, and it blew the fire, and we couldn't stop it and put it out."

He looked as if he was about to cry again.

"I'm sure they'll understand. Accidents happen."

"But I'll get in trouble for running away."

Madeleine shook her head. "I think it's those nuns who might get in trouble for child abuse," she said. "It looked like a terrible place."

Oliver shuddered. "It was. It was like the worst place you can imagine. But I don't want to talk about it. Are we going back to London, or to Paris?"

"Wherever you want," she said. "I promised your grandmother that I'd help her get the château restored after the Germans wrecked it."

"Grandmother?" Oliver frowned. "You mean Papa's mum? I thought she didn't like us."

"She does now. She'd want to meet you. You are the heir, after all."

"Crikey. I hope I haven't forgotten all my French."

She glanced up, saw Tony's face and read the disappointment. "But you know what?" she said. "I really like it here, in Australia. I think it might be a better place to be for now. While we get to know each other again."

Oliver shrugged. "I don't care. Anywhere is all right with me. Now that . . ." He stared at her face as if he still couldn't quite believe his eyes.

"You need a decent school, Oliver," Mr Baxter said. "And university. Your good brain shouldn't be wasted."

"We will definitely make sure he gets a decent school," Madeleine said. "We'll take our time to decide if it should be here, in Sydney, or in Paris or London." She put her arm around Oliver's shoulder, hugging him fiercely to her. "Although let's not worry about that now. Let's just enjoy this miracle."

Oliver looked at her, beaming. Then he shook his head and pulled away. "But what about Charlie? We can't leave him here. He deserves a good life, too."

"Charlie?"

"The boy I escaped with. He's always stood up for me at the farm. He's a good sort, and he's had a rotten life so far."

Madeleine exchanged a gaze with Tony. "We'll see what can be done for Charlie."

They met Charlie, and later that day the local policeman was called in for the boys to make their statements. They explained how they had only meant to cook something to eat but the wind had come up and the fire had spread. The officer listened in silence, then he said, "But why would you want to run away? Weren't they good to you at the farm?"

"Good to us?" Charlie exclaimed. "You want to see that place, mate. Pay a visit when they aren't expecting you, and you'll see what it's really like. When people come on visitors' days, they put out toys and let us play and eat decent food, but the rest of the time it's working in the fields and not much to eat."

"But you get your schooling, surely?" The officer looked worried now.

"I go out there two mornings a week," Mr Baxter said. "I have observed what the conditions are like, but I didn't want to say anything in case it made it worse for the children. You'll find it really is a most depressing place."

"And we ran away because they were about to sell Charlie," Oliver said.

"Sell him?" The policeman sounded shocked now. "What do you mean?"

"I'm turning fourteen, see?" Charlie said. "That's when they look for a farmer who wants a big strong lad who'll work for room and board. And the nuns get a finder's fee. But they were going to send me to a sheep station out miles from anywhere. Back o' Bourke. I thought I'd be trapped there. No hope of escape, so Oliver and me got out while we could."

"My word." The policeman exchanged a glance with Mr Baxter. "If you weren't verifying some of this, I don't think I'd believe it. We'll certainly start an investigation."

"Go and talk to the kids when the nuns aren't around," Charlie said. "They'll tell you. Nobody escapes because we're orphans. We've nowhere else to go."

Madeleine looked at him and wanted to hug him. Instead she put her arm around her son.

"You've got us now, Charlie," she said.

CHAPTER 55

The boys stayed with Mr Baxter while Madeleine completed her recovery at the hospital, then Tony arranged for them all to go to Sydney. He rented a flat for them on Manly Beach while they made plans for the future. The boys were thrilled about the ocean, behaving like normal children who hadn't a care in the world. Madeleine watched them, feeling as if her heart would burst with joy. She and Tony had to meet with government officials to give their accounts regarding the New Australians killed in the fire, and there was communication between the Australian authorities and London. Dental records were being requested to identify the dead. It was suggested that Madeleine return to London to complete her assignment. When Oliver heard this, he asked, with concern, "What about Charlie? Can we take him with us?"

"Back to England or France?" Madeleine had asked.

"We can't just ditch him, Mum. He was my best mate all this time. I'd still be at that place if he hadn't taken care of me."

"Why don't we ask Charlie what he wants to do?" Madeleine suggested. She questioned Charlie whether he wanted to come with them and if he had any relatives she should get in touch with if they went back. Charlie shook his head.

"I don't have no one, missus. My mum put me in the orphanage when I was two because she couldn't take care of another kid. So there's nothing for me there now."

Madeleine looked at him with concern. "So what would you like to do, Charlie?"

"I don't mind hard work, missus. I'd like to work with me hands."

"All right. Let's see what we can do," Madeleine said. They visited child services and were told that a foster family would be found for Charlie. Maybe an apprenticeship, which seemed to satisfy him.

Oliver and Charlie both testified before the board of education about what they had experienced at Ferndale. Madeleine tried to hold back tears as she heard what her son had been through.

"Let's hope the authorities will close it down and punish those awful nuns," she said. She couldn't bring herself to tell Oliver that she, too, had suffered, come from hell, and survived. It was not a time for looking back but looking forward, and she had so much to look forward to. She was still torn between taking Oliver back to meet his grandmother and fulfilling her obligations in Europe or staying in a place she had come to love.

One evening in Sydney, she went for a walk with Tony along the oceanfront in Manly. The breeze in her face was balmy, tinged with the salt of ocean. Madeleine thought of cold and rainy England and sighed.

"So you have made up your mind to go?" Tony asked.

"I have things that need sorting out. I did promise my mother-in-law, and I'd want to see her settled. Olivier should meet her, and see my father, too. But then . . ." She paused, looking up at him, "Would you want to come with us?" she asked. "Won't you have to report to your organization, too?"

He shook his head. "I am never going to Europe again. Too many bad memories."

"So what will you do now? Is your assignment complete?"

He shrugged. "There may be more Nazis to hunt down. But anyway the community hospital where you were treated has told me they are desperately short of doctors in that region. They will sponsor me to complete my studies and retake my exams on the condition that I go to work there for a while."

"But you're a qualified doctor. Why should you have to study again?"

"They have to make sure that foreign qualifications are up to Aussie standards, I suppose. I need to learn the names for everything in English," he said. "And how things are done here. But I do not think it will take long. I should have my qualifications within a year. And if I am a proper doctor again—a respected man—then I wondered if one day, maybe, you might consider returning here, and perhaps . . ."

She saw his eyes, the flicker of uncertainty, and of hope. A good man, she thought. One who had suffered like her. One she could respect and maybe come to love someday, if love was still possible.

"Yes," she said. "I would like us to return, when I have sorted things out in England and France. And I would like to know that you are here, waiting for me."

His face lit up with pure joy, making him look suddenly like a young man again. "Really? That's wonderful. I have come to admire you greatly, Madeleine, and I think what I feel for you is more than admiration."

She nodded. "I think I feel the same way."

His face clouded. "You are not concerned that I am half-Jewish?"

She smiled. "My husband was also half-Jewish. And this is Australia, where such things do not matter." She hesitated, then added, "Tony, you should understand I have only ever loved one man. He meant everything to me. And I have been deeply hurt. I'm not sure what I can feel again. If I can ever learn to have those feelings again."

"But you are willing to try? To get to know each other better and maybe one day . . ."

"I'm willing to try."

He nodded, then asked, "Your son—what will he think about this?"

"A boy needs a father," she said.

Tony nodded agreement. "And speaking of that, I have decided to take Charlie in myself. It's not right that he should go to strangers. He needs to get a feel of what a family is like."

Madeleine looked up at him. "You're a good man," she said, feeling her eyes brimming with tears.

And so it was arranged that Charlie would live with Tony and attend a trade school, which seemed to please him enormously. "Car mechanic," he said. "That sounds bonzer. I've always wanted to get my hands on a car engine."

~

Tony came with them as they boarded the P&O liner. He brought Charlie with him.

"Goodbye, Charlie," Oliver said. "I'll miss you."

"Go on!" Charlie shoved him. "You won't miss me. You have a family now."

"But I will," Oliver said. "You saved me. I won't ever forget you."

Charlie looked embarrassed and shrugged. There was an awkward silence.

"We'll be back soon, Charlie," Madeleine said. "And maybe you'll come and live with us?"

"Really?" He beamed.

Tony turned to Madeleine. He took her hands in his. "Well, I suppose this is goodbye."

"Au revoir," she said. "We will come back soon, I promise. And I'll write."

He nodded, his eyes holding hers. He started to say more, then released her hands and turned to the boy.

"Take care of your mother, Oliver," Tony said. He held out his hand. "Until we meet again."

Oliver shook it solemnly. "Right-oh," he said.

"Goodbye, then." Madeleine hesitated. Then she came towards Tony. "Don't be so bloody formal," she said. "You know you want to kiss me."

He gave a little laugh as he took her into his arms.

HISTORICAL NOTE

If you have felt uncomfortable at reading what Oliver had to endure in Australia and feel I am exaggerating or overdramatizing his plight, I suggest you read many of the online accounts of what abuses orphaned children endured when they were shipped to these "farms" in Australia, often at the hands of nuns.

ACKNOWLEDGMENTS

I wish to thank my editor, Danielle Marshall, and the whole team at Lake Union, also my wonderful agents Meg Ruley and Christina Hogrebe at Jane Rotrosen Agency, who make working with them such a joy.

Thank you to John, as always, for being my first reader (and critic).

I should also thank my parents and brother for moving to Australia, after I myself moved there, so that I could visit them every year and thus know my way around the Bush.

ABOUT THE AUTHOR

Photo © Douglas Sonders

Rhys Bowen is the *New York Times* bestselling author of more than fifty novels, including *Where the Sky Begins*, *The Venice Sketchbook*, *Above the Bay of Angels*, *The Victory Garden*, *The Tuscan Child*, and her World War II novel *In Farleigh Field*, the winner of the Left Coast Crime "Lefty" Award for Best Historical Mystery Novel and the Agatha Award for Best Historical Novel. Bowen's work has won twenty honors to date, including multiple Agatha, Anthony, and Macavity Awards. Her books have been translated into many languages, and she has fans around the world, including sixty-seven thousand Facebook followers. A transplanted Brit, Bowen divides her time between California and Arizona. For more information, visit www.rhysbowen.com.